# CONSOLATION

# MICHAEL REDHILL

# CONSOLATION

*A Novel*

WILLIAM HEINEMANN: LONDON

Published by William Heinemann in 2007

1 3 5 7 9 10 8 6 4 2

Published by arrangement with the original publisher, Doubleday Canada,
a division of Random House of Canada Limited

First published by Doubleday Canada in 2006

First published in Great Britain in 2007 by William Heinemann
Random House, 20 Vauxhall Bridge Road,
London SW1V 2SA

www.randomhouse.co.uk

Addresses for companies within The Random House Group Limited can be found at:
www.randomhouse.co.uk/offices.htm

The Random House Group Limited Reg. No. 954009

A CIP catalogue record for this book
is available from the British Library

ISBN 9780434011797

This bookproof is printed and bound in Germany
by GGP Media GmbH, Germany

The man who commits suicide
remains in the world of dreams.

*Seven Nights,* JORGE LUIS BORGES

In my solitude
I have seen things
that are not true

"PROVERBS," DON PATERSON

LATE SUMMER, THE AUGUST AIR ALREADY COOLING, and some of the migrators are beginning south. Hear the faint booming high up against windows before sunrise, pell-mell flight into sky-mirrored bank towers. Good men and women collect them and carry their stunned forms around in paper bags, try to revive them. Lost art of husbandry. By the time the sun is up, the reflected heat from the day before is already building again in glass surfaces.

A man is standing by the lakeshore at the Hanlan's Point ferry dock. Cicadas in the grass near the roadway, cars passing behind the hotel. The ferry rush hour is over already at 8:15, and the Hanlan's Point ferry is the least frequent of them all, as it takes passengers to a buggy, unkempt part of the Toronto Islands. But it is the most peaceful ride, ending close to wilderness. *The Duchess.* He sees it departing for the city from its island dock, on the other side of the harbour. He stretches his arm out at eye level, like he once taught his daughters to do, and the ferry travels over the palm of his hand.

At the kiosk beside the gate he buys a Coffee Crisp, struggles with the wrapper. He hands it to a woman standing near him at the gate. "My fingers are useless," he tells her.

She neatly tears the end of the package open. Such precision. Gives him the candy peeled like a fruit. "Arthritis?"

"No," he says. "Lou Gehrig's. Sometimes they work fine. But never in the mornings."

She makes a kissing noise and shakes her head. "That's awful."

"I'm okay," he says, holding a hand up, warding off pity. "It's a beautiful morning, and I'm eating a chocolate bar beside a pretty girl. One day at a time."

She smiles for him. "Good for you."

The docks are two hundred and forty feet out from the lake's original shoreline. Landfill pushed everything forward. Buildings erupted out of it like weeds. The city, walking on water.

All aboard. The woman who helped him with the chocolate bar waits behind him—perhaps politely—as he gets on, but says nothing else to him. There are only six passengers, and except for him they disappear into the cramped cabin on one side of the ferry, or go up front with their bikes or their blades slung over their shoulders. He stays on the deck, holding tight to the aft lashpost, watching the city slide away.

The foghorn's low animal bellow. The ship moves backwards through the murky water fouled with shoes and weeds and duckshit. This close to the skyline, an optical illusion: the dock recedes from the boat, but tiers of buildings ranging up behind the depot appear to push forward, looming over the buildings in front of them. The whole downtown clenching the water's edge in its fist.

The lighthouse on Hanlan's Point has been there since 1808. It marks the beginning of the harbour, and in the days of true shipping, if the weather in the lake had been rough, the lighthouse signalled the promise of home. He can't see it from the rear of the ferry, but he can picture it in his mind: yellow brick; rough, round walls. A lonesome building made for one person, a human outpost sending news of safety in arcs of light. A good job, he thinks, to be the man with that message.

Five minutes into the crossing, he removes a little ball of tin foil from an inside pocket and unwraps four tiny blue pills. Sublingual Ativan, chemical name lorazepam, an artificial opiate. Four pills is twenty milligrams, at least twice the normal dose. He puts them under his tongue and they dissolve into a sweet slurry, speeding into his blood through the cells under his tongue, the epithelia in his cheeks, his throat, up the mainline to his brain, soothing and singing their mantra. *You are loved.* He's taken this many before, and ridden the awesome settling of mind and soul all the way down into a sleep full of smiling women, bright fields, houses smelling of supper.

Marianne is still at home, in bed.

He can see the whole city now, a crystalline shape glowing on the shoreline where once had been nothing but forest and swamp. After that, the fires of local tribes, the creaking forts of the French, the garrisons and dirt roads and yellow-bricked churches of the English and the Scots. It's only overwhelming if you try to take it all in at once, he thinks, if you try to see it whole. Otherwise, just a simple progression in time. Not that far away in the past at all, even—the mechanisms that make it seem to be are simple ones. Just a change in materials, a shift in fashion.

This joyous well-being holds him. He doesn't mind that it's chemical: everything is chemical. Happiness and desolation, fear of death, the little gaps between nerves where feeling leaps. He holds tight to the lash-post and shimmies around to the front of it, drinking the moist air in ecstatic gulps. The vague slopings of the deck are transmitted to his brain as an optical illusion: the city pitching up gently and subsiding, up and down, his senses marvellously lulled. Water moving under the boat. Sky, city, blue-black lake, city, sky. The peaceful sound of water lapping the hull. He lets the swells help him forward and up. More air against him now, his thin windbreaker flapping, his mouth full of wind, the sound of a long, deep breath—

*One*

~

# THE HARBOUR LIGHT

~

*Toronto, November 1997*

## I.

MARIANNE HELD THE PHONE TO HER EAR AND WAITED for her daughter's voice. Outside the hotel window, the dark was coming earlier than it had the night before, a failing in the west. There was, at last, a slow exhale on the other end of the line: unhappy surrender.

"And you really wonder where Alison gets her drama gene?"

"She gets it from your father."

"There's a difference between passion and spectacle, Mum. This is spectacle."

"I'm fine." She scuffed her bare feet on the hotel carpet, thinner here, at the side of the bed. She lifted her face, breathed out quietly toward the stuccoed ceiling with her mouth wide. "How is your fiancé?" she said.

"Like you care how he is. Don't change the subject."

"I do care."

"So you want to talk to him then? I'll put him on." Bridget lowered the phone and Marianne heard the close, hollow sound of the receiver being muffled. Under it, John's voice saying, "Me?"

Bridget came back on the line. "I'm just going to come down there, okay Mum? I'll bring you something to eat."

"They have room service."

"You know what I mean."

"And you know what I mean."

"You want to be alone."

"Yes."

"And watch a hole in the ground."

"That too."

"And is Alison coming?"

"Your sister's in Philadelphia."

"I know that, but is she coming? Did you ask her to come?"

Marianne had thought of calling Alison, but her younger daughter had a second child to worry about now and didn't need to know her mother was having an interesting reaction to the death of her father. "I haven't spoken to Alison," she said.

"She'll freak."

"Bridget, your opinion of your sister's—"

"She will."

"She'll understand. It would be nice if you could do that too."

"I *understand* but that doesn't mean I—"

"I'm glad you understand," said Marianne. "I'll talk to you tomorrow, I promise."

She hung up before Bridget could say another word and kept her hand closed around the receiver as if pressing her finger against those lips. She took the phone off the hook and lay it on the bedside table. They charged two dollars for a local call here, but at the kiosk on the ground floor you could buy a phone card and, for eighty-five cents, talk to someone in Lithuania for an hour. She didn't know anyone in Lithuania. She hardly knew anyone here, except for the room service people, and they never said anything but "Will that be all?" and "Thank you, Mrs. Hollis." She stared at the silenced phone, imagined Bridget calling back and getting the hotel operator again, being asked if she'd like to leave a message. She didn't want to hear it. This silence was necessary.

Through the room's north-facing window she looked at the upper halves of downtown buildings that ranged up into the centre of the city. At her feet, the room was tight with clutter, like something shattered and held in a fist. She got up and stepped over discarded newspaper sections and books splayed open on the floor where they'd fallen, their dustjackets loose. Moving closer to the window, the object of her attention hoved into view: a slowly deepening hole at the foot of the hotel. From where she stood, she could see what anyone on this side of the hotel above the fifth floor could see: the whole expanse of a construction site, congested with yellow machines twenty-four hours a day, and the busy bodies of men and women ranging over the acre or so of dirt, with its steel framing, PVC piping, and heavy wooden beams. But to the occupants of room 647 or 1147 or 3447—the room directly above hers—the busy excavation was just some faint hint of the future, like all the

holes in this city were that eventually generated condominiums and shopping centres and bank towers.
Marianne was the only person in the hotel for whom the
pit at the foot of the hotel meant the past.

They were digging out the foundation of a new arena.
A boondoggle of municipal and private money had been
dedicated to the creation of an unnecessary new hockey
palace. They'd broken ground on the new arena just as
fall began in earnest, the leaves radiating back the whole
spectrum of light they'd absorbed since April, fading out
yellow, orange, red, and the builders were already three
months behind schedule. They'd started gutting the old
post office in June, but had spent the rest of the summer
wrangling with the municipal government, fighting with
the National Hockey League, the National Basketball
Association, the neighbourhood associations, the seeming swarms of local citizens' groups and area historians,
all of whom wanted their say, and who were finally dis-
patched with reassurances that the local ecology
(crushed Tetra Paks, rotting blankets and parkas,
pigeons) would be respected, and any finds of interest
turned over to the correct authorities. If she had learned
anything from her husband's life work, however, it was
not to trust the promises of developers.

That bed of dirt was nothing more than landfill
honeycombed with a century's debris, but it had been of
great interest to David Hollis. He'd spent his working
life teaching "forensic geology"—a field he'd invented
that combined landforms with sleuthing. He took his
students out to local fields or caves with little hammers

and corked phials of sulphuric acid to hunt down speci-
mens and take note of various topographical events.
They became adept at following old river paths, and
learned to date settlements, when they found them, by
overgrowth. Abandoned cemeteries presented fascinating opportunities for in situ casework: he'd ask them to
determine the year of the last burial by comparing different stages of gravestone erosion and making calcula-
tions. All of this was actual geology, and by the third
time he brought the same group out, they all came to
within three years of the date of the last burial. Standing
there, among the living, he felt the beautiful and numi-
nous relationship of his young students to the commu-
nity of these dead, whose last official moment they'd
teased out of the silent witnesses to their lives. The forest that those people had built their houses and coffins
out of now gave testament by counting out the hours and
years *since*. There was (it had come to him in a flash, he
later told Marianne) a science to determining how time
passes. Human beings interrupt the natural cycles of
growth and decay with their communities and their
structures, but they don't stop those cycles. Rather, the
processes continue, like river water flowing around a
stone. Except the river water is made of cities and buildings, and the stone is pushed underground and lost forever. Unless.

Before his death, he'd published a monograph about
these shorelands Marianne looked out on from the hotel.
The booklet suggested there was greatness in that anonymous dirt, but his colleagues had ridiculed him, had

accused him of inventing his source. These people ("those fuckers" was their official designation) had paraded him in front of committees, and only the intervention of his oldest colleague at the university had saved David from complete ignominy. But not, of course, from death. The lakebed accepted all manner of discards.

David's source had been a diary he'd turned up in the rare book library at the University of Toronto. Pyramids of Bankers Boxes there held the barely catalogued papers of perhaps eight defunct archives dating back to the beginning of the nineteenth century. Squinting academics had stroked the John Graves Simcoe papers with cotton gloves (the city's founder! the holy grail!) and taken down every last *bon mot* muttered by him or any of his bucktoothed relations; Simcoe and Mayor Howland and William Lyon Mackenzie and Timothy Eaton had spawned biographical industries. And yet, David had somehow ferreted out an unknown eyewitness with a story of early Toronto.

But David refused to produce this diary—*let people show some faith*, he'd said. His dean, Gerry Lanze, had all but begged him to produce it—or at least, for God's sake, a *call number*—but David had declined. *Proof lacks the power of conviction*, he'd said.

He'd been made a laughingstock. The abandoned post office, still owned by the city, remained unexplored and the area was a hodgepodge of expressways, steakhouses, railway lands, breweries, shipyards, and printing plants. Faith in the "city before we arrived" did not hold any allure to the municipal klatch. Hockey and basket-

ball did. Ten weeks after the publication of his monograph, they dredged him out of the lake.

She came to the hotel as October ended and requested a
northwest corner room on the thirty-third floor. She
wanted to plug in her own lamps and use her own linens.
She would take care of the place herself, wanted to be
undisturbed—intended to finish a novel there, she said,
and she required the utmost privacy. Once the manager
determined to his satisfaction that his hotel would be
home to an *artist* (and was told he would personally be
thanked in the acknowledgements), he admitted her on
her terms. Five porters accompanied her to the thirty-
third floor, moved her things into the small but comfortable room, and then clogged the little space in front of
the door like Keystone Kops. She handed the one in front
a twenty.

   It had taken her a few hours to pack a bag of her
things at the house and then two boxes of books and
papers from David's library. Some of these were his
writings—older monographs, or books including chap-
ters he'd written, books on urban development at the
turn of the century, pamphlets done for the department
of earth sciences on specialty subjects such as archival
practice before 1920, reverse erosion (a computer program that retro-modelled shorelines based on historical
snow- and rainfall measurements), and air-to-ground
cartographic reconciliations. He'd also written a text-
book on forensic geology and topography that was the
standard in many American schools (and as a result was

coming into use in Canada). Marianne gathered up her copy of his damning monograph, a maquette of the city in 1856 that one of his students had made for him, and a tower of photocopied newspaper pages. Lastly, she took two art deco standing lamps from the front room (David had hated these lamps), some blankets and pillows, and called two cabs to bring it all downtown.

One of the lamps she placed beside the bed, a trilight that provided mood, reading, and daytime settings. She put the other one near the door, beside the bathroom, to give the impression of a larger space: when lit, it made the little entranceway look more like a foyer. Hotels never wasted lighting on entranceways, but she hated the darkness of exits and entries. They'd installed key-lights on a track down the middle of the front hallway at the house to make that space glow with welcome.

From a market below the hotel, she bought a bag of apples and a box of clementines, which had just made their appearance in stores. They'd scent the room of home and fall, and if she'd had so much as a hotplate, she would have boiled a cinnamon stick on it too. In the room, she peeled three of the clementines and scattered the skins under the beds and along the wide ledges, and sucked on the sections while standing in the middle of the space, looking for gaps where the hotel's soul showed through too plainly. She unloaded her books and papers, and organized them in piles on the west-facing ledge, as much in categories as she could manage, so she'd be able to find sources if she needed them. She suspected she would not need them: in the main, her work was observation. She'd brought the books, books he had loved, to have his company while she was there.

She imagined Bridget's voice trapped in the cul-de-sac of the disconnected phone. She looked at it from the window—just a harmless thing when unplugged—and resolved to keep it off the hook for a couple of days. Knowing it would not ring made the room feel a little more lonesome, and she went to sit at the desk beside the television where she kept her copy of David's monograph, leaning upright against the wall. She'd wrapped the cover of the little book in a protective plastic sheeting, and when she sat at the desk at a certain angle— which she avoided doing—she could see her face in it. The cover said:

A Deduction Using Forensic Topographical Methods in Conjunction with Archival Source Materials of the Location of the Plate Negatives of the 1856 Toronto Panorama and 352 Other Items, with Some Comments.

And centred below it:

David M. Hollis, Ph.D., A monograph published to mark the opening of The Symposium on the Victorian City in Canada, University of Toronto, May 30–June 2, 1997.

She picked it up, as she did many times in a day, and tilted it into the light from the window. It reflected the white-and-blue sky and elided his name in clouds. She put it down and crossed to the window. Maybe the hotel would not be an unpleasant place to be holed up with grief, she thought. Its windows drew in a clear bright light from the north and the west, and it would not be any harder to sleep alone in one of its two double beds than at home. There were sounds of machines from outside, and voices through the walls, and even art to look at: two lithographs on the walls, of the models of the solar system preferred, in one, by Copernicus, and in the other, by Ptolemy. They flanked the television set.

Bridget said, "What I understand is that you're acting like a madwoman." She looked across the living room at John, who was sitting at attention on the couch, a book open in his lap. "Mum?" She shook her head slowly. "She hung up on me."

"Let her be for now," John Lewis said.

"Do you know what she's doing?" He closed the book and pushed himself up from the couch, took the phone out of her hand. He tried to kiss her and she pulled her head back to see his eyes. "Do you?"

"She's taking a break."

"She's living at the Harbour Light Hotel. Watching the Union Arena excavation." She took the phone back from him. "Now do you think she's crazy?"

He slipped the book back into its space on the shelf, running two fingers along its spine to ensure it was flush with the others. It was the sort of gesture Bridget noticed and made fun of from time to time, but she was silent now, looking through him. "I think you should leave her alone," he said. "It's been two months. She should do whatever she needs to help her cope."

"She doesn't want me down there."

"You shouldn't take it personally."

She laughed at him.

"I have to go to Howard's," he said. "I have stuff for him. Have a drink, take Bailey for a walk." The dog snapped to attention at the sound of her name. "You'll feel different later."

"That would suit you."

"It'll suit you too."

She stood with her arms crossed, an obelisk. Then she seemed to decide to drop it for now. "Will you ask your employer to actually pay you?" she said. "Tell him you can't wait until his next hit play."

He kissed her and held her face against his. He felt the tendons in her neck standing up beneath his palm.

## 2.

TWO YEARS EARLIER, ON A SPRING AFTERNOON, John Lewis had been in the Hollises' living room waiting to see if he'd be needed. *TV Guide* open in his lap. *Jerry witnesses an accident—and is attracted to the victim.* In the kitchen, two rooms distant, all four Hollises were around their table, discussing what they knew, what they could not know, what they feared to know. David Hollis had been diagnosed with Lou Gehrig's disease. John heard Bridget crying and he readied himself, wiping his palms on his pants, but then there were voices again.

Bridget said, "Normal for who?" and then he heard the murmur of David's voice, calming some rush to judgment. Her father brought a measure of courtesy to a household of bull-headed women. He had honesty on his side, the women had bluntness and charm. If one of them disliked something you said or did or wore, you knew about it immediately. You heard *we're not having this conversation* or *are you done with this?* or *are you really going to wear that?*

From the kitchen, Marianne: "We *are* getting a second opinion. And a third if we have to."

"You can't shop for a diagnosis you like," said David. "This is what it is. But we don't have to lose our heads over it."

A chair squeaked backwards and there was the sound of a pile of something hitting the tabletop.

"Get those fucking handbooks off the table, Bridget. He's a person, not an appliance."

"You don't know the first thing about these."

"Mum sent them down to me."

"Well, of course she did."

"Trust me, the only thing they don't have is a chapter on how to slit your wrists. They're total downers."

"Well, he doesn't have the flu!"

"Come on, girls."

"She thinks 'Be Positive' is a treatment option!" John could see Bridget gesturing with both her hands. About now he imagined she looked like the Greek men who sat all afternoon in the cafés near their apartment. "Are you going to sit here and meditate? We have to get to know this thing whether we want to or not."

"The storm before the storm," David said, and he laughed alone. John heard one of the sisters begin to cry. His money was on Alison, "the passionate one." Her domain was the big emotional moment. Bridget's famous story about her sister involved a drive from Toronto to Disneyworld when they were kids, during which they had so enraged Marianne with their incessant complaining that she'd made David turn around at the

Florida border. An hour later, stopping for gas near Glynn, Alison used every last penny of her spending money to buy them all plastic Mickey Mouse ears. Then she sat weeping in the back seat until everyone put them on and Marianne agreed to point the car south again. Sometimes Alison frightened John, but she simply infuriated Bridget, and her living in the U.S. suited them both. John heard the passionate one say: "No matter what, you can't give up, Dad."

"Don't be so dramatic. Of course he's not—"

"I know he won't."

"Well don't even suggest it."

"Maybe I should move back," Alison said. "To help you guys. Just for a while."

John could hear Bridget's thoughts as if they were being megaphoned from a passing truck: *GOD NO.* She said, "You have a six-month-old. He needs you too."

"I'm just saying."

"I know," said Bridget, and there was relief in her voice. Her sister would get credit for the intent.

Alison's penchant for emotional cabaret came from David, who once cried during a Campbell's soup commercial. He'd wept when Alison called with the news that she was going to have a baby, and he'd cried when John and Bridget announced their engagement the previous fall. He even hugged John before he did his own daughter. They'd announced it in this very room, and John had been sitting in this same chair, with the same view of the closed television cabinet, appliqué flowers over yellow paint. He'd felt frightened then, as if what he and Bridget had chosen could be annulled by a secret word. This fear had translated itself into the two of them sitting at opposite ends of the small room. David came over to John and clasped both his hands in his. "John Hollis!" he said laughing. "You really think she's going to let you keep your own name?"

"Lewis-Hollis actually sounds really nice," Bridget said.

"Or Hollis-Lewis."

Marianne had not moved, and when David sat back down she said, "Any reason in particular why now?"

Bridget gave her mother an underwhelmed look. "Do you mean *am I pregnant*?"

"I know you would tell us that news first."

Bridget was sitting with her arms crossed, physical shorthand, John knew, for *come and get me*. Because she was innocent of her mother's accusation, Bridget would refuse to say so. "If I am pregnant, then have I done a bad thing by not telling you first, or because I'm getting married for the wrong reason?"

"I'm saying I'm certain you would give us the benefit of the right context and then we could be very happy to hear all of your news."

"So you would be equally pleased with *Mum, I* want *to get married* and *Mum, I* have *to get married*, as long as we told you the news in the right order? It has nothing to do with the fear that you'd look bad in front of your North Toronto chums if I were standing at the altar already knocked up."

"We're not pregnant," said John. "We're not."

"A wedding!" said David, clapping his hands together. His wife and daughter looked into their laps.

After another moment of silence, Marianne breathed in brightly and said, "I'm sorry. You caught me by surprise is all. I'm thrilled for you both. For all of us."

~

"You're not my frigging valet." Bridget was standing in the doorway of the living room. "Why do you insist on waiting out here?"

"I don't want to intrude."

"If anyone's the intruder here, I am. To judge from how much Alison already knows."

"You guys should keep talking. Anyway, I don't think your mum wants me in there."

Marianne's voice carried from the kitchen. "I don't care where you are, John. At least if you're in here, no one will think you're eavesdropping."

"See?" said Bridget, and then more quietly, "If you're in there, I might be able to keep myself from garrotting my baby sister with her own fucking necklace."

He went in and sat down. Cups of tea in front of them, David at the head of the table, spent and pale. John had only met Alison once before, at her wedding two summers ago. The last happy family occasion? She was living in Philly with her husband, a baby, and another on the way, but she flew up as soon as she heard the news. She said, "John," as if they were meeting in a boardroom, and he took a seat beside her.

There was a pile of pamphlets at Marianne's elbow. The one on top was called *Living with ALS: Managing Your Symptoms and Treatment*. She saw him looking at it and slipped it over to him, and John instinctively covered the title with his hand. "We all know what it says, John. You can read it."

"Plenty of good stuff in that one," said David. "Cramps-slash-spasms, urinary urgency, swelling of hands and feet—none of which I have. Fatigue—I have fatigue, but I've always had fatigue—"

"But not like this, Dad," said Bridget.

"Drooling-slash-salivation, thick phlegm–slash–postnasal drip, quivery jaw . . . anyway, what I'm trying to say is we need to be vigilant, yes? But for now: *I'm fine*. We don't have to fight amongst ourselves, we don't have to call in the army—"

"No one is calling in the army," said Bridget. "But shouldn't we be prepared? We have to know what to look for. Because we know you won't ask for help when you need it. Right?"

"That means you want me to ask now, Bridget, but all I need is my family around me, and for everyone to stop panicking."

"No one's panicking."

"Bridget's right," said Alison. "We have to meet this head on. As a family. You too, John."

Bridget clenched her eyes to slits. "What the hell does that mean?"

"That he's part of the family."

"No, that's your way of saying that even though he

lost his parents he can probably still understand how these things work."

"Bridge, I don't think that's what she means." John tried to take her hand; she slid it away from him. "I consider myself a part of the family, Alison. Thank you."

"So how does he look to *you*, John?"

He braced himself for Bridget to boil over. She had never mastered the art of letting her sister roll off of her, and in the past couple of weeks her Alison threshold had become perilously low. Marianne had called Alison a week ago to tell her what Dr. Aubrey said about a twitch in her father's cheek. "Bell's palsy, right?" she'd said to the doctor, but it wasn't that harmless, almost comic response to stress. "Never sick a day in his life," she'd said to Alison, but she waited a week to tell Bridget. "I didn't want you to freak out while you were cramming for the bar," Marianne had said, meaning, *you have limits, but your pregnant sister can handle anything*. It had taken John three days to calm her down after that.

"Just tell yourself she was being thoughtful," he'd said.

"This is what happens, just like I told you. The old alliances."

"They're not an alliance, Bridge." He remembered the look on her face, as if suggesting that there was no familial conspiracy called his own allegiances into question. "People in families express their love differently to each other."

"And are you an expert on families?"

What he didn't say was that Alison couldn't hold a candle to her, but he had to be careful saying anything positive to Bridget when she was in a mood like that. She would take it as coddling and turn into a porcupine. He noticed lately that he was measuring what he said to Bridget more than he had before. He told himself it meant that he knew her fully now, but it worried him that maybe it meant something else.

"Cadet Lewis, are you going to answer me?" Alison said.

"Yes," said John. "I guess he seems fine to me. Right now."

"Thank you," said David, and Bridget glared at them all.

She took the symptoms-and-treatment book from in front of John and squared it on top of the pile. Four neat colour-coded spines with gleaming staples all lined up in the middle of the table: her father's future spelled out in positive, but firmly realistic, language. ("*Power pudding* can be a helpful recipe for constipation. It consists of equal parts prunes, prune juice, applesauce, and bran.") "Never mind," Bridget said. "He's not fine. And we're not lighting candles or going to herbalists or hunting down a doctor with an alternate opinion."

"I don't think it's up to you what we do," said Marianne.

"I want a beer," said David, pushing himself up from the table. "I'm alive for the time being, so I'm going to watch the ball game."

Bridget pushed her own chair back. "You're not supposed to drink."

"Why not? They give you a cigarette when they blindfold you, don't they?"

She stood in front of him, as if to block his passage to the fridge, but he took it as an offer to be held. He pulled her to him and Bridget hugged him with one arm around his wide back. John marked Alison's face, Marianne's tears, and watched Bridget stretch her other arm out, open a drawer, and put a bottle opener on the counter beside her father.

That night, John and Bridget slept in the bed they'd bought only a week earlier, the dog wedged into the space between them, and Bridget dreamt about the afternoon, seeing it on the screen of her mind almost exactly as it had happened. Coming up the steps to the door, her mother standing there with that twitchy, excited expression on her face, the four of them in the kitchen, John sentinel behind the wall. Watching her father trying to return a teacup to the tabletop. Everything the same in the dream until her father got up and left the room. In her dream, when he closed the kitchen door, a skin grew over it instantly. It spread in a rash over the walls and ceiling in all directions, fresh pink skin that suddenly dried to a white cake, then cracked and fell away and came down on their heads like old paint, heaping up around their feet.

She woke, the end of an unconscious exclamation on her lips, and moved closer to John. She wasn't used to the bed yet; it was softer than the futon she'd slept on since university, and having a proper bed raised off the floor made her feel as if she'd invited adult things to roost in her life. And so now she was living with a boyfriend, engaged to him, and her father had fallen ill, and her sister was pregnant with a second child, and how did this happen, how did you fail to mark the little changes that brought you to such a place in your life? Everything was different now, so much in her life was new, but it wasn't newness that distressed her, it was unfamiliarity, it was this deeper gravity. As if the ground drew her footsteps down to it. She pushed against him. "You asleep?"

His breathing didn't change; she draped an arm over him, the ball of his hipbone accommodated in the crook of her elbow, her fingertips against his thigh. Her eyes were adjusting to being awake and she could make out street light through the curtain, the window behind it was lambent with it. It was deep in the middle of the night. "John? Are you asleep?" She heard him murmur that he was. "Maybe I should ask Alison to stay with us?"

He shrugged and with the logic of a dream, he saw the release of his shoulders pull a bright light down from the ceiling. It was Bridget switching on his lamp. He burst upright, completely awake. "Where," he said.

"I didn't mean to wake you."

"I'm awake."

"Maybe I just want to keep an eye on her though."

He nodded, still swimming in a dream that involved a road. "Sure . . . maybe it would be good for the two of you to be together right now. You could sleep with her in here."

"She'll say Mum needs her. There's no point in asking."

If he let her now, she'd dash exhausted down some looping conversational path and then end up crying. He pulled her over to him and drew her head down against his stomach. Her shoulder was cool against him. She tucked an arm under his leg and pulled it close to her, like a blanket. His body stirred despite him.

"I don't think you really get what's going on in my parents' house."

"In what way?"

"Just how it is. With everyone fighting for possession of my father. It's sick. You don't know how sick families are."

"I still had a family after my parents died, Bridget. I wasn't raised by wolves."

"You always say 'my aunt's kids' when you talk about them, though. You don't call them your family."

"Well, they were my family. And now you are. Just because I don't work up your sister's hysteria about it doesn't mean—"

She sat up and he could see it was too late to prevent tears. His erection vanished. "Then why did you have to wait to be invited before you'd come and sit with us this afternoon?"

"I'm sorry."

"Why? You knew how alone I was there."

"I didn't want to do the wrong thing. With everyone so tense—"

"And standing by me could be the 'wrong thing'?"

"You know how your mother is, Bridget. When she's like this."

She shook her head. Without knowing how, he'd confirmed something for her. When had this talent for taking everything the wrong way emerged in her? She slid back down under the covers and turned her back to him.

"Bridget . . ."

"You let me know when my mother's stress levels reach a point where it's safe to pay attention to mine."

"I don't want to make things any worse."

She said nothing. After a moment, he lay down and turned the light off. He reran the conversation in his mind, trying to find the place in it where he could have turned, where he would have made her happy, where she'd have been comforted. But he could not find it.

SHE TOLD NO ONE WHERE SHE WAS. SHE UNPACKED her clothes and put them neatly away, placed a couple of framed pictures on the small desk beside the TV: one of the four of them; another of David taken a year after their wedding, him reading the *Toronto Telegram* in their garden, a mug of coffee sitting in the grass.

She spent her first night in the bed closest to the west-facing window, and shed photocopied pages of the *Globe* from 1855 to the floor beside her. Government lands for sale, new goods arriving daily at Rutherford's. This world that had so possessed David seemed unwilling to impart any scent of itself to her. She'd heard his stories on an almost daily basis throughout their married life, and yet she knew now that she'd listened to so many of them only passingly, as one does when the commonplace is spoken of. Reading these papers, she tried to imagine men in costume standing on wooden sidewalks, snapping open their fresh, linen-like newspapers and scanning for tell of England. She read "Death of a Canadian in California": a man "foully murdered" while on his mule. People gone a century and a half, but freshly dead in those pages, their bodies only just committed to their graves and the widows still keening. For some reason, Marianne had always thought that in earlier times people took death in stride, that they weren't as attached to each other as people were in her own. It was to be expected that, in the rude, unfinished world, people would be lost. It bothered her to think that her pain was part of a tradition. That people so different from her could partner her in grief.

She could not sleep and focused instead on relaxing her electrified limbs and trying to breathe. Now and then she was surprised to wake up and realize a little time had passed. She imagined she would probably sleep in fits for the rest of her life. Anything approaching normal in this room was not to be wished for, and yet, within a couple of days, she'd established a routine of moving to and from the bed all day, alternating lying in it with sitting on the north-facing ledge against a large throw pillow, reading. Sometimes she would move to the small desk to search the Web on her laptop. She felt sleepy occasionally, and when she tried to focus too long on something her eyes would become heavy, unless she was reading the monograph itself, which held her attention like a voice crying her name. She'd open it and it would hold her, saying—

Men and women who were not our fathers and mothers brought us into this world. They made this city before us. We know that a man once stood on a scaffold eighty feet above the ground and painted in brilliant white the words GELBER BROS. WHOLESALE WOOLLENS on the side of the red-brick building at 225 Richmond Street. We know because we have seen that sign since we were children, we have watched it slowly fade—the brick rising through the skin of the weathered paint like a welt—and although we do not know the name of the man who put those words there, and surely he is dead, we cannot doubt that he lived, he lived here, he worked here, he was a Torontonian.

—and she might want to put it down, to return to the uninsistent view outside the window, but in this little booklet lay all his faith—

So too the women who sewed fur collars at 121 Spadina at the dawn of the century, one of whom photographed her co-workers and wrote their names on the back of the print that resides in the Toronto archives at St. Lawrence Hall. *Gusta, Hattie, Freda, Channa, Marie-Caroline.* And before them, the men who baked bricks at the works in the Don Valley, and the men who mortared them for the houses on Palmerston before 1870, and the men who buried the gaslines that lit that part of the city in 1901. Go back farther, however, and our proofs are thinner. Someone made an ink drawing of Bishop Strachan's house—the Bishop's Palace—before it was torn down in 1890. I have seen a picture of Front Street's grand Iron Block, destroyed by fire in 1872. But what of the city we know—should I say, *we believe?*—

existed before then? Didn't those men and women, whose names we have all but lost, wander home in the evening to their hearths and speak of their future here? We are only faintly aware of the city they lived in—it is just an intuition, a movement in the corner of the eye. Of that city which must have stunk of horses and offal and pine oils and roasted fowl, of that air that rang with the cries of newsboys and the sounds of boots on hollow walkways and hooves on stone. But a hint of it is all we have.

Here, then, is something to buttress our faith: we already know of a thirteen-plate panorama of the city of Toronto. Made close to Christmas of 1856, the images were taken from the roof of the Rossin House—once located at the southeast corner of York and King streets (and demolished in 1969). The pictures were collodion positives pulled from glass negatives, and have always been attributed to the Toronto photography firm of Armstrong, Beere, and Hine. These pictures were the extent of the city we knew of before 1860. And until now, we have believed these pictures were all we would ever know.

Allow me now to set forth the outline of an incredible discovery. This monograph—using modern methods of cartographic reconciliation, computer imaging of known weather patterns in the Toronto harbour of 1857, shipping records, as well as newly discovered source materials—will show that an unnamed photographer (who is unlikely to be any of the principals of Armstrong, Beere, and Hine) took the Toronto panorama, and also took *a nearly complete photographic record* of the city of 1856: its streets, its parks, its houses and industry, its people. Further, it will show that the original glass negatives and their positives were displayed in England in early 1857 and were returning to Toronto when the ship carrying the photographer, as well as his trunk of photographic documentation, was swamped in a violent storm about two hundred metres from shore in the Toronto harbour. The photographer was also a diarist who survived the storm to describe it in his journal, where he gives the date of the sinking as April 28, 1857, but does not name the ship. However, he describes a harrowing barge rescue "in waters so enraged that though Brown's Wharf be nearly made when the boat capsized, the journey to land with our rescuers seemed as epic as another ocean crossing." Six ships sank that day in the lake, but the only one that close to shore was a screw steamer called the *Commodore Walker*.

The remains of this boat would have sunk approximately six hundred metres from the 1857 shoreline. This shoreline, long since elided by landfill, would have run approximately twenty metres south of the railtracks behind the present-day Union Station, which is due north of where Brown's Wharf was located.

This monograph will show that somewhere within a five-square-kilometre area due south of Union Station lies the ruin of the *Commodore Walker*, and that in its stowage remains a steel container holding almost four hundred never-seen images of this city. These pictures, still graven on the original glass plates, will constitute the earliest photographic record we have of Toronto.

Finally, she'd have to push it all away, push his passion out of sight.

He'd surprised her one night in the spring of 1996, calling her name from the driveway. She saw him fumbling up the dusky incline to the door and rushed out, the air still warm from the afternoon, and pulled him into the house. She put a cup of tea in front of him, mopped a light cover of rain off his hair with a paper towel. Two Coffee Break cookies on a plate. She watched his mouth as he worked the cookies against his back teeth. He'd been spending his days hunched over papers in the Thomas Fisher Rare Book Library at U of T, hunting down information even he admitted was dull. The Fisher was his heart's home— old teak cabinets full of file cards with the fading handwriting of dead librarians, local history, broadsides carefully peeled off last century's lampposts by some archivist type just like himself. Newspapers, maps, advertisements for land, everything filed away in crisping folders, laid back to front in Bankers Boxes. A room full of voices. He was talking about a misfiled dossier. The phrase *emotional lability* scrolled across her mind as he fought to chew, catch his breath, and tell her of his find all at once. But that was excessive laughing or crying, wasn't it? At least he didn't look crazy.

He was coughing out tea. She got up and rubbed his back with a circular motion until it was over. Dr. Aubrey had told her not to thump him on the back unless it looked as if he were really choking. David held up his hand for her to stop.

"The wet and the dust is just a super combination for you, David."

"Will you listen to me?"

"I am listening." She stood, hand at the ready, behind him.

He tucked his forearm behind one knee to pull the leg closer to the other. "That place is a giant jigsaw puzzle, you know? Three million pieces. Someone starts a thought in 1870, and then someone else completes it in a pamphlet a hundred years later. All you have to do is fit it together."

She was thinking about the air in the library—she couldn't help it—and how often David yawned, his brain oxygen-starved. And the particulate matter, that's what Dr. Aubrey called it, not just regular dust but flakes of insect exoskeletons and dander and mites' legs and dead white blood cells, none of it worth breathing. She pulled her mind around to him again, the way she'd once had to turn the girls' faces to her to make sure they were paying attention. "So you found something? That's good."

"Will you sit *down*," he said.

She poured more tea for them both and furtively dipped a pinky into his cup to test the heat. She was trying, as she always did now, to keep her mind focused on the present, where he was alive and speaking to her. *This moment is still happening*, she thought.

He watched her settle into the chair across from him with her cup of tea. He held her eyes. "I found a diary. An Englishman who came to Toronto in 1855. Faded grey ink and actual fingerprints in the margins. You can feel him sitting at his table and writing everything down in that very book. Drinking tea like I am right now. He was a photographer."

She felt a little calmer with a hot mug in her hands, and the present holding them in it. "They had photographers in the 1850s?"

"They had them before 1850, Marianne."

"What are his pictures like?"

"They aren't with the diary."

"Okay."

He drank. Hands relatively steady. "They're lost. He lost them in a storm. All of the original plates. But he could be the fellow who took the Toronto panorama. That was 1856. Or '57, I think."

"They know that man's name, don't they?" she said, trying desperately to hold on to his story, but he frowned at her. "What?"

"Why would I say he *could* be the same man if I knew his name? Of course they know who took the panorama, but most people don't address themselves in their own diaries, so I have no way of knowing if this is the same man. That's why I said *could be*."

"All right, I'm sorry. It's very interesting, David, for sure it is."

He nodded once, emphatically, and began to give her more detail, making links for her between times and seasons, but she couldn't follow again, she was pre-occupied with danger, with how excitement of any sort was no good for him. His words closed over her like a wave: he was talking about photos of the city, he said something about London (he must have meant England—no, he was talking about Toronto again), and there was even something about Queen Victoria, but all she could really focus on was his building, childlike excitement. "Hold on, though," she said, backtracking to regain purchase on the story, "he lost the plates where?"

"In the lake." He stopped to breathe and gulped for air, jaw unhinging fishlike. "He brought them back from overseas and his steamship foundered in Lake Ontario. They were in a leather-bound steel strongbox. Glass plates."

"But people dive in the lake all the time, David. Anything that went down a hundred and fifty years ago is long gone."

There was a corona of white around his pupils. "The box isn't in the water, Marianne. The steamer was close to the shore when it went down and the city's filled that area in long since." His eyes went up toward the ceiling and for a moment it looked like he was going to close them. "It's in landfill. It's buried in the dirt somewhere close to where the old wharves were."

"But doesn't the panorama exist, David? You've shown it to me in a book . . ."

"For Christ's sake, Marianne! I'm not talking about the *panorama*! What I'm talking about is other pictures taken by the same man, hundreds of other pictures, all intimate pictures of Toronto—stores and houses and people and streets and signs! And if it's the same man, then the original plates for the panorama are down there as well." His eyes were bright and glassy. "This is the motherlode."

She remembered that he hadn't taken any medication since noon; he'd missed the four o'clock chemical correction, having overstayed his time in the library. She knew he wouldn't eat dinner until he'd had his tea, so now the after-dinner pills too, with their tiny powers, were not at work in him keeping various symptoms in abeyance, systems in balance. This was why she'd had the odd tingling of danger: he was failing in that minor way he did when too much time passed between medications. At this time of day there was baclofen for stomach cramps, glycopyrrolate to keep salivation down, lorazepam for anxiety and shakes and to relax the breathing (to relieve "air hunger"—too beautiful a term for what it was: the sick-making sound of her husband snapping for air with dry lips), calcium pills for bone density, Mylanta for constipation, Rilutek to slow the decay (but she'd forgotten it had to be taken with food—*shit*—and now she'd have to convince him to eat something else just to get it in him), and finally a vitamin pill. The capsules were arrayed inside little dovecotes that had the hours of the day, rather than the days of the week, embossed on their individual lids. When shaken, after being filled in the morning, the container sounded like an African rainstick. "We forgot your pills," she said.

"All I need is a couple of maps and I can triangulate the position. There's probably even records of the wreck. Measurements."

"I think it's terrific, David." She pushed her chair back to rescue the neglected pill container from the window ledge above the sink. "You have to take these with something more hearty than biscuits."

"I can take them later. Gerry's going to love this."

"It could be something, it really sounds like it could be."

"Don't condescend, Marianne. It is something. I'm going to talk to him. This could keep me busy for years."

"The pills, David." He reached for them, a gesture that would have been sharp and angry if his muscles were still listening to his commands. She held the container back. "Do you want toast or a banana with them?"

"I'm not hungry."

"A bit of rice then."

He shook his head. "Give me a couple more of these." He pushed the empty plate across to her and the few crumbs on it coursed over the side and onto the table.

"The sugar can aggravate your shaking."

"Damn it, then just give them to me. I can take them on their own."

She didn't feel like fighting him, and she popped open the two compartments that said "4 p.m." and "7 p.m." and tilted the case into his hand. He took them one by one, placing them near the back of his throat on his thick greyish tongue (the pale handwriting he'd described suddenly flashed in her mind, a strange cognate) and he washed them down with water. One round red, two long thin yellows, a pentagram in blue, a tiny white pill, one after the other like the beads on an abacus vanishing down into the dark of him, pills to count days by. When done, he opened his mouth wide and moved his tongue around, like a prisoner.

*When it was all over, she remembered one of those evenings—they flew back to her unbidden, those last days they'd had together. She came upon him sitting at the dining room table, the whole surface colonized by paper. She'd passed behind, remembering to take the huge iron key out of the standing cabinet: he'd given himself a bruise walking into it once. "It's right there," she said, pointing at the jagged line below Palace Street that marked the lakeshore on his map. 1860. He turned stiffly in his chair.*

*"Marianne, I can see where it is on this map, but do you think I could walk down to Union Station right now and trace it for myself?"*

*"Don't get mad at me, David." (To have him mad at her once more! To have the pleasure of a disagreement!)*

*"I have to go up in a helicopter. You can probably still see the outline from the air."*

*"You're not going in any helicopter, hon. Forget it."*

*She continued on into the kitchen, and when she turned back to look at him, expecting to have to argue the point further, he was standing on the chair, trembling, staring down at the city in the old, photocopied map.*

*In this other life, her afterlife, she kept the table clean.*

## 4.

DAVID HOLLIS WOKE AT SIX, A WAVE OF AWARENESS moving over him, and he began to lever himself against the bed to push his lower half out and over the edge of the mattress. His arms were weaker than his legs, it took a concentrated effort to get himself sitting upright, digging the heels of his palms into the bed. The movement woke Marianne; she sat up on her side, blinking hard, and threw her covers off, a lofting air carrying her scent over to him. He felt her steadying hand on his flank. "Everything okay?"

"I just have to pee."

"Use the bottle."

"I'm going to go like a man, Marianne. Just go back to sleep." He let his top half tilt sideways until he was face down on the bed, then pushed himself up to standing, as if he'd been kneeling beforehand on a pew. Everything shook as he did it, his spine and legs a tower of teacups, but then he was erect, and the habit of being upright steadied him. Standing for almost sixty years had to be worth something.

She let him go, tracking his progress with her eyes. The bathroom was ten feet from his side of the bed and required walking around the foot of it: the southern passage. He'd refused to change sides because he'd slept on the right his whole life, and there was no sense in trading that comfort for the convenience of being four feet closer to the toilet. He closed the door and Marianne lay back down again.

These days, his body felt both light and leaden at the same time: his muscles had wasted, but despite the loss of body mass he still felt like he was carting around an increasingly inert weight. He'd learned, in the past eight months, to balance natural momentum with muscle control: he could get himself moving and then continue by using the natural forces of walking or turning. His arms had become pendulums.

He urinated and washed his face—in the mirror it was long and slack. He tried to smile at himself and saw a novocained grimace. He would not shave, just as he wouldn't cut anything with a sharp knife anymore or lift anything heavy. Gripping was one of the chief problems: he could not hold a fork anymore, and to stir a cup of tea he had to put his shoulder into it first and transfer the rotation down his arm and into his hand. Just to dissolve half a teaspoon of sugar into a mug required a motion that looked like he was churning butter. He had been balancing himself against the cream and sugar table at the local Tim's when, without asking, a strange woman had plunged her stir stick into his coffee and finished mixing it. "My father had it," she said, and she smiled kindly at him, but on her face he saw his own future.

Marianne had fallen back to sleep, and he watched her, his head tilted birdlike. He dressed quietly, negotiating the various garments with the new skill set he'd been taught by an occupational therapist. The trick to getting into a pair of pants was to sit on a chair and put the pants on the floor and arrange the two legholes so they looked like a figure eight. Then you put your feet in the holes and pressed them flat to the floor before threading the pants up your legs. You only stood when you had to, and if someone was needed to button and zip them for you, well then, so be it. T-shirts were out of the question, but he almost never wore them anymore. A button-up could give you grief if you put it on standing: it was almost impossible to get the second arm in if the sleeve fell behind you. So you had to arrange it on the bed and then lie down on it. On this morning, he took his chances, standing in the closet and swinging the second half of the shirt around until he caught it. Socks were still a breeze, so too a belt.

He returned to the room ready for the day and stood near the bed, watching Marianne's ribs rise and fall. She wouldn't wake now, was off-alert, thinking the danger had passed, seeing him to his oblations. She'd sleep deeply now till perhaps eight, thinking him propped up beside her with a book, or drowsing, and he felt, standing there in his own silence, that the present moment was reaching out to her, that his watchfulness would permit a long peace to descend on her before waking. The still and dreaming face of this good woman, heart of his heart, this woman who had seen him to this point in his life but could go with him no farther.

They'd installed a banister lift to get him up and down the stairs. He had to manacle himself into a little fold-down seat and push a button, which would then deliver him in a graceful spiral to the main floor. But when Marianne wasn't around, he liked to walk it, turning to face the other banister and negotiating the steps like going sideways on skis down a hill. It gave him a powerful sense of accomplishment to get all the way down. Edmund Hillary returning to base camp.

He went down and set the coffee maker for eight a.m., poured water in for three cups. He ate four low-sodium Triscuits out of the box while watching the weather on TV. It would get up to twenty-eight today, with clear skies. A storm building off the coast of Georgia, people nailing down the things they cared about, attaching themselves to the known world as the unknown rotated toward them.

At seven, John arrived.

*Two*

~

# BALSAM OF PERU

~

*Toronto, Fall–Winter 1855–6*

MEASURING WITH A DROPPER EIGHT MINIMS OF *Tinctura Opii* into a glass of sherry, the chemist J.G. Hallam, late of Camden Town, said to himself, *I am an average man.* This was a somatic measurement, not a judgment, as twelve minims of laudanum was sufficient to put an average man to sleep. A full dozen would permit up to eight hours of rest. Hallam reduced the dosage to account for the depressant vehicle, and as a professional apothecary he knew a full dose of the addicting drug was excessive if all he wished was to sleep. The night before, twelve grains had combined with the sherry in an unpleasant way that was both stimulating and exhausting. He wanted sleep, needed sleep, and on this night doubled the sherry to ensure he could overcome the inciting qualities of the drug. Strange that there existed in the plant world a compound as likely to instill in one a "creeping thrill," as a writer in *The Knickerbocker* had put it, as it was to induce pure catatonia. Pain was the main cause of prescribing the drug, not nervous sleeplessness. For this condition, Hallam almost always gave potassium bromide. That he gave himself the good stuff reflected the creed of chemists everywhere: careful with the needs of their customers, liberal with their own. Hallam's father had known a fellow apothecary whose regular dosings with silver nitrate (for a gastric ulcer, when bismuth would have done just as well) had turned his skin blue, and yet he would not sell the same caustic in his own shop. *Too dangerous*, the old man had once told Hallam's father. *It will transform you into a dolphin.*

Even so, he splashed the droplets in his drink and watched them spread in an oily slick on the dark surface, mesmeric. He drank it down and went to the hard bed on the other side of the room. He lay on it and faced the iron grate in the pot-bellied stove, watching the wood coals glow. The deep red light was the only illumination in the room; its bars reached across the floor like a maroon-coloured paw. It grew until it held Hallam in its grip, and he slept.

In the dream that he would not later remember, he was back in Camden Town with his wife and two young daughters. He sat at the table with breakfast in front of him, a boiled egg in a cup, a glass of tea, a rack of toast. When Alice spoke to him, he heard her with perfect clarity. *Is there anything you want, darling?* and *Drink up that tea, don't keep your father waiting.* But when she spoke to their children, he could not make out the words, as if Alice spoke to them under water. He heard a songy echo.

The girls' faces were turned up toward their mother, listening. Beloved faces, black curls framing the baby's

eyes, her older sister with her head tilted in an unconscious imitation of her mother. He turned his attention
back to the egg, pried off the lid and scooped out a shiv-
ering mass of white. He salted it and laid it on a point of
toast, put it in his mouth. He saw the black top of the
yolk, idly thought: *ferrous sulfide*, and pushed the spoon
down into it. What came out was solid black though, and
the cut through the centre of the egg showed a yolk as
dark as India rubber all the way through. The smell of
ash rose from the egg cup, and he raised his head and
called out, "Alice?" but neither his wife nor his daughters
were in the room anymore. Rather, a picture of them in
the very attitude he just moments ago had seen them
in sat upright on the floor in a gutta percha case, velvet on
one side, silver and light on the other. His children's eyes
as sharp as stars.

After this J.G. Hallam slept for six more hours, and for
each hour an inch of snow fell on the new city of Toronto.

Winter had begun quietly at the beginning of November,
after sending its card round on October's cold salver.
Only a flurry for a day or two, but then, like a guest
who'd peeked in the door and heard no protest at his
arrival, the snow came to stay. It fell ceaselessly, piling
up on streets and roofs, a weather that stifled the city as
if in a huge blanket. Hallam began to understand why
the slapdash wooden ladders leaning against every second house in the city were left up in winter. They were
used in summer to gain access quickly to a burning roof,
but in winter were needed to get up and broom off the

weight of the snow. It was safe in the main in the damp and temperate median seasons, but in summer people died from smoke and flame and in winter might perish beneath a thin creosoted roof holding up a tonne or more of snow. A Toronto winter was a thing beyond imagining. Never in England had Hallam seen this kind of persistent snow or its attendant temperature. English snow was damp and sticky, white for only moments before the smoke from the day's coal stoves (stoked high against what *seemed* to be cold) brought a familiar bilious tinge to it all.

Here there was no language, no simile for this shut-in weather: a city so benighted by snow that it was as if thousands of people were living, perforce, alone in it. Social intercourse had to be managed indoors, but few were willing to seek it out in such a punishing environment. And if one were to walk the covered streets in violent winds, then it seemed that the city was inhabited by a dark sect, its aspirants walking with their heads lowered, their eyes shrouded, their bodies hidden beneath thick exteriors.

In the middle of the third week in November, Hallam marked four months in his shop under the sign of the mortar (a costly wooden carving that was meant to impart seriousness and authority), and although he didn't feel in the least celebratory, he did feel cheered by the thought that time was moving on. He mentioned the minor event to Mr. Terrace, the server at Jewell & Clow's. He'd made the restaurant his regular, having only to pass south of King Street on Church to reach it, and from there it was only a short walk back to his shop. Hallam took breakfasts and suppers there, and it was a way to be around other people, something that in this unsociable town was essential if a man did not want to feel that he was travelling alone in a groove of his own making.

Mr. Terrace brought a pot of hot tea, and Hallam ordered the oatmeal as he usually did, but added a single egg on the side. "To mark one entire third of a year passed and survived," he said. "A little splurging."

"You're entitled, Mr. Hallam." He admired the waiter, well placed in his work. To feel that you were doing well the job suited to you: was it too much to dream for? Maybe Hallam was born to drink tea. Just to sit in a place like Jewell & Clow's like a fixture, a part of the atmosphere. He was certainly good at it. The idea of being a regular held a mysterious sway over Hallam, as it did for many of the single businessmen whose faces he would see only in this place before they all drained away into the general population. Their society was made of two meals five days a week, with only rare conversation, but it was continuity, and it was nourishing. Sometimes Hallam imagined the restaurant as a trench full of men, and you cast your eyes around looking for the others who were in there with you, counting them off silently in your mind: *there is Russell, and Burke, and Samuels is over there in the corner.* But he would notice the absence of one of them, and before long word would go round that something had happened. Russell had taken to drink worse than ever, or Burke married, or Samuels felled by

a bad heart. And the survivors would trade a sympa-
thetic word, as they would in his own extended absence,
and shake their heads. Strange, thought Hallam, that this
minor society would convene at first at random and then
by choice. And in a restaurant. These moments in his
day filled him with a feeling not unlike hopefulness, and
he brought that mood back out into the street with him
like a scent of something freshly made. But then it would
disperse and in would come the pong of creosote and
dust, milk and offal. And a few moments later, unlock-
ing and entering his shop, so would float in the scent of
chemicals and disappointment.

In the beginning, when the days were still full of
light, he'd taken his meals at the American Hotel at the
bottom of Yonge Street. Because of its situation so close
to the main docks, the hotel took its fair share of travellers fresh off the boats and, to Hallam, this meant the
possibility of hearing news from home that was only
three weeks old, and seeing faces still uncreased with
the worries of the so-called New World. He remembered freshly his first glimpse of the city, as the ferry
came around the western side of the island that lay off
its shore: a vision of spires and yellow brick and white
stone set against a wall of trees. And from that distance—even as the ferry bore down on Brown's Wharf
at the foot of Yonge Street—the seeming feebleness of
the little twists of smoke and steam rising up from different buildings, Lilliputian industry while all around it
raw nature went about its effortless business. *Who thinks
of making a city in the rough?* he'd thought, seeing the

place for the first time, and he knew from the expressions on the faces of the newly arrived that this was the wondering thing that occurred to everyone that made landfall here.

Some greater shocks were in store for those brave enough to leave their ships. Streets paved with little more than the accumulation of grit pressed into them by boots. Wooden sidewalks put together with penny nails. Tar-acrid log shanties with bank buildings made of Kingston stone in their backyards. German and French spoken freely in the streets and canoes out in the lake with actual Indians in them, spearing salmon at the river mouth. Then that same lake, frozen to stillness between December and April, ice-clenched with nothing coming in or out of it. And centred in it, with misplaced pride, a stuttering attempt at making an English town out of nothing, like a voice straining to be heard from a great distance. It would actually be funny, Hallam had thought, if he didn't have to live here.

When he'd first arrived, he needed those new arrivals to remind him who he was and what he'd come from, and one could also stop to ask after them a question or two about the war in Crimea or some late happening in London they may have been present for. And he could put forward a welcoming face for the city, since it lacked warmth, and that was something anyone would want to do for his countrymen.

But it aggravated his melancholy. He didn't want to turn a lunatic face on those arrivals, and he himself had been warned not to fall in with the desperate. There was contagion in the looks of people; he'd already seen this in the distracted or haunted faces of people who walked from one place to another without purpose, as if attending a bell that would call them in for a meal, or worse, wake them up. He couldn't think of a circumstance more chilling than to be the reason someone might avert their eyes, or move away from the bar with a full glass in hand because he'd turned too suddenly or spoken too loudly, perhaps blurting out *how nice to meet you* before proper introductions were made. And to see those fresh but exhausted faces full of hope and interest, the baggage lined up so neatly in the foyer to be taken to their rooms by the negro men in white gloves. Why ruin anyone else's hope? He found himself laughing nervously at the fantasy of himself dragging a piece of that luggage back up the gangplank, struggling with its owner, all the while babbling on about saving the poor fellow the trouble of unpacking and then packing again and booking passage home and the disappointment of crushing failure, ha ha, no need of a gratuity, off you go lad. It made good sense to stay closer to home and work so as not to relive their expectations, and see their belongings trot up and down the stairs with such deceiving pomp. Once the days got shorter, he could no longer risk having his meals there.

Terrace moved Hallam's paper aside without saying a word and put the egg in its bright blue cup under his nose, the oatmeal to the side. Hallam chipped the lid off the egg and a faint memory of burning leaves at his father's country home entered his mind and then dispersed. "More slaves coming north," Terrace said, lifting the corner of the paper toward his eyes. "They're saying we ought to brace ourselves for another raid."

"Another?"

"The Fenians came bounding up here only forty years ago, Mr. Hallam. Our guard is down."

"I thought the Fenians were in Boston."

"They could be here within days."

Hallam skimmed the spoon around the inside of the egg lid. He brought out the bright white disc of albumen with a sucking sound. "But it's the southern slave owners we'd have to be careful of, isn't it?" he said. "About the slaves? I grant I'm not completely certain of my American history." Terrace was still standing beside him, in an almost wifely way. He was occupied with another part of the paper now. "And do they care so much that they'd risk their own lives coming up here to collect them?"

Terrace closed the front page on the news before folding the paper in four and tucking it under his arm. "Would you sand the rust off your musket to protect an escaped slave, Mr. Hallam? I think we'd need two weeks' notice just to oil our mechanisms."

"I thought they came here because it was a haven."

"You can't be a haven if you share the prison fence, Mr. Hallam. More hot water?"

"When you have a moment."

*Bisous to the girls,* he'd written in August. *Tell them their papa is going to build them a house with green shutters and hiding places. In truth, I haven't yet found a suitable place for such a home, but I am making my priority getting through this winter. I am still in the rooms I took on Duchess Street, which point toward the late-day sun, so if I am able to get back there before the very end of the day the rooms glow with an orange light, and I imagine you sitting in that very light, which will be on its way to you, while I sleep.*

In his letters, cheeringly written, he'd enclose little scraps of things the girls might find amusing, although enclosures were expensive to send: bits of cigar paper, a raggy strip torn from the top of the *Globe* with the date on it, as if to reassure them that he had lived through the same days as they. In the privacy of his mind, however, he could not imagine their lives in London. His keepsake box had no power over him. In it, a lock of hair from each of the girls (one a flat bronze, the other black as tar, each smelling faintly of roses) and a tiny daguerreotype of Alice's face, a round glassen image that sat in his palm like an egg. He'd tilt his hand back and forth to see her eyes flash to life in the changing light, but the sudden illusion of her face brightening could move him to helpless tears. Most of the time, he kept the box closed and hidden. When he could bear it, he took out the least personal of its keepsakes, a sampler sewn by his eldest with the letters of the alphabet and a tiny house stitched in blue thread.

That he had crossed an ocean to get here, and could trace the route back in his mind (and it was not one memorialized by ocean and the occasional broken horizon, but by motion and illness and the smells of animals, people, and salt—by time) didn't lead to the conclusion that they were *there* and he was *here*. His faith in "home" was shattered; he believed in it the same way he believed in the sun when it was nighttime. And that he had touched those beautiful little bodies, that he had smelled and tasted his wife so many days and nights, these were also anomalies to his senses as he knew them now. Reality was a dirty little city on the verge of either becoming a dirtier, larger city or being returned ignominiously to forest. To be aware that he woke as their day concluded, and that when they rose from their beds he was asleep as if dead, an inconceivable distance from them—nothing mitigated against the sense that they no longer existed. And that his letters, when posted, went flitting bootlessly out between the planets.

I continue to build up my business, which you will be pleased to hear has attracted some of the custom that was left without a regular chemist when Mr. Allen on Front Street passed away. I had understood that his son would take over the shop, but then I learned this was not so, and through local intelligence was given the impression that Allen Jr. would pursue medicine instead. I overheard a conversation that took place in the Rossin House one week past (I was delivering a box of pills to a young woman who was rooming there and I will tell you it is probably the finest hotel in the city). I later confirmed what I had heard by visiting the shop. I offered my condolences to the young man for his father and told him I was new to the city and wished to open an account (I counterfeited a bile complaint) and the young gentleman confirmed that he was not taking on any new custom, as he was going to leave for Montreal to attend medical school. He recommended me to F.R. Lewis on King Street, or Cockburn Druggists, who are on Yonge Street. I know both businesses, and they are commodiously appointed with every jimb-jamb known to the trade, and therefore it is hardly possible to compete. But is it? Size and inventory are not the only recommendations. I therefore took out an advertisement in the *Globe*, which fancies itself (and is thereby fancied as) the paper of record. I attach a cutting as illustration, and assure you that its effectiveness has convinced me it will not be the last time I purchase advertising space in this newspaper.

AT THE SIGN OF THE MORTAR
No. 81 King Street East

—

J. Hallam, Apothecary

WOULD respectfully announce that his stock is
now complete with a large and varied assortment of

HEALTHFUL MEDICATIONS
GARGLES, DECOCTIONS, PILLS, LOTIONS

HE would like to direct the particular attention
of any custom without a regular Chemist to consider

THE LATEST FORMULATIONS AVAILABLE
THE MOST MODERN METHODS

ALL is offered for sale at prices to suit purchasers.

J. HALLAM
TORONTO, Nov. 22, 1855

So you see, I am now a local impresario. Shameful, I know, but there are few enough mouths to pass word around in, and I will admit that competition is strong.

I am sorry I have nothing else to tell you. My life is that of a clock-dove. I wake and drink tea, eat a bowl of gruel, potter up to my shop and polish bottles. December is near and I cruelly wish a harsh winter on the populace, so that they may bring themselves with their aches and catarrhs to J. Hallam, Apothecary. An unfortunate derivative of these healing professions is that we cannot survive without the bad luck of the sick and dying. Less their misfortune, ours follows. So wish me a terrible winter, my darling, and know that I think of you constantly and of the girls, who I know are doubly loved by their mother, doing the loving of two. I enclose an amusing drawing I made of the corner of my room, where the light disappears last in the evening.

(As I write this, a fine rain has begun to fall, and I suspect that by morning it will be snow.)

J.

And he had sealed up this letter as if he were drawing a curtain on a cherished view, and prepared his evening drug.

2.

BILE PILLS AND FOREST LOZENGES, SAUGEEN OIL, Pastor Levi's Emetic, Doctor Jamieson's Palsy Rub (in powder as well as in liquid form), bowel stimulant, Queen's Liniment, pyramids of red-and-yellow boxes, clean jars with clear liquids within, the labels only slightly faded in the window-sun, a scale perfectly balanced with a one-ounce weight in each pan. Perhaps a voice will say, *Where are we?* and another answer, *You are in Hallam Chemist, under the sign of the mortar, where there is something for every ill.*

This was the motto—*Something for every ill*—under which his father and before him his grandfather had conducted business in England. It grated on Hallam that Lewis, the chemist at King Street near Bay Street, had already adorned the space over his door with this motto, one he'd clearly stolen from their family. Hallam had even gone in to the old apothecary and glanced about admiringly, and when Lewis had asked him what ailed him, Hallam wanted to say, *Your gall*, but instead told him he was only looking around, and this he did a few moments more before beating a quick retreat back to the sidewalk. Above his own door Hallam had placed a little painted sign that had cost him three bob, and it said, *Enter Ailing, Leave Hale.* A little dramatic, perhaps, but a motto.

He was not clearing his costs, even with the advertisement, but at least his stocking fees were nominal owing to the fact that when his father had purchased the store from the previous chemist—a Mr. Lennert—the shop came with its stock intact. Hallam even wore Lennert's apron, with its slight discoloration under the arms, since his father had made certain to purchase the small supply of linen as well. Two other aprons hung on little hooks in the backroom, one small enough for a boy. To imagine a business healthy enough to require the services of a full-time delivery boy was beyond dreaming.

He didn't get to know his few customers well at all. Sometimes he'd recognize a face but could not be certain if he'd seen it in his store, or just out in the streets. Despite this, he made it a habit (taught to him by his father) to greet everyone who came into the shop as if they'd seen each other only yesterday. And to ask after their health and their family in the knowing way of someone who would naturally know to ask. *How is your dear mother handling the wet air?* Because, of course, everyone's dear mother was struggling with the wet air. But the effort was exhausting. He was no better off than a travelling salesman hawking unctions from a wooden cart, a piebald donkey nervously waiting to move on before someone got wise and laid a beating on him or his master. People seemed to materialize in the store, drift through, lay a coin on the counter for something they might as well get there than go elsewhere, and that would be the last of them. Hallam became more aggressive in his newspaper advertisements, stating there was "no need to go anywhere else," and referring to himself as a "master apothecary late of England, where the most recent physicks are currently taught."

"What unique approach would you take for a persistent catarrh?" asked a man one December morning. It was bright and cold outside, and the man had brought a swirl of snow in behind him. His voice was clear.

"Your wife?" said Hallam.

"A good friend," said the man.

"I trust he's tried Irish moss."

"To no effect."

"And elecampane? In pure extract?"

"He has had the tincture as well."

Hallam nodded thoughtfully. If he were to develop a reputation for curing stubborn illnesses, his business would take root much faster. He brought down a small phial from high up on a shelf behind him. It was a rarely used compound that the previous owner had probably never opened. The cork was hard and dry. "I brought this from England directly. I doubt you will find any shop in town carrying it. Do you know it?" He held the small container out toward the man.

"*Balsamum Peruvianum.*"

"Balsam of Peru," said Hallam. "From Central America. Commonly used to dress ulcers, but of late I've found it very effective on stubborn mucosa. I'll make your friend a syrup. You can pick it up around suppertime."

The man nodded, his eyebrows raised in admiration. "Balsam of Peru," he said.

"I'll take down your name."

"Wilcocks," said the man, drifting away a little, staring down into the glass cases. Hallam wrote the name down on an order ticket. "I've never heard of Balsam of Peru."

"Why would you have? It's rarely enough used as an astringent, but its application as a respiratory aid is brand new."

"It must be," said the man. He was staring intently into the cases, running his hand along the topglass.

"Is there something else?"

"No," said the man. "I used to come here when it was Mr. Lennert's store. It looks the same."

"I imagine it would. You've seen one apothecary, you've seen them all. Although of course they are not all equal." He was making idle conversation while trying to figure out his fee. It would have to be reasonable, but too reasonable and the man might doubt the value of the syrup. Hallam was certain that the decoction would work, but it was the first time that week he'd been called on to mix anything.

"Did you ever meet him?"

"I'm sorry?"

"Mr. Lennert."

"Oh, no," Hallam said. "We purchased the shop while still in England. We exchanged letters."

"It's a pity what happened."

"Yes," said Hallam. Two shillings for a week's dose was reasonable. *A pity?*

"You must own the building now."

Hallam glanced up, oddly certain that someone else had entered, but it was still only the two of them. Why would the man have asked such an impertinent question? Hallam nodded, although in case of fact he did not own the building. It was none of the man's business. With one shop each to carry back in Camden Town and Clapham, Hallam senior and junior had agreed it was wise not to carry more paper on bricks, especially when they would need funds to get through the mild spring and summer seasons, when people had less need of apothecaries.

"I thought I recognized some of this stock." The man displayed an amused face.

"As I say, there's little enough to distinguish between stores like mine. It's the expertise that is different." He stood now, his hands flat on the glass countertop. Mr. Lennert's pill tile was to his left, a piece of white and blue porcelain with a dip in the middle from many years of use. It had the faded insignia of a griffin in it and Hallam imagined it might have come from home, wherever Lennert's home would have been. He'd seen such an insignia on German products. He wished his father had presented him with his own tile on leaving home; he'd anticipated a gift like that, but instead his father had pressed two ten-pound notes into his hand at the docks in Thamesport.

The man was drifting away now toward the back, looking down into the top of the cabinets. His hand trailed behind him in a showy way, and he drew it in to stomach level and stared at his fingertips. He made a turn of the room, coming down beside the opposite counter, his back to Hallam. He appeared to be trying to remember something, or bring the right words to mind. What if Lennert had owed someone money, such as this Mr. Wilcocks? They hadn't asked Lennert what his reasons were for relocating to Buffalo: they seemed clear (why stay in Toronto when you could live in Buffalo?). And his reputation was sterling. But it seemed to Hallam that this Wilcocks could be a debt collector, or an unhappy supplier. For all he knew, this man could have more claim on the inventory than he did. And then Hallam saw something very interesting. With a precise gesture of an index finger (capped with a perfectly formed white nail), Wilcocks pushed a box of gripe water back into place on the top of its pyramid at the end of the horseshoe counter.

"How long were you with Mr. Lennert?" he asked the gentleman, who now made slowly for the door.

"Some time."

Hallam kept pace with the man, coming down behind the counter on the other side of the store from him. "His apothecary was satisfactory?"

"It was excellent."

"I have your ticket, Mr. Wilcocks." Hallam held out the little slip of paper and Wilcocks took it without looking at it. "Have your friend come around five. What name will he give me?"

A flicker in the man's eyes. "He's too ill to come. I'll have to pick it up for him."

"It's my responsibility to ensure the patient understands the dosage. And counterreactions can be very dangerous. I should have to tell him what compounds to avoid while on the medication."

"I see," said the man.

"I'll go to him then. Just let me write down the address." Hallam returned with purpose to his position behind the counter and brought out a pencil. "Is he nearby, or should I hire a trap? I'll have to add the cost of travel if I can't walk it."

"Why don't I see how he is, then?" said Wilcocks. "I don't want you to go to the trouble if he's improved." The man nodded, then held the ticket up in the air between himself and Hallam, as if it were proof of something. "I will see him later today, and I'll ask him if he's well enough, and if he isn't, I'll come with the directions."

"You are something of a good friend," said Hallam. "Fine then. I'll wait to hear from one of you. His name? Should he come in?"

"Peter," said the man. "Peter Burns."

Hallam came forward and shook Wilcocks' hand. "I'll see one or the other of you then."

"Yes," said Wilcocks, and he bent down to put his hat on—half bowing, half retreating—pushing his head into the empty bowl of the hat as if an invisible force prevented him from lifting it any higher than chest level. It allowed him to hide his face.

Hallam turned back into the shop, to exchange one lungful of air with another, and then strode back behind the counter, as if a wind were coming and he had to lay his hands on anything not stuck down. He watched Mr. Wilcocks's form in the right-hand display window as he started off to the west, and he wondered idly if the man's presence had somehow changed something, like a dash too much of salt in a plain soup. But of course the interior of the shop was the same as it had been all that morning, and the previous night, and all of the week and month before: generally empty, a shrine of old burnished oak shelves and labelled bottles. Hallam counted to five, then snatched his coat off the back of the tall chair behind the pill counter and stepped out onto the sidewalk. Wilcocks was in front of him, proceeding at an easy pace toward Yonge Street, and Hallam followed him. In the street and on the sidewalk, the marks of different species of traffic were imprinted in the snow: on the sidewalk, bootprints had made a series of grey lines into which shadows fell; there, in the street, wheel ruts and hoofprints dug up the dirt beneath, mixing it in to make a hard beige slurry. By day's end it was a more uniform brown. Snow, thought Hallam, is the only weather that makes stillness seem busy.

"Dinner already?" said Mr. Boyers from his doorway. He owned a thriving hardware business with two shops in town, a wise business to grow on in just about any place, but best of all in a new one. There was no season for two-inch iron floor spikes, nor wire, nor bolts. The man was useful to everyone at all times. Better to sell hardware, or sugar, or raw cloth, or just about anything that a healthy populace goes out of an afternoon to pick up a little of, for who doesn't need a patch for their pants? A gill of sugar for his wife's tart? Or a screw to hold together the chair he sits in, attired in those new pants, while waiting for the rudely healthy English Rose to place the slice of still-steaming pie in front of him? No wonder Boyers was fat. He was a drunk too, and by three in the afternoon smelled of two if not three little jars of whisky. If he managed to snare Hallam in conversation, it could take the better part of an hour to escape.

"Someone forgot his change," Hallam said, holding up a closed fist to pre-empt his neighbour.

"Off with you then, Honest Tom. Drop in for tea if you like." A toothy smile.

"Yes," said Hallam, shaking his empty fist. Ahead of him, Wilcocks turned north on Yonge Street and Hallam began to walk faster, shifting sideways to pass two women coming the opposite way, his greatcoat flapping open like huge black wings. It occurred to him that he might have left the door to the store unlocked, and he wondered if perhaps the women were on their way to the sign of the mortar and would find the shop empty. With his luck he'd have two customers in the same hour and not be there to mark the occasion. Still, he rushed to the corner and around it, the wooden sidewalk planks offering the faint resistance of a sprung dance floor, an extra punch in his step. Wilcocks was further up the street now. He passed Adelaide and continued north, and Hallam followed under the ever-swirling snow, keeping his eyes fastened to the back of the black mantle; there were more people on this stretch of the street, most of them heading south to King, perhaps one of the only features of the city accurately advertised to them back home. As they went by, little bursts of conversation enveloped him, words strung on the air—on the health of an unfortunate relation, the state of the streets, the cost of household articles—the real stuff of daily life. Approaching Richmond Street, Hallam kept his pace steady, lost somewhat in the stray detonations of speech, but then, as if having seen a flash of light out of the corner of his eye, he was brought back to the moment and spun around and walked back two paces, the wind biting at his cheek. A little piece of yellow paper lay crumpled in the impression of a boot: the ticket for an order of Balsam of Peru.

Hallam stood straight and looked down the street toward the lake. He resumed his walking, going faster now; he clocked Wilcocks crossing Richmond Street and the man almost reached Queen before he finally turned and disappeared into a doorway. It felt unseemly to run, so Hallam lowered his head and tried to make time by walking quickly, his legs pumping like twin pistons. He held the damp ticket tightly in the palm of his hand. He passed Richmond and finally came to the plate window of Cockburn, Chemists where he saw "Mr. Wilcocks" pulling his coat off behind the counter. The inside of the shop was clean and bright, as if the sun had twisted past all celestial obstacles just to find this one little place. Hallam shoved the door open hard and stood glowering silently in the diminishing echo of the bell. His erstwhile customer turned in mid-gesture to look back through the store, and Hallam let the little ball of paper tumble off his palm and onto the floor as if he were rolling a die. "You dropped this," he said.

"Ah, excellent," said the man, who walked casually back through the airy expanse of the shop to pick it up. Hallam stood motionless as the man carefully uncrumpled the paper. "Balsam of Peru," he said. "For a stubborn cough."

"You owe me two shillings."

"You mix quickly."

"And you tell lies."

This brought a pitying smile to the man's face. "Peter Cockburn," he said, holding out his hand. "Your surveiller."

Hallam did not take the proffered hand, but glanced back through the shop, which was in possession of at least four aprons: one for this Peter Cockburn, and three for the other men, two behind counters on opposite sides of the well-lit store and an older man who had just then come out of the back. He'd been right in saying that all chemist shops seemed alike, but of course one with light, and busy employees in it, had it over a store with but one worker and a few dim corners.

"These are my brothers, Adrian and Randolph. And our father."

The man at the back of the store was his own father's age. He was drying his hands on a cloth, both of his sleeves rolled up, and looked out over the scene in his shop. The scents of mixing alcohol and carbonized sugar wafted through the space, a smell that spoke of industry. Mr. Cockburn opened the countertop to come through. "What's the problem?" he said.

"Your son placed an order in my shop under false pretenses."

"Your shop," said the older man, coming nearer. He glanced at his son.

"He took over from Lennert," said Peter Cockburn.

His father turned his eye on Hallam. For a moment all he did was absently rub the cloth over the back of his hands. Then he passed it to his son. The gesture made Hallam press his lips together.

"So *you're* the tout who's been placing those ads in the *Globe*?"

Hallam blinked a couple of times. "I have been placing ads, yes. So have you."

"I don't make miraculous claims, though, Mr. Hallam. And *my* education is complete." He scanned Hallam. "What are you? Fourteen?"

"I'm thirty," he said, inflating his age by three years. The man's devious son was not yet twenty-seven. Of that, Hallam was sure. The elder Cockburn could have no objection to him on the basis of age.

"You're not a day over twenty-five, son, and you'll not make it to twenty-six beating your chest like a fool. This is a place where people actually work to make their livings." He snapped the little ticket out of his son's hand, accidentally ripping it in two. He took the other half more gently and held the two parts together. "You told him you had an infection?"

"A bad cough," said Peter.

His father returned his attention to Hallam. "Balsam of Peru?"

"It's often effective," said Hallam, looking back and forth between Cockburn and his sons. The other two men had not moved at all, standing either in fear or at the ready, four more fists. Cockburn put one half of the ticket neatly on top of the other and held out the two portions to Hallam without saying anything. "Elecampane is overprescribed," said Hallam.

"Close your mouth. I know elecampane is overprescribed. Are you going to teach me to mix gripe water as well?"

"Excuse me."

The bell then rang again and an elderly lady came in and nodded in the direction of Adrian Cockburn. She went by the clutch of three men standing frozen at the mouth of the store, and passed a glance at them. Mr. Cockburn and his son nodded politely at her. If she had any awareness that she'd interrupted a disagreement, she showed none of it.

For Hallam, the disruption was much welcome; he imagined his dressing-down might have gone on until a natural break occurred, such as nightfall. The elder Cockburn followed the woman to the counter, gesturing for Adrian to retreat. He would take care of this loyal customer; he would show his eager colleague how to run a shop.

"Mrs. Hastings has been coming here for years," Cockburn said over his shoulder. "She has ongoing laryngeal complaints." Mrs. Hastings turned at the sound of her name. She was a stout woman who, Hallam could only imagine, had a great deal more complaints than laryngeal.

"We'll prepare a fresh batch of Mrs. Hastings' inhalation, boys. This bottle is already two days old—into the trash with it." Mrs. Hastings smiled regally, as if a maître d' had just ordered a bottle of the best champagne sent to her table.

Adrian and the youngest brother, Randolph, snapped into action, and Hallam felt he could do nothing but stand there like an animal in a snare while three of the Cockburns busied themselves with making their livelihood. In the meantime, his original tormentor remained within arm's length of him, should he feel the need to sock him in the eye.

Adrian Cockburn handed Randolph a slip of paper on which he'd written the order; the latter brought down the bottles of the necessary compounds, assembled them on the countertop, and weighed ingredients before putting them into a base of sugar water.

"Inhalation of benzoin," said Peter quietly, in a tone of voice that might have been more appropriate for *prepare to die*.

"I know that," murmured Hallam.

Mrs. Hastings took note of him then and looked at him steadily. Through a crack in Hallam's coat she noted the off-colour apron still tied on. "Are you taking on a new boy?" she said.

"Perhaps," said the elder Cockburn. "If he passes my test. Mr. Hallam?" Hallam's eyes moved dully from the old woman to Mr. Cockburn. "*Unguentum benzoini*. Describe three applications, two topical and one as a basis for another compound."

"Perhaps I will come back at another time. Sir."

Mrs. Hastings tilted her head at him with mock surprise. "The Cockburns are the leading chemists in the city, young man! Don't turn your nose up at an opportunity. Why, mark how well fed these boys are. You look like you could use what they've supped on."

"Cracked skin," said Hallam.

"Where?" said Cockburn.

"Usually the nipples. Fissures of the fundament."

"Mrs. Hastings has heard of the anus, Mr. Hallam."

"She is before one right now," whispered Peter in Hallam's direction.

Hallam stepped back out of range of Peter Cockburn's arm, the heat building under his coat. He had the urge to start shouting.

"That is one use, Mr. Hallam. What of one admixture?"

"That means how would you mix it," said Peter.

"I don't know," Hallam said. "I don't recall."

Mrs. Hastings' eyes flew wide. "Wrack your mind, boy! These Cockburns will have another candidate in your apron before you know it!" She separated herself from the counter and came over, wobbling, to stand beside Peter Cockburn. "Make something up," she stage-whispered to Hallam. "Say something."

Peter leaned in as well. Hallam smelled mint on his breath. "Surely a master apothecary late of England such as yourself," he said loud enough for everyone in the shop to hear, "would know something about the most modern uses for such a physick?"

Hallam took one step back and shouted, "BENZOIN OINTMENT!" The barracking ended suddenly. He trained his eyes on Mrs. Hastings. "It may be applied in a thin layer to a cracked anus!" he said loudly. "But beware you don't lather it on or you'll find it worse than the disease." He faced the counter and continued speaking loudly as he backed out of the store. "And benzoin vapour is indicated more for the pharyngeal mucosa than the laryngeal. It is absorbed into the mucosa readily and quickly. An inhalation of thyme with a bit of magnesium added would be much more effective." He reached the door.

Mr. Cockburn called to him, "I can block supplies to your fine establishment with a single handwritten note."

*These are apothecaries!* thought Hallam. "You are a powerful man, I can see, Mr. Cockburn."

"You'll be selling talc and baking soda if I care to make it so."

"But I import from England. Are you in charge of the harbour as well?"

From his outburst, Mrs. Hastings had laid a protective hand over her heart. "Who *is* this man?"

Cockburn came out from behind the counter and held a hand up to her, indicating he would take care of everything. "This is Mr. Lennert's replacement."

"Poor Mr. Lennert!"

"Yes," said Cockburn, and continued toward the door. Hallam did not like the expression on his face. And there was that *poor Mr. Lennert* again—what had he and his father stumbled into? He braced himself for what he was certain would be an embarrassing and perhaps painful end to the encounter, but Cockburn passed him and simply pushed the door open. Hallam hesitated for a moment, but then squared his shoulders and went out, back into the cold weather. Cockburn stuck his head out slightly. "I don't think you got the job, Mr. Hallam," he said, and pulled the door to before Hallam could wedge in a retort. Instead he watched the proprietor of one of the city's most established druggists walk confidently back to his counter and talk in what he imagined would have been the soothing tone he used for all his best customers. Hallam felt the eyes of the man's three sons on him, and their stares were like a weight, something with the power to push him down. He walked a few feet south, taking in deep draughts of air, until he was out of their sight, then reached out with his hand to steady himself against a wall of brick directly south of the store. *What a brotherhood is this!* he thought wonderingly, and shook his head. He looked under his outstretched arm to be sure no one was coming for seconds and remained in that position. He was feeling pain in his ribs, and presently it got worse; it seemed quite sudden, as if a vice had been winched tight on his chest. *My God*, he thought, *an infarction?* but there was no pain in his arms or along his jaw, he was just unable to breathe. His eyes began to water and he pushed his head back, stretching his neck, fighting for air. Through the smudge of his sight he saw Yonge Street in front of him, and the buildings appeared altered, as if reflected in a slick of black ice: they seemed huge and glassy, carved from crystal.

They loomed black and red and silver, and he closed his eyes and collapsed against the wall, his hand cradling his side.

He thought he would die, but then he was on the street again, he was walking south, he was fifteen feet from where the attack had happened, and yet he walked calmly and the air passed through him, cold and metallic, as if he were immaterial.

## 3.

WINTER DRAGGED ON. CHRISTMAS AND NEW YEAR'S in the city had seemed sick with tragedy: men and women freezing in the cold; bleary fires burning in the bad parts of town. Hallam stayed at home, or shuddered in the store, alone it always seemed, and dreamed of another life. February would pass in a smear of despair. Hooded men (or were they women?) pushed on to their business, stopping only as briefly as their tasks demanded; even nodding a friendly greeting could cause people to stop too long in the screeching wind and cold. Sometimes a voice could be heard to say to an unseen hearer, "Nothing like it!" or something along those lines, and what little comfort this gave was in the suggestion that maybe they would never see another winter like this.

Every day of those impossibly cold weeks there were boys out skating on the ice of Lake Ontario, taunting those who could see them with their easy capering, as if they were immune to the shattering cold. But immunity was not reality. On New Year's Day they'd discovered two young boys in ragged clothing, frozen to death by

Beard's Wharf (had they thought it possible to stow away until the opening of navigation four months hence?), and Hallam's gloomy reaction was that they had been lucky not to have to continue. His thoughts surprised him—why else would he have chosen his field, if not to give aid, succour those in need? But what life is it to freeze, he thought? To imagine that passage in the frigid hold of a vessel you are not welcome on will take away your suffering? The cold hurts for only moments anyway, and then it coddles you and you sleep. If you must die, why not freeze?

Out of a morbid sense of obligation (sympathy, perhaps, for those who saw hope in a ship), Hallam trudged out to the boys' funeral in Potter's Field, the last stop for unclaimed bodies. If the tragedy had happened on any other day but New Year's or Christmas, the funeral wouldn't have excited the imagination of the working populace the way this one did. The *Globe* reported that the boys died on the first, and the funeral was held on the second, in the great unkempt field at Yonge and Bloor, just feet from the houses in Yorkville. A small group converged on the place, wandering in as if just happening by the site of the burial. The air felt as hard as something solid against their faces; the two graves were among the last ones dug in early December in anticipation of occupants through the winter months. They had the bodies wrapped in cloth and tipped them into the holes once the chaplain had commended their souls in general terms (their religions were unknown). And so they entered time, a conveyance more reliable than boats.

Hallam trundled out with the crowd of forty-or-so fellow citizens, his eyes tearing with the wind. *What true sadness was there in that frosted field?* he wondered. It seemed to him the emotion in the graveyard was like the one you sometimes encountered at hangings. The pleasure of being permitted to go on with one's day after such a thing.

The death of these boys was not the only evidence of a rift in the natural order. In January, there was much excitement about a man the police were interested in, a gentleman who'd begun appearing on King Street once or twice a week in the evening, dressed as if for the theatre in a greatcoat, top hat, cane, and glistering spats. On the nights of his appearances, he stopped under a street lamp and pulled from the inside of his sleeve a sheaf of letters, which he would then read from. Out of the other sleeve, he drew a handkerchief and performed mysterious gestures in the air, like a prestidigitator, in the direction of a window across the way. What he was doing was not illegal of course, but in a winter month when there were few arrests but for drunkenness and disorderly behaviour, he was certainly of interest. The amount of attention he attracted was manifest in the way that people who lived on the south side of King Street, nearest his location, would put out their lamps early, in the hope that he would not stay away for fear of being watched.

One night near the end of the month, a small group of men gathered on the southeast corner of Yonge and King streets, in front of Eastwell, Woodall & Co's School

Book Store, and watched as the gentleman made his way to his regular spot. When he got out his handkerchief, they rushed him in a body. He was fast and made for York Street, where the gaslamps ended and he could take cover in darkness. The following week, a second group hid itself at Simcoe and Bolton streets, and the two groups leapt on him as he turned north into the darkness.

Once brought to the police station, the gentleman's hat and coat were removed and it was revealed to the surprise of everyone that he was a she, a girl of no more than twenty years. She was charged with appearing in public dressed in an attire not of her sex, a misdemeanour that had been freighted with meaning for twenty years in Toronto, ever since W.L. Mackenzie had evaded capture in Oakville by disguising himself in the stolen garments of Mrs. John F. Rogers. Of the young woman's motives, however, or the meaning of her actions, nothing could be concluded, since she refused to speak. By the time she was arrested, the local papers had been following the adventure for nearly three weeks and expressed their dissatisfaction over the abrogation of the court's responsibility in uncovering the meaning of her behaviour. At least to Hallam and his comrades in Jewell & Clow's restaurant it seemed that the poor woman had simply gone mad, perhaps from grief. She kept her own counsel in front of the magistrate, a silent unhappy figure. They also searched the rooms on the south side of the street, looking for the object of the young woman's signals. But no one ever claimed any relation to her: the girl had been supplicant to a ghost.

Although the sun set later in February, the extra light gave no promise of anything but the joyless days lasting a few minutes more every evening. When, in the middle of the month, the temperature rose, it presented Torontonians with the vision of dead birds revealed under the snow, half dissolved in the grass, as well as grey litter and decomposing dog scat. The worst thing of all, however, was the spectre of a man who had hanged himself on the windmill you could see at the lakeshore from most vantages below King Street. At the beginning of March, when the worst seemed over, a vast storm blew into the city and dropped temperatures to well below minus twenty, and the wind came in on the back of it and made it impossible to walk or speak or hold a coat closed around oneself. *Abandon all hope*, the storm seemed to say, *winter is not leaving this country after all.*

The man had made himself a noose and slipped it over his head, then tied the other end onto a heavy gaff that he eventually managed to jab through a passing mill blade. No one wanted to speculate how long he'd stood in the wind-thrashing dark, throwing the end of his life into the air, hoping to lash it to the elements. To imagine how determined he was on death would be to invite thoughts of where one's own limit lay. What if there was, in every person, a threshold beyond which only death could sate you? After succeeding, the suicide spun in a small circle around the centre of the windmill, and wilted there for three days, a ghoulish figure in the squall, seen in the distance through the snow, rising and falling like a marionette. When they cut him down the blood had pooled in his feet and frozen solid and his leather shoes had burst from the pressure like overripe gourds.

A death, it was said in the restaurant, that could have come to pass only in Canada.

Hallam had never really seriously contemplated failure. He'd always thought he had been chosen over his older brother to bring the family name to Canada because his father had more confidence in him. Now he thought perhaps he was Isaac sent up the Lord's mountain. And yet his lot was worse than that of the original son betrayed: his father's face was hidden. Who would accompany him? Who would intervene on his behalf?

He'd long since cancelled his ads in the papers, but he continued to advertise his success to his wife and his father. If anything, his letters became more fulsome with news of his burgeoning affairs. He thought perhaps he could dream his life into existence by writing it down. But what was more, he had plenty of time to write letters. After the encounter at the Cockburns', business continued as usual, "usual" being the glacial pace of custom in and out of his door. The elder Cockburn's influence, if in fact he'd tried to exercise it, would not have had any effect on Hallam's business as he had had no cause to try to replace any of his stock yet.

He buffed bottles with an application that seemed to him theatrical. He made perfect towers and pyramids out of popular brands, tins and boxes that would seem to crow their efficacy even to those who walked on the south side of the street. But a caul had grown over his door, no one entered but for those few souls immune to the mischiefs of fate. He sold a powder for bunions here, a box of liver suppositories there, even had the pleasure, in an otherwise empty day, of explaining their use to the unfortunate young man whose lot it was to take them. He'd kept a strict professional manner while describing their use to him, altering his expression not a whit while the man's face whitened, and was able to say with the utmost professional comport, "Not very," when the man had asked how big they were.

But otherwise, his pleasures were restricted to meal-taking and sleep induction. In the evenings, he made himself a supper of bread and honey, drank tea, opened a book or a newspaper (a book was safer, with its promise of order), then poured a sherry or two, or a whisky or two. When the dark was full enough and he could begin to feel the little waves of panic lap at him—these little waves like childhood fears and their attendant revelations of utter loneliness, the feeling that there was nothing safe in the world, not one's favourite foods, nor one's parents or friends, nor the promise of getting older and being able to do whatever one wanted, there was no succour in any of this because it was dark and night was begin-ning—Hallam would dose his drink, a little more each night, and let the drug settle on his mind like a shade. In his sedated state, he sometimes imagined a bustle of activity in the darkness of the rear of the apartment: he'd learned from other tenants in the building that an enter-prising Christian gentleman of some description had occupied his tiny home before him. He'd used the back of the rooms to operate a printing press on which he produced religious tracts. It was fortunate there hadn't been a disaster, thought Hallam, with two apartments below. No one had said anything, of course; such an enterprising person would be allowed to go about his godly business even if it presented a hazard. Imagine the noise. Then the man went out of business and vacated the rooms, leaving the cumbersome press behind. Hallam imagined them taking the machinery apart and putting it in boxes, or better, throwing the whole thing out the window, a splinter and crash in the street. The demolition of a room where God had failed to turn a profit. What hope had he? With the aid of his sherries and decoctions, sometimes Hallam thought he could hear the desperate man bootlessly clacking out his salvation on the huge machine, and no one listening, not even God Himself.

One visitor to the shop had more to offer him than a small purchase. Adrian Cockburn emerged from the shadows one night as Hallam was locking up and looked at him in such a way as suggested it would not be dangerous to reopen and go back in. Adrian was the mildest-seeming of the three brothers, all of whom could fairly have been called strapping, and his face was kind and open. He waited until Hallam's door was shut again, and the lamp relit, before speaking.

"My father asked me to come speak with you."

"Did he."

"I know you must be heading off to Jewell's for your supper, so I won't waste your time. My father offers to buy out your lease as well as your inventory. We know that your agreement with your landlord runs to the end of August. My father thought you might welcome the opportunity to recoup some of your losses."

"Your father is a very generous man."

"There's something you don't know, Mr. Hallam. Joseph Lennert isn't in Buffalo, he's in jail. Here in Toronto."

"That's no concern of mine," said Hallam, keeping his expression flat. Was this the "pity"? That Mr. Lennert was in jail? He barely heard Adrian Cockburn continue as he tried to calculate the cost of the remaining inventory in the shop.

"He got old and his eyesight got poor. He couldn't tell the difference between a minim and a drachm. About three months before your family bought the business, he killed, in succession, a child, an elderly woman, and a pregnant woman with two children already in her care. Accidentally, of course. He wasn't a *murderer*. But he couldn't read his formulary anymore and started guessing."

"Mr. Lennert sold this business free and clear. How stupid do you think I am?"

"He's in a cell right now, a seventy-year-old man. A murder convict."

"An accident is not murder."

"It is if you are charged with ensuring the public's health. People go to doctors and druggists to get better, not to be put down like animals."

Hallam could not reply to this. If it were true, it was terrible, but it would be easy enough to find out. And yet you would think that this small detail might have come out in the negotiations. Mr. Lennert had written them himself.

"This is why you have no customers. People do not want to come into this store."

"There's a different name out front, Mr. Cockburn. People aren't blind."

"People are informed, you're right," replied Cockburn. "They know you bought Lennert's supplies."

"Ah, but you just said it was human error. The chemicals are blameless."

Adrian nodded the way one does when an acceptable argument is forwarded in service of an entirely erroneous presumption. "The magistrate may have concluded that there was nothing wrong with his physick, just his measurements. And yet people know you're pouring and measuring from the same vessels, they know whatever emanated from this store started in those bottles and tins. They're not interested in gambling with their lives. My father, on the other hand, will come in here, put our name on the door and above the counter; he'll throw out all the old stock and invest in new stock and we'll put our regular ads in the papers, stating we're on King Street now, in the heart of the shopping district, in fine new surroundings, with all new supplies of the most valuable and healthful compounds known to man. And people will not say, *Well it's no longer Lennert's*, or *That Mr. Hallam no longer owns the shop*. They'll say, *That's Cockburn's, the most trusted name in chemistry*. That's what it will take to make this store profitable in this location. Can you argue with it?"

"Fine surroundings . . ." was all Hallam could say. Adrian Cockburn started to make a round of the shop, leaving his host to think, and looked the shelves up and down. It struck Hallam that when he'd been visited by Adrian's brother, that Cockburn had also gone around taking the measure of the place. Peter Cockburn had been sent by his father as well, and Hallam had been under siege ever since he arrived. The moment his ship put in at Tenning's Wharf, it was done but for the weeping.

"Nothing short of starting over will give this shop back its livelihood," said Adrian. "And you can't do it, Mr. Hallam. My family is prepared to pay you the cost of your remaining lease, plus the cost of all your stock— even though we plan to dispose of it—plus fifteen percent. My father calculates you will be able to leave the city with much of what you came with. Less your passage home."

Hallam regretted having had even one charitable thought about this young man, and he went directly to the door, which he wrenched open. The bell erupted into sudden peals. "You tell your father," he said, "that I will go home on my shield before I sell this business to the Cockburns."

Adrian Cockburn smiled warmly as he walked toward the door. "My father is a reasonable man, Mr. Hallam. I'm sure he'd throw in a shield if I ask him to."

"I'll run this business into the dust before I willingly give your family a grain of it."

"It'll cost us less then," said the young man. "We can wait."

"Get out."

Adrian Cockburn began to leave the store but then stopped and held out his hand to Hallam, as if the ferocity of his denials only underscored that a deal would very soon be struck. With every fibre of his Englishman's being, Hallam resisted taking the young man's hand (either by instinct to shake it, or by inclination to haul him near and shatter his nose), and closed the door behind him. He stood then in the open space, which he had thought he was done with, finally, for the day, and for the first time felt a powerful affection for the shop, which was his, his family's, and which suffered, as he did (he now understood), from ghosts.

The feeling of being cursed—the proof of it—lightened Hallam's spirit considerably. He felt that there was nothing to be done and nothing to fight. And so he went back and forth from his home to the store in the lengthening days of March and waited to see what would happen to him. It was not at all like being mid-ocean in a storm-tossed ship; it was like being in the ocean itself, under a warm and invigorating sun, whilst clinging to a bit of wood. No immediate threat was obvious, but the situation was, like life itself, clearly fatal.

In the middle of March's idle hopelessness, the first atom of a new life drifted into Hallam's shop in the guise of a man with a rare request. He was a shambler in a ratty coat and straw hat, and he placed on Hallam's countertop an empty bottle of lunar caustic—*Argenti nitras*—and asked if Hallam could replace the contents.

Hallam wasn't at all certain that he actually carried any silver compounds. It was difficult to discern the man's condition, since he appeared so generally unwell. One eye was almost eclipsed by a growth that could have been anything from syphilis to fungus. He warned the man that if he'd already consumed the contents of one bottle, he was well on his way to being unpleasantly tinted, but the customer laughed this off, saying he was a photographer. The same reaction that turned a man's skin blue could render his image on a piece of glass, he explained. Hallam hunted through the tall shelves behind him and did find a single full bottle of the compound, and he put it beside the old one. The man sighed with pleasure on seeing it, like a drunk at a bottle of rum with the custom house label intact.

"There it is," said the man. "I am still in business."

"That makes one of us."

The photographer looked around the inside of the shop. "The place seems a little lonesome," he said. "It could be the light. You put an armature beside the window out there and put a mirror on it, it would brighten this place considerably."

"It's not the light," said Hallam, trying to imagine what the store would look like with actual sunlight in it. "There's a curse on the place."

The man pulled his head back on his neck and turned his face away. It was a fierce expression. "Which one?"

"Which one, what."

"Which curse?"

"It's a general one, sir. Do you want this or not."

"General curses are harder to deal with. Try dowsing."

"Does it work?"

"No," said the other. "But it can make you feel better, if and all you believed in the curse in the first place." He smiled. "I don't believe in them."

"I didn't used to," Hallam said, "until I got to Toronto."

"A lot of people say that."

Hallam pulled the empty bottle off the counter and put both of them into a paper sack. "I'll charge you one shilling and you can keep the empty one. I doubt I'll restock it."

The man paid Hallam in small coin. "I'll tell you what. Say I guarantee return business, would you agree to carry it again?"

"That would be difficult," said Hallam. "It's little used and I order direct from London, from my father, and—"

"It's a risk you'd rather not take."

"There are other chemists who may already have it in stock," said Hallam.

The man nodded, his thick hands laid on the counter. He had fingers like bread rolls. "My credit's all used up is the problem," he said.

"Well, I can't afford to give you any."

"I understand." The man took his bag and rolled it up before dropping it into a pocket. It clanked against something and he instinctively put his hand over the pocket to hush it. "What if I put you on commission?" he said. "You front me the silver, I give you what you're owed out of my portrait fees, plus twenty percent."

His mother had always told Hallam he had an innocent face. He wasn't sure it was the best quality to have in business. He felt insulted that the man thought him so easy a mark that he hadn't even bothered warming up to the subject. "Why would I want to do that?"

"I can't see why you wouldn't. You're all alone in a dark store with no customers and a curse to boot."

"But I just said I don't have the means to give you credit."

"Fine," said the man. "Let's start over." He took the bag back out of his pocket, and removed a small snuff tin as well and laid it on the counter. "Open the tin." Hallam did. There was a total of eight shillings in coin, just about. "You keep the money, and the bottle you just sold me, until you gather enough to fill an order for nine shillings. That's nine phials in total. You've made a tidy profit, plus I give you twenty percent of what I clear with the pictures I make from all of it. After that, you give me the compound on credit, I pay a wholesale cost, and I continue to share my profits with you. Now who's the sucker, Mr. Hallam, me or you?"

"How did you know my name?"

The man speared him with a concerned look. "It's on the door, man! Do we have a deal or not?"

Never in his life had Hallam bargained before, so he wasn't sure where the sudden instinct to say forty percent came from, but it was out between them before he could think of a reason.

The man was staring at him. "Good," he said, and he held out his hand. "Samuel Ennis."

"J. Hallam."

Ennis held his hand tight. "J? You lack a first name?"

"In a business venture, I prefer to remain J."

"Very well," said Ennis. "Thirty."

"Thirty what?"

"You have a scant memory, J. Hallam. Thirty percent."

"Oh. Let's say thirty-five."

"No, son, I say twenty, you say forty, I say thirty and we're done." He pumped Hallam's hand and released it.

"How do I know I can trust you?"

"What is there to trust? You have everything I own in the world in front of you."

"But this is too easy."

"You're right. No one stranger should trust any other. That is, I grant, the very best way to be. You can't know if you should trust me."

*The man couldn't have said anything more inspiring of trust than that. Right? This is how my fool's errand ends,* thought Hallam. "Fine," he said. "We have a deal."

Ennis looked at him with admiration. "If you were my son, I'd have you on the first ship home and I'd put you back in school so fast your teeth would rattle. But I think you're going to save my life."

"I am quite certain, Mr. Ennis, that this will make not a whit of difference to either of our fortunes," said Hallam.

"You're young to give up, son. You should wait a few more years, you'll enjoy it more." He laughed, expecting to be joined in it, but he wasn't. There was an awkward pause. "This is the moment you give me back that bottle of silver nitrate, Mr. Hallam, in a show of good faith."

"Oh," said Hallam, feeling a little numb. "All right then."

Ennis held out his hand and Hallam put an ounce of the man's livelihood back into his palm.

It has always been a popular pastime to think of the last moments of an old life, before two people set eyes on each other for the first time, or the instants before an unfortunate choice is made. All of past time is erased in tiny moments like this. That people begin somewhere and end elsewhere is never in doubt, but there is the larger, and less obvious, mystery of how all the threads of a person's life converge in a weave that eventually becomes a pattern.

Sam Ennis was a portrait photographer working on glass (Hallam had seen daguerreotypes in London, but they were made on copper), and his business, he later explained, had begun to slow. His was a luxury service, and if his business was waning, then worse things were already beginning to happen higher up the economic chain. This was his theory, and why Hallam felt inclined to listen to an Irishman's economic theory he'd be hard pressed to say, but the man could be convincing. Ennis had concluded it would be wise to hoard material while *anyone* could still afford it—the first things to go in a crisis are luxuries, after all—but he could not raise his prices in order to counterbalance his expenses for fear of losing his remaining custom. Hallam was unsure of Ennis's strategies, but he placed his first order with his father's man in London in a spirit of hope. Out of curiosity, he consulted Toronto's city directory and found five portraitists in business and one firm that billed itself as municipal and industrial photographers. He amused himself with the thought that he could beat the Cockburns to the silver nitrate trough by ordering in a tremendous stock and becoming the sole supplier to the city's photographists. It struck him in the midst of plotting like this that specializing was a talent that evaded most businessmen. What if Mr. Boyers became the only source for doorknobs in the city! What if the haberdasher on Queen Street cornered the market in straw? It was a brilliant idea.

The shipment came one month later. In a kind of delirium, thinking that the income from the silver would offset it, Hallam drastically lowered the prices in the store and placed a new advertisement, this time stating that he now offered twelve of the most common medicines and cures at prices less than half the next lowest price in the city. The Cockburns, Mr. Lewis, and the chemists below the synagogue on Richmond Street took out adverts severally announcing that *they* were all changing to a one-price system so that their customers could be certain in all seasons that they were getting the finest apothecary money could buy, with no hint of tainted quality. The Cockburns' ad even featured a little mortar and pestle, but the pestle had a crest of the skull and crossbones. Hallam braced himself, the way a man might when he feels the chilled horror of his bluff about to be called. What custom Hallam had now dwindled to almost nothing, and most of his business was restricted to gripe water and barley candy, of use only to mothers close enough to his door to make a fast trip out in service of quieting a child back at home. Once, in the week after the competing ads, he heard a child screeching, a door slamming, the ring of his bell, the chunk of his cash box as a young woman paid for a sucking cane, the slamming of that distant door again, and then silence. All in that order. A miniature opera of the quotidian, worth two entire pennies to him.

With the shipment came a letter from his father, and a bill of exchange for ten pounds.

Dear Jem,

Use this money carefully as we are skint until the summer. The three businesses are stretching us, as I'm sure you understand. I know and trust all is well with you. I have seen plenty of Alice and your dear children and everyone is in rude health. Your mother sends her love, although you will note you do not yet get letters from her (no point in dulling either of your resolves!!), as does David, who will be taking over the Clapham store come May. I should note that you will not be able to return the $AgNO_3$, as Fulton and Co. had to make up the order special, but I trust you wouldn't have ordered it if you didn't need it. I am picturing dolphins crowding the waters of Lake Ontario! But I salute you, my boy. I think it shows ingenious initiative to stock the unusual as a selling point. If I may advise you, I suggest a sign describing its unusual and far-reaching applications. *An astringent! An antispasmodic! Effective in dysentery, epilepsy, and cholera! It will arrest gonorrhea in its first stage.* Although depending on the custom, you may want to advertise that last somewhat more discreetly. There is nothing more counterproductive than making unwanted suggestions, and we do want your counter to be productive.

A happy new year to you, we all wish you well.

Father

The ten pounds would pay his rent and food for six more months; the rest was a wash. The bill of exchange, he knew, was a mute testament to the end of his fortunes. To receive an order for but a single chemical, one that was itself as uncommon as scammony, was clear word of the fate he was in the midst of suffering. His father had been kind enough to fetch out a complimentary interpretation of the order, but realistic enough to provide him with passage home. The cost of that ticket was two pounds eight; his father was telling him to give it four more months, not six. If he could not pay his own way back, he would be stranded.

To return to his family and the world he knew, this was something dearly to be wished. But to fail, and hear the jeers at his back as he climbed the gangplank . . . it was difficult to deny the power this held over him as well. Hallam saw himself as his father's prodigal but reviled as a pariah in his new home, prey to gossip and embarrassed by his own innocence. He saw himself as a bright-eyed fool, invited to throw dice with new friends, his measure taken.

He took walks at night, still unable to sleep, but worried about how inviting he found the drugs. Although the nights were more temperate now, he went with three layers under his coat, and passed under the lamps like a phantom, his shadow stretching back as if unable to go on and then thrown forward again against its will. Candles burning in the windows of cafés, promises of fellowship. He badly wanted to step into them, to beg for the succour of a glass of beer and the time of day. He wanted to make new acquaintances, to tell them of the people he loved, so those people would be seeded in this place within his stories, in the minds of his listeners. But instead he kept Alice inside of him like a secret, he kept Jane and Cecile inside of him. He felt he burned with them, gave off a light that was of them, that would cause those who saw that light to ask who he was, who he belonged to, what place was his home. But he lurked outside of those windows, unable to see himself in that society, with this blemish on him of his coming ruin.

He imagined, in the darkness of his rooms, abed and awake, that if he stood up and crossed the cold, pocked floor of his bedroom to the window, he would look down into the street and see a figure gesturing to him from under a gaslamp. Lips moving, incantatory but silent, offering up the contents of a message essential to his understanding but which he would never be able to hear. He knew, somehow, that the form (if he'd had the courage to move to his window to look at it) would have white eyes glowing steadily underneath its hood, eyes of magnesium, and he began to fear this spectre he'd never seen. He sensed it was allied with the bottles and tins in his shop, whose levels of powders and crystals rarely changed—that in its imperturbable patience, it was the manifestation of the stillness that had come to descend on the middle of his life.

~

Samuel Ennis chose not to live in MacCaulaytown, where he had many relations, but stayed alone in a shanty on Adelaide Street, west of the college. He had divided his shack into two rooms, one to live in and one to work in. The work half was well appointed: there was a sitting chair and a lace-covered table with a silk hanging behind it and a red curtain tied off to one side with a sash (the curtain simply hung from the ceiling, but in the pictures it completed the feeling of elegance). The profession of photographer attracted both the artiste and the filth-maker, and anyone meeting Ennis for the first time would not have hesitated to conclude his specialty. He cut a frightening figure. A childhood illness had left him partially elephantized. He could see out of both eyes, but his left was occluded by a fleshy growth that hung over it, the eyelid was thick and convoluted as a cauliflower, and the pupil appeared incapable of rising above the midway point in its socket. Certain of Mr. Ennis's expressions seemed perfectly normal, but for the lid, while others required him to lift his chin and tilt his head, a posture quite in keeping with madness. And yet his custom, which generally found him by reputation, held him in the highest of esteem. Hallam, upon first visiting the studio, saw examples of the man's work, and although Hallam could not understand how Ennis could even see straight enough to produce a picture, he had to admit the results were handsome. He saw the studio when he delivered Ennis's second purchase, the eight one-ounce phials of silver nitrate that had arrived with his father's letter. It was a lot to ask people to come to a part of town where nightdresses hung out of windows, but the fact was Ennis's skill exceeded those of the photographists who had studios in better neighbourhoods. Those studios (some of which Hallam would have cause to visit in the upcoming months) were tricked out with mirrors for gawking in, pots of flowers, and even chocolates for the ladies and their dogs. Children as well.

Ennis had none of this, but he had a *way*, as he put it, and this way produced superior results, regardless of the impediments. His images were sharp and clear. The eyes of children registered the presence of living souls; the stray wisps of hair that fell from a lady's bonnet almost begged to be wiped away with a finger. And so the stalwart British of the city and the few well-off others tramped down past the Bishop's Palace to have their pictures taken in a part of town not yet worthy of street light.

There were customers waiting for Ennis when Hallam arrived with the order; they sat in a frigid, cramped foyer with their hands folded in their laps. Ennis admitted him and invited him to stay and observe, to "take an active interest in your investment." Apart from the sitting area, which stood out like a theatre set, the room was spare and unfinished. The camera itself, a polished oak box standing on a high wooden tripod, stood six feet away from the sitting chair, facing it like a guard dog.

"Why don't you play assistant," Ennis said. "It'll make you and the subject less nervous. And you may even learn something."

There was no risk, thought Hallam ruefully, of anyone recognizing him here; those odds were about seventy divided into the whole population of the city. Ennis took a thin black robe off the back of his door and tossed it to Hallam. He slipped the garment on, a muslin thing that smelled of hay, and stepped back against the wall as Ennis brought in the first of his clientele, a newly married couple who appeared to be no more than twenty years of age. The husband was thin as a horsewhip, but wore an expensive coat and tails, and held his hat nervously in front of him. His wife was a fetching girl of perhaps eighteen, with a fine figure and long, thin hands. She took her husband by the forearm and put him behind the chair, which she then sat in. She was not new to the photographer's room. She sat and angled herself flatteringly, her head nestled in the iron headrest, cast a glance over her shoulder to her husband and uttered a single word, "Closer."

"Mrs. Arnold, if I may ask you to turn slightly back toward me now," said Ennis, "then I shall have you in three-quarter profile, which is a most appealing posture for you."

"Of course," said Mrs. Arnold.

"And shift a little to your left so we may have the slightest hint of contact between you and Mr. Arnold.

That's it." Mr. Arnold, hearing his name, straightened. "That's excellent," said Ennis.

"Am I all right then, sir?"

Standing now behind the camera, Ennis cast a cursory glance at Mr. Arnold. To Hallam's eyes, it looked as if a series of broom handles had been put in the groom's sleeves and pant legs, but Ennis just nodded to him and lowered his head again into the eyepiece at the back of the box. "Hat, though," he said apparently to no one, and Mr. Arnold placed the hat on top of his head, completing the look of a country mouse poured into a suit chosen by his father-in-law.

Mr. Ennis leaned into Hallam's ear. "You will find a crate behind the curtain," he said. "If you will take it and stand on it, you will see, directly in front of our friends and in the ceiling, a little sliding door that can be opened. Since you are here anyway, and I dislike having to look upward, you will kindly open it."

He went as instructed. Standing on the crate, he slid the small trap door along the ceiling, and light and cold air dropped in. Mingled in this air was the faint scent of roses trailing off the young woman below. Hallam found her eyes on his, a small smile on her lips. Her husband looked straight ahead, perhaps thinking his photograph was already being taken. Hallam realized this was one of the only instances since he'd arrived in Toronto that he'd smelled the fragrance of a woman younger than fifty— none but the most piercing scents travelled through the crystalline air—and a shock of grief sped through him, as if in the scent he was able to feel something that would otherwise have been lost to him. He stood a moment longer and let a deeper draught of this young woman flood him until Ennis called, "Everything all right?" and he snapped out of it. Hallam stepped down from the crate and Ennis instructed him to prop a thin white-painted board against it, angling the light down and in. A warm glow bloomed against the back wall of the studio, and held his subjects in a ball of light. Ennis came forward and reangled the board so that more of the light caught Mrs. Arnold. As Ennis's back was to Hallam, he could not see his expression, but Mrs. Arnold lowered her chin, her lips pursed.

"The heat from the reflected light should help mitigate the cold, my dears," he said. "Now cough or scratch one last time, and we'll begin." The husband shifted around inside his suit and then came to stillness, while his wife moved not at all except to bring her clear brown eyes up again, an expression of calm anticipation on her face. She had a lovely face: white skin with high colour in her cheeks, her black hair tied back. When Hallam looked at the husband, however, all he could see was family money. It could be the only explanation.

Ennis held his hand up for stillness and went behind a curtain. Hallam heard the photographer shuffling back and forth quietly and then the sound of something being dipped into liquid. He emerged with a wooden frame, which he put into his camera. "A piece of see-through glass given the power of vision," said Ennis. "Would that we could submerge our politicians in silver and get the same result!" Mrs. Arnold twittered and then returned to stillness. Her husband had not moved, as if he were trying to attract a bird. He was as still as a painting. (Hallam's father had paid for a painted portrait to be made of Alice and his son. The painter had meticulously made their likenesses in long sittings, and then excused them, their heads floating in gesso, alone in midair. He then had invented the couple's wardrobes, perfect garments neither of them would have had the resources to buy. Hallam wondered, flashing on the fantastical picture of him and his wife, if he would even achieve the happiness hinted at in that image.)

"And now, in the dark, the glass awaits and . . . careful, careful, finally we are ready." The other three exhaled, as if they'd watched a high-wire walker cross from the ledge of one building to another.

"Now," he said to the couple, "silence and stillness are our touchstones." He lifted the cap off the lens and gingerly brought his hands away from the apparatus as if he'd been building a tower of cards. "Whatever you are focused on, don't look away, or your faces will have dead, empty eyes. The light is carrying you now, like a word into an ear, through the lens and onto the glass. Thirty seconds is all I need. Be still, still now. Think that no matter how life treats you, no matter how old you grow, how prosperous—steady, don't look away— even though you may suffer illness, you will yet be young and only just married. This little instant of your lives will not go on into the future but will remain here, seeded in time as you grow leaves above it. Three, two, one. Relax."

But they did not, they were mesmerized by the process they had just participated in. Hallam found it remarkable, this communion. Even as Ennis moved smartly to close his shutter, they remained fastened to the moment of the photograph. Then the young bride leaned forward in her seat, breathing out, and the two lines in time separated themselves, one moving forward, the other fixed in a past that had just begun.

"Lovely," said Mr. Ennis, putting the protective sleeve back into the camera to remove the sensitized plate. "Come back tomorrow for it."

The couple stood, and the husband removed his hat, looked about as if refreshed by a catnap. He smiled at his bride and led the way out. Mrs. Arnold did not look at Samuel Ennis as she left his room, but she said, "Tomorrow."

"Tomorrow," he repeated to them as the door closed. He spun on the toe of one shoe back to Hallam. "I hope you enjoyed that."

"It was extremely interesting," he called after Ennis. The man had vanished behind his curtain again. "You obviously know your craft well."

"It takes less skill than it would seem, to master a mechanism that excites people's vanity. They do most of the work."

"May I see how the picture is coming out?"

"I'm not working on the positives right now, Mr. Hallam. I must fix this image and get ready for three more customers today. You can see I've a going concern here—you'll have your percentage in no time."

"I'm not worried," said Hallam. "In any case, I quite enjoyed watching you." He chose not to say that it may have been the most interesting thing he'd witnessed in Toronto since arriving. "I'd always wondered how a photograph was made."

Ennis emerged and crossed the room to go through a second curtain, this one a soiled muslin drape that separated his studio from the other half of the room, and there was the sound of one metal object clacking faintly against another. "I owe you six bob," he said, coming back through. "From the time I have used that first instalment of my order—the beginning of our arrangement—I have made one and ten in portraits. I can show you my receipts."

"That won't be necessary."

"You should verify them, Mr. Hallam. You needn't make a fetish of being trusting." He removed a cloth purse from inside his coat and poured a small handful of coins into his palm. "Have you ever had your picture taken, Mr. Hallam?"

"I haven't."

"Would you give three pence in exchange for a likeness of yourself you could send home? I'd make a quarter plate for you—just a good, close likeness. Mr. Arnold is paying ten for a half, so it really is a very good trade."

Even though this suggestion agreed with his earliest instinct that he was going to be railroaded by Mr. Ennis, Hallam still agreed without hesitation; the thought of a portrait had of course occurred to him from the moment he walked into the studio. To be able to give his family such a keepsake and have it cost him next to nothing (even if he were about to be fleeced) was irresistible. He proposed returning to his rooms to change into something more appropriate, but Ennis demurred. "You're no bride, Mr. Hallam. You're a missing man to all who love you. Let them see you as you are."

"I'd rather something more formal, Mr. Ennis. Something that won't worry them."

"A picture of Mr. J.G. Hallam, apothecary."

"No, not quite that. Just myself a little spruced up."

Ennis shrugged and stepped aside so Hallam could go back into the street. In the cramped foyer Ennis saw the next two customers, both young women. "Come back at the end of the day, Mr. Hallam. Before the sun goes down, and we'll do it then." Ennis looked at the rest of his day's work and knit his brows as if facing a trial. But Hallam had seen the women and knew this was a man who loved his work. "Miss Read?" Ennis said, and the one with the dun-coloured hair and tiny red mouth stood and went through his door into the studio. The shaft of light stood within the room like a pillar of alabaster.

When their eldest daughter, Jane, was still a toddler, she wandered out of the house one morning with nothing on but a little white dress. Alice ran to the shop, thinking Jane might have gone there to visit her father, and he and Alice rushed out onto the Hampstead Road calling her name, Hallam still in his frock, Alice six months pregnant with Cecile. They must have looked to all as if they'd just been robbed, frantically searching back and forth down the street, falling to bickering over which direction to take, each trying to think like a child. What had her conversation been like over breakfast? Had she said anything that might yield a clue as to where she had gone? He begged Alice not to weep as they swept down toward Harrington Square and Arlington Street. *If lost, Jane may have tried to trace her way back to the house on Albert Street*, he thought aloud. But here, at the fork of three major byways, where the Southampton Arms stood, any wandering child would have been in danger of being hit by cabs, carts, or just horses and riders. *You won't be able to see*, he said to Alice angrily, *stop crying*. They halted people on the sidewalk, hailed the hackneys to ask if they'd seen the child. Alice ran with one hand over her stomach.

He thought: *What will be the last image of the girl I carry in my mind? What will be the final expression in my memory, always, that I will think I had not paid enough attention to? Your father loves you*, he thought, pressing this sentiment to the air around them, urging it to its home. *Beloved, listen to my voice.*

The shops and people in their workaday clothing sped by. *Alice should not run like that*, he thought. Bells and organ music filtered past. He insisted she sit and he crouched in front of her as she rested on a barrel outside of Hamilton's Meats. "She is *somewhere*," he said. "You wait here for us. Don't move."

"What if she went to the canal?"

"Maybe she wanted to watch men fish?"

"What if someone took her?"

Hallam stroked her hot, pale face. "I'll return with her. You stay here or go back to the house."

"I won't go to the house," she said.

He untied his frock and handed it to her; it had impeded his legs. "She's but two," said Alice quietly as he took off toward the canal, down Mornington Crescent toward the tracks where there was a bridge, but in imagining Jane standing at the edge of the canal, he hit on an intuition. They had always taken her for walks in the pram, but lately had let her amble where it was safe (a grave mistake now!) and she had peered down into the tracks on the Birmingham Line and said, "River?" and they had corrected her, delighted with her. For the lines had been built deep below the level of the streets, and where they had walked that afternoon, the tracks sat down in a gulley. Hallam turned left on Mornington Road now, away from the bridge, and, as if materialized by his terror, he saw the clean white dress at the crest of the hill above the tracks only a hundred feet in front of him. She was only half a mile from her front door. He stopped dead on the spot. He could not see, from the flatness of his perspective, how close she might have been to the edge. The distance to the bottom, everyone knew from the *Times'* article, was ninety feet; it had taken the men seven months to drill and carve out the enormous ditch. If they'd chosen just to run the line at street level, he would not have stood in such deep awe as he did then, fearing that moving a yard forward could displace air down the street in the direction of her back. "Jane!" he called to her, but she was just a dot of white with tiny dashes of pink legs below, and she could not hear him. Still he called to her, "Jane——" until the urgency he could not muster in his voice reached his legs and he exploded into a panicked dash. He came up behind her (she remained unmoving, gazing into the activity below; he had even forgotten about the trains—there would be no surviving the fall) and stood ten feet away, staring at her form. She turned to him then, unsurprised to see him—for two-year-olds expect their parents to be wherever they are—and turned back to the scene in front of her. He went and gratefully clasped her hand. "No river," she said.

"No, darling. This is for the trains."

"Come," she said, and led him back in the direction he, and he presumed she, had walked. He brought her back to where her mother sat, although upon seeing her daughter at a distance Alice stood and, riven to the spot, simply began crying uncontrollably until they reached her and she could be sure it was not her fevered wishing that revealed to her this vision of her daughter still alive. Alice picked up the child and held her tightly to her.

"Where did you go!" she asked now, letting Jane lean back from her to look in her eyes. "Must I tie you up?"

"Ah, ah, ah," said Jane, "*train*."

"She was at the trains?"

Hallam shook his head wonderingly. "On the top, staring down."

Alice brought her eyes back to Jane, who was smiling at her and playing with her collar. And then Alice slapped her. It was quite sudden. Jane froze, a surprised expression on her face, and then the blood filled her cheeks and she burst out wailing. "Home is the only place for you!" shouted Alice. Passersby quickened their pace. "Not trains, not rivers, not streets!" She was fairly quaking. "This is what will happen every time you step out of your house without your mama or papa! Do you understand me, Jane?"

"Alice," he said, reaching for the baby.

"No. I'm speaking to Jane. Do you understand, Jane?"

"Love you Mama," said Jane, her voice contorted.

"Only home is safe," Alice repeated, and she pushed the girl's head into her neck and held her there.

*Only home is safe*, he thought, walking back to Ennis's in his day suit under a grey mantle. Ragged fat sparrows had made their reappearance in the city and sat on fence posts twittering at each other. Hallam had shaved the day's stubble off his cheeks, ran his hand over the raw skin. *If only my own father had punished me for wandering rather than encouraged it*, he thought, *what hot drink might I be taking in front of the fire now, my daughters involved in their books? Wish such independence on a child and they may well be shipbound*. He realized that his own sense of desperation had developed to the point that when he thought of his wife and children, he could only think in emergencies. His imagination pressed on him terrible outcomes to the daily dramas that must, still at that moment, be going on at home. And yet, the plain white dress did not tumble into the breeze, flying up around the little legs like a flag. He could not help seeing it in his mind, however unencumbered by the reality of his daughters' ongoing survival. He stood at the top of the railway crest and saw his two-year-old child's body dashed on the stone and the iron rails below, a knot of people already gathering, their eyes following the line of the gulley up to where he helplessly stood. He had to shake the image out of his head.

"Ah, you're respectable now," said Ennis. "Too bad."

"Too formal?"

"It's your picture. You wait here—it's something of a tip inside."

Ennis rearranged items within, and then opened the door into the foyer and stood aside, making a grand gesture toward the reset room. Hallam went to the chair and sat, pulling his pant legs down to cover the tops of his shoes (a lesson his mother had taught him as a boy when they went visiting and he would sit there looking as if, in her words, he were ready to pull them the rest of the way up and go hunting for frogs). Ennis went behind his camera and framed his subject.

"Does your wife call you Mr. Hallam, Mr. Hallam?" He stood in front of his subject with arms crossed. Hallam laughed uncomfortably. In nine months, it was the first time anyone had brought up his wife.

"Not normally."

"And your children? Mr. Hallam, or Papa?"

"Papa."

"Mmm," he said. Ennis approached him and lifted the hat off his head, stepped back to regard him. "Still too much Mr. Hallam here," he said. "Let's see if we can get Papa in the room without making you seem too ragamuffin."

"You want me in shirt sleeves."

"Maybe one like that for your wife. What does she call you?"

"Jem," he said quietly. It hurt even to hear his own voice say that private name. "It's short for—"

"Good enough, Mr. Jem. Now tell me why you are so keen on sending home an image of Mr. *Hallam*, a man your loved ones hardly know, when just a layer or two down, Jem and Papa are available to be photographed?"

Hallam understood the point, but presumed the picture would be shown around; he had to admit he was thinking of his father's interests. A prosperous-looking man of twenty-seven was more likely to be given some room to fail and then rebound; the man Mr. Ennis wanted to photograph might have to be rescued.

"Let's not mull it too long, Jem Hallam, I'll do it both ways for the same price. You'll choose the one you like and I'll scrub the other. What do you say?"

"It's more than fair," he said, holding his hand out for his hat. "Thank you. Let's do the scion of the family firm first."

Ennis returned to the huge camera and slid a black metal plate in through the top. He leaned down into his eyepiece. The bad eyelid poked out from the side, like a toadstool on a tree. "With less light, we'll need almost fifty seconds, so hold still. Think of this photo on someone's wall, and their saying, *That's Jem Hallam, he started all this.*"

"My grandfather did."

"Time to stop talking. Shutter open."

He took the cover off the lens and Hallam saw himself upside down in the glass, his hat spread out in a comical crescent at the bottom. He held still, focused on one of his black buttons in the middle of the lens, and Ennis counted off the ten-second gaps between silences. He did not attempt to make the wait more comfortable by regaling him with a distracting fable about the power of the picture they were now making. He simply stood, as before, with his arms crossed and his head turned ever so slightly to his left, to compensate.

"Forty-nine," he said, and finished the picture. He took out the masque and went into the back to fix the plate. He returned with another holder. "Now stand up and get that hat and coat off."

Hallam did, and stood in his vest in front of the chair.

"Good. Now sit down and let me see a little of Jem Hallam." Hallam sat again, and turned away a little from the camera, as he'd seen Mrs. Arnold do; it was a pose that seemed both decorous and relaxed. Ennis stood staring at him, an unnerving vision that Hallam imagined must take some getting used to. "Fetching," he said. "A little too much so. Turn back straight. No. Uncross your legs, hands on knees." He contemplated Hallam a little and checked in his eyepiece before returning his unhappy gaze to the scene. "Can you let your shoulders go, Mr. Hallam? I mean, try actually to sit in the chair. You appear to be levitating."

Hallam tried to push his shoulders down and he stretched his neck forward to release the muscles in his back, wrung his hands out in front of him as if they were wet, and then settled again. He tried to fix an expression on his face neither pompous nor uncertain. He felt very much like a monkey on a stick, but sat there in silence, gazing straight ahead at the lens cover, waiting. But Mr. Ennis was laughing into his fist.

"Is there something the matter?"

"No, Mr. Hallam," he said, "only mausoleum portraits are extra. Will you please come with me? Please?"

Hallam followed Ennis through the curtain that led into the man's private room. It was a jumble of chairs and clothing, much ugly crockery standing in a tower in an upright metal sink, and staves from a long-broken barrel scattered about. The bed leaked straw from inside its cloth and showed long signs of habitation: a deep trough was pressed into the middle of it where Samuel Ennis had slept for the two years he'd lived in the city. Hallam had suspected some misbehaviour on Mr. Ennis's part when he'd left him alone with the two young women in the afternoon, but the state of his personal room cast doubt on that, for he could not think of a woman of any standing consenting to be in this room, with or without Mr. Ennis.

There was a squat can against the wall, a milk can of sorts, and Ennis brought down two teacups from a doorless cupboard and passed one over.

"Now truly, Mr. Hallam, d'you trust me?"

"We've been through this."

"Now's the time to make your mind up."

Hallam regarded the milk can with some worry. "I don't think there's any advantage in turning back now, Mr. Ennis."

"Excellent. Do as I do then." Ennis lowered his teacup into the can, producing a faint bubbling sound as he did. It echoed around the inside of the metal walls. He removed his cup, and Hallam stepped forward and did the same, withdrawing a clear liquid from inside.

"What is it?"

"Mother's recipe," said Ennis, and threw the contents of his teacup directly into the back of his throat. "Go on now."

Hallam did the same. It went down like water, cool and refreshing, although somewhat more *viscous* was the word that came to his mind. It reached the pit of his stomach (which was empty, he now realized) and began to warm it. It was very nice, this whatever-it-was, some kind of Irish bitters perhaps. Then, without any discernable transition between *very nice* and *violently unpleasant*, something like brimstone seemed to explode in the space behind his eyes and nose. He staggered back as if from a blow and handed Ennis the teacup in order to have his hands free. *I might need my hands now*, was his dumbstruck thought as the heat from the liquor began mounting throughout his body at once, like a flame climbing a wall. Finally a flavour—or was it a fragrance?—became apparent, a full five or six instants after ingestion: burning hot bile, a greeny acid, the taste of one's insides cauterized. He thought that maybe smoke would come out of him. He held his breath, frightened to risk even a cough, his diaphragm pumping in and out, and then, as if a blockage had been broken, it was all over, and a sudden warmth settled in his limbs. Ennis, apparently long acclimatized to the effects of his refreshments, had calmly watched the whole reaction.

"There you go," he said.

"This is your *mother's* recipe?"

Ennis smiled broadly. "She's quite dead now." He held back the curtain and they re-entered the studio, which looked brighter to Hallam at this moment, even though it was past five o'clock and there couldn't be more than an hour and a half of sun left. "Back to your little chair, Mr. Hallam. Smartly, smartly."

He sat again, and Ennis moved his apparatus closer. "You know what to do, so let's begin without delay." He pulled away the lens cover and Hallam saw himself again in the ground glass, clownish and upside down. But now he sensed that the inverted image in the glass was a kind of translation of his earthly self, and that the light which entered his eye and allowed him to see that image of his distorted form was the same light that was entering the camera and scarring the plate within. And at some level, it now seemed quite clear to him, his eyes that received this light also cast it, and this was why the image could be made upon the silver.

Hallam fixed his eyes unmovingly on the lens and looked past it to concentrate all of himself on the plate. He pushed his tattered, flagging spirit along the wire of his gaze and embedded it, so Alice would have him, so their children would have him. He felt the liquor of his self crawl along this wire of light, a fluid like that which seeps out of a burn.

"Ah, I see Jem Hallam now," Samuel Ennis said quietly. "There he is in front of me. We'll need fifty-five seconds of him now. I see him with his wife . . ."

"Alice—"

"He's with her, drawing back the covers of their bed. He blows out the candle and fits his arm around her. This is her, her lovely self." Hallam was certain they could both smell the warmth of Alice's bedclothes, the sharp-sweet scent of her skin. "Her hair drifts across the pillow. Everything you care about is this simple. In the morning, the children come into the room."

"Yes."

"Don't move your mouth now. Thirty seconds. The children clamber up onto the bed. Times are different now, your parents would have frowned on such permissiveness, but you love these little bodies. Alice lifts the covers." Hallam felt the heat of the nighttime billowing around him. "They tuck in, their cold little children's feet. Laughter. This is what they have of you, what they think about and what they miss. Not that man in his waistcoat and garter, his tall hat. There you are. There is Jem Hallam, the father of two. Stay still now. Not long now." Hallam sent his whole self into the box, down the arrow of his sight. "Done," said Ennis. "You can rest."

"And what was that I drank?" Hallam said quietly, still in the thrall of the photo, as Mrs. Arnold had been.

"Potatoes."

"Really."

"They have souls, you know, but you can't get at them until they rot almost to hell. And then they become something quite as pure as a child's soul and as clear. It's very handy of them."

"I feel a little brutalized." He realized the small amount of light in the room was hurting his eyes. He closed them and rubbed them with his fists. "But I'm happy."

"Wonderful," said Ennis. "You can come round for the results tomorrow. In the afternoon, I'll be guessing."


Hallam walked home in the full dark, the sliver of a new moon casting a fog-like glow on the city, and above that moon, an ancient sky of stars. Along Adelaide Street, under the protection of the near-dark, women stood speaking with men, and other couples passed by. Even Camden Town, transformed like this at night; it was no longer a source of surprise to him. But that it had reconstituted itself this completely, like a powder poured into the water of a new city, was startling. Toronto was but fifty years old, and already all level of trade existed there.

"You need a lie-down, burgomaster?" said someone in the shadows. She laughed, a musical sound that was out of place.

"No, thank you."

"That's a fine suit of clothes to be walking crooked in." She'd stepped out. She was young, with bright, clear eyes. "I can help you walk straighter."

He tried to smile in a sophisticated way. "I'll be fine on my own," he said, bowing slightly, and pulled his eyes away from the woman. He took Peter Street south in the direction of the lake. For some distance down this way (a street he'd never been on day or night), there was not a soul, and not so much as a candle burning in a window. A single bat burst from the underside of a bare tree and shot past his head like a shuttlecock.

On Wellington Street, he turned left, coming within the ironish scent of the still-frozen lake, and passed the Parliament buildings and Bishop Strachan's Palace, back into the comforting light of the gaslamps. At the very first of them, a pair of men sat huddling for warmth under its meagre heat, and Hallam passed them each a coin, which they received with silent nods. Along here, he'd seen families begging in the warmer months, groups of four, two children and two adults, all revolving within the sphere of the Parliament, where their troubles were ignored. *There but for . . .* he thought, feeling grateful.

It felt warmer, or perhaps he was warmed still, whether by the lethal cocktail Ennis had given him or by the seeming closeness of the people he loved, and he had an urge to visit the lakefront, to stand where he'd first stood almost nine months earlier, full of arrogant wishes and simple hopes. He walked down to Front Street, where people of a more familiar class were now to be seen near the American Hotel, standing in knots of conversation. He returned a happy wave of the hand to one of them, and inside the ground-floor windows of the hotel, frosted around the edges and fogged, he could hear the revelry of the guests in their grog, and a pianoforte playing in the background. *I could close my eyes and be home.*

Hallam continued to the base of Brown's Wharf and stood there surveying the expanse of frozen lake. There was slurried water where ships' hulls made contact with the ice, tied up at their wharves and scratching at their element like animals in cages. Spring would come now—one could feel it in the air. Out into the dim light, the lake lay pale and off-white, encased in its icy sheath like a plate of tin covered in crystalline silver. Lunar caustic, that substance which drank light. Hallam stood before that expanse, a shiver of joy and fear in his muscles, looking at a giant photograph being made by stars.

*Three*

~

# THE EARTH MOVERS

~

*Toronto, November 1997*

I.

AT SEVEN, JOHN ARRIVED.

David came out the front door and walked to the curb. The whole neighbourhood smelled of August flowers, the phlox blooming at last, a tang in the peach-sweet air.

John watched the way David moved and it made him want to jump from the car and take his arm. But he knew better and he let Bridget's father make his slow way, his ankles loose, the backs of his hands somehow leading his body forward. John's only concession was to reach across the passenger seat and push the door open an inch. David got in with a heavy exhale. He settled himself in the seat and struggled to bring the belt around.

"Was Bridget awake?" he said.

"No."

"I woke Marianne. But she was asleep when I left."

John took the end of the seat belt out of David's fingers and snapped him in. "Are you going to be all right without a jacket?"

"I don't want a jacket." He twisted stiffly in the seat. His clothes seemed to move independent of his body. "Are you okay, John?"

"Are you?"

"I'm ready." John sat with his hands on the wheel, the street over the dashboard soaked in light, and he tried to think of something else to talk about, anything to keep them there, in front of the house. He began to speak, but David put a hand on his, and said, "Come on now, no more small talk. Let's go."

Driving south, John saw the car as if from above, a view of the little red Corolla taking the side streets out slowly toward Eglinton Avenue and then joining the morning traffic there. Going south on Bayview toward the lake. A slow-moving form taking on the heat of other cars and the sun, and below them the huge expanse of lake. It hurt his eyes to look at it. At Bloor Street, passing under the viaduct, John realized he was probably equidistant from both of their women, both still sleeping, unaware of this invisible line he was drawing between them.

They were talking as if merely passing the time of any day—David saying something about the smell of bricks baking in the old valley kilns—but John was distracted by the image of his car as a bead on a line and his mind ticked over into a strange consideration. The actual distance in feet or miles between two places would be constant, but the time it would take to bridge them was flexible. Distances between things had at least two independent qualities, a spatial one and a temporal one. This wasn't a new thing, even a six-year-old would understand that if you ran home you'd get there quicker. What distressed him was that the speed at which he drove the car correlated to the establishment of a moment in time. David was asking him something about Bridget and John answered by saying, "Until now, as well as you might expect. Although after today . . ."

"Yes," said David. "Of course."

"Little explosions."

John kept his attention on the traffic, which was building the further south they went, collecting cars from the Don Valley Parkway and the side streets. He didn't want to invite David this morning to enlarge on anything very much; he didn't want to be too direct about anything. There are forms of knowing, he thought, and many are better unacknowledged. He noticed his legs were shaking, and to cover, he patted his thigh, as if to music. But the car radio was off.

He slowed down. He liked being with David, no matter why, liked the way David talked to him. None of the Hollises spoke to him the way David did. Not even Bridget, and although it would seem natural that one might expect a different kind of intimacy with one's lover than with her father, John still felt it as a lack. David had said, during an odd half-hour the previous spring, *Will you begrudge me a drink?* as if he actually believed it was in John's power to deny him anything. Except that afterwards, John realized it hadn't been a question, but a test of kinship. Before this, he had done a number of small tasks for David—he'd realized long ago that his destiny was to be called upon—and he'd collected a book for David or looked up some small matter like a date or a street name. John's so-called expertise was only a convenience, though. The two men were too far apart in age to settle on simple friendship, so their relationship was sown on the berm of being useful to each other. David, over the five years John had known him, had confided many of his passions: the city's history, the Blue Jays, the lives of his daughters, certain flowers in certain seasons. But now, it felt to John, all of it had been leading to this morning. Fate employing them both in its inevitabilities. It came to him in a worrying flash that he didn't know of a single city where you drove north to get to water.

"Did you eat?" he asked.

"I had a few Triscuits."

"We can pull off here and go to the Canary. Get a real breakfast."

"Why don't you stop on the way back, John. Take some time for yourself. What do you think?"

"I might do that." John let the thought of how he'd be feeling slide from his mind and he drove past the exit to Eastern Avenue, another spot in the city it would be difficult to look at.

Simply by living in a place the parts of it become invested with the power to memorialize pleasure or pain. He'd lived in Toronto since high school—only fourteen years, less than half his life—but the entire city was flecked with significances. The apartment his Aunt Cecilia and Uncle Jason paid for at Mount Pleasant and

Eglinton when they sent him to Toronto to "start new"—an intersection that still filled him with hopeless loneliness. There, too, the North Toronto high school that, when he had reason to pass it, still emanated the stink of cigarette smoke and wet concrete, as well as the faint aural scar of the music he was forcibly loyal to in those days. ("The Lovecats"? "99 Luftballons"?)

They came out onto Lakeshore Boulevard, which (David had once told him, and was now telling him again) had been built on debris. Directly behind them the abandoned industrial lands ranged back—tall grey stone faces at their edge and behind them squat weathered brick buildings and wild scrubby fields and a breakfast dive or two still pulling in enough people to keep opening their doors, fifty years beyond the last active days of that neighbourhood.

The Harbour Light Hotel was coming up in front of them on the left. Strangers still in their beds, stacked to the sky, unaware of anything but what was going on inside their minds, to be forgotten on waking. What slim thread of the world at street level might infect the place, John wondered, and turn the late dreaming within it darker, like a dropper of black ink squeezed into a swimming pool. He knew that every inch he proceeded with David in the car he shared with his fiancée would push the edges of that stain farther in all the directions of his own life.

"Will you let me take you home?" John said, and David's answer upset him, and he spun the car hard against oncoming traffic and swerved to the opposite curb. His face was hot and red. He suddenly tasted bright iron in his mouth and a wave of electricity flowed through the marrow of his teeth. They were at the walkway west of the hotel, near the ferry docks. John undid his seat belt.

"Don't get out," David said.

"I didn't go through this to let you stumble the last steps to the docks. It's three hundred feet to the turnstiles."

"I know how far it is," said David. He leaned across the seat and kissed his future son-in-law on the cheek. "I love you," he said, his hand cool against John's face. "Take care of my girls."

## 2.

HE SAW THE LIGHT IN THE EYEHOLE BLOT TO DARK-
ness and he felt her staring at him as he stood in the hotel
hallway. He could sense the waves of disbelief penetrat-
ing the door. She'd called Bridget for the first time
almost a week ago; she had every reason to believe the
knock at her door meant a thaw in relations. A moment
of discomfort displaced by a tearful hug. He wasn't sure
she was going to open the door at all, but then it swung
wide and it was somehow a grand gesture of displeasure.

"I guess she must really be pissed off at me," she said.

"She's concerned," said John Lewis.

"Well, you tell her I'm fine."

"Are you?"

Marianne stared blankly at him, leaning on the door.
He was trying to gather as much as he could, knowing
the door could close at any moment. He smelled citrus in
the air, a watery, thin thread of it, and soap coming off of
Marianne. Home smells. She was wearing taupe slacks
and a T-shirt David had bought her on their last
Christmas. "Can you tell me what you're doing here?"

"Well, John, I'm having a vacation."

He stepped back from the door. "So I guess you're fine, then?" She let him back up a step more. "Should I tell Bridget that?"

"Sure. Tell her that, since she's so worried about me." He stood in the hallway, his hands deep in his pockets. "You're just going to go?"

"I guess."

"Fine," she said.

She walked back into the room and stood between the two double beds, leaving a right of way in front of him that led to the windows. He wiped his clean feet thoroughly outside the door and then entered with his eyes lowered. He inventoried the lamp outside the bathroom before he crossed to the windows, glancing around the room as he went, although not at her. The room was clean, if cluttered. One bed of two unmade. He could scratch utter madness off his list. The lake, glowing dully in the large west-facing window, drew him to the other side of the room. The early November light turned the water into a slowly undulating movie screen. The other window faced north onto the monolithic-seeming city, a window that took up only half of that wall. He stood there, looking down along the row of condos ranging westward along the lakefront, then faced the city in the other view. There was the muddy excavation at the foot of Bay Street.

"This is what you're doing?" he said, still looking through the window.

"I have a hobby now. They're always telling widows

to get a hobby, so this is mine. Like trainspotting, only without trains. Or tracks."

"Or a destination."

"If you're going to nitpick."

He stood straight. The door was still open, fifteen or so feet away. "Did David ever say he thought there'd be something right here? Right at the foot of the hotel?"

"I don't know, did he?"

"Not to me."

"It's a grand conjecture," she said. "I'm not afraid of the outcome."

"Maybe some people are going to get put in their place."

"We'll see."

"How long do you think?" he said, turning to face her. "Until they get down far enough?"

She came to stand with him in the quay-facing window and he moved slightly to one side. At street level the site was walled in with pastel-coloured boards painted with the images of local hockey heroes. From above, the walled hole looked like a grave. "Well, how far are they now?"

"I have no idea," he said.

"Forty feet?"

He tried to calculate if it was, but applying his brain to something as mechanical as a measurement was impossible in his current state of mind. His hands vibrated with pins and needles. He compared the depth of the wall on the far side of the hole to the machines and people he could see in it. There was no scale. "You think forty?"

"Forty feet down, under the fill, that's where the water's surface would have been. The lake of 1850."

She went over to the little hotel desk and fished through the mess on it. The desk was the room in miniature: paper, books, scraps of hotel stationery with illegible notes and diagrams on them. Scribbled arrows pointing at boxes. He made out the word *wharf* under one of them. Cylinders of photocopied newsprint leaned against the wall at the back of the desk like spent uranium rods. There were more paper tubes on the floor, a few of which had burst their elastic bands and flopped open there. Strange white paper blossoms. She brought out a press kit. "This says the foundation is going to be poured at fifty-two feet."

"It's not even fifty feet yet."

"You sure?" She handed him a pair of binoculars. "Now look through these and tell me."

He had questions for her, but she'd already driven him from his purpose and he went along with it, waiting for the right moment. He lifted the binoculars, and through them he saw the dirt and the machines and the bits of garbage. He couldn't think very well, aware that her eyes were on him. He tracked past the two or three large yellow machines making busy over the surface of the site, went up as far as he could and then back down when he saw cars, and refocused. He figured he could pile three bulldozers on top of one other and reach street level. Was a bulldozer seven feet tall? He'd never considered the height of a bulldozer before. He held the glasses steady and looked away to see if he could judge size by comparison. He had no idea. He said so.

"Okay then," said Marianne. "So you have nothing to offer me?"

"I'm not good at guesstimation."

She laughed. "Add it to the list, John."

"I'll go."

"And tell Bridget what? Now that you've *veni*ed and *vidi*ed?" She held out a hand and he put the binoculars in it.

"I'll tell her she should come and see you. Or call you, at least."

"I don't want any more phone calls, John. She knows where I am."

Once he'd had to level a swing seat at his uncle's farm by evening out two ropes tied to either end of it. By the time they were each a foot shorter the seat was still uneven and he gave up, and it struck him that this was a perfect image for Bridget and Marianne's relationship. He could never tell Bridget this thought. Or tell Marianne the kinds of things her daughter, wrongly, thought of her. An agonic love held them together, and the strongest force in it was a complete and basic misunderstanding of each other. He said, "I guess the two of you are coping with David in your own way."

"Diplomacy is another way of lying, John."

"I hadn't thought of it like that."

She closed her mouth tightly. Stepped around him and went over to the north window. "This was all water up until 1890. We're standing on top of the lake from 1889 right now."

"David talked about that."

"He talked to you a lot."

Marianne was staring at him and it made him feel oddly seasick. After a few seconds, she seemed to lose interest in him, and drifted back to the window. It had felt, in that moment, that the truth was going to be towed out of him. He watched her watching the excavation, and he realized that for her, he was no longer in the room.

3.

WHEN THE FUTURE STILL HAD DAVID HOLLIS IN IT,
John and Bridget were living together in a part of town
called Riverdale. David had educated them (whether
they wanted to be or not) in the history of their neighbourhood. He explained to them that at the turn of the
century, when the land to the east of the Don River and
its deep, almost impassable valley was first developed,
the acres of thick forest gave themselves up reluctantly
to cutters and road-layers. Access south to the lake was
not as direct here as it was from the middle of town, and
the promontories not as pleasant. A road had been cut in
the valley, but if you wished to live in Riverdale, your
horses had to be strong for the uphill slogs to and from
town. It was said that if you stood at Yonge and King
streets at nightfall you could hear the curses of the tan-
ners and the coopers and the housewives beating their
way back into the dark part of town.

Now, of course, Riverdale was almost gentrified, and
the city extended so far east that it changed names sev-
eral times before it subsided to country again.

They lived on a pleasant avenue south of Danforth Avenue called Hogarth that went down between a church and a coffee shop—so you could have any part of you woken up, David had once joked—and there was even a good bookstore across the way in case Jehovah or mocha Irish cream failed to do the trick. North of the main thoroughfare, the big houses that had been subdivided into apartments in the fifties and sixties were slowly being returned to their original forms, with two-career families snapping up the properties at second-best prices and refurbishing to their hearts' contents. But south, the houses were smaller; they were still better earners than sellers, and the area was full of tenants. John and Bridget were on two floors—a half-floor with a bedroom and an office, both with slanted ceilings, and a main floor with a big open plan and a hard bright view of the street. Old chestnuts and oaks and silver maples up and down the street, where Norway maples hadn't taken hold and sucked off the top of the water table. He loved it there and was happy enough when Bridget suggested her kitchen table and newish Ikea drinking glasses and side tables were probably suitable, and so down into the shared storage area went John's scratched cobalt blue drinking glasses that he'd bought at Honest Ed's discount emporium and his mispainted yellow-and-green wood table that he'd carted around from apartment to apartment when he'd gone to university. Bridget had better taste than he—they both admitted this—and when they set up the apartment he felt a little more sophisticated and he liked that.

"They called it Riverdale, and the Playters even came up here and built a little enclave, so people started buying up the land. Even before there were streets." David was talking to them both as they buzzed around him getting the place ready for a dinner party with three couples from the office at the ministry of the attorney general, where Bridget was now articling. He'd begun dropping in on them once or twice a week; he wasn't one to call beforehand. "I had plans all my life, now I'm flying by the seat of my pants."

He was talking to them from the living room as they milled about in the kitchen. "Go see if he wants anything to eat," Bridget said.

"Why don't I bring him some of the soup."

She flung a hand out toward the stove to ward him off. "We're having six people here tonight, John. Make some toast or something."

"One-eighth a bowl less each won't make a difference." He made his point by ladling out a generous serving for her father and bringing it to him in the living room. She heard her father's surprised exclamation of gratitude. There was a carpet under the table and she imagined the soup dripping onto it.

"Come and be closer to us while we cook," she said, going out and carrying his soup back into the kitchen. Sitting level with him at the kitchen table, John saw the glassiness in David's eyes, the "drugged" look that Marianne had once or twice referred to, but rather than giving him a soporific expression there was a shine in the man's eyes, a pleasant, vague sheen of something one might even have been tempted to call health if one didn't know better. It was, John thought, a luminousness that came from knowing something.

He listened to David free-associating on some of his pet topics, rates of erosion and bicycle lanes, and at one point, when he was in the middle of a sentence—"This is why you get so many willows at the edges of promontories"—Bridget recoiled from a crisper drawer in the fridge and muttered, "Shit."

"What is it?"

"I have no lemons," she said, and she stared wildly around the room as if she might find one dangling from a corner, an expression of full pre-party dementia on her face. "You go," she said to John. "Go to the Loblaws on Broadview. They'll have the big ones."

"No problem," he said, patting David on the forearm. "Hold that thought."

"Take him with you," said Bridget.

David put his palms flat on the table. "*Him?*"

"Sorry, Dad." She threw John the car keys from the bowl on the sideboard. "Don't be long."

It took some effort to settle David into the passenger seat, and once John let go of him the older man released a long breath. He drove slowly, but David said, "I won't break if you change lanes."

John left him in the car in the no-parking lane beside the doors and ran in to collect the lemons. A quivering pyramid of them stood at the head of the fruit-and-vegetable aisle, glowing unnaturally. He couldn't recall if it was oranges or lemons that were artificially coloured before being sent to market—maybe it was both. Oranges were green, he thought, as green as limes. He carried six lemons in the crook of his arm to the shortest queue, his thoughts jumping. He couldn't see the car from the checkout. He should have brought David in; it was an insult to leave him in the car like a dog. The clatter of cash register drawers was getting to him. He strained to see out the front of the store.

"Sir?"

He put his purchase on the conveyor. *If someone tries to give me a ticket, David will probably attempt to move the car himself, won't he?*

"One ninety-eight."

How had David got to their house, anyway?

"Three-oh-two your change. Your lemons, sir?"

"Right. Thank you."

Back in the no-parking lane, there was a ticket under the windshield wiper, but David was gone.

"Hey!" he shouted as if he'd been robbed. "David!" Spinning in a circle, panicked and sweating, already deeply into the frantic conversation he would have with Bridget—"You're the one who insisted I take him!" / "I didn't insist, John, I suggested"—but then he saw David in the checkout line of the little liquor store attached to the Loblaws. He was reaching forward and holding on to the counter, almost leaning against the man in line ahead of him. John pushed the ticket back under the wiper and went into the store.

"Yeah, we got a ticket," David said. "I would have run out—"

"What are you doing in here?"

David held up a mickey of Jack Daniel's. "Will you begrudge me a drink?"

"I don't think you should get that. Come back to the house and have a beer or something." David shook his head. "Won't that interfere with the medicine you're taking? I mean, it's not my place to—"

"No, it isn't," David said. "Go wait in the car."

Maybe it was eminently sensible. To drink in the face of dying. *Go ahead*, John thought, *take that old medicine*.

David lurched back to the car and directed John out of the parking lot. He asked him to go south, and they drove to the tail end of a forgotten street. John imagined that the squat red-brick buildings were probably lofts now, or were about to be. David passed John the mickey and asked to be taken out of the car, and John put the little bottle into his back pocket and helped him out. He held the weight of David's body in his arms until he could feel the man's spine engage with gravity, and then followed him to a strip of grass at the top of a hill that went down fifteen feet to the parkway. It was a desolate place, with the sound of cars sweeping by in both directions. Across the asphalted valley the city was a flat mirage of towers above a hem of trees. David descended the incline a couple of feet, standing high above the traffic, tilted back to stay plumb, and John could see his pale white scalp under wisps of hair at his crown. David pointed to where a pedestrian bridge spanned the

Bayview Extension. "That was the edge of town for sixty years—the necropolis is right behind those trees. And you go down here"—his arm tracked slowly south—"and that was the middle of town. I guess it still is. Generally, you moved into the necropolis by the time you were fifty-five. That was old age. That makes me a lucky man, doesn't it?"

"If you feel lucky." John waited a moment, making an effort to see the place as David was seeing it, to grasp the connections. "We should go back."

"I'd like a drink." He turned to see whether John would dispute drinking out there in the open, but John drew the bottle out of his back pocket and cracked the cap in his fist. "You can make the first toast," David said.

John thought: *Life has not made me smart enough to know how to deal with a situation like this. Does one give a man with a degenerative motor disease a shot of hard liquor while he is teetering on the side of a hill overlooking traffic?* He passed David the bottle. "To the future?" he said.

"A brave toast to a dying man."

"Something else then . . ."

"No," David said. "That's good. Thank you for it." He raised his arm stiffly, weak even with the faint weight of a thirteen-ouncer in his hand. "The future, whatever it is."

"Whatever it is," said John. He listened to the whisky plunge in David's throat, and then accepted the bottle from him. David was staring out at the city, his eyes blank.

"The future is nothing, though," he said. "The present is nothing. It's already gone." He stumbled, turning for the bottle, and John caught him by the elbow. "I'm not drunk."

"I know."

"Yet." John passed him the whisky and David drank, more deeply this time. "What do you imagine the average person thought about? Back then?"

"Probably what we think about now," said John. "Food. Work. Sex."

David considered that for a moment, shaking his head a little, although John thought it might have been a tremor. "Maybe it's a mistake to think they were like us. We have no idea, really. What they were like when they were alone, how their shoes felt on their feet. How food tasted to them. No one cares about this. They want a list of wars and casualties, big numbers, historical roll call." The whisky went into him like water. He held the bottle tight to his chest. "Do you think you're awake, John?"

"I don't know what you mean."

"Aren't we just dreaming? All of this? Living in some agreed-upon fantasia?"

"If we are, then I guess I'm asleep."

"Would you wake up if you could?"

David was staring at him, his gaze flicking from one eye to the other. "I don't know," said John. "I like the dream I'm having."

"Good answer," David said, his smile lopsided. "Plus, it's hard to get back to sleep." He considered his feet, pushed the toe of one shoe into the yielding dirt. "My wife humours me, you know? And your fiancée thinks I'm a fool who should be dying in bed."

John shifted back up the hill a bit and found himself suddenly looming over David.

"That's not what Bridget thinks. She's just worried you're exerting yourself too much."

"And what do you think?"

The spectres of the three Hollis women stood behind him, waiting for him to deliver the company line. But John said, "If I were you, I'd want a drink and whatever freedom I could get my hands on."

"There you go." Tilting the bottle into his mouth. They stood gazing down at the traffic, the silver-and-gold flashing cars speeding by in packs where salmon had once run.

"Should we go back?" The man's eyes were wet. "David?"

"Never mind me." He poured out the rest of the bottle into the grass and turned away from the scene. "You're a good kid."

He'd never been called that in his life. *A good kid*. An unexpected boon to be loved, after a childhood of dutiful care under his Aunt Cecilia's roof. Her family had done their best to enfold him in their lives, but he was an only child with dead parents, a cursed child, and he knew he was a raw wound in their home. He'd never dreamed of another family.

He watched the only true father of his life struggle back toward the car and after a suitable moment of leaving him to his dignity, John stepped back down into the grass and put his arm around David's waist. He brought him around to the passenger door, and braced him as he opened it. David's skin smelled like wet cardboard. A death smell. John's cellphone rang and both men looked at each other with dread.

"You answer that and we're both in deep shit."

"It'll be worse if I don't." He let it ring twice more, then opened it. "Hi."

It was Marianne. He passed the phone over with as apologetic an expression as he could and David put the cell up against his ear.

"How did I get here?" he said to John.

"I drove you."

"There you go, he drove me." He listened, apparently bored. "No, I walked to Bridget's."

The word *walked* erupted from the phone and David passed it back to John.

"Mrs. Hollis?"

"Put him back on."

"It *is* springtime," David said to no one in particular.

"John, you put him in a cab right now, do you hear me?"

He felt the blood pounding in his rib cage. It made him feel faintly sick. "I'll drive him," he said.

"People should be out smelling the flowers, Marianne!" David was trying to turn in a wide circle, like they did in some commercials, but he was beginning to gasp for air. "Not being prostrate. In bed, dying. But . . ." He stopped and leaned over, holding his thighs. "If it's any consolation, I didn't walk *all* the way."

Marianne hollered into John's ear. "I don't care how far you fucking walked!"

"David, I think you should—"

"Oh, give me the bloody phone." He snatched the cell away and John stood aside, running his hand over his scalp. His forehead was slick. "I didn't walk, okay? Are you crazy? You think I could walk all the way from . . . what? A nice lady picked me up. She gave me candy and I got into her car." John could hear Marianne roaring on the other end of the connection. "You *do not* get to tell me how to spend my time on earth," he said. "Do you understand me? No, I won't calm down. Yes . . . yes, I know, but I'm not going to disintegrate out in the spring air! Well, better that than rotting in a mechanical god-damned bed. . . . If you're planning on ditching me at home with nothing but a television and a pill-holder to mark the time, then you're damn well right I'll be making my own fun." He snapped the cell shut, then leaned over and put a hand on his thigh, laying the phone in John's palm. "She wants me in a cab."

"I told her I'd take you."

"Not if you cherish your life." He turned his greyish, gleaming eyes to him. "I'm to die like a moth in a bottle, did you know that?"

John offered a half-nod.

"Should I sit at home?"

"I don't know."

He was shaking his head, snapping his jaw for air. "I'm awake," he said. "I'm awake and I'm alive, and it hurts like hell."

4.

MARIANNE OPENED THE DOOR FOR HIM AND STOOD there momentarily, looking at him with—if anything—amusement. It was the day after his first visit, and yet he saw she wasn't the least bit surprised to see him again. She walked back into the room. "So?" he said.

"So, you're impervious to hints."

"I mean *them*."

She waved a hand in the air. "Oh, *them*. They dig. Dig, dig, dig. Busy as beavers." She was wearing a robe she'd brought from home, and walked barefoot on the hotel carpet.

He sat on the end of the unused bed. Housekeeping had more or less been barred, but apart from the clementine peels under the beds, the room was still clean.

"I see the trucks making new groupings in the back there," she said, and he thought she was deigning to make conversation with him. "They must be getting ready to pour." Her shoulders went up, bearing the weight of her body as she leaned into the glass. "I read all about construction sites," she said. "They'll put down an iron grid first. Then they'll drown it in cement, and that will be that."

"Why don't you go down and talk to them?"

"And say what? Dig a little more for me? Just in case?"

"Someone might be willing to investigate a bit. It wouldn't harm anyone to ask."

She regarded him with mock pity. "John, if I go down there and they get one whiff of me, they'll pour the concrete that instant. You think they want someone making a claim on their dirt?"

"It's not a claim. And anyway, by the time they get to the point where they want to pour, they'll be past forty feet. Right? They'll have found it by then."

"Or not." She returned her attention to the window. He could hear the distant mechanical sounds from three hundred feet below them. Whirrs and clanks. He closed his eyes and felt the whole of it in his mind: the big dirty space, the machines avoiding each other in their slow progressions, the earth being removed. He saw the land as a cross-section and imagined a shape just below the surface, rising. Or the land falling, like water receding and revealing. It would be a miracle if there was anything there, he thought, but it was something worth hoping for.

He considered Marianne as she stood in the window, seeing echoes of Bridget in her spine, in her neck— Bridget's form embedded in her mother's. He'd noticed these similarities before, but had averted his attention from them because he was busy being in love and couldn't imagine Bridget any other way than as she was. As an adult, he had no person around whose older body he could see himself winding like a vine, but here was Bridget, the future's Bridget, standing in front of him. Into the window, Marianne said, "Should we make small talk?"

"Do you want to?"

"Bright for November," she said.

"I never notice those kinds of things."

"You don't notice November is dark? Don't you usually feel like killing yourself in November?"

"Not especially in November, no."

She laughed; he imagined she'd thought him clever for a moment. "Well, fine, how's work? You do someone's bookkeeping, right?"

"It's more research."

"Right." He heard her fingertips ripple along the top of the ledge. "I guess it's hard to apply an accounting degree when you hate accounting."

"I thought it was a practical major. I didn't realize I didn't have the talent for it."

She looked at him with what seemed to be something of a leer. "Was it really a matter of talent? Does one need talent to use a calculator?"

He gave a faint shrug. "Do you know *bookkeeping* is the only word in English with three double letters in a row?"

"You're a panic, John. I've never been able to think of you as an accounting type."

"I guess I'm not."

"Would this be why you work as a researcher for a failed playwright rather than raking in the bucks on Bay Street?"

"Could be," he said.

She fell silent. He released his breath, controlling his rib cage so it wouldn't make a sound. "Are you going to be useful to me, John?"

"Useful?"

"I'm just wondering if you're here to perform some kind of a service. Maybe I can't afford you."

He went along with the joke, but he knew his face looked wrong. "This is a special offer," he said. He felt stupid.

She came closer, but he stood his ground in front of her. She was entitled, he thought, but he hoped she wouldn't hit him. "Come back tomorrow," she said. "I've had enough company for today."

"I thought we could—"

"You thought wrong."

On Wednesday, she called him a cad and told him to go away again. Her eyes were grey and red. That night, while he was sharing a pizza with Bridget in front of the television, she'd debated aloud whether it was time to call her mother. He looked at her without moving his head. "Do you think you can talk to her calmly?" he asked.

"Do you think I can?"

"Maybe wait a few more days," he said. She subsided to silence then, her attention on the TV and his secret was still safe, although "safety" was not on the spectrum of feelings he was having these days. She was lethargic at night, willing to eat whatever John brought home, but she only picked at her food. He noted her skin was pale, as if grieving for her father was leeching the colour from her. In the middle of the night her groaning woke him up and all he could get out of her was the word *foot*. When he lifted the covers off her legs, one of her feet was cramping—her big toe pointed at an almost ninety-degree angle to her instep. He held her foot against the inside of his leg and pushed against the long muscle running down the edge of her sole. When the cramp subsided, she began to cry, but the entire time she had remained asleep. He tried to imagine how her sleeping mind had coded the pain and release as a dream.

He left Marianne on her own on Thursday and spent the day on the fifth floor of the Toronto Reference Library looking up the symptoms of legionnaires' disease for Howard Rosen. It rained all afternoon and then the sun came out just as he left, a benediction.

Late on Friday afternoon she said, as if in hope, "I thought I'd scared you off for good." She'd opened the door and then gone back to the window. Now she was in jeans and a black blouse. A room service lunch, a linen napkin covering a plate, was waiting on a wheeled table near the door. She asked him to leave the door open.

Even in the house on Banff Road he'd not felt he was in her territory as keenly as he did now, in this space that was, temporarily, hers alone; he'd never felt he was taking his life into his own hands. Here now, there was nothing but Marianne, Marianne detached from the grid of her life and her mind pointing down into the dirt like the head of a shovel. She would not be moved and he had already decided, anyway, not to try to move her. She could uncover her own version here and it would disturb nothing that he knew. He could probably live with that.

He pushed the lunch table into the hall.

"I spoke with Alison," she said. "She told me she was disappointed. Do you think a child should say she's disappointed in her parent?"

"She's trying to be honest with you. I thought you wanted that."

She *hmph*ed and pointed at the unslept-in bed. There was a pile of books on it. "I think you may last longer if we don't speak. I made you a reading list."

"Is it for me or for you?"

"What do you mean?"

"Do you want me to make notes?"

"If you want." She yawned as if considering the prospect of having to read a dozen précis. He'd begun to see that the piles around the room hadn't changed much in his four visits. They kept an unread shape. Perhaps they were there only to buzz and whisper. Conversations heard through a wall. "See if you can't tease out a salient detail or two." She tossed him a small pad and a pen.

He let her go back to what she was doing at the window (he'd been careful, this time, to appear uninterested) and sat on the bed. The first thing in the pile was not a book, but a photocopy of the sort of thing he never knew had existed before the 1930s: a travel guide. It was for people planning to visit or move to Toronto in the mid–nineteenth century. Beneath it was *The Annals of York*, which appeared to collect the goings-on in city chambers to well back in the nineteenth century. Then *Canada and Why We Like It*, by Mrs. Edward Copleston, and at the bottom of the pile, like a nostrum vouchsafing sleep, was *Smith's Canadian Gazetteer* for 1846. He'd had to rifle through one of these catalogues for David himself, to confirm the name of a wharf. That was in 1996, when David had asked him to help with the monograph, his hands too unsteady to take his own notes anymore.

Six hundred and ten barrels of ash exported from Windsor Harbour in 1844.

He glanced up at Marianne to ensure he was doing what was required of him. She was drawing concentric circles in a notebook. Twenty-three pages of the city guide offered the Latin names of local trees and animals and bugs, most of which no one had seen in the city since the First World War. (He had the image of berobed monks walking the streets in a long line, reciting these names in a long chant.) In the winter of 1854, *Vespertilio noveboracensis*, the "New York bat," was found by a local entomologist, a Mr. Couper. John wrote down that the man "stuffed it and sent it to the celebrated naturalist L. Agassiz, to whom it was of the utmost importance." Further on, there was a section enumerating the professionals in various trades. Two basket makers, two hundred and three tailors, thirteen artists. Ages, nativities, religions. Fifty-seven Jews in the city in 1856. *Howard might want to know that*, he thought, and wrote it down as well. Their sole synagogue was located at Richmond and Yonge, above "the apothecarists."

The writer—he was signed *a member of the press*—wrote in a personal tone, as if he were standing right there beside you, pointing out a clever gilt vane here, a peculiar odour there. John found himself engrossed in that voice, happy to be anywhere but in Marianne Hollis's bedroom, the voice so alive despite its calling out from a distance. He wondered how difficult it would be, if a person were so inclined, to manufacture a case for one thing or another, abetted by a witness like this.

"Do you think my behaviour is 'disappointing'?" she said, and he lowered the book to his lap. She'd crept closer to "his" side of the room.

"No. I understand it."

"And what does Bridget say?"

"She's frustrated."

Marianne's laugh was crisp and mocking. "You *are* a diplomat, aren't you? Is that a euphemism for she thinks I'm nuts?"

"No."

"It would be courteous, you know, if you insist on showing up here, to stop the embroidery. Don't make me prod you like we're on a date."

"If you're asking me what I think—"

"I'm asking you what you know."

"What I think is that the two of you should be talking."

"We are. Through you. Just like David did. I hope *that* makes you feel useful."

He held her eyes steadily now. "I don't tell her anything, Marianne."

"Why."

"Because she doesn't know I'm here."

She became very still and instinctively, he leaned back on the bed. "*Really*. Are you threatening to become interesting?"

"I will tell her."

"And here I thought she was getting a front-row seat to my misery."

"Are you miserable?"

"I thought you knew." She stared at him with a menacing blankness. "Avert your eyes is the first rule of someone else's suffering," she said, "but you're far too earnest for that. My daughters have figured it out, but not you. You want to be helpful! Wow. You'd probably rescue a parakeet from a burning building."

"I'm not here just for you."

"Get your own room then."

"Marianne—"

"What did I do? Tell me what I did." There was that expression of almost comic bewilderment he'd seen on the faces of others from time to time. An unravelling he could cause. It told him he had the power to affect others, even though he felt he was somehow an uncharged particle, a conduit through which a force could travel but not remain. "So you're here for yourself. You're here just to see for yourself?"

"It's more than that," he said.

"But basically."

"No."

"You know what? I should be watching people dig instead of trying to figure you out. I don't care why you're here. I know why I'm here." She turned away from him again, and looked outside.

He went into the bathroom and filled a drinking glass with water, drank it, and then washed the glass out under hot water, running soapy fingers around the rim. He took in his plain, unmysterious features in the mirror and wondered if Marianne thought of him as a con man. He came back out and noted that the light was beginning to fade. She was sitting on her bed, facing the one he'd been on, lost in thought, holding the Copleston book.

"What David did wasn't because of you," he said.

"And you know."

"You know too, Marianne."

She rubbed her hands along the top of her legs—a gesture so familiar to him that he was embarrassed to see it.

5.

ON THE WEEKEND, JOHN AND BRIDGET SAW LITTLE of each other. She worked both days at the ministry, catching up on work she'd let slip in the confused week and a half of her mother's strange behaviour. She was still trying to impress her superiors, working overtime when she thought she'd be seen and taking paperwork home with her every night. John stayed in the apartment, cleaning and taking the dog to the park every couple of hours. He ran with her there until they were both exhausted, and then she slept on the couch, a small beige oval, her back leg twitching once in a while and pulling his thoughts back to her.

On Sunday night, Bridget reached across him in bed and switched off his light as he was reading, took his book from him and dropped it to the floor on her side of the bed. Then the sound of fabric lifting, her arms near him and the smell of the inside of her shirt: detergent, her skin. "I don't want to talk," she said, and she put her mouth to his to prevent him from even agreeing, and he was glad for it. Anything he might have said would be an omission of the truth: not speaking at all was somehow more honest. She moved on top of him and he knew what she wanted, put his hands on her hips and pulled down on her as she fought him, and he arced his back and drew her down. Then held her against him, biting her mouth, the heel of his palm hard against the scoop of her lower back.

Howard Rosen backed away from the door. "You're kidding me."

"I'm not," said John. He listened to Howard gather up the tea things—this was how all his visits with his employer began. Rosen lived on the top floor of a rundown three-flat house on Brunswick Street, just above Harbord, an area he frequently eulogized as the lost heart of the city's Jewish culture. John's regular day was Tuesday, usually for three hours in the morning, and for this Howard gave him the unlikely salary of four hundred dollars a month. It nearly paid a third of his and Bridget's rent on the Hogarth Avenue apartment. It was as close as John got to holding his own.

Below Howard, in the other two apartments, lived tenants John had never met, and the glass doors on the main level were obscured from the inside by a bedsheet. The whole house smelled stale; John was certain the other two tenants were men as well. Howard Rosen's life was emblematic of a certain kind of city living: boxed in by the many, but basically alone.

Howard came down the hall with the tray in his hand and they went into the front room—the bedroom, library, and living room—and John stood in the verge, reading this Tuesday's disarray. More index cards had been added to the display on the long wall beside Howard's bed: the makings of a new play, *new* still being the only word to describe something that, if he ever finished it, would be Howard's first play in seven years. Every six months, like clockwork, the artistic director of the theatre that produced his work held a reading of the thing "in progress," and this was enough to renew the funding for Howard's so-called residency at the theatre. The residency consisted of an office on the third floor of the theatre with a chair and a table in it, a room Howard had never actually seen and which was increasingly being used to store boxes of Styrofoam cups and photocopying paper.

Howard had hired John after advertising for an "amanuensis," a job title that was more likely to attract applicants than "general dogsbody," which was closer to the truth. For John it was further proof that his degree was useless. He was primarily a stacks-sniffer for Howard—which talent was not completely out of keeping with his "training" (what is accounting if not the excavation of patterns?)—but he was also company, and he let himself be treated as on call. Once or twice a month an "emergency" required John to do some shopping or faxing or interference-running. And sometimes, to show he liked him, John would arrive unannounced and cook Howard supper and stay and eat with him in the battered, horrible kitchen. It seemed to John heroic that Howard went on when there was hardly a point. "A cul-de-sac," Howard had once said, "gives you an excellent vantage point on the direction to go in." The man's mind was like a high-octane engine with a faulty carburetor: his ideas flashed and sputtered and all of his progress in life after his play of seven years ago (not such a giant hit as to trigger writer's block) was really more a fitful kind of inertia than forward motion.

"You like things complicated, John. You should be a writer."

"And give up everything I've spent my life building?"

"You're right. My mistake. One doesn't ditch an empire on a whim." Howard's voice was like a cheese grater on leather: the result of a severed nerve during bypass surgery at forty-eight. He had shoulder-length straight grey hair and since the life-saving operation five years earlier, he'd managed to smoke and eat himself back into the danger zone. The topic was off-limits. "So what's with the shacking up with both mother and daughter then?"

"I don't sleep at the hotel."

"See, if this was a play, you would. And Bridget would show up and either kill you both or join in—no matter, it's a smash. Can I have it?"

"You should finish this one first."

"Ah, yes." He cast a forlorn glance at his planning wall. "I've moved some more scenes around. You should go look. I'm starting the play with the home movies now, and then later on I'm adding some scenes from those movies, verbatim, but the adults speak the lines."

"Home movies back then were silent," said John. "Bridget's dad had a bunch."

"Say these are videos then. You can talk your face off in a video."

"Not in 1935, you don't." He spent a moment orienting himself to Howard's latest structure. Rewriting hadn't been working, and he'd spent much of the year moving scenes around, waiting for something in the moribund play to ignite. "Back then, it was all silent eight millimetre."

"Well, write it down for next week," Howard said with a dismissive wave of his hand. "Find out if there was any eight millimetre with sound. And if there isn't, we'll figure out how to work in some dialogue over the movie. Maybe the mother speaks the children's lines as their mouths move—you know, she has complete recall of every last thing that ever fell from their darling mouths."

"I'll look into it." He joined Howard on the couch and took his tea. Like most people without much of a life, Howard had found some little things to focus on, such as obsessively archiving his work, buying antique paperweights, and becoming an expert in tea. The pot he was serving contained Monkey-Picked Tie Guan Yin, which he explained was no longer picked by monkeys, but was very rare indeed. They sipped it, and John guessed correctly it was an oolong. "Top note?" said Howard.

"Honey."

"Not quite. Orchids." He sipped. "Pollen."

"Yes, well, I haven't had either in a while, so it tastes like honey to me."

They drank quietly for a while, John in a faked tea reverie while Howard swished his around in his cup and thoughtfully chewed some of the leaves. A black fleck lay on his bottom lip. "So what does Bridget think of your new hobby? What would you call it—? A cross between visiting the sick and hostelry, I'd think."

"She doesn't know."

Howard's eyes widened. "I really am going to have to start writing some of this down. How is it that she doesn't know? Are you lying to her?"

"She hasn't asked."

"You mean she hasn't said, 'John, you're not visiting my mother in a hotel room these days, are you?'"

"That question has not been asked."

"I think your very soul may be in danger here." John didn't reply, and the expression on his face made Howard add, "But perhaps this is just what it needs."

"I don't know what it needs. Bridget once told me I float above everything, and at the time I didn't think it was true. But now . . ."

"You're feeling a little disconnected are you?"

"Yeah."

"That can happen when you start living in a play by Sophocles."

John put the sickly-sweet tea down on the table in front of him and moved some papers out of the way. His mouth felt dry, the way all of Howard's teas made it feel. "Bridget isn't even talking to her mother. Or me, really. And no one's talking about David. So however crazy this thing is down at the hotel, I think I should be a part of it."

"You owe them that, you feel."

"I should be present. David more or less asked me to be."

"Well, Marianne, at least, must be pleased to have your support. A show of faith."

"I'm pretty sure that's not how she sees it."

"Two beds, right?"

John laughed. "I don't think I want to talk about this with you anymore, Howard. I don't like the way your mind works."

"I really had no idea you had a death wish."

It pleased John a little that Howard was surprised by him. To be, for a moment, unpredictable. "I just feel I should try to be of some use."

"Build houses then!" Howard threw his hands up and let them fall with a heavy slap on his legs. "Hiding out with your girlfriend's mother isn't necessarily the way to develop a sense of purpose."

"Write a scene with the father taking the home movies," said John. "Then you can show the movie itself later in the play and we'll already know what the kids were saying."

Howard leaned against the back of the couch and thought for a moment. "I'd have to cast children. Matt would have a cow."

"Just the voices. The dad alone onstage and the voices of the children as he's filming them, but we never see the kids until the mother watches the film."

"I put ghosts in my play."

"Why not? Isn't that what it's about?"

He'd done this more than once for Howard—somehow thought of an elegant solution to something left-footed in his conception. "Well, geez," Howard said quietly. "That's very good. And it gets rid of the technical problem."

John stood and put his teacup back on the tray. "That's what I was thinking. So for next week, no eight millimetre stuff? Or do you still want it?"

"No," said Howard. "In fact, I'll go to the library. You stay here and write the bloody play. I'll take a story editor credit."

"I'd love to," said John as he silently slipped his cheque off the mantelpiece, "but I think I'll be spending most of my time with my own lies."

## 6.

THE STEEPEST DECLINE IN LIGHT ALWAYS CAME IN the middle of November. There was a point every night now when the sun suddenly plunged below the horizon and dropped the city into a blunt, grayling light. The shock of darkness before five-thirty snapped the cord that connected people to the vain dream of summer, and confirmed that the only way back to daylight now would be to put one's head down and push on through December, January, February. But it was really February—that month of wet lungs and bird-choking fog—that November's desolation looked forward to. They were bookends, these two months, one buried in a dead year that said *abandon hope*, and the other in a fresh one that said *what hope?*

This November—even with its grief and the prospect of a first Christmas alone—appeared to have an entirely different effect on Marianne. John almost thought he could attach the word *jolly* to her mood, if only he believed that her jolliness wasn't *schadenfreude*. He knew that Marianne was so inclined; it was one of the qualities

Bridget had ascribed to her mother that he never argued with. The failure of the plans of others and their consequent unhappiness did not actually make Marianne *happy*, but it confirmed for her a certain view of the universe. In school, John had read about the despair of short-sellers in bull markets; how their philosophies of loss were unshakable, and that there was no joy more lunatic than when these investors began finally to make money, when the markets downturned and all the bad bets they'd placed began to pay off. It was this wet-eyed worship of ruin that John thought he was beginning to detect in Marianne.

He'd found himself less frightened of, and feeling more in common with, Mrs. Edward Copleston, whose memoir he'd read when he'd been alone in the apartment on the weekend, a tiny fire burning off a Java-Log in the shallow fireplace. Her arrival in Toronto had been nothing like his (he took the train, she a boat; there were plenty of roads in his Toronto, in hers you had to hack them into existence), but there was the generous melancholy of wondering what on earth she'd done to her life. Except, for Mrs. C., there was no turning back. And she had three children and a husband in tow and a wet, dark homestead waiting for her up north in Haliburton. He wasn't sure what, if any, connection there was to David's work in this slim diary, though. More, he suspected, there was a life lesson to be had in it, and that was why Marianne had put the book into his reading pile. He was worried he'd glean the wrong lesson—the one about persistence and fortitude—when perhaps she was just telling him to get out of town.

He'd placed the little booklet on the second bed upon being admitted to the room, hoping she'd not quiz him on it, and she didn't.

The five-thirty sundown had already passed, and all the lamps were burning. They glowed, Orion-like, in the monograph's acetate covering. John had brought food for both of them and on seeing two plastic bags dangling from his hands, the corner of Marianne's mouth rose and she said, "Is one of those for me?" By bringing food, he imagined he was performing a proper service, one that could eventually be relayed back to Bridget when the time came to reconstruct these visits. Each day that passed without his telling her compounded his sin. The fact that he told himself variously that he wasn't doing anything wrong, and that he was entitled to live a life of his own even within her family, only abetted this sensation of guilt that filled him like a bucket catching runoff.

He sat in the room's one chair, his back against the wall, facing Marianne in her pillow nest up on the north-facing ledge. She'd transferred her meal of Korean chicken and chap chae to a hotel plate; he ate his noodles right out of the takeout container. "Are you interested in knowing what they found today?" she asked.

He swallowed and put his fork down on the Styrofoam tray. "I thought you'd tell me as soon as I came in," he said. "I presumed nothing."

"They found *something*," she said. She left an annoying pause. "A flugelhorn."

"A what?"

"A flugelhorn. *A brass wind instrument whose valves and shape resemble a cornet.* I looked it up on the Internet. There are very few pieces written for solo flugelhorn."

"Maybe that's why the owner threw it away."

"That's what I thought," she said. She expertly plucked a chunk of chicken with her chopsticks and put it into her mouth.

"Is that it?"

"It was flat." She tucked the meat into a cheek. "Like a cut-out. They were laughing at it and pretending to play it. Marching around like idiots."

"Is it the one you have to put around your body?"

"You don't know your brass instruments, John. This is a major failing." She said this with, perhaps, an edge of tenderness. He couldn't be sure.

He knew that soon they would turn the kliegs on in the site below, and a cool blue light would glow up from it, as if a moon were embedded down there in the earth. It was in this light, with its sharp shadows and contrasts, that small objects could best be made out in the dirt and in the piles of twisted waste the machines had heaped all over the site. None of what the machines dug up was of more than passing interest to Marianne. If it wasn't a strongbox encased in leather she didn't want anything to do with it. A flugelhorn in broad daylight, though—that was an exception.

Through Marianne's binoculars John had found the mass of uncovered silver-and-turquoise bottles, yellow brick, and bits of crockery fascinating. Some of the workers had started their own collections, and a row of liniment bottles and powder tins was spread along one of the steel girders on the perimeter of the yard like an open-air shooting gallery. When they turned the kliegs on, some of the bottles glowed with a waxy blue lustre, a phosphorescence in their makeup. Their presence, delicate and seeming rare, struck John as an impossibly whimsical counterpoint to the rugged hole and its machines.

Around six, the lights came on and the room took on a hue that suggested the entire city behind them had turned into a single, enormous television set. Marianne looked down to the ground and marked the change, as common now as natural shifts in light. This, however, told of another day of digging over and a night of digging about to begin. They both heard the sound of a machine coughing to a stop. He went to the other window. Two large yellow machines had stopped. In the hard, slanting artificial light, they looked like toys left in a sandbox. "That was a short shift," he said.

"Site manager's probably off duty. Sometimes if a couple of the young guys are alone, they'll park their machines side by side and get out and stand in the light together. Smoke, or just stand around talking."

"It must be pretty dull work."

"If only they knew what they were standing on." John pulled away from the window. The cast of light made a sharp blue shape in her window where her face was reflected, a Noh mask floating over the night. "It used to anger David that people were ignorant of how the places they spent their lives in grew," she said. "He would say, 'Neglect of the past is a form of despair.' I bet the people who started all these places didn't give a shit about the history they were creating. They just came to make money and that's the way it's been ever since."

They heard a motor starting below, the sound a dull popping in the distance. Marianne finally turned back into the room and settled against the pillows again. "David thought if people were surprised by what had come before them, they'd get interested in it for their own sake. They might see the connection between those people's *now* and their own."

"It's hard to make people care about anything that came before them."

"He thought if he made it personal . . ." She paused for a moment and John felt certain that, in her mind, she was taking a long drag on a cigarette. "I had a sick husband going on about buried treasure. I didn't really think hard on what any of it meant. I just wanted to keep him alive." She pushed her chopsticks around on the plate. "I'm not sure I was listening all that closely." She came down off the ledge, collecting her plate and held up his nearly finished container of noodles. He nodded.

"What happens if something shows up down there, Marianne?"

"Then he'll have been right."

"What if it's not what he said it would be?"

Something in his voice brought her attention back to him fully, and she tried to read his face. "What does that mean, John? Do you already know what's down there?"

"How would I know that?"

"That's not really an answer, is it?"

"There's got to be something," he said. "I do believe that."

She had her fists on her hips and he thought she could see into his heart at that moment. He felt pierced by her, and ashamed of what he possessed that she did not. Those moments with David, in the car on that bright, dread August morning. He had usurped Marianne, replaced her at the signal moment in her own history. Asking him to watch over her was like sending a thief to guard treasure.

"You don't want to talk about David anymore," she said.

"I do," he said. "We can."

She went into the bathroom and began to run water over her plate. When she came out she held it at her side and it dripped onto the carpet. "You never told me what you thought about the Copleston book."

"I was surprised that they said *snooze* back then."

"Did they." She remained where she was, just outside the bathroom door, in the dimness of the little foyer, her eyes shadowed. He felt faintly endangered.

"When they get off the boat," he said, "officials take them to the Swords Hotel, and they give all the travellers dinner, and when her husband goes off to make arrangements at another hotel, she and the children all have a *snooze*."

"Snooze," Marianne said. "Anything else?"

"She has a *quinzy throat-attack*."

"So they had naps and sore throats in 1856. Is that what you got out of it?"

"I got out of it that not much has changed."

"Do you like that thought?"

"I don't know."

~

She wanted to take a nap. She said she napped for an hour after supper each day now, and then rang down for coffee. She liked to be ready for the night shift, since whatever might be revealed in the excavation would appear with a certain kind of stealth after sundown, and this meant staying up most of the night. Since his first visit ten days earlier, they'd deepened the hole to what looked closer to forty feet. It was impossible to judge the depth: John had discovered the odd fact that his mind (perhaps most minds) was attuned more to horizontal measures than it was to vertical ones. Car lengths, street widths, kilometres per hour—all of these were units that made absolute sense to a life lived on a flat plane. Time was linear: it went forward and back. But up and down was organic, it was growth and decay, it was time as experienced by vegetation. It was history itself. He looked down into the hole and tried to measure it by the time he imagined it would take to fall from the lip of the hole at street level to its black clay depths. Somehow it seemed like thirty-five or forty feet.

Whatever its measure, though, he knew Marianne was aware now that a skin was about to be pierced and the workers were on the threshold of the old lake. She could not afford to sleep a whole night now. There would be time enough for sleep later.

She meant for John to leave, but when she turned over and faced the windows, her back curled toward him, he simply stayed. He sat quietly on the other bed, and after a few minutes her breathing deepened. It pleased him that she could sleep in front of him. He had stopped being a threat. He had the urge to call Bridget and tell her what he was doing, but he also sensed that the time was coming when nothing could remain hidden. His anxiety was fading now, replaced by purpose. There was something he could give them, to vitiate his treachery. He saw something emerging from the darkness.

Marianne's voice woke him. He shook himself, surprised that he'd drifted off. "I want you to talk about this," she said, and he saw a pinwheeling light that he realized was the monograph. She had thrown it at him, and it spun open, its brilliant plastic cover flashing under the light like a blade. "Open it up and tell me what you believe."

The booklet landed on his belly. "I only know what it says, Marianne. What he claims."

"I'm not asking you to explain it to me. I want to know if you believe it. If you believe him."

He closed the monograph and lay it on the bedspread. "No," he said. "I don't."

"Then why are you here? To lessen a blow?"

"I'm not."

"You have no faith in him."

"I never said that."

"If you don't believe him, then you don't have faith. There's no distinction."

He saw out of the corner of his eye that Marianne had made the bed. He wondered if he'd slept long. "I think the distinction is that I don't necessarily accept the facts as he has them. But I believe in why he wrote that monograph."

"Which was *what*? I'm doing this for David. Can you say the same thing?"

"Absolutely."

"We're not going to have any secrets if you plan on showing up in my life like this. Do you understand? I want Bridget to know what you're doing, I want Alison to know, and if there's anything you're holding back about David, I want to know it. I don't care if it makes things worse."

"I don't want to make things worse, Marianne."

"This is your whole world, is it? A widow, a blocked writer, and a woman you're lying to."

"That's a lot for me."

She leaned over his bed and picked up the monograph, held it up to him and shook it. "*This* . . . this is important to me. This is what I have. It matters if you don't believe him."

"I want him to be right," said John, and he had raised his voice for the first time in her presence. They both marked it. "But I don't know if that's belief."

She held the booklet with both hands and tilted it up toward herself. The light swam over her face. "Why do you want him to be right?"

"Because it would make his dying less awful."

She turned to the desk and carefully put her burden down, not showing her face to him. "Are you ready for a life with someone, John? Do you really think you are? Because this is what it comes to. When you start out with someone, you're signing on for the long haul even though you have no idea what it's going to be like."

"You didn't know what it would be like? At all?"

"I knew what David was. Who he was. I can draw a line back to the day I met him and he fits on it all the way. Everything he was, and all his choices in life, came out of the same man. I married him because he was bringing something to the table, do you know what I mean? I didn't know always what shape it was going to take, but all of it—his work, the kind of father he was, the husband he was to me—all of it was a bud in him that was there from the beginning."

"You're saying I don't have that?"

She turned her face to him, her eyes hooded by a fringe of her hair. "How are you going to contribute to Bridget's life? What do you bring, John? You're a decent person. Even though I haven't always been on your side, I think I can say that about you. But what do you bring? You make no choices. You allow yourself to be moved by other things. David, who you obviously admired so much, *did* things his whole life. He invented his bloody specialty, for Chrissake. You finished a degree by inertia, not because you loved it. You're like a powder that has to have some ingredient added to it to make it active, and you think Bridget is going to be that for you?"

"Bridget is finding herself too, Marianne. I'm not standing in her way, and I'm not asking her to make anything happen for me, either."

"What a fine pair you are then. I dread your marriage, John. You're like two little lost storm clouds, drifting around."

"And you have too low an opinion of Bridget."

She laughed at him. "Think about what I'm saying. You don't have to respond to me, but think about it. What can you give that makes you worthy, more than your decency, John? Because she's going to need more than that. We're all going to need more than that."

After he left, Marianne lay in the bed in the near-dark, the faint, bluey light from outside the only thing to see by. She shut her eyes and laid her hands palm down on the blanket and listened to the rooms around her. A woman's voice from two or three rooms away, talking on the phone. Unintelligible words separated by silences. In the walls, the sounds of water coursing in pipes above and beside her, an invisible body containing her.

*He would curse in the shower, furious with himself for not being able to do even the simplest things. This came back to her when she cleaned, her arm sweeping in slow arcs over the surface of the tub. She recalled the squeak of the rubberized feet on his special stool. One night—was it the spring before he died, or a whole year earlier? Time had compressed itself since his death—one night, she put her book down and called to him. "Do you want help?"*

*"I can't reach up."*

*She'd gone into the bathroom. Rolling clouds of steam puffed out on either side of the tub, around the curtain. She worried he'd scald himself, his skin insensate to the heat, but that wasn't supposed to happen, he was supposed to be able to feel it still. "How hot is it in there?"*

*"I need you to wash my back." She drew open the curtain, and he tried to shimmy the chair sideways, but couldn't manage the movement. "For Chrissake," he said. "This is pathetic."*

*"You know what? Wait here a second—"*

*"Where else would I go?"*

*"I'll be right back."*

*She went out through the front hall into the garage, through the door they'd once argued over when designing the house. It was a kind of bourgeois sickness to have a door leading directly from your garage into your house, he'd said, but she'd carried the day on that one: just think of the convenience of not having to trudge into and out of the snow once you'd parked. Over the car's hood was a ramshackle shelf piled with the summer things; she pulled down one of the plastic garden chairs and carried it back in. "Move over," she said, pushing the curtain aside and lowering the chair. He watched her, amused, as she stepped out of her clothes and got in beside him, sat under the too-hot stream of water. "We're going to turn into cooked shrimp, David."*

*"I can reach the bottom of my back, but not the top. I can't lift my arm up high enough."*

*"So I'll do it."*

*"You're going to wash my back every day now?"*

*"Do you want to go around with a dirty upper back?"*

*He passed her the soap wrapped in a wet facecloth and she manoeuvred her body and chair so she was behind him. She revolved the soap in her hands and pushed the cloth around on his back. She felt the muscle there, trying to compare it to the texture it'd had in August, in June, but the deterioration was too gradual. She couldn't detect the change. She brought the shower head out of its holster and ran it against his skin so the soap ran off him in sheets and his skin glistened. He said, "Showering together never lasts."*

*"What do you mean?"*

*"It's something you do when you're young. When you take every opportunity to be naked with the other person. Showering alone, a waste of time."*

*"And after, there's not enough time for it."*

*"Mmm," he said.*

*She kissed a shoulder blade. "Do you miss being together like this?"*

*He didn't answer and she realized she'd asked a question canted toward her own future, a question he didn't want her thinking about right now. She leaned into him and pressed her mouth into his shoulder, the skin there so hot that its heat pushed up into her eyes. She had a flashback to being in a hotel room with him. Twenty years ago? Thirty? In some European country, maybe it was the Italy trip. Sleeping beside him in the August heat and this very smell, this fleshly radiance, coming off him. And then it was gone, and it was just the heat again.*

*She stroked his leg and brought her hand back up the inside, and held his balls and his cock, and he twitched, pushed her hand away. She kept her mouth against his shoulder, rolled the soap in her palm, returned her hand to the other side of his body. The smell of him.*

*"Mare," he said.*

*"Shush."*

*"Come on——"*

*She wrapped her other arm around his chest and slid off her garden chair so he could feel her against his back. "Relax. It's just us."*

*Could you heedlessly give yourself over to pleasure when you had to focus on the remains of your time? It was an unsensual state of mind. He held on to her arm with a motionless grip, trying to will her not to move. But she bent around him and kissed his mouth, felt his arm moving under her breast. His facial muscles had continued to weaken, so he could not kiss her back the way she wanted him to, but he tried, wanting not to disappoint her. He pulled away to fill his lungs with air, then took her against him again. She remembered how, once collapsing together against the sheets, catching their breaths, he'd joked that there couldn't be an afterlife, not when this was what life itself offered you. His palm on her belly, him saying, What could an afterlife give you that would make up for losing this? Now she imagined him much closer to finding out the answer to that question. He concentrated, trying for her, her hand stroking his cock, locking her motion to his, and felt in him at last nature's mulish insistence, the old ways of the body. Lovemaking was once for pleasure, she thought, and then its worlds opened up. You knew the cosmos was using you to make the future happen, and it may have been frightening, to be caught like that. But then you wanted it to, you gave in to it. Later, it was a retreat to the way you once were, long past the point when you could be of any value to the cosmos, sex as a marvel of uselessness, a pension given the body.*

*For a few moments, she forgot she was trying to make a dying man come, and she leaned against him, loving him, knowing she'd remember being like this when the future arrived. She was too lost in her thoughts to notice that he was trying to lift her up, he wanted her to come around in front of him, and now she gladly did, raising her leg around him and using her palms on the shower seat to bear her weight. She took him into her. He could not move, so she did, but she could not look at him. She watched what they were doing, seeing the water pool in their lap when she pushed against him then sluice away between them when she lifted up. She did this, mesmerized by the filling and emptying, until he pulled her mouth up to his and drew in a deep chestful of air through her, gasping unlike the way she'd become used to, and she felt him come. He leaned against her and his body shrank as if the weight inherent in his bones, in his muscles, had left him all at once. She felt the fight go out of him, and held him under the drape of water, riven by joy, listening to him breathe.*

~

In the blue of the kliegs and the burning white of the truck and backhoe headlamps and the flashing red lights of braking machinery, the nighttime digs were a confusion of swimming colours and retinal flares. Pale grey rocks appeared purple past dark, the dirt was a chiaroscuro of pink and green. There was only one woman on the night crew, Inger Wolfe. Her partner, Allan, waved her forward and she lowered the scoop to drag out another pile of dirt. She broke her nights up into one-hour periods. After one hour, coffee; after two, coffee; after three, ten minutes of talk and jokes and being flirted with. Then lunch, then coffee, then the sun would start to come up. The nights went quickly, and after four hours of sleep she'd spend the day designing her clothing line, the line that would get her out of the night shift.

The scoop struck a rock and Allan went down into the hole to chip at it with his shovel. He disappeared behind the scoop and she could hear the repeated dull report of his blade. Sometimes he'd put a big slab of stone into her load once he'd got it out, other times he'd try to impress her by hauling it out himself and hurling it whatever distance he could manage. He was a nice guy, but she wasn't interested. After a minute, the noise stopped and he reappeared below her door. He gestured to her to open it.

"Back it up a bit," he said.

She pulled an earguard away from her head. "What is it?"

"Just back it up."

She put the machine in reverse and cleared the middle of the hole, climbing the edge of it so her head tilted down. She could see through the dirt-encrusted window a pipe lying in the earth, yellowed from years, like ivory. She watched him dig more delicately now, scraping around the edge of the pipe, and she lowered the scoop to the ground to stabilize the backhoe and stepped out onto her footrest. "Come on, Al—I'll go around the right and come at it from the side. How big is it?"

"I think it's huge. It comes out here and goes back in there."

"It's old PVC. I'll smash it up with the scoop."

He stood up and faced her in her door. "It has rivets in it."

"What?"

"It has rivets in it."

"What the hell are you talking about?"

"Will you get out and look?" She jumped down to the ground and stood opposite him at the other side of the hole. He crouched down beside the object, pointing, and in the steady white light of the backhoe, she could see what he was talking about. Round, crusted brown rivets stuck out at regular intervals along a slightly curving old hardwood slat, four or five feet of which he'd been able to expose. He stood and faced her with an expression of boyish pride. "Holy shit," he said, and she locked eyes with him. "It's a boat."

*Four*

~

# IN CAMERA

~

*Early spring 1856*

NEAR THE END OF APRIL, AFTER HIS FIRST ENCOUN-
ters with Samuel Ennis, Hallam hired a trap and went
west to Niagara where he'd contacted an older apothecary by mail with a request for advice. The man, Mr.
Taylor, had an excellent reputation, and Hallam's
father had consulted with him on the suitability of the
Lennert property. He believed the man would answer
him frankly.

The eight-hour drive down the King's Highway was
not as terrible for Hallam as he imagined it must have
been for the nag and the driver, but it impressed on him
the notion that in no way must this country have first
been visited during the rainy season. And had Simcoe or
his wife set foot ashore in weather as unsuitable for
human habitation as this winter had offered, he had no
doubt there would be no Toronto. What excuse for
Kingston or Cornwall, he could not imagine, and the
existence of such colder, wetter cities as Montreal and
Quebec only suggested that the French were a different,
hardier branch of the species.

He entered the other man's shop with trepidation, as he knew whatever came of the discussion it would direct his life for some months to come, and this would determine the length of his stay in Canada. Hallam nursed some fantasy of failure: returning home, even under the shroud of defeat, appealed to him. In the worst hours of January, he'd been horrified to realize he was unable to bring his family's faces to mind, and he was forced on more than one occasion to treat the intense panic that attended this disintegration with a significant dose of valerian in hot water, a cure that made him completely useless the following day but at least curbed the hysteria.

Mr. Taylor listened patiently to Hallam's tale of the Cockburns and how his business had suffered. Without inquiring any further, the older apothecary offered Hallam a loan, which kindness nearly reduced him to weeping. But Hallam explained he had come for advice only: this third outpost of the family firm was his own responsibility; the question was what to do to ensure its viability. This speech Mr. Taylor met with a tolerant silence. "If you wish," he said, "I would be prepared to purchase your inventory at a fair market value."

"As I told Mr. Cockburn's son, my business is not for sale."

"Do you read the papers, Mr. Hallam? We are at the beginning of an international decline that will see all unsecured businesses swallowed up. And if you are not in the absolute pink, you will be winnowed with the rest of them. Think of it as a gale wind that is going to sweep everything up that is not nailed down. I know of three chemists in New York State alone who are going begging for buyers. Not for their medicines, but for their front doors, along with the keys. If you sell, you can return home and regather your strength for when the storm lets up. But you describe yourself as half-undone, Mr. Hallam. I have no advice for your recovery."

Mr. Taylor's wife had prepared them some cold meats with fresh bread, and Hallam realized he was being shown compassion. He presented the aspect of a hapless, lost boy. He finished his food and thanked the man. As he took down his hat, Mr. Taylor held him back from leaving.

"I know the Cockburns," he said. "I am friends with them because I deem it in my interest to be. They are true Scots and they see their interests as sovereign, and if they have determined for themselves that you will not survive in Toronto, then you will not survive. You should consider my offer."

Hallam walked back to the hotel, and in the morning collected the driver, and they started back to Toronto in the needled air. He thought on his luck in exciting the attention of a gang upon his arrival on these shores. A gang was the best way to describe them, all professions have such an element in them, a grouping formed around a protectionist idea and reinforced by exclusion and, if necessary, threats.

All the way home, he weighed his options. He had but one customer to count on—Samuel Ennis—and against his custom he had hostile competition and a city whose economy was in decline. Converting the business was not out of the question; men in dire situations had done worse before. He could sell groceries; he could stock books. He could, he realized with a heavy heart, do anything but sell drugs.

Hallam wrote to Mr. Taylor immediately on returning home, and told him he would accept his offer if he was still tendering it. By return post Taylor sent an outline of prices he would pay for various compounds: the inventory his father had entrusted to him would net one hundred and fifty-six pounds odd, plus some coin, and with that windfall the business of chemistry could be left behind. Hallam collected all but the compounds he might need for daily use and emergencies, and then boxed the contents. The shop stood all but empty, except for a surprisingly tidy collection of crates. He shipped the contents to Niagara. Mr. Taylor's bank draft arrived the following week and Hallam's career as an apothecary was over.

With the money realized, he travelled to upper New York State, and posing as a photographer himself, bought up as much of the silver compounds as he could in Rochester, Syracuse, and Albany. When he came back to Toronto, Hallam was the sole supplier of photographic salts west of Kingston, east of London, and north of Buffalo, and he had forty-nine pounds sterling to his name. Before the end of the spring he would have all seven photography firms in Toronto as his clients. He brought Sam Ennis over to the now-curtained store (he'd taken the sign down, and the wooden carving of the mortar lay across one of the empty glass cases like a reproach).

"You've been robbed," Ennis said, gazing around at the cold, echoing shop.

"I've done the robbing, though." He went into the back, uncrated one of the cases of silver nitrate, and placed a bottle on the table. Its label was as white as a cloud; the freshest bottle of anything that had been in J. Hallam, Apothecary since they'd bought the shop. "There are fifteen more boxes of the nitrate and ten of silver bromide. All told, I have almost sixty pounds avoirdupois of silver in here. That's almost half-a-million grains, Mr. Ennis. Enough to photograph the country end to end in a travelling cart and some left over to make rings. I've cornered the market."

Ennis was fairly impressed, a wide amazed grin on his face. "You turn out to be a pirate," he said. "Let me shake your hand, captain." He held out one of his large, dark paws, and Hallam thrust the bottle of silver nitrate into it.

"This is to thank you," he said. "For pointing me in the right direction."

"Oh, don't put the blame on me, Mr. Hallam. If you've lost your mind, that's on your ticket." He rotated the bottle label side up in his hands and read it carefully. One of those bottles would realize two shillings—three if the local supply appeared to be dwindling—at a cost of ten bob each, all in. "Your father threw you to the wolves, didn't he?" said Ennis.

"He couldn't have known. He thought Toronto was trees and rivers with Londoners wandering in the clearings.

He didn't know the only person in the entire place to offer me his hand would be an Irish picture-maker."

"You've fallen."

"I have."

Mr. Ennis offered him his free hand, and the two men shook. "Here the true adventure of your life begins."

2.

Dearest Alice,

I imagine by the time you get this, the worst of your winter will be past. So it is here as well, with the sun out for longer periods every day and even bird calls beginning in the trees! Tell Jane I have seen chimney swallows and purple martins, and the golden-crowned thrushes are coming back and bringing the best of spring. There is not yet enough industry in this little town to convince the birds to nest elsewhere, so we live in our little brick houses beneath an aviary.

I am busy with the shop, building clientele and meeting my business neighbours. I expect at this rate that we will be able to plan for next year before the end of the summer. I mean to write my father and give him some of the fine details, but for now, when you next see him, pass on news of my well-being.

I will write you and the girls a longer letter very soon. For the time being, I am enclosing a little picture made of me by one of the city's talented photographists. I trust I am neither too fat nor too thin for your liking.

I am wearing my father's topcoat in it. I am a Hallam family man here, and before long you and the girls will come to join me and we will have a house in town and a cottage by the lakeshore with horses to convey us one way and the other.

How I miss you! I cannot say, my dears,

Jem

The coarsening of his character had begun the moment he made landfall in Toronto, but now, almost ten months later, he could feel the gold of his self more adulterated every day. He thought worriedly, man's nature is such that the purifying agents of church and marriage are the only countervails against his welcoming misuse of his spirit and his body. Man is a creature of dirt and woman is one of air and God is the element in which they are co-tempered. Toronto was a city of men. Men built the edifices and waited for other men to fill them. Men, such as himself, came without their women, without their families, and felled trees or dug holes, conjuring an English village in the woods. What women there were came to serve, or had arrived with brave expressions on their faces to be with their men, to plant themselves on this naked soil and start their families. They came in their dresses and walked in the mud. Some laughed at their predicament, many went mad. The asylum out in the western part of the woods, above the garrison, was filled with their weird mirth and their weeping. And on Sundays, those who had kept their minds intact assembled at church and listened to a hopeful message. Bless and keep those who are far from home.

But being a man alone in this church society meant one of three things: you had lost your wife and were trying to find a new one; you were a bachelor and looking for your first; or you were alone in a strange country while your people sat by their fire trying to remember what your voice sounded like. Those in that last category were by far the most numerous, but they were the ones for whom nothing could be done. He was one of those for whom there was no point in making introductions, no point in bringing home to supper; his habit of taking his meals in the company of labourers meant he was not suited for dinner parties. Perhaps this wasn't true, and Hallam knew a great many men who would have given their eye teeth for some gentleness and some conversation about home, but with a sour smell in the air and resources dwindling, entertaining was something people had begun to ration. If it meant bringing together a man and a woman who might increase the town's numbers (and therefore its shoeless feet, its hatless heads, its unfilled stomachs), then this was a worthy goal. Those labourers and forward scouts would be left to fend for themselves, and Hallam knew that keeping their company (and swelling it) meant they would all become common. There was another category of woman in Toronto, as well as men who had lost their wives, and more who were abandoned. In this respect, the little town was already worldly.

To keep the scent of civility on him, and to see those who were, in his mind's eye, still his kind, Hallam continued to attend the church at St. James'. And although many of its congregants knew he had been ruined in business, he was a welcome member of the flock. The Cockburns and their constituent attended the kirk of St. Andrew's just up the street, but he was lucky not to run into them, and now that the sign of the mortar lay on one of his cabinets like a discarded shield, he liked to imagine that they had moved on to the next pressing threat. Before long, Mr. Taylor and Sam Ennis's intuition on matters economic seemed to be prescient: the papers told of a general decline in fortunes throughout the United States, especially in the north, and however the north suffered, so would they. There were whispers of Fenian troubles brewing in Massachusetts (which made Mr. Ennis laugh mockingly; he referred to the Fenians as a file of drunken gits), and, as in 1837, editorials recommended that the local populace keep their powder dry. It was the first time Hallam thought of the Cockburns as rifle owners, and he felt relieved anew that he had changed course. Before long, he was certain, the wisdom of his decision would be borne out.

On a bright Sunday at the beginning of May, Hallam left services and went up Church Street, thinking to take a sandwich into Moss Park and sit a while trying to identify the spring birds. He'd been present the previous year for the southern migration and it had given him the sensation, for all of September and October, that he was being left underground by canaries. Now, despite the tenacious cold, the birds were coming back. To belong in a place, one must hear the homecoming of birds: they suggest, in their innate wisdom, that wherever they alight is a place worth being in. For Hallam, the sounds of birds pressed the sky higher into the atmosphere; they made manifest the existence of a world above. Their reappearance brought relief.

He walked in his heavy boots up Church Street, past the kirk and the New Mechanics' Institute, with its imposing granite pilasters and handsome windows, and he would have continued if not for a voice that came from the west. A man in a flapping mantle held his hat down as he crossed the street and hailed him again, calling him by name. The wind seemed to pick the word up and dash it against the face of the Institute. The man was one of Hallam's customers, the photographist Mr. Peter Bryant, of West William's Street, by St. George's Square. He owned one of the pleasant houses on the side of the square and catered to the very well-off, making coloured photographs by means of hand-mixed colours, a technique Ennis called bastard painting. Mr. Bryant gripped Hallam's forearm and caught his breath. "Excellent to find you," he said, gasping a little. "You were at St. James'?"

"Yes. Reverend Merrifield spoke on the importance of modesty."

"He is an excellent man."

"Yes."

"Well," said Bryant, "I was intending to stop by your store, but you are so little there, I thought I might have some luck if I came over to your house, but here you are!"

"Yes, here I am, as Abraham sayeth to the Lord."

"Haw, yes! Well, this is what I mean to ask of you. I understand that you have an interesting arrangement with Mr. Ennis, do you not?" Hallam, caught off guard, stared dumbly at the man. "Of course you do, but no matter. I find the terms excellent and should like to subscribe myself."

Hallam found his voice. "I extended an offer to Mr. Ennis which is part of a business arrangement between himself and me, Mr. Bryant, but I'm afraid it is not generally available, as I'm sure you understand."

"Well, no, of course not, sir. But I am not all of your clientele and given that my purchase of last week was sizable, I think it would be more than reasonable for you to furnish me with a return of a portion of my funds in exchange for a percentage not unlike Mr. Ennis pays you. You know I have a large and loyal custom."

Hallam stood with his arms at his side. He had known Ennis for less than two months and already he regretted entering into "business" with a man possessing an Irish mouth. It was a half-hour walk to Ennis's studio, but Hallam was certain he could make it in fifteen.

"And glass is expensive, as it turns out," continued Bryant. "The nitrate lasts a long time, though. You sun the bath once a week and flush out the filth, but you always need new glass. You'd be surprised how many people purchase their negative along with the prints. You can black it and put it in a frame. It looks just like a daguerreotype."

*You should have bought up all the bloody glass in New York!* thought Hallam. Indeed, but if he had, they would have started to make photographs on air with the use of saliva and gun cotton and then he would be in the same position.

"You know what my terms are with Mr. Ennis. I cannot refund half of your order."

"I imagined you would say that. Then let's compromise and say a third."

He recalled his earliest lesson from Mr. Ennis in negotiating. "A compromise would be a quarter, I believe."

"Let's be fair," said Mr. Bryant, his tone changing minutely. "You want to ensure my business survives so I may continue patronizing yours. It will be a painless transition."

"Not if Kaufmann comes to me, and Sullivan, and Tullamore. All they have to do is ask for a third of their money back and I'm ruined."

"Have they asked you?"

"No."

"Well, if they do, and it will ruin you, then say so. But my request will not ruin you. So I expect you will grant it, and in turn I will pledge my ongoing business to you. It's a changing world, Mr. Hallam. You can't expect your best customers to accept your worst-customer terms just to suit your account books, can you, hey?"

Of course he would give Bryant his money. He would give Sullivan, Tullamore, and anyone who asked for it their money as well, and then the city could auction his stock at pennies after they'd lowered his emaciated body into a hole in Potter's Field. "I cannot pay you all the money at once, but you will have it if you insist on it."

The chummy glow returned to Bryant's face. "You *must* come and see my new studio! I have an enlarger now that works through a hole in my house! Sunlight and a mirror—I can make you a picture of your eye as big as a pullet. Come see!"

"I don't need a picture of myself, I know what I look like. But thank you."

Mr. Bryant tossed his hands in the air, light-hearted and pleased with himself. "You can cash the offer whenever you like."

"From whom are you purchasing your glass, if I may ask?"

"Mr. Whelan has lately laid in a good stock of it. I've reserved a fair order for myself."

Hallam's neighbour on King Street. He held his tongue. Tomorrow or Tuesday, Whelan would be depositing money in the bank that was right now in Hallam's pocket.

He sped past Osgoode Hall and on into Ennis's neighbourhood. He rehearsed his outrage: *how dare you* and *I am fatally exposed*, a tidy phrase he thought would cut Ennis to the quick. *I extended my goodwill to you and now the silver-blued wretces of this town will line up at my door seeking a partner in their miserable businesses!* He feared that to passersby he looked faintly mad, his hands rising and falling with his unspoken monologue.

He calmed himself and breathed out, shook his head. Twenty minutes earlier he had been contemplating a picnic in the park and now he was ruined. Bloody Ennis! Bloody Bryant! And to accentuate the insult, he was now in a part of town a man of his standing should never have called familiar, but it was now. He rarely took this walk in such clear daylight, which made his presence here seem even more furtive. On one side of the city, Toronto was still the little British hamlet with treed avenues and good shops, but the well-wrought illusion of a town growing at a regular rate burst apart once one came east of College Avenue. That wide avenue, with trees growing in the middle, had been based on the Parisian model, but as a boulevard it marked a hard barrier between the accustomed-to-having and the never-did-have. Although Osgoode Hall rose above the street like a vision out of Araby, below it were the roughest kinds of log huts. The fug of creosote and human effluvia floated over the whole place. Mr. Ennis was farther west than this, where the concentration of unhappy humanity was not as dense, although, Hallam knew now from witnessing it, it was as unhappy. At night, many of the little abodes west and south of Osgoode Hall became disorderly houses or gin dens, and worse festered there. He knew Mr. Ennis to be a patron of some of those businesses. It would have been fair to say that if one were a denizen of Portland Street below King and one wished to buy an apple, it would take a walk of at least a mile to get it, but at all hours a glass of rum could be easily had. One could stick out a hand in the middle of the street after nine in the evening and be certain a most illicit treat would fall into it. Very little of the local fermentation was bottled at Gooderham's, or came to shore on a steamer. Most of it was of the same provenance as Ennis's gullet-burner. Homemade spirits and a homemade economy allowed neighbourhoods like this to carry on. Mr. Ennis, with his still and his photography, was a veritable captain of industry here, and some of the recent immigrants to the area had nicknamed him *padrone*.

Many of those who lived in the ramshackle houses were still snoozing away their mornings while church-goers in the better part of town had filed out for their lunches. Hallam passed through the dark country below to Brock Street and knocked on Mr. Ennis's private door. He steeled himself to begin speaking the moment the door opened, but getting no answer he fell back into himself and went to the other side to enter the foyer, where he pushed the door open to Ennis's studio. Here was the smell of woodsmoke, as Ennis had a fire going in the little stove he kept for tea. But he was not at home. Rather, a young woman stood by the stove, warming her hands. Red sparks flew up from the open hob. On seeing Hallam she withdrew her hands, as if he'd caught her stealing Ennis's personal store of heat.

"Hullo," he said, peering around. Mr. Ennis's set was not present; rather, his shapeless mattress had been brought in and was draped with relatively clean white linen. "Is Mr. Ennis here?"

"Is he expecting you?" She spoke in the clear, clean tones of a Londoner. She would have been perfectly at home on King Street, or in his local in Camden Town. She would be here having a picture made for her parents, he thought.

"He's not, but he wouldn't be surprised to see me. He's doing your portrait?"

"He is." She took a chair near from the wall and brought it back to the stove. "He said he'd be back in ten minutes. He went to get me some medicine."

"Oh," said Hallam, worried that he and Ennis had passed in the street. "Did he say where?"

"One of the neighbours. I have a cough." She demonstrated for him. It was a wet cough, with a rattle under it. He took off his gloves and tucked them under his arm. He realized the colour of her face was not from the heat of the fire.

"I'm an apothecary. If you don't mind—" he gestured to the chair, and she sat in it. She turned her face to him. Her eyes were a fawn brown, but from close up they were polished tigerwood. He thought perhaps she was sick with something more than a catarrh. "If you don't mind, ma'am, I'd like to touch your hand." She held it out and he put his own hand under it, judged its weight. It was thick, heavy with edema, and the skin was pallid. "How long have you felt unwell?"

"Some days. Mr. Ennis has been most helpful." Her voice, he realized now, was from somewhere farther north than he'd originally thought: she was speaking more slowly than she might usually, dulled by her illness.

"You're from Manchester."

"Bath," she said.

"Oh, I see. Yes, Bath. You need some lozenges. I can make some up for you."

"I have no money, sir."

"You are a friend of Mr. Ennis's. You can pay when you're able. I will make you a capsicum gargle. Not very pleasant, but it will restore your energy."

She smiled, but then her gaze went past him to the door and the smile broadened. "Sam," she said, rising. "Did you get it?"

"I have it right here. Hello, Jem Hallam. You've met?"

"We have," Hallam said, straightening and remembering his purpose. "Nice to make your acquaintance," he said to the woman.

"Claudia Rowe. Late of Bath. Pleased to meet you." She held her hand out and he took it again. "Mr. Hallam is going to make me some cap—a gargle," she said to Ennis. He had proceeded to the mattress, and she followed and eagerly sat. As if aware that Hallam had come to talk, Ennis held up his hand, that official gesture of his. He took from inside his coat a pipe, which he put in her open mouth and lit. She took a deep draft and lay down.

"Well, yes," said Hallam. "Tobacco has excellent restorative qualities. More women should smoke it; it reduces hysteria and is good for the organs." Miss Rowe held the smoke, her eyes closed, and exhaled. Ennis took a draft of it as well. The smoke was oily, and black. "Oh," said Hallam, catching its sweet fragrance. "Oh."

"Will you take some, Mr. Hallam?"

"No. I will not. Mr. Ennis, I'd like a word—"

"You may have many when our *pause fumée* has concluded, sir!"

"You must be very cautious with that. It's addicting," said Hallam.

"We are doing portraits," Ennis said, smiling joyously at him. He removed the opium pipe from Miss Rowe's reach. "That's enough. We don't want you dropping off." He rose from a crouching position and went to his camera, and Hallam crossed the room to meet him there, his attention divided between his reason for coming and what he'd found on arriving. "You've been to church?" said Ennis.

"You haven't."

Ennis laughed. "Just as you were, then," he said to Miss Rowe.

"I ran into Mr. Bryant this morning," he said. "The picture man on St. George's Square. I gather you know him."

Ennis brought his gaze around, his eyes swimming red. They reflected him like a pair of shined doorknobs. "A fine fellow."

"Yes. He wants me to refund a third of his money. Can you imagine why?"

"Poor stick. I knew his business was faltering."

"No, Mr. Ennis, his business is quite fine. But he is a little put off paying full price for my goods. Strange, that."

Ennis frowned. Hallam couldn't tell whether it was at the conundrum or the way Miss Rowe was sitting. "Ah," he said at last. "I have been a little Irish, I see."

"I won't be the only supplier of silver salts in this town forever, Mr. Ennis. I cannot cut deals with every person who comes with his hand out. Do you see what you've done?" Hallam followed him around the back of the camera. "He's investing in glass, and he thinks I must subsidize it now by refunding him a *third* of his chemical costs. *My* salts, Mr. Ennis, at a third off! Does that sound familiar?" He was trying to keep his voice down, but he was upset at Mr. Ennis's seeming lack of interest in these troubles.

"It may not be as bad as you fear," Ennis said. "Is that comfortable?"

Miss Rowe called out that it was.

"Will you be my light man, Mr. Hallam?"

"What?"

"We will solve the problems of the world once we are done with Miss Rowe here. Who is getting cold, I imagine."

Hallam was calculating the loss. "If I give Bryant back even a quarter of his funds, and the others insist on following his example, I will lose on the order of twenty pounds! And then I must wet-nurse these men and collect their fees and check their logs—it's an utter disaster. Are you even listening to me?"

"Jem, you're going to make yourself sick with worry like this. Give the gentleman what he asks and stay on him to make sure he's fair to you. Tell him the terms are secret and any communication of them will render your arrangement null."

"I see. And are you pledging yourself to this as well?"

"Hand to heart," said Ennis. "From this point on I will be as quiet as the grave. Now, the light?"

"Fine," Hallam said, "I will hold you to this." It was a sound idea, he had to admit. He would even prepare paperwork for Bryant obligating him to keep the terms private. "Yes," he said again, relieved somewhat, "but if the situation worsens, I'll hold you responsible."

"There will be nowhere I can hide," said Ennis. Hallam turned from him to put the reflecting board in place under the skylight (and such a pure, fresh light it was that came down from on high), and directly in the line of his sight as he turned was the milk-scented Miss Rowe sitting before him, without a stitch of clothing on her, and stretched out in the fashion of a Renaissance bather. He brought the white board up in front of his face instantly. "Mr. Ennis?" he said.

"Yes?"

"It is pure daylight in here. I don't think you need my assistance, but thank you for your advice." He put down the reflector and made for the door. He thought he could feel Miss Rowe's skin sending off heat like a miner's lamp behind him.

"Stop, please," said Ennis. "Stop now. You're being foolish. How do you think some of the world's best-loved paintings were made? From memory?"

"You are not painting, Mr. Ennis. You are making a picture." He spoke over his turned shoulder. "Miss Rowe, you are already unwell. Raw air will do nothing to improve your condition."

"If you will direct the light toward me, sir," she said, "I'll be able to warm up some."

He stood between them, unmoving but trembling,

and Ennis stared at him as if his eyes were a camera rendering Hallam on a silvered plate. The image, perhaps, was the reluctant face of a trapped animal, its snout narrowing in disbelief.

"You are left alone to fend for yourself in a strange country," Ennis said at last with a broad, open gesture. "Allow yourself some beauty."

"It's all right, Mr. Hallam," said the soft voice. "I'm not embarrassed."

He spun toward her and her skin flashed behind his eyes, but he did not look away. "You're not! Well, this is an excellent advance for you then!"

"It's only a human body," she said.

"Miss Rowe, you are alone in a room with two grown men. Either of us could do you ill, and one arguably already has, and if you chose afterwards to relate your misfortune to the police, it would be our words against yours. Who would they believe? Two businessmen, or a woman who has thrown off her clothes for supper?"

She pulled the linen over her lap, but made no other effort to cover herself. "If what's in store for me is further humiliation, then let me have it. I've resisted it before to no effect. Why resist it now?"

*This country is marvellous soil for despair*, Hallam thought. *Are we all marching down a narrowing corridor to the same place?* He took off his overcoat and threw it toward the woman. "If you won't cover yourself, I will," and proceeding to her, to ensure her shame was hidden, he said to Ennis, "You are indiscreet in more ways than I had thought."

"I have fallen in your eyes, Jem. This is a sad day."

On the mattress Miss Rowe was like a shot bird; the weight of his overcoat was almost too much for her to bear. "Look at her! She's half dead. Get up." He pulled her to standing by her shoulders, and instinctively she held the coat tightly around herself.

"I won't be paid," she said quietly.

"I will pay you whatever he owes you."

"I *work* for what I—"

"Stop speaking." Hallam pulled her toward where her clothes lay in a heap by the stove. Luckily, they would be warm. He put them into her arms and pushed her through the muslin curtain. "Dress yourself and I'll take you back to your house."

"Good luck with that," said Mr. Ennis. "Her house is a half-burnt-out shack on Niagara Street."

"And this is your idea of charity, then? You will seek an advantage no matter what it costs others!"

"I have a stove. And I pay for her modelling."

"Modelling."

"Photography is going to be an art form, Mr. Hallam. There are people who want to be transformed by it. Mrs. Arnold, whom you met earlier, has been Cleopatra in here, as well as Mrs. Nightingale."

"But she has not been forced to humiliate herself for you, for your money."

"I was not forced!" shouted Miss Rowe behind them. "And he never came closer to me than where he is right now. I am here of my own free will."

This left Hallam unhappily silent. He simply took

her under the arm and led her out into the afternoon, directing them south. Behind, Ennis called from the doorway, "Whom are you saving, Mr. Hallam? You are separating us both from our suppers. Is that your calling now?"

He pushed on past hearing. If he was going to take Ennis on over any of this, he'd be certain to do so when the larger man was not so medicated. Perhaps the smoke had lent him a shamelessness that would fade when he sobered. He could hope. "I'll take you home," Hallam said to the young woman who now stood at his side, appearing even more tired in the clear early spring light.

"You'll take me to England, will you?" The air had revived her somewhat, and now for the first time she appeared to be hearing directly; the filter of the drug had evaporated.

"Would that I could snap my fingers and transport us both to safety," he said. "But since that is not in the offing for now, I'll see you home to Niagara Street."

She gestured with her hand to show the way, but Hallam held his out as well, as if they were two very English sorts of gentlemen standing before a door. When she went ahead, he thought it best to follow somewhat behind so that no one could connect them in any way beyond that they were on the same street. As it was, King Street was nearly empty, and the angle of the road passing south gave an aspect on the lake that made it seem as if they could have been walking off a cliff. The lake often had this kind of presence in the city, a visual primacy that made one feel encroached upon, even if—

especially if—a person turned his back on it. Clippers, cutters, and screw steamers gathered in the harbour basin, aiming themselves in a seemingly random way at the shoreline, as if they would smash into each other and then just make it to land. Steam and smoke knotted the air as they approached, and a busier sight than the lake-front could not be had, generally, in the city. He had to admit that, in the more temperate months, it even gave the city the aspect of a going concern.

But here, as if warned of their presence, not even the impoverished denizens of Brock Street bothered to show their faces in their windows, and Hallam continued on with his charge without witness.

Miss Rowe's swayback gave her an easy lope that was attractive to look at, but Hallam made an effort not to. All women with their youth so manifest (Alice was but twenty-four) had a ruddy health about them that could not easily be broken by self-abuse or poverty, and Claudia Rowe possessed a kind of unimpeachable vital-ity. The city had examples of Irish waifs so pitiful in their circumstances, and yet so beautiful—despite the grime, the grey-green teeth, the shabby clothing—that it moved him to despair to think their maker would mock them and yet still leave them the vain gift of their looks. It was not so for men, and a man like Samuel Ennis was a good example of what effect hard living could have on such a body.

Miss Rowe took him on a similar route to the one that he'd walked the first night he'd been at Ennis's studio. The tenor of Ennis's parting with Mr. and Mrs.

Arnold that late afternoon took on new meaning now, as it seemed clear in retrospect that he and Mrs. Arnold had set a separate appointment for the following day, not just so he could show her the results of her sitting with her new, rich, and ugly husband, but so that she could trick herself up in the garb of a courtesan or a squaw or a pioneer wife. For all Hallam knew (and he imagined the scene with a shudder of revulsion), Mr. Ennis had a makeshift stake for tying his Joan of Arcs to, and God only knew what he did for those with a leaning toward Héloïse.

"You must be careful with unmarried men in a city where so much is unsettled," he said to the back of Claudia Rowe's head. "There is no safe place for a woman who is alone."

"So I'm unsafe right now?"

"You must presume so, yes. I know you are safe, but you do not. And you'd be inviting catastrophe to think otherwise. As you clearly already do." She had nothing to say to that, so he carried on berating her. "Who taught you to be so incautious?"

She turned sharply and Hallam had to stop to avoid walking into her. "Necessity. And who taught you to presume so much?"

"I make no presumptions about the behaviour of men." She gave him a disgusted look and continued walking.

"My house is coming up," she said. In front of them stood a line of broken-down shacks, any one of which would have been unsuitable to live in. They were black from tar as well as fire, and a couple sported the mockery of already-charred ladders leading to their roofs. The worst of the row lacked a full corner, as if a giant with a cleaver had simply hacked it away. A sheet had been draped over the missing corner (the burnt remains of which lay under a peaceful cover of the last of the snow), and this, of course, was Miss Rowe's home.

"Is this really where you live?"

"I'm thinking of putting in a carriage house." He could not laugh for her, even though it would have been a welcome kindness, he was sure. She looked at the sorry thing, and Hallam tried not to fix his mind on the image of her going into it and wasting whatever fuel she had within to heat it, heat that would only be sucked out through the gaping hole in the side and distributed amongst the stars. "What was Mr. Ennis going to pay you?"

"Four bob. And I would have stayed warm for the whole afternoon without burning a stick of my own wood."

"I'm a meddler."

"You're English. We think we know what's best for everyone. We sweep in to clean up and leave everyone to fight it out in better clothes."

He reached into his pocket and took out what he had—two shillings—and folded them into her hand. She gave no modest show of refusal. She took them and put them into a cloth purse. "Please promise me you'll spend that on food or firewood."

"You have no business pretending to be my father. If you were so good with money yourself, I doubt you'd be availing yourself of Sam's business."

"Fine then. I will express my desire as a wish that you will not smoke those coins."

She laughed quietly. "I own this house. Could I have spent my money any more foolishly than on a house put together with fire starter? A single match could transform any of these little huts into signal flares that would burn for a week at a time. Slow and steady: you could watch everything you own slowly melt." She stood square to him, as if issuing a challenge to contradict her unhappy logic. "If you want, you can have your money back, but I won't make you any promises."

"No. You're right."

"In your honour, however, I will spend some of it on a proper meal and a room for the night at Mrs. Chesley's on Adelaide Street. She takes only women and only cash. I will have a healthy serving of boiled ham, a hot bun, and a cider. How's that."

"I approve," he said. "And I won't even offer to walk you there. I'm sure you know your own business."

"Sirrah," she said, bowing slightly, then rising with a mock sweep of her arm. Hallam tilted his hat to her, earnestly as he could, and continued on his way. But he was pleased to hear, after he'd walked some distance, "Thank you, Mr. Hallam," said just loudly enough so that he knew she wanted him to hear it.

## 3.

Toronto was a city that sopped up one's dreams; at night, abed in his anonymous flat, Hallam drifted through the silent, colourless landscape of the deepest kind of sleep, a dead sleep. Dreams had once brought him news of an inner heart, and he was reassured to think that his spirit carried on with its work in an absurdly colourful underworld, the regulations of which only it knew. Awake, he would recall them wonderingly, never so wild a man as he was in his dreams. That anyone had it in him to be another person struck him as miraculous. But in Toronto, he did not dream, he was no one when he slept. Drugged or hard-won, when he came out of these featureless sleeps, it was as if he'd spent his night locked in an empty vault.

Because now there was no point in going out every day (there were no customers to see after and no inventory to keep track of), and because the rains and intemperate bursts had all but ended by the beginning of May, Hallam stayed at home with his windows open. He'd broken off all contact with Ennis, knowing the man to be flush with supplies (enough, he thought sourly, to take a naked record of the whole city), and he tried not to think how he'd handle himself when next called on for reprovending. He made the rounds to his empty shop once in a while to ensure all was well, and took iodine and silver salts to his other accounts. Although the rent on the shop was steep, he thought of it as insurance against his father discovering what he'd done with it. Perhaps there would come some as-yet-undiscovered purpose it could be put to, at some point in an inevitably happier future. It was not legal to offer it as a residential property—a pity, since he could have rented it out ten times over. He tried to picture the place as a pub, or a little hotel, but no matter how he imagined it, the shop would not be transformed in his mind. It could be nothing else to him but a charnel pit for his hopes.

He tried to batten down his wandering mind by going to the bookstalls in the market a couple of times a week to exchange reading materials. He finally read Cervantes, and was cheered by the image of the old Spaniard attacking his windmills. In his mind, Quixote chopped at a murderous windmill on Toronto's own shoreline. He had the poetry of Charles Sangster (a Canadian) thrust upon him, as well as *Moby Dick*, by the author of *Mardi*, a book he'd enjoyed, but after those two recommendations he gave that particular stall a wide pass. There were copies of *Uncle Tom's Cabin* everywhere, that favourite of abolitionists, anti-abolitionists, escaped slaves, negro workers, angry northerners, angry southerners, and so on, and the fact that it was everywhere to be seen in preread condition suggested that no one found it particularly satisfying. Although in more than one place Hallam was told to read it for its depictions of *Canada*, as if having the place of his imprisonment described to him by one who had never been so detained would be enlightening.

He continued to write letters to Alice, but he finished few of them, and mailed none. They lay about, half written and full of lies too egregious for sending, and were increasingly about his so-called leisure time. He gave the impression that to tell her any more about his business would simply be repetition of past letters, but all was well, and things were picking up and so on. To his father, Hallam's lies were somewhat more careful. He'd found stock closer to home, he told him, a half-truth, but the stock was not what his father would have expected. The elder Hallam wrote warm letters back, in that rambling verbiage that brought his voice so rawly to Hallam's mind that it hurt. His father had made Alice a gift of handsome new luggage in the new year, telling her she would have need of it by the fall. *To move to smaller lodgings,* Hallam thought sourly, where the suitcase would probably be the finest of the house's furnishings. Hallam envied the thought of his father with those two plump little girls sitting on his lap being fed sugar cubes while Alice loaded up his plate again with stew and potatoes. All of them, all the while, imagining the spread of the Hallam name in Canada. Alice's letters he, at first, left unopened and unread in a pile on the windowsill. And then he simply stopped picking them up at the post office altogether.

One such afternoon—spent committing lies half-heartedly to paper—was passing with morbid slowness when his bell jangled. It was the end of the first week of May, and he'd just spent an entire weekend without going out of doors, so evidence of the world beyond his windows was something of a revelation. He was in a shirt and long drawers, with the curtains drawn on his own funk, and he now opened them to see Claudia Rowe standing in the street, having stepped back from the stoop where she'd rung the bell. Hallam snapped the curtain shut, and the bell rang again. He pulled on pants and swished a mouthful of water around to rid his breath of the smell of stale tea, and rushed down the stairs to the street door. He stood behind it, his mind empty, believing he could actually hear her breath through the door. The bell jangled once more in his room above him.

"Miss Rowe?" he said opening the door, and he shot a glance down the street in the direction she must have been walking. "How did you get my home address?"

"There is the city directory, Mr. J.G. Hallam."

"Oh. I see."

"Mr. Ennis says he hasn't heard from you since our friendly meeting. You've broken off with him?"

"No." Hallam was aware that the longer they stood in the door, the worse the encounter would appear. He stepped aside and brought her into the foyer. "He hasn't sent word for more supplies, so I presume he has what he needs for the time being. You've seen him?"

"Just to say hello."

"I see."

They stood in a tortured silence. He wasn't sure what etiquette demanded of him: would one behave differently if an unexpected visitor was *not* someone one had seen naked? If unintentionally? He waited for the inevitable door to fly open on the main floor or one above, and for a neighbour to see him with this unfamiliar girl. "You formed the wrong impression of me," she said.

"How so."

"For one, I'm married."

Hallam stared at her.

"I should say I suppose myself still to be married. My husband was employed by the Atlantic Telegraph Company and went early last fall to set up some lines that would connect Fort William to Toronto. But he vanished in November. It was six months on Friday."

She waited for him to say something, but he didn't.

"Six months means he's deemed dead by the county coroner," she said. "I suppose it was a good thing he had life insurance. But they won't pay it, will they? Because there's no body and no witnesses that can vouch he's dead, and even if he is, they don't have proof it wasn't a suicide, even though I tell them he would never have taken his own life. Do you understand?"

"Mrs. Rowe—Mrs. Rowe, I don't know what to say."

She continued, explaining that no authority would take possession of her particular case, how her letters went unanswered, and she pushed him into the hall walking toward him, her hands now freed from her sides where they moved through the air angrily. "I have a husband, Mr. Hallam, who by law is half-alive and half-dead, and I am powerless and friendless and have nowhere to live and nothing to eat and it is the *street* for me if I don't figure out what to do—"

She had set her jaw just enough to prevent tears from pouring down her face, but her whole body was shaking. Hallam's face reddened not only because of the horror of this nearly weeping woman in the vestibule of his tenement, but because he'd fixed a picture of this woman in his mind so uncharitable that it was hard to correct. He'd seen her as one of the myriad hangers-on, who would do anything to cadge a meal or a cigar, not as someone who had lost everything. It was beyond his powers to imagine how his cruelty must have felt to her, and he felt profoundly ashamed. Without another thought, he led her upstairs to his unkempt room and put a pot of water on to boil.

She collected herself in silence, sitting in the chair he'd been in only moments earlier, staring out of the window, where he'd spent aimless nights, alone, scribbling his fantasies home. When the pot boiled, he filled a silver ball with fresh leaves and steeped her something strong. He thought of adulterating it a little with whisky, just to pacify her, but he thought better of it, knowing first-hand that her system was already too receptive of such balms. She held the hot cup in her hands. On passing it to her, she covered one of Hallam's hands with her own, and her touch was waxy and cold, even though it was a true spring day outside.

He pulled along a stool and sat near her, at the side of the desk, his breath coming in nervous rags. He sent his mind back to recall all the harsh things he said or suggested when he dragged her from Ennis's house that afternoon.

"You must accept my apology," he said. "I imagined your circumstances somewhat differently."

"You thought I was a whore in training," she said.

"I don't know what I was thinking."

"Yes you do." She drank gingerly from the cup, her hands shaking only a little now. "At last you know I'm a widow. Well, I am enough of a widow to take on his debts."

"Is there nothing the company will do for you?"

"It is through them that the policy was purchased! They garnished the monthly fee from his wages, but now that there are no wages to be paid they have kindly offered to continue accepting payment on the policy. Should their 'terms' be satisfied, they will need to have the policy in good standing, which in plain English means that if I am so fortunate to recover my husband's body one day, I will have to have paid into the policy right to that bloody moment!" She was splenetic now, but Hallam held his tongue, hoping her mood would spend itself, although he could scarce but imagine a crowd of curious neighbours gathering in a knot outside his door. "So either I save my eight shillings a month and forfeit my right," she continued, "or I pay on until such time as they admit what everyone seems to accept, *or* they decide the case is closed and the terms unsatisfied. It's only a matter of choosing when I am to lose everything: now or later." She took another deep draft of the tea. She seemed immune to the heat and swallowed without moving the liquid around in her mouth. Perhaps all of her was numb. She sat with her eyes closed over the steam, letting it soothe her, and when she opened them she allowed herself a look around Hallam's living space, taking it in over the rim of her cup and then sending him a sideways glance. "You weren't expecting me," she said smiling.

He cleared his throat rather than laughing. "I don't expect anyone."

She peered down at the rag plugs in the floor. "Those are a unique way to stop the drafts."

"They're bolt holes," he told her. "There was machinery in here before I took the room. A man who printed tracts."

"What came of him?"

"He stopped paying the rent." She nodded, her eyes still taking in the room. The curtains were drawn, and she put her cup down and leaned across the desk to shift one open and look out, then let it fall again. An arrow of light pierced the room as she did, and then vanished. "You might as well open them if you want," Hallam said. "I doubt your presence here is much of a secret anymore."

"I'm sorry," she said, and then she did open them, standing to do so. She pulled a strand of hair out of her mouth and pushed it over her ear, then turned to the room and saw it in all its murk. The late-afternoon light probably showed the place to what advantage it had, but he was aware that no amount of light could have made it homelike. He remained where he was as she stepped farther into the room, looking back once to mark any objections Hallam might have had. But he remained silent, and she went over to the stove and held her hand over it, then peered into the dry sink, at its dirty contents. She came back toward the centre of the room, briefly scrutinizing the bed. She stood against the wall opposite the window and held her arms apart, her palms facing together. "One machine here," she said, and then she shuffled sideways, turning and keeping her arms stiffly out. "Another one here."

"I imagine."

"Where did he sleep?"

"Perhaps the floor."

"That couldn't have been very nice. Although back at home, in England, I knew a preacher who slept on his own pews. Maybe the discomfort reminds them of something."

"I think most of them sleep in beds," he said. He found himself watching her carefully, as if he'd encountered a nearly domesticated animal in his flat, a marten or a raccoon. Best to keep one's distance. Mrs. Rowe remained on the other side of the room, taking in the small cloth-covered crate he used as a bedside table, his slippers pushed neatly under the bed, a drinking glass on the windowsill. He saw it all as he imagined she saw it, following the line of her vision to all the forlorn objects of his own life, but when he brought his eyes off the glass and back to hers, she was looking directly at him.

"Pretty cozy though," she said.

"Yes."

"One could never have fit two people in here with all that machinery."

"Well, no," he said, and thought to mention that he knew some married couples in the building with rooms just like his, but before he could form the words her meaning was borne in on him like a blast of heat, and he realized why she had come. She stood with her arms at her sides, and there it was, in the open between them.

"Mrs. Rowe," he said. "I wish there was some way to show you I'm not a *complete* brute, but . . . I can give you . . ." He thought for a moment, trying to appear as if he were calculating something, rather than reining in his flailing mind. "I have to spare perhaps—"

"No," she said. "I don't want money. I want to know what it means that you cared about what I did with myself. An utter stranger. Hundreds of women in this city fall to all sorts of predation. Some of them live very well on it. Will you ferret them all out and save them from their worser instincts?"

"I felt . . . involved . . . somehow, in your case."

"Why did it matter to you?"

"I suppose it was because it was my supply of silver that was allowing him to abuse you in that manner."

"I was not being abused."

"Of course, yes. And I see now that I was overzealous. It was wrong of me to presume to—"

"You can't withdraw your concern now." She still stood across from him, her arms folded over her chest. He felt surprised to imagine that he was now in *her* space. "Not when you are being asked to make good on it."

Unwelcome heat seared his face and sped down to his stomach. "It's not that," he said. "It's only that it was your business, and I would have done well to assume you knew it better than anyone."

He expected that she would counter him with a new assertion of his obligations, but instead he saw that her face had softened, or fallen even, and her expression was one of complete despair. He turned away again from her startling nakedness. She spoke quite plainly now. "I'm here to throw myself on your mercy. I need your help, your good graces. And in exchange I offer you my friendship."

"My God," he said. "Look around, Mrs. Rowe. Judge for yourself. And what about Mr. Ennis's mercy?"

"You've seen his rooms. They're even worse than yours. And do you think he has mercy in him?"

"You know him better than I do."

"But I feel I know you better than him." She came back to the desk and removed the same cloth purse she'd dropped his contribution into the previous month, and drew out a small roll of paper money. This she placed on its end on the desk. "I entrust you with my entire life savings. My husband's bank saw fit to allow me to empty his account. *Be rid of her*, they thought, *there's no more where that came from*. There's six pounds there."

"You could pay rent on a room for almost a year on that, Miss Rowe. Mrs. Rowe."

"And then face death in the middle of winter? You take that money up front and we'll enter into an agreement. A companionable arrangement. You need help in here, and I need sanctuary. I'll come and go in darkness if you like."

Having entered now into a conversation he would not otherwise entertain the merest thought of, Hallam felt compelled to speak to her proposal, but another part of him wanted to grab her by the shoulder and march her down the stairs. Her tone of voice—one that suggested that only the details needed working out—could have been applied to the most absurd petitions, such as suggesting they rob a bank or burn the customs house to the ground for the sheer thrill of it. *You needn't answer her directly*, he told himself. *She may have laid the grounds for one conversation, Hallam, but you lay the grounds for another.*

"I've read of confidence men, Mrs. Rowe, and probably their tricks aren't restricted to their sex."

"I have to believe in you as well, that you'll treat me honourably. You said I shouldn't place my faith in men. But I think only an honest man would say that."

"I'm not worried about my own behaviour. I'm married with two daughters."

"You have two girls."

"Yes. But, that, that is *not* the point, Mrs. Rowe. The point is, I am not a bachelor, and even if I were, it wouldn't be correct—you must understand what I am saying?"

The light was fading now, and the lamps had come on, and he imagined she was visible to anyone who cared to look in. "I'm someone's daughter," she said at last. "Would you be the kind of man you'd wish one of your own daughters on if ever so unhappy a fate as mine visited her? Would you want her to find a man like you?"

"If she had to find anyone. But if he were sensible—"

"If he were heartless."

"What about your parents, Mrs. Rowe?"

"An ocean away."

"It sounds as if you have enough savings to afford the passage back."

"Would you go back if there was a chance your life was going to return to you?"

"I don't understand," he said.

"Are you advising me to give my husband up for dead?"

"I thought you said you'd—"

"Is that what you'd have me do? Lose faith entirely?"

He stopped speaking.

"Shelter me for your daughters' sake, Mr. Hallam. I am in a world that has no use for me on my own, and doesn't care what happens to me. It's not aware of my beginnings, the hopes of my family, the future I wanted. But you are sensible of it. I'll sleep on the floor. I'll work for you in your shop if you like. And we can, at night, trade books and . . . and even discuss them, civilized conversations about things that interest us. I have a good mind. I'm a fine conversationalist. And if you are, eventually, displeased with the arrangement, you can turn me out and keep my savings."

He listened to these words, this desolate argument, but what he could not defend himself from was how she looked in his room, standing before him in a filthy coat that hung shapeless on her and did not reach her feet and the grey stockings poking out of black shoes, one foot pointed awkwardly away from the other. She had dressed as if she had come to fill a position, and his heart was breaking at the sight of her. "Do you really think I would keep your money?" he said almost inaudibly, but she had heard him, and it fired her courage.

"No," she said firmly. "I know you won't." She picked up her teacup and finished it, then took it to the dry sink and poured some cold water into it, scrubbed it briefly, and put it down on the countertop. "I have some hand towels in my things. I have a roll of clothing and other items with a neighbour. You might think of keeping a warm pot of water on the hob for the dishes."

"It wastes fuel."

"Your home is neglected, Mr. Hallam. *You* are neglected. I can help you."

Hallam nodded at her, feeling weak and sick and fallen. It would be a sin to agree to her request, but so would it be to send her back to the street. And had he not been sworn to protect the well-being of others? He saw that, once he understood exactly what was being asked of him, he could not refuse her. Given the chance to provide succour, one must do it: the alternative is not much more than murder at a remove. He had, it was true, recoiled at the mere horror of an erotic photograph, but would he seriously consider sending another human being back into the elements?

Even so, this sensible, moral justification only masked that he'd been offered a solace of his own, and once he was done arguing with himself he would see the conclusion was foregone. Her offer of company, even if it were only to be the sound of another human being breathing in the darkness, was not a boon he could refuse. If it meant the sacrifice of his good name, his future hopes, then so be it. He was too lonesome to turn her away.

So he sent her to collect her worldly things, and despaired.

4.

AS IF BECKONED BY A STRANGE GESTURE OF HOPE, the spring came in earnest the week after Mrs. Rowe moved into Hallam's rooms. It was hard to believe, after a winter such as they'd had, that the cold was not somehow still invested just below the surface, and that anything that tried to grow would hit its head against the underside of the earth. And yet all the incipient charms of the city were suddenly manifest. The smell of sweetgrass in empty lots, the honeyed air, the lovely breezes off the lake. And where before the city had seemed a subterranean nightmare of hidden faces and hushed voices, Hallam now nodded at his fellows in the street and received the most friendly time of day in return from them. Perhaps because English winters were not as cruel, never before had he encountered spring with such a sense of gratitude, and this sense was shared by everyone else who survived the winter of 1856. He found himself laughing unaccountably as he walked down King Street. The warm light inspired people to have their joyful faces photographed for posting home, and more than once he came to the shop to find a note tucked in behind the handle asking for his services at one or another location. Bryant had kept his word, and to Hallam's even greater surprise, discharged his percentages as promised on a biweekly basis. Sometimes he even made deliveries (or Mrs. Rowe made them) to hotels or private homes where one of his photographers was so busy he could not meet at his regular place of business or the shop to take delivery of a much-needed silver salt. And his earlier fears of the nitrate lasting too long did not figure either, as the need for silver salts in exposing paper positives exceeded the need of simply sensitizing glass plates. If one or two paper pictures were affordable, then why not three or four? Silver was not going out of style.

During the days, Hallam and Mrs. Rowe went their separate ways, unless there was some agreed task to be done that required them both. Hallam deposited her six pounds to his general account at the Bank of Montreal and kept careful count of the interest that accrued to her capital. He had no intention of keeping her money, but as it was the cornerstone of their agreement, he felt he had to honour the terms that found him holding her entire personal reserves. Between the two of them there was a worldly fortune of nearly one hundred pounds, about a fifth of the amount Hallam would have expected the shop to bring in by 1857, had he not scuttled it to live. But one hundred pounds was enough to survive on, and build on, and he allowed himself the luxury of some hope.

At first, when together in the room, his discomfort at the new arrangement overwhelmed any other feeling.

There was no privacy, and he had the instinct to announce himself if he were about to so much as shift in his chair, for fear it would startle her. The effort at politeness exhausted them. Never had either said *Oh yes, thank you* or *Oh that would be very nice, yes, thank you* or *Oh, well, no, I'm fine, thank you* so many times, and Hallam began to feel as if he were playing a role in an amusing satire on newlyweds.

Bedtime was, as he had imagined, exquisitely painful. He allowed Mrs. Rowe to sleep on the floor, as she had originally suggested, since there was no way he could allow her to take the bed he'd slept in all those months and also retain any sense of propriety if she did. To send her to the floor was for certain ungentlemanly, but he felt keenly, and she agreed, that this part of their agreement had to remain sacrosanct to ensure there was no illusion of greater familiarity between them. And once she had unrolled her belongings, a layer of sweaters and the unneeded winter coat made fine bedding, and Hallam felt convinced after the first week that she was not uncomfortable.

At night, bowing with excruciating politeness, their bodies twisted as far away from each other as possible, changing into their nightwear under the bedclothes like children playing at a game—it was profoundly embarrassing, but to Hallam (and, he allowed himself to imagine, to Mrs. Rowe as well) it was also replete with pleasure. To scent another body nearby! To hear the happy, unconscious sigh as her tired body settled into the bedding . . . it did his spirit good to be in the span of such simple human moments.

With time, they gradually unknotted this unease. Mrs. Rowe was good company and a good guest. She eased them into their queer arrangement gracefully, never displaying any discomfort greater than her host's. Hallam allowed himself to think that if Alice knew the whole truth of his situation, and knew his heart then as he did, that she would have approved of the arrangement. It was felicitous to his mental health. Mrs. Rowe was funny and clever, and within two weeks (working with an agreed-upon budget that she believed burdened their finances equally) she transformed the little box he lived in into something almost like a home. She bought an inexpensive rug and put it down over the most conspicuous of the bolt holes, pushing the rag plugs down level with the boards. It was as if no violence had ever been done to the floors. She purchased a heavy white curtain as well as a hanging rod, which she herself installed, and divided the room into two clean halves, including the window, so to allow each of them moonlight and a portion of the sunrise. The curtain was drawn after supper if either wished to have privacy to do whatever they would, or it remained open until their game of chess or discussion of the evening was complete. Hallam endeavoured to stop drinking tea at an earlier hour than he normally would, and ensured that he made water before retiring, although he kept a pan beneath his bed in case an urgency arose in the middle of the night. This way, Mrs. Rowe had use of the hallway water closet and he did not have to pass through her side of the room. He found the pan an infernal discomfort when he did need it, and the effort to relieve himself silently was excruciating. He entertained the thought of an open window, but being well-born, he suffered with the pan when absolutely necessary.

Mrs. Rowe also entered a subscription with the ice man, and took delivery of a block of ice twice a week to place in the hayed icebox Hallam tricked up out of a couple of crates and a tin tub. The ice melted much faster than it would have in an expensive, insulated larder, but he didn't have the money to risk on a proper one, and they made do with the toy icebox he felt proud to have constructed. Into this new cabinet, Mrs. Rowe placed such rarities as butter and fresh meats and occasionally cheese—never more than they could consume in a week—and so to the lonesome dry goods that sat dejectedly in Hallam's cupboards were added such things as might result in a good toad-in-the-hole or even a chicken vol-au-vent, should the person in control of those things have the knowledge of how they might be so transformed, and Mrs. Rowe did. This was achieved with the assistance of a wedding-gift copy of *Mrs. Beaton's Book of Household Management* she had brought with her to Toronto. On Friday mornings, she told Hallam to call a number at random upon which she would open *Mrs. Beaton* to the same page, and announce what the Friday supper would be. Boiled round of beef one week, sheep trotters another. As he did not like wild birds or rabbits, he learned not to choose the page numbers in the vicinity of four hundred and fifty.

To be at home while the scent of something a man could not possibly prepare on his own (or even, perhaps, know to order in a restaurant), and then be sent to the table to taste the proceeds of his good luck . . . the improvement this provided Hallam's body and soul was hard to measure. For the first time in nearly a year, he fattened. Not so that it was obvious, but he could feel himself fitting his garments better, and Mrs. Rowe herself observed that his cheeks had filled with flesh.

Mrs. Rowe did not go to St. James'—his church—as this would have invited the kind of scrutiny they could not answer to, but he did introduce her as an employee of his to the pastor at St. Michael's, and she was welcomed to that congregation. She did not wish to go back to the church she and her husband belonged to because she could not bear the looks of pity she got there. Once they returned to the flat of their separate Sunday afternoons, however, they had sermons to compare. And although they recognized quickly that neither was as observant as they were presumed by the other to be, the questions brought up by their respective pastors were interesting to them. Charity was a popular subject at Mrs. Rowe's church, as the building was on the border of MacCaulaytown, and it frequently took up collections for widows and children in that part of the city. She came back to Hallam's rooms on one June Sunday disturbed by the pastor's assertion that a legitimate child was more deserving of charity than one had outside of marriage. That there were "true" widows and "false" widows. "But imagine punishing a child for the sins of its parents," she said. She had made some beef rissoles from a rump she'd roasted on the Friday, and she had put it before them with a pot of good gravy on the side. As was their habit, through some unspoken agreement, they served themselves, although this made sense to Hallam. Alice would have served him, and Alice was his wife. Serving the person you love, with whom you've chosen to share your life, is a kind of joy and a duty. Here, he and Mrs. Rowe did not have those sorts of duties to each other; there were no rituals to reinforce the meaning of their lives together, as their "togetherness," as he saw it, was a side effect of his social obligation. Her word *arrangement*— which she always used to describe how they were living—seemed to him a good and true way to describe them to themselves. So he served himself some lemon-fragrant croquettes and poured his own gravy and ate in utmost contentment with, as time went on, less and less of a sense that he was living in a state of gross betrayal.

"Maybe your pastor wants to reinforce the importance of the marriage sacrament," Hallam said. "It wouldn't be unusual for him to do that. If the women of MacCaulaytown see their married neighbours receiving more of the church's aid, they'll think twice of getting a child outside of that sacrament."

"That species of morality is a luxury for educated people, Mr. Hallam. Everyone else lives in hordes and gets by as best they can. I think outwardly *condoning* immoral behaviours is not in the church's interest, of course, but could anyone condone giving a child less to eat only because his mother is unmarried?"

"No," he said. "I see what you mean. Sin should not be hereditary."

"Indeed, but more importantly, charity should be blind to everything but need. Our personal feelings should not determine whose starvation is legitimate."

"Are they our personal feelings, or are they laws?"

"They're *our* laws, if anything, and I've been subject to them enough to know that they are applied unevenly, depending on how things appear. Imagine this. If you were a doctor, and came upon an accident in the road, and there were two men lying on the cobble bleeding, and one was drunk and the other not, who would you treat first?"

"The one who was more badly injured."

"Fine. Then say they are injured about equally, and the sober man is quietly waiting for attention, while the drunk is shouting and cursing and waving his hands in the air. Now who receives your ministrations?"

"I understand the point you're making," he said, and halved a croquette with his fork. He wished to change the subject, worrying that he'd accidentally reveal some native flaw in himself that would show him inclined, say, to turn a blind eye to the suffering of someone he disliked. There were relatives in life that tended to sink you in logical discourse. "We should try to depend upon our reason when in situations where we might be tempted to react with feeling. Is that not so?"

"I think we have to see our responsibility to all people as equal. I don't believe a thin line of spiritual alikeness connects me to the child with an unmarried mother, and a thicker line connects me to the one who was born in wedlock. That makes me an agent for something morally odious, and I don't want to be that agent."

"Well, that's brave of you. Because you can even out the thickness of all the lines that emanate *from* you, outward to humanity, but you'll never have the luxury of controlling those directed *toward* you."

"I've managed well enough, though. Here I am, fed and with a place to sleep, right? When a mere three months earlier, I was a fallen woman."

"Touché," he replied, and he rose to get them both a glass of beer. "But you are probably the exception."

"If you're talking about the lines of connection that come to me from elsewhere, then it's you who are the exception, J.G. Hallam." She took the glass and poured herself a draft of ale, then raised it to him. "Thank goodness you work from a different spiritual account book than Father Caufield's."

"To your health," Hallam said, and they clinked glasses.

She drank, watching him, thinking. She'd barely touched supper, even allowing for the fact that she usually ate about half of what he did. She put her glass down and made a sound like *hmff*, and then picked up her fork.

"No," he said.

"No what?"

"No to whatever conclusion you just drew. Don't think I can't hear the gears spinning in your head."

"I'm gearless, Mr. Hallam. I plot nothing. Except that I just realized that I can ask you something and you'll do it."

"And what is that?"

## 5.

THAT TALK IS A FORM OF ACTION IS NOT WELL
understood. One should not agree to the terms of something in debate, whether heated or polite, but neglect
these terms in life. Many people do, but most try not to,
and liking one's morals only in theory is likely to lose a
person both friends and business.

In agreeing, theoretically, to Mrs. Rowe's terms in
their discussion about charity, Hallam agreed, without
knowing he was doing so, to remake his acquaintance
with Mr. Ennis, who was apparently suffering alone in
his cottage on Adelaide Street. Hallam had not known
that Mrs. Rowe had continued, throughout May and
into June, to visit with Mr. Ennis, although she insisted
that she was not posing for him, and he believed her. By
her estimation, whatever natural syndrome afflicted him
had worsened and required better medicine than he
could ferret through his own channels. And so it was
agreed that Hallam would withdraw whatever money
was required and take the man to a doctor in the good
part of town.

Hallam found a cab waiting outside of St. Lawrence Hall and took the hack out to The Ward. The driver was instructed to wait while Hallam went inside to see for himself how Ennis was. He found the older man covered in a worn blanket lying on his pallet. *A pig in his sty*, thought Hallam. It would have been difficult to judge the place a greater mess than it had been when he'd last seen it, but it was even more neglected. He noted two glass jars full of a clear liquid on each windowsill in Ennis's little chamber. A suck of the good stuff within arm's reach, no matter where he was in the room. And the milk can was still in its place beside the bed. Ennis could have a gutful of drink without having to sit up straight.

Ennis was dozing on his back, his breathing apneic. Hallam calculated in his mind the levering force it would take to get Ennis onto his side, where the weight of his body would not afflict his lungs so. With Ennis incapacitated, it occurred to him that he could go into the studio and try to find out how much of his photographic practice was illegal. If the use to which he had been putting Mrs. Rowe was typical, only God knew what examples of his work might be in the drawers in the other room. But he was at Ennis's home on a supposed mission of mercy and so he shook him awake. When the man opened his eyes it was immediately apparent that his palsy had worsened: he seemed to have suffered a paralysis, and the left side of his face had fallen down like a torn drape, drawing his cheek and mouth away with it. "My old friend," he said, blinking. He held out a hand to be helped up and Hallam pulled at him until he was sitting upright. Ennis's left arm seemed all but useless, and Hallam realized that the Irishman had suffered a stroke. He would have to carry that great bulk out of the cottage and into the hack. "Have you come to rescue me as well?"

"You already have your freedom," Hallam replied.

He found his anger still fresh, but in coming to know Mrs. Rowe's character it should not have been so, since she was clearly never as helpless as he'd imagined her. In thinking of the episode when he first met her, Hallam still felt the bite of distaste, but now it was caused by something different. It was that he'd been betrayed by this man, whom he'd allowed to take him on as something of an apprentice and friend.

"I have a horse and carriage outside for you, Mr. Ennis," he said. "I have a medical man willing to see one such as you." Hallam helped him up to standing and put a dead arm over one shoulder. Ennis steadied himself and glanced around the dirty room as if he were leaving it for the last time. From Hallam's point of view, it would have been cause for celebration to be delivered of this place, with its bowed floors and shabby, broken furniture, not to speak of the human and chemical funks that met like two weather systems and became a dank stench.

Ennis's arm was strangely pliable, as if the muscle had changed to taffy, and cold as well. His legs were steady, but nearly all his energy was sapped. "How bad is it?"

"It doesn't hurt," said Ennis. "It's as if I went to bed drunk one night and woke up with only half my body sober. But it doesn't hurt."

"As *if* you went to bed drunk? When do you not go to bed drunk, Mr. Ennis?" Hallam pointed his jaw toward one of the windows. Sunlight processed through the glass jars spread a fan of colour along the greying sills. "The air in this room could make an entire household drunk."

Ennis's eyes drifted from the windows and back to Hallam, and he laughed in a halting fashion. "Those are concoctions of your own making, Mr. Hallam."

"That is no medicine of mine."

"No, you're right. They're jars of silver nitrate solution. You have to sun it, don't you know? To clean it."

"You have to clean it," said Hallam, his voice flat.

"It becomes adulterated with filth. But if you expose the impurities to sunlight it becomes elemental silver and sinks to the bottom of the jar. Then you flush it out, recharge the solution, and off you go." He laughed more heartily now, searching Hallam's face. "You think me so perverse, Jem, that I would drink my own silver?"

"No, I did not think that."

"But you would begrudge me it, a dying man by rights, if I had a thirst for it, wouldn't you?" His face had become solemn now. "You hate me, Jem Hallam."

"I don't. I am uninterested in you now."

"I see. Well then, I suppose you had better get me to your undertaker. Perhaps he will have an opinion."

Doctor Cotter had his surgery at Queen and Church streets. The office was a few doors away from the general dispensary, and Hallam believed that if he explained his former profession and spoke knowledgeably enough, the doctor might be able to obtain Mr. Ennis's medication at a fraternal rate. His room smelled of oiled wood and rubbing alcohol. The doctor's portrait hung behind a heavy mahogany desk and an imposing leather chair: it was a place to instill confidence. He had Ennis sit on his examining table and looked at his eyes and in his mouth. He ran a stick along his tongue and examined the damp sludge that came off it. "Your breath is rank," he told Ennis.

"I don't have the money for parsley."

"You have enough for wine, I'd judge."

Hallam stood off to the side, listening quietly and observing the doctor's technique. He listened to Ennis's chest and tapped his entrails with his hand flat against Ennis's belly. Hallam had seen this particular sleight performed a number of times and had never had the courage to ask what was discovered by the resulting sound. However, the secrets of Ennis's moist insides were hardly necessary; his most obvious symptom confronted them both factually: his face was hanging from his skull.

"When did this happen?"

"I've had it in my eye for some time. Then I woke up one morning a couple of weeks ago and the rest had followed suit."

"Do you have pain?"

"No."

"If I can help you, you'll have pain. And even then, I don't know what kind of improvement you'll have."

"I've had pain my whole life," Ennis said. "I know how to deal with it. But I can't practise my profession with half my extremities out of commission."

The doctor nodded and returned behind his desk to take down some notes. "Have you been bled?"

Ennis raised the eyebrow that could be raised. "No, and I don't plan on it either. That's English medicine. I need Irish moss."

"You've had enough Irish physick, Mr. Ennis," said the doctor. "We'll bleed you here for a few minutes and see how you do. Are you his brother or his son?" he asked Hallam.

"I'm an acquaintance."

"What do you think of blood? Will you be sick?"

"I don't think so."

"What about me?" said Ennis, looking back and forth between them. "Does my opinion count here?"

"No," said Doctor Cotter, and then to Hallam, "hold his arm."

"I can hold my own lordly arm," said Ennis, and he swatted at Hallam, but the doctor gestured at the palsied one and had him hold it steady along the side of the examining bed.

"I'm sure you'd rather be lanced in the one that can't feel it." He took an armature with a curved blade and expertly opened the vein in the crook of Ennis's elbow. Ennis flinched, but only because he expected pain. He felt nothing, and after the initial puncture stared at the wound with curiosity. A dark slow blood leaked out of the opening, thick as paint. Doctor Cotter lifted the arm and put it in a receptacle made for the procedure, and Ennis's blood ran down either side of the cut, collecting in the black hair of his forearm, and finally drip-

ping into the porcelain tray, as slow as molasses from a
tap.

The doctor marked the running blood and listened
again to Mr. Ennis's chest, then tucked the earpieces of
his stethoscope back into the pocket of his gown. "That
you will die is more or less a certainty," he said.

"I can make the same diagnosis of you, sir," said
Ennis.

"I'm a man of almost seventy, however, and I would
place a bet on my surviving you at, what is it? Forty?"

"I celebrated that birthday some years ago, but you're
close."

The doctor leaned forward and closely examined each
of Ennis's eyes. Hallam looked as well, unsure what to
make of his eyes beyond the obvious differences. "Do
you want to know how it will happen, or just an approx-
imation?"

"Give me the testimony entire," said Ennis. "I
embrace my fate."

The doctor's narration lasted less than a minute, and
although Ennis nodded through it, his face drained of
colour. They took him outside, respectful of his silence,
and put him in the hack. Hallam went back into Cotter's
surgery and, mentioning his late business, said that he
would prepare Mr. Ennis's physick himself. The doctor
had said *oh* at one point, making some connection to
him from a tale he'd heard going around, and perhaps it
was this that prevented him from offering to use his dis-
pensing privileges on their behalf. And so Hallam spent
the better part of two pound three at the dispensary,

buying—at nearly twice the cost it would have taken to stock it himself—bryony, guaiacum resin, and pleurisy root. He took it all in a small box and then returned to Sam Ennis and brought him back to his house in the near-dark.

The two men proceeded west along Queen Street in the hackney carriage, each in his own silence. Hallam watched the northern side of the street pass by in a drab dumb show. Shopkeepers drawing down their grates, or simply locking their doors. The sounds of the day-end carried on the slow-moving breeze, along with the scents of the street, the dust in the macadam kicked up all day by traffic, the pervasive smells of wood, of sawdust, of cut lumber and planking. The forest, so recently standing in these places and still surrounding and within the city, lay down blond and dead in the middle of it, put to civilized use, bent to human will. In his mind's eye, Hallam imagined a pantomime in which the trees shed their barks, their branches, stood naked in their living wood and then fell to in long planks, stacking up and becoming houses, becoming doors and countertops and cabinets and beds. The trees spun themselves to dust, distributing their parts into lathes to be transformed into newel posts and table legs. So willing, so selfless. He thought of Mr. Ennis, whose death was upon his huge body like a broadsheet on a hoarding, and wondered what people's passings lent back to the places they'd lived in. There was no similar transformation in store; their bodies would not help build the cities they'd carved out of forests, they would not rewater the rivers that had been filled with dirt. "Sometimes I think," he said, "that no one will ever know we were here, but for the damage we did."

Ennis brought his face around from his side and peered at Hallam with rimmed eyes. "We'll know. Who gives a good feck about anyone else?"

"At least you make something."

"Pictures," he said almost inaudibly. "The rich in their glory and the desperate poor in theirs."

"It's a better legacy than mine."

He looked over and put a hand on Hallam's shoulder. "Keep the finer points of my condition from Mrs. Rowe, please. She has no need to know."

"She'll ask."

"Tell her nothing can kill me. She'll laugh at that."

Back at his shoddy little house, Ennis limped inside, refusing Hallam's aid, and collapsed on his pallet. His weight on it sent up a sour odour. In the winter months, Ennis did not smell as strong as he did now, with the spring air an ideal vehicle for the scents of disease and uncleanliness. Hallam sorely wanted to get out and go home to face Mrs. Rowe's impatient questioning, but he had first to administer the guaiaci and it would take preparation. "I'll open a window so you have some fresh air."

"The authorities disagree on fresh air," he said, wheezing on his back.

"You've just had plenty, so a little more won't hurt you."

"I've heard that there is a particulate in air that can lodge in your lungs and kill you. And that it is out there all the time hunting for victims."

"I think it depends on a person's constitution," Hallam said. "But you are right, there are plenty of things we can't see that we encounter daily and could make us quite ill. That we wander around in such air, and touching unclean surfaces like doorknobs and other people's hands, it's a wonder we don't die ten times over every afternoon. We must be doing something right."

"Some of us are." The air was clearing the closeness in the room as Hallam made up a half gill of guaiacum syrup. "I'll have a pipe before you indoctrinate me with your witchcraft."

"Go ahead," Hallam said. "It'll restore your nerves."

Ennis's pleasure in his pipe bought the apothecary a few minutes of quiet, in which he could concentrate on quantities and processes. It was amazing to him that a mere three months away from the only profession he'd ever had was enough to render his fingers thick and useless. He had no formulary with him, and had to rely on dim memory to remind him how much resin to dissolve in the gum arabic, what colour indicated the correct potency, how much of the mother-water to incorporate back into the syrup.

His attention, directed as it was to his hands, did not at first detect the sweet odour of the opium paste with which Ennis had doctored his tobacco, but when he smelled it he spun around and leaned over to pluck it out of Ennis's mouth. "I won't have you speeding your end along while I'm over here trying to delay it."

"It's a painkiller," he said.

"You said you don't have pain."

"See?"

Hallam took up the tray with his preparations on it and drew the only chair over to Ennis's bedside. "I'm paying for your recovery, Mr. Ennis, because I feel bound to. But I won't do it if you plan on counteracting my good physick with your bad drugs. Do you understand?"

"So I'm to have no pleasures?"

"Will you settle for the pleasure of being alive?"

"With you as my nurse?"

"You can be reassured that under my care you're safe, Mr. Ennis. Could you extend that guarantee to all who have passed under your thumb?"

Ennis regarded him with frank wonder. "A man with your imagination should have been writing romances, Mr. Hallam. Not even in my most sinful dreams have I done the kind of evil you think me capable of. But fine, so I am a dark soul. Why come to my aid, then?"

"At Mrs. Rowe's behest."

"Ah, that unsullied creature." Hallam didn't reply, setting out his medicines. "So where are all the women carrying my spawn, Jem? Lurching about the back alleys crouching over their birthing pans? Or, or, the dead-eyed supplicants queuing at my door, ready to trade their mortal souls for a picture of themselves? Surely in my rapaciousness, I'd be running my dirty thumb down the shank of some ten-year-old, even as you brought me back to health."

"Do you want me to go?"

"No. I want you to tell me where are my victims, Mr. Hallam."

"Am I not one of them?"

This caused the jolly look on his face to fade. "I never touched Mrs. Rowe with anything but my eye. Or any of the others. I was a young Jem Hallam myself, a married man come to a new world to make his name for his loved ones, to set up a doorstoop and light a fire, and I failed as well. I have a wife in Kerry, Jem, and four children, and all I want is to go home. And if that means a bare loin in here to quench the market for such things, then so be it. It will pay my passage home and I can't see what business of yours it is."

"You're not married."

"With four littlies, Mr. Hallam: Peter, Ceiran, Martina, and Sèan. Eight, ten, fourteen, and seventeen."

"Then in their name, how can you do what you do in here? Hopping yourself up, your door wide open to whores?"

"I NEVER TOUCH 'EM!" he fairly roared, and his voice died at the end of it. He lay on his bed, panting. "And I live alone, Jem Hallam; you've got nothing to say to me. Give me my medicine and you can take your lectures home."

"I won't do anything for you," Hallam said, and he stopped what he was doing. "You're poison, and you're an addict. There's no percentage in you."

Ennis hoisted himself up to sitting, groaning like a rusty bellows, and with further effort pushed to standing, his great form tottering in the air. To Hallam, his weakness was awesome to see, but he proceeded to the cupboard above his sink and from within brought out a small wooden box such as was used to keep butter in. His breath was coming ragged and raw and with one big hand he scrabbled out the contents of the box and hurled them at his unwilling saviour. Hallam had the impression of a book missing its boards, but instantly it burst apart: envelopes and papers, a scatter like a flock of birds suddenly put to air, that fluttered to the dirty floor. The two men stood facing each other, Ennis supporting himself against the dry sink. He nodded upward with his chin, too winded to speak. Embarrassed, Hallam leaned down and scraped up a couple of the bits of paper from the floor. He saw the same handwriting everywhere: a salutation: *Dear Sam*, words here and there with place names, weather, the names he'd spoken: *Peter*, *Martina*, and as if to brand Hallam's eyes, a drawing in pencil of a man on a winged horse, a child's effort: the horse had three legs and no tail.

He took the box from Ennis's hand and carefully replaced its contents, gently shaking out the letters that were covered in grit. Hallam moved them out of his direct line of vision, so he would not see again any of the private words of love and sorrow that came from home. He stacked them carefully in the box. "They're out of order, I'm sure."

"Now you know my real sin."

"What is that," said Hallam quietly.

"That I convert my coins to paper at the going rate, and mail it off to home, where Brianna converts it back to coin—at the going rate, mind—and she writes letters on paper she buys with that money, and buys postage and converts my meagre earnings into messages she sends back. To keep me company here. Have you ever known such a rich cold city as this, Mr. Hallam? That a man with my love of life should be dying alone without so much as conversation or someone to lift a yard with? I send my pennies home and beg my wife to give me the time of day."

Hallam went to take his arm, which Ennis thrashed off.

"This place has made me mean," said Hallam.

Ennis went and sat in his chair. "You're not entirely wrong. I *am* an addict."

"So am I. I can't sleep without my preparations."

Ennis nodded, lost in himself. What could be worse than being accused of criminality, Hallam imagined, but being forced to think of what you are, what you've become. It was like this for Hallam now as well, and this realization shocked him, with its reminder of how long he must already have been here to get like this. He thought, *Mr. Ennis's palsy is nothing compared to our underlying condition, that* systema *of unhappiness that makes all thoughts of joy afflicting to think of.* It would be the pipe for him before long, he thought. His careful plans were not yet at an end, but looking at Samuel Ennis, he saw that they would be.

"I give up," Hallam said. "I surrender."

"To what."

"To this." He swept his hand through the air, taking in all of their present reality. "The only way you, and I, and Mrs. Rowe will survive is if we throw in our lots together. There's no point in pretending any longer. Between the three of us, we have one means of making a living, so we should accept that."

Ennis contemplated his guest. "Are we to open a grocery stall, Mr. Hallam? With me wheezing over the rice and knocking cantaloupes?"

"No. You will train Mrs. Rowe and myself in the operation of your equipment. We will all share your knowledge and then we'll figure out what to do with it. We'll combine forces. We'll look out for one another."

Ennis laughed. "And I suppose Mrs. Rowe is at home this very moment knitting another curtain to divide your commodious rooms in three?"

"No, Mr. Ennis. There's hardly room for the two of us there. I'd have to bed you on my countertop, and that won't do."

"No it won't," he said. Hallam helped him back into his bed and formed the two pills Ennis would have to take before retiring. His expression had not changed much from that look of perplexed wonder he wore when the argument had ended. *I will be a better man now*, Hallam thought. *I shall be a good man in the realm where such goodness can make a difference to those whose lives are joined to mine.*

What stood now in this place as home, as family, was all he had.

*Five*

~

# THE WORLD BELOW

~

*Toronto, November 1997*

I.

IT WAS COOL AFTER DAWN, EVEN ON THIS DAY AT THE height of summer, and John thought, *Here is the hidden nature of the world: it holds back until you're looking.* He got into the car in the almost-dark and crossed the city to David and Marianne's house. The streets were empty except for a few cars and one or two pedestrians.

When later he thought of the morning, he'd realize he had no memory of being alone in the car, in those last minutes approaching the Hollis house. Perhaps he'd daydreamed, made logy by fear, but more likely the tail of some thought had appeared and then vanished, leaving no trace of itself. Because he remembered getting into the car and then, in the next instant he was at the top of the Bayview Extension and David was beside him, his hands folded in his lap. For a moment, before the road dipped down into the valley, John had seen the lake. The windows were down and the last of the wet night air rushed through the car, and David breathed in great drafts of it as if it tasted of something.

MICHAEL REDHILL

"They did nothing down here for eighty years but make bricks," he said. "Half the houses south of Eglinton began their lives in kilns beside the river. Do you know what it smelled like?"

John shook his head.

"Some people thought bread—that it smelled like bread."

"Was that in your photographer's diary?" He kept his eyes forward.

"No. Not that I recall," said David.

They passed under the Bloor Street Viaduct, and the moment it was behind them, John heard a train rattle onto the undercarriage of the bridge. It was always something to be in the dark underground and then burst into light over the valley and the roads. From the windows of a sub-way train, the full denuding of the river and its wetlands below bore in on you: the roads on either side of the thin waterway rhymed with the paths cut through trees that had once been used by industry, now reclaimed by hikers and bicyclists. There were defunct train tracks down there as well, and he wondered who apart from David could picture the sound and smoke that must have choked the place once, except that he himself could now. John had listened to all of the stories, and there was never a single time present for him in Toronto anymore. After today, he would smell bread in the Don River Valley.

David said, "They never regarded this as pretty, you know. The river and the trees. A tree was an obstacle or a table, and a river was something wild that could do your work for you. The idea of a nice Sunday walk was not an amble in the woods. This here"—he tapped the window with his ring-finger— "this was the factory floor." They had come out onto the flat that ran down against the side of the river. These days, people kept tents in the trees and hung their laundry there; in the winter, you'd see flashes of colour through the branches. "There hasn't been a salmon in the Don since 1920."

He'd slowed the car to give David time. Time to look around and see the place behind which everything that mattered to him flickered. Almost everything David told him John already knew, but hearing it the same way twice reaffirmed the presence of that world. Now David was telling him (again) that the land they were on had been built of garbage. All through the end of the previous century, they'd trucked soil and stone and unwanted building materials down past Front Street and dumped it into the lake, and the city had pushed forward onto it, as if it were walking onto a bridge as it was being built.

"The city grew by five hundred metres," John said. "Right?"

"About that. Maybe closer to seven hundred."

"Why do you think, in all the time your guy was in Toronto after his boat went down, did he not find some way to get that box out of the lake? I mean, the wreck must have been sitting there in the harbour. How deep could it have been?"

"Impossible to know how deep it was," said David. John took his eyes off the road long enough to look at Bridget's father—his eyes were bright, as if his face had been overexposed in some chemical bath, and of course they had been: the medicine that flowed through David's veins could probably change your name.

"Maybe he was lying," said John. "Maybe there were no pictures. Or boat. Maybe there was no man, even."

"There was a boat, John. You traced it in the records for me."

"I know."

They came out onto Lakeshore. A hulking black Russian ship was taking on sugar at the bottom of Yonge Street. They were driving now over the old wharves; the splintered remains were mixed in with crushed stone and old planking that lay under this part of the city. The Jarvis, Brown's, and Evan's wharves— these places where almost everything the city had worn or eaten or survived had landed. Brown's Wharf was where the *Commodore Walker* had been swamped by the worst storm in a century—so violent, it had severed the harbour's ancient peninsula and created the Toronto Islands. All of it, all of this unquestionable fact, swam through John's mind.

"If you want to ask me a question, you should ask it," said David at last.

"Will you let me take you home?"

"I don't think that was the question."

"If you come home, I'll take it as your answer."

David shifted in his seat. He had to use both hands to push himself upright against the seat back. "I'm not ashamed of myself, John. Or anything I've done. You can't be direct with people if there's something important you want them to understand. If you say to them, *There is something here of great value*, they will stare at you until you produce it, and then they will wait for you to name it and catalogue it and square it away for them. But if you say, *I believe there may be something here*, then there is a chance, however faint, that they will want to look to it for themselves . . ."

"So there's no diary. Just say that to me."

"There is a vast part of this city with mouths buried in it, John. Mouths capable of speaking to us. But we stop them up with concrete and build over them and whatever it is they wanted to say gets whispered down empty alleys and turns into wind. People need to be given a reason to listen."

John swung the car across the opposite lane and stabbed it into the curb facing the wrong way. A cold wave had passed over his scalp. They were now at the base of the Harbour Light Hotel. A path beside the hotel led to the lake and the ferry docks. "You've given them a reason to care even less. That's what your legacy is going to be, David. A lie in an empty hole."

"They're going to find something there. And it will matter to them simply because they chose to look. Something different but worthwhile."

John stared out the windshield at the road curving along the lake. He'd had the instinct, even as a small child, that the world may be made up of things you cannot see, people who are gone, knowledge you may not speak of. And if that was most of it, then the day-to-day was just skipping along on the surface of an accord, an agreement about time and place.

He had his hand on the seat-belt catch, but he moved it to the door and pushed the lock button, not taking his eyes off the middle distance. "Let me take you back to Marianne. Please."

David unlocked the car from his side and pushed the door open. He said, "Don't get out," and a moment later John felt David's hand, light against his face.

## 2.

THE HOTEL DOORMAN STOOD AT HIS POST, THE PANE of glass a cold white flare. Marianne pushed through into the light, John behind her. He nodded at the man in his uniform, in league, as ever, with the fallen world of helpers. Marianne's wide back blocked out the sun beyond her, a late fall sun with a hint of the last of the good weather in it. The sweet leaf-rotted air was disorienting, its crispness so unlike the stale air of the room. She stood in it, not moving, and John thought she'd suffered a sudden return to her senses. He even prepared himself to give solace, to answer *what am I thinking?* with solicitous murmurs. They'd go back to the room and he'd help her pack it up. But then she pushed on, crossing as the light turned yellow, as ever a woman out of phase with the rest of the world.

"Wait up," he said.

"Keep up."

"Where is it you're going? The site is huge."

"I'll start with the closest gate," she said. He imagined tugging on an invisible leash to haul her in. If she showed up at the site and started flinging commands left and right, they'd have the cops on her instantly. At the very least, he should be able to control her most immediate impulses. This was a talent he'd never developed with Bridget, who wore her impulse receptors on the outside where they could be activated by passing breezes.

"Marianne? We should plan what we're going to say."

"We're going to ask them why they've stopped the excavation."

"Why should they tell us anything? It's a private site, they can do whatever they like—please wait for a moment."

She stopped short and almost seemed to recoil backwards. The hem of her coat swirled around her legs. "Look, this is what I've been waiting for, for two weeks in that stinking room."

"A few more minutes won't make a difference."

"They promised to act responsibly if anything of interest came up; the dig got delayed for two months while citizens' groups got them to agree to a code of conduct."

"You don't really think that means anything, do you?"

"It better."

People crossing with the green light passed on either side of them. His mind sidestepped the problem of the moment and saw through the eyes of others that a young man was arguing with his mother. "Listen," he said, bringing his attention back to Marianne, "just think—if we go over there and give them any clue that we're interested in whatever that thing is, they'll shut the whole place up and start digging double time. We have to be curious bystanders." Two little girls, twins in white coats, drifted past them like falling stars.

Marianne dismissed his concerns with a wave of the hand.

The night before they'd watched the two workers track around the object with flashlights and it immediately had confirmed for her that this was the beginning of the truth appearing, this was the utterance she'd waited for. They stood in the windows watching, but nothing had happened. After another hour, the woman who'd been operating the backhoe switched off the machine's headlights and she and her partner trudged back to one of the two trailers at the edge of the site. They both emerged without their hard hats and reflective pinnies and went out through the gate, and as the next shift started no one went near the stilled backhoe or approached the object in the dirt. Marianne told John he should go home, that nothing would happen until the main superintendent came in at eight or nine the following morning, and they could wait until then. She would not agree to call the historical society first: she wanted control, wanted to be the first one to speak her terms so that even if some group took over the investigation of the object, her desires would be on record.

As midnight came and went, they stared down at the edge of the object as moonlight played over it, picked it out like the rim of a huge cup and gave it a dull glow. Marianne muttered, "My God," and shook her head with slow wonder. "That's really it."

She continued toward the Lakeshore gate, walking past the huge hockey greats rendered in unlikely pastels. At street level, the whole construction site was much larger, like a walled city. Even the gate was not a simple opening: there were two walkways on either side of a large steel-post door reinforced with fencing, and a man stood beside a windowed box signing people and trucks in and out. Even approaching at the tightest angle to the wall, they could not see the southwestern corner of the excavation, although John marked that none of the motion on the site was directed over there. Little meshed windows were cut into the wall every fifteen feet or so, and he peered through them in passing, seeing busy tableaux beyond, the moonscape of digging and scraping, machines scattered purposefully, the perspective changing in each cut-out.

Looking through holes in other construction walls over the years, John had had the thought that buildings seemed to emerge out of a process of discontinuous specialties. In all the buildings he'd watched go up, the likelihood of a finished structure with working electrical outlets and stairs that led to the right floors always seemed like a stroke of luck. How could the guy with the nail gun on ground level be making the same building as the guy sixty feet away and two floors up pulling a pallet of glass through a gaping hole? And where was all the paper, all the maps and instructions telling everyone step by step, diagram by diagram, what to do? He'd thought of the time-lapse film he'd once seen of a dead fish being eaten clean to the bone by bugs: that film in reverse—

bone fulfilled with muscle and flesh—was how the making of a building appeared to him. Fanciful. Impossible.

They were at the gate. "We're just curious citizens," John whispered urgently to her. "We're only going to get one first chance here, Marianne."

"I'm doing the talking," she replied.

They waited as a worker handed a clipboard to drivers and walk-throughs, checked ID cards, and issued stickers. He was in his late thirties, but he wore braces on his teeth. John wondered if the company had posted him here for maximum humiliation. Neither John nor Marianne seemed in the least official, so the man ignored them. Finally, Marianne stepped right up to the vehicle gate and looked through. "Can I help you?" he said.

"Yes." She stepped back. "My husband's in there. He left his cellphone at home."

The gateman inspected his clipboard. "What shift is he? What's his name?"

"He's actually doing an inspection. He's a representative of one of the rights-holders' groups and he's supposed to call in some specs, but I have his cellphone. Well, John here has it." She shot him a look, and John jiggled his empty hand in his coat pocket.

"He has a name, though?"

"Daniel Hass. He's with Hass, Logan, and Munny." It was not safe to be around an inventive person; John knew this about himself and perhaps he even already knew it about Marianne, but it surprised him unpleasantly. Marianne had leaned in and was speaking quietly to the gateman. "His visit is supposed to be under the radar, if you know what I mean. I'll just go in and give it to him."

"He still had to check in." The guy was flipping pages, going back and forth between two to see if the name popped out at him. "Closest I got here is Danny Ng, but he's a crane operator."

"That's probably him."

He closed the clipboard pages and stared at Marianne. They weren't going anywhere, and now if they showed their faces here again, someone in one of the trailers with a gun in his belt would be getting a call. "Your husband shows up incognito at construction sites pretending to be a Chinaman, huh? What's he do, squint?"

"Do you see any cranes on the site yet, young man? Why would there be a crane operator showing up to work when there's nothing to be lifted or laid? Explain that."

"I don't know, ma'am, but if you want to leave your husband's cell with me, I'll make sure Mr. Ng gets it on a break. How's that." He'd crossed his arms now, and would unleash his best language pretty soon. John had stopped listening. Instead, he stared despairingly through the gate at the measured chaos beyond. Most of the work was still dirt disposal, but there were a few men going around with cables or long iron shafts. Things were going to be put in their right places, in preparation for the pour. They'd lay a gridwork of shafting through concrete posts first, then pour the foundation, flowing it through the grid for interior stability. Everything moved at an easy pace, despite the deadlines and a late start. It came to him that this was just one hole of many hundreds these men and women would make and fill in their life-times. What was here or not here would never matter much, or for long, to them. The appearance of a strange hunk of wood had no weight at all: uncovered and filled in, it was so much waste no matter its shape. He and Marianne were the only people who cared at all about this insignificant thing buried in the ground.

Marianne had crossed her arms now as well, full engagement with the enemy. How many times had he seen her like this at the Hollis house, mad at someone and puffed up like a goalie. She could be immovable if she wished to be, but the gatekeeper was having none of it, this woman was staying out. It was bullshit that there was any kind of expert disguised as an Asian taking notes somewhere on the grounds anyway; he'd know. But he'd also seen this type before. She wasn't going anywhere unless she won something. This talent he had, for running the right kind of interference, was surely why he was at the gate, not because his dental hardware would make him a laughingstock. He switched on his walkie-talkie and murmured something into it. The thing cleared its throat at him. He showed them his back and talked quietly, listening to the squawky replies. John watched the man give a good show—nodding, protesting, acquiescing—but he was sure that he was talking to static.

"The super says he's expecting a walk-through later today, not this morning. So maybe you got your husband's schedule mixed up. He's probably at home right now wondering where he left his cellphone."

Marianne nodded. "I think your super's wrong."

"Yeah, he wasn't sure," said the gateman. "He told me to give you his card and you could call in if you liked."

The night before, John had got back to the apartment well after midnight, his mind pulsing with the image of the bone-coloured shape in the dirt. Bridget was asleep, the sound of her long breaths intermingled with the dog's. He was cold, and he unwrapped a log to put in the fireplace and sat on the futon-couch waiting for it to catch and glow. After a while, it started to burn with that slight odour of creosote that he had come to like: it reminded him of lovemaking. The little store-bought logs would burn for the better part of a night, and the scent of their bodies and the fire was a uniquely private thing to him.

Bailey came out of the bedroom and stretched her front legs, then stood at his feet, shaking her rear end. The constancy of dogs. He patted the couch and she leapt up, turned around twice, and settled against his leg on her side. He put a hand down and held her ribs and belly.

When they'd first taken the apartment, the dog had urinated in all its corners and they'd discussed getting rid of her. A good rug her parents had given them was another of Bailey's favourite spots and now the tassels at one end had been stained a stiff yellow and would not come clean no matter the effort. But it was the dog that had actually brought them together, one afternoon in a park (how many times had they told the story entitled "The Dog Introduced Us"?), and sending her away would have felt like daring the gods. That first sense of permanence.

Choosing the hard path meant, to him, that they could weather a lot. They could deal with her mother's truculence toward him, her father's illness, his own general sense of homelessness, which intensified even as he appeared to all their friends as more settled than he'd ever been. A job, a girlfriend, a home, a real life in the making . . .

Even so, he couldn't ignore a sensation of restlessness that had possessed him since David's death. He went back endlessly to the image of the man making his slow, deliberate way to the turnstiles at the docks, fishing clumsily in his back pocket for his wallet. Why was it that of all the moments of that strange morning, it was witnessing David following the rules of common commerce that stayed with him, that wounded him? That he'd had to pay to get onto the ferry where he'd spend his last few moments on earth . . . shouldn't that trip have been free? John felt he should have gotten out of the car, even if he'd been told not to. Either dragged David back against his will or gotten on the boat with him. Why pretend that he was not a full accomplice, no matter the outcome? Not having followed David in reality, John found he was following him now in a waking dream of that morning that went on and on. He was on the boat, ceaselessly. Looking over into the blue-black water and thinking about what was down there now.

In the last few weeks, his distraction had finally breached Bridget's force field. "Where are you right now?" she'd asked him.

"You want latitude and longitude?"

"Just a planet will do."

To these anxious questionings he'd reply by pulling her closer, or laughing, or turning it somehow back on her, but privately his blood would go surging in his chest.

And where were they when this had happened most recently? It might have been last weekend. Her hair blowing across her brown eyes. A little tin cup of gelato in front of her. Their coats still on even though they were sitting inside. "Are you angry with me?" she asked.

"I'm furious," he said, smiling broadly.

"The new John Lewis." She tilted the melting remains of her ice cream into her mouth. "Inscrutable and entertaining all at once. Should I get used to it?"

*Yes*, he thought now, his hand on the dog's belly, his fingers moving gently up and down with her breath. *Whatever "it" was, they might both have to get used to it.*

He heard Bridget throw off the covers and pad out of the bedroom. Her eyes were shadowed; she was asleep. He'd seen her do this before when he'd stayed up in the kitchen reading at the table or trying to write some-thing—this was her animal self: beautiful, uncivilized. The person he'd meet for mere seconds if he woke her up too early, or on these rare midnight sleepwalks when he himself wasn't asleep. Once, before her father died, he'd followed her out and stopped her on the way back to the bedroom and kissed her, slipping his hand down the back of her pyjamas, and she'd returned his kiss deeply, never waking. Now she passed across the hall, the firelight playing against her, and went into the bathroom where she sat and peed with the door open, and then plodded back facing him, her eyes open but unseeing. The dog raised her head briefly, scenting her, then dropped it back down and he was alone again.

He fell asleep on the couch, his head slumped against the back. He woke up before sunrise with a stiff neck and drool on his cheek, and the dog was back in the other room under the covers. He went to the bed and got in, folded himself against Bridget. When he woke again, she had already left for work and the dog was stretched against his chest, her back against his ribs. The clock said 7:30—she'd risen without waking him. He could only imagine what she must have thought, going to bed alone, perhaps aware of him in the night, out there where he did not belong, then finding him insensate beside her in the morning. He got up, washed, made a coffee for himself, and brought out a sheaf of paper he'd started keeping in a junk drawer below the cutlery and the tea towels. He read the pages over and drank his coffee. He made a correction here and there, but otherwise felt that increasingly familiar trance overtake him in the presence of those words, this thing emerging from darkness. An hour passed. He was beginning to discover what Howard must once have felt: something blossoming under his hands. And a sense of betrayal, as he turned his attention away from the world he supposedly lived in.

He was back at the hotel by ten. "You're late," said Marianne, taking her coat off the back of the door and bodying him out into the hallway. "Let's get down there." He went and pushed the button for the elevator.

TORONTO'S CENTRAL REFERENCE LIBRARY HAD BEEN built during a dark moment in the civic architecture. Made of red brick and glass on a design that seemed to be dreaming of cinder block, the structure rose on its street corner in ever-expanding layers, like an inverted rice paddy. Whatever professional life John had had, he'd spent it in this hangar for books and he was used to it, but he hated it just the same.

Marianne was an interested amateur, which was worse than just being a hobbyist, and John had already, even before that morning, intuited that she would almost certainly and by instinct do the wrong thing. Her failure to outsmart a grown man with braces on his teeth was confirmation enough. If people with professional interests weren't involved soon, she'd lose whatever chance she had to explore what was in that pit. He went up to the main reference desk and Helene was there, as ever in her thin pink sweater, in front of the computer, staring at the screen over the tops of her glasses. She greeted him and examined his accession slips. "Howard's changing tack, is he?"

"It's not for him this time," he said. "I'm looking into a few things for someone else."

She riffled the little papers. "Shipping records and early photography . . . and council Hansard?"

"I think the subject of local heritage laws came up in the council. I just want to see what they actually said."

"Well, it's a change of pace, at least. A couple minutes, John," she said, and went back into the stacks, what the workers there called *the tombs*.

He sat down at one of the scarred wooden tables near her desk, and cast a look around at the others bent over books and papers. There was always the feeling here that those people who haunted libraries were all working together on some mysterious work of revelation that, once completed, would blow the lid clean off reality. He knew that the man sitting at the table near the back wall, Yuri, was working on something like that, a book that cross-referenced the Old Testament with the Al-Khwarizmi's arithmetics. He'd once asked the old Jew a question about the Zohar and gotten a wide-eyed lecture about opening the heavenly *guf* and letting the bad spirits drop down. "These spirits will change the nature of our rational numbers," he'd said, and John avoided him after that.

Helene brought his books and set them down lightly. One of John's searches had brought up city council Hansard for the second half of 1995, but he had no idea where in the volume he should start. The definition of an awning had been hotly debated in March, it appeared. Could a huge papier mâché nose over a door be considered an awning? Yes, it could. He lifted about five pounds of pages and pushed them over. In July, it was determined that there would be a public competition to name a new park to be built on Augusta Street in Kensington Market. He'd been down that street many times and couldn't picture a park at all. The books contained all the minutiae of the day-to-day workings of the city, but there was nothing, as far as he could tell, that could predict the fate of a boat lying in the ground.

He pushed the book away and drew a history of photography toward him. In the period David had been interested in, they'd figured out how to print a photograph on just about anything. Pictures could be taken quickly, and the chemicals weren't as deadly—the previous chapter had described men dying of mercury poisoning, and pariah photographists with hands and mouths turned blue from silver. A small outfit, or even a single man, could have photographed an entire city—David's monograph hadn't been far-fetched on that account—but the likelihood that the man would have shipped his glass plates anywhere, never mind England, was laughable. The plates were expensive, fragile, and reusable, and a person could easily get a thick stack of paper positives out of one glass negative. If David's diarist had existed, his entire portfolio would have fit into a large envelope. It was a detail no one—not even David's academic tormentors—had caught, and seeing it himself made John feel that he held David's fate in his hands.

He stretched his neck, feeling utterly lost. He should have gone to the historical board, or right to city hall, but he was worried he'd somehow set something in motion that Marianne would murder him for. His eyes caught an older man's across the table. John had never seen him before and he gave him what he hoped was not a pained smile.

"1995, huh?" said the man. "They lost their minds in October."

"Oh yeah?"

"Bike paths. For a few days there it sounds like punches were going to fly." The man scanned the spines of the four volumes. "You don't have October."

"No," said John. "I'm not sure I need it."

"What is it you're seeking?"

John flipped randomly, hoping somehow an answer would appear, but the page he turned to presented only a swarm of numbered subparagraphs, and the word *WHEREAS*, which appeared boldly here and there. "I don't know how to describe it," he said.

"Maybe you have the wrong years?"

"You don't know how right you are."

The man half-stood and tilted his head so he could read what was in front of John. "Disposal's a huge issue," he said. "That what you want?"

The page John had turned to was concerned about subcontracting for waste disposal. Suddenly he remembered the mayor on television talking about barges carrying trash across the lake. "No," he said. "I'm actually interested in . . . I don't know what you'd call it. Local archaeology."

"Ah!" The man retracted into his chair. His exclamation was judged too exuberant by a woman one table over and she gave him a forceful little *shh*. He lowered his voice. "So old liniment bottles, that sort of thing."

"Maybe," said John. He leaned on his forearms. "Like, for instance, what happens if you decide to build a new concert hall or something, and while you're digging the hole, you find, like, an old statue or something? What happens?"

"You dig faster and hope nobody noticed it."

"What's supposed to happen?"

The man glanced over at the woman behind his desk. "Is this what you asked Helene for and she gave you orders in council for 1995?"

"One of the things."

"Maybe's she's in on it."

"What?"

The man got up and strode to the stacks facing the table area. He ran his finger down a list of subjects posted on a shelf end, moved to his left, read another list, and then confidently disappeared between two rows of shelves. When the man stood, John noticed ink streaks on his pant legs. He waited for him at the end of the row and shortly he returned with a slender unmarked book bound in red boards. "Anyway," the man said, handing John the book, "it's not even up to the city. This is the Heritage Act—it's a provincial bill. It sets out what's protected in the province, whether it's on provincial, municipal, or private property. If you want to know the truth, it's a toothless bill and most of it's about how many appeals you get if you *really, really* want to tear something down. March of progress and all that, good luck if you're an Indian burial ground or a nice old house standing on some expensive dirt."

Now patrons in the carrels near the half-wall overlooking the atrium were casting glances their way. "How do you know all this?" John asked.

"I'm a regular."

John nodded. "I've never seen you here."

The man leaned in toward him. "I'm going to run for mayor," he whispered.

John nodded. "*Okay*. But now let's say this thing's a boat," he said. "Something that was originally in the lake."

"You found one? That's good—if it's in the water—"

"What if it's in the ground?"

The man pulled his head back, confused. "In the ground?" He thought about it for a minute. "If it's wooden and still in one piece then it's probably too new to be of interest, and if it's old it's probably too rotten to be of use. Now, if you found a German U-boat, then you could probably get someone to take a gander. You got a U-boat?"

"No," said John. "I don't even know what it is. But I guess—from what you're saying—that an old wooden boat would probably not be enough to get work stopped on a construction site."

"I doubt a four-foot piece of the True Cross would be enough to stop work on a site in this city. You find a three-week-old potato chip in Montreal, they raise a velvet rope around it and have a minute of silence. But here, no. If you're hoping for a work stoppage, you'll need a lawyer." He waved the Heritage Act in the air. "This thing doesn't make any noise without a mouthpiece attached to it."

"I get it." He looked down at the thin red book. "Um, what is it, exactly, that Helene's *in* on?"

"Helene?"

"You said she was 'in' on something."

"Who's Helene?"

John nodded without looking up at the man again. "Okay," he said. "Thanks for your help." Libraries and madhouses. He walked away. He knew a lawyer, but he was pretty sure she wouldn't be happy to volunteer her services. As he descended the carpeted stairs, the capsule elevators across the atrium rode the rails in the wall like two pills sliding down a huge throat.

Mail in her mouth, cloth bag under one arm, and a knee up against the door, Bridget keyed the lock to the apartment and pushed in. He could see from her instant turning toward the bedroom that she'd expected to arrive home to empty rooms, and John stood in the kitchen, stirring a pot of sauce as quietly as he could, hoping she wouldn't jump out of her skin. He heard her singsong greeting to the dog—*Where's my little girl? How come you didn't come out?*—and he thought to himself, *Because Dad's been home for an hour and all is well with her world*. He dinged the side of the pot quietly and she called out from the room, "Hello?" with just an edge of fear in her voice.

"It's me," he said. She stepped into the hall that led to the kitchen. "I guess you weren't expecting me."

"The past week or so I seem to be living here alone." She went back into the bedroom. "I did your laundry."

"I made you supper."

"I guess we're even."

She came and kissed him, but the tone of her voice told him his endless day wouldn't be over anytime soon. After the morning spent trying to rein in Marianne, and the afternoon at the library, he felt that nothing would have pleased him more than to simply board something bound for any other place. But instead he'd collected the makings for dinner and come home. Bridget went and changed into jeans and a white T-shirt, then stood beside the fridge with her hands tucked into her back pockets.

"So, what's the special occasion?"

"It's just supper."

"Well, now I don't believe you."

She sat down and he went back to his burners. He poured the pasta from the colander into the pot of sauce and kept the heat on it. Ghosts of her cooking flocking near—she'd taught him to let the pasta cook in its sauce.

"Knife on the right," she said. He looked over his shoulder and she was shifting cutlery around. "You're still a bachelor in the kitchen after all these years."

"And the plates?"

"Those are fine. But we have proper spaghetti bowls, you know."

He brought the pot over and dished them each a serving. His movements felt artificial, as if someone were directing him in a scene—a bad domestic moment from one of Howard's plays. She watched the food. "That smells good. How'd you learn to make this sauce?"

"Osmosis," he said.

She picked up her fork and paused, then tilted her chair back and got them both spoons from the drawer. "How did you spend *your* day?"

"The library."

"Something for Howard?"

"Various things."

She squinted at him. "Uh-huh. What's going on, John? You're talking like you're afraid I might actually be listening."

"I'm sorry." The pasta and the different colours on his plate struck him as too complicated. "I'll start again." She twirled a few strands of pasta onto her fork. "Can I ask you something?"

She held up her hand and displayed her engagement ring. "I already said yes, but you can ask again."

"Why haven't you gone to see your mother?"

"You want to ask me about my mother?" She lowered her hand to the table. "You were in the room when I attempted that, remember? You were the one who told me to leave her alone."

"Not permanently."

"It's been, what? Ten days?"

"You've turned your back."

"I haven't turned my back. Don't say that."

"You don't talk about her."

Bridget slowly turned some spaghetti on her fork, and he watched the strands meld together into a ball. "Just because I'm not talking about her doesn't mean she isn't on my mind. I'm not heartless."

"I'm not saying that."

"I can barely sleep these days, John. You know that."

He reached for her, put his hand on her arm, but it frightened her and she withdrew. "It's just strange to me that after that phone call you had with her, it's like she's the one who's died. You were angry at her, but you've said nothing about it since. I find that strange."

"My father is the one who's dead. My mother is something else. She's chaos. I don't need chaos right now, you know? I'm hanging on by my fingernails as it is, and if I let her, she'll pull me right through her looking glass." She let the pasta fall from her fork back onto the plate. "You have no idea what she's capable of."

"I have an idea."

"You might think you do, but you really don't."

"I do, though, Bridge."

She frowned, trying to read his tone, and then turned toward the living room, as if he'd said *don't look now* and she couldn't help herself. "Has she called again? It'd be like her to call during the day. Leave a maddening, cryptic message." She wiggled her fingertips in the air. "*Do not go gentle into that good night.* Something like that, right?"

"She hasn't called." She'd had a hopeful, amused expression on her face, but now it vanished. "But I have spoken to her."

"Oh no," she said. She closed her eyes, then stood up and her chair shot back and hit the wall. "Don't say another thing. I don't want to know."

"It would help the both of you, if you would—"

"No no no." She put her hands out in front of her as if to ward off blows. "We are not having this conversation. I am not having this conversation with you." He sat still. "You've been to the *hotel*!?"

"I understand why she's there."

"What's to *understand*, John?"

"Don't shout at me."

"This is sick."

"There's a point. You need to listen to me."

"My God, what are you doing down there with her?"

He didn't answer. It was unwise to defend himself from even the faintest suggestion of impropriety. He got up from the table. The dog rose, ready for the customary leavings. "There's nothing for you, Bailey," he said quietly, and took his and Bridget's dishes to the stove. He scraped their meals back into the pot and covered it. He thought for a moment that he should tell Bridget everything he knew—about the diary, about her father's resolve—but he realized that even if he could say it all, she wouldn't hear him. She was standing in the middle of the room, shipwrecked. "There's something down there," he said at last. "Like your dad thought there would be."

"He was guessing."

"And what if he was? And what if he was right? Isn't that better than everything they said about him? We have to talk about this, Bridget. I know I've gone about it in the wrong way, but this should matter to you."

"Of course it matters to me!" He could feel how unhappy he'd just made her, as if it were a type of weather crossing the room.

He sat back at his place and she lowered herself to the floor against the fridge. The mottling in her skin was picked up in her eyes. In some lights Bridget's face looked as though gold dust had fallen onto it. "I suppose you must be memorizing all this for Howard. I hope he'll send me tickets to opening night. I'd like to see how it ends."

"Don't be like this."

"Oh, I'm sorry, like *what?*"

"Look, Bridget, it's a boat. It's probably a boat. They've stopped working where it is, so they know it's important. But we think——"

"We."

"You have no idea how much you sound like your mother sometimes."

"Christ——"

"Listen to me. They're going to try to get around reporting it. They want to start pouring the concrete as soon as they can." She stared down at the floor. "There's probably less than a week to find out if what your father was looking for is down there."

"So go look."

"We can't get into the site. The minister of culture can put some kind of a stop-work order on the site, but someone has to write a letter." He wanted her to figure it out for herself, but she was saying nothing. "A lawyer, Bridge."

This brought her back and her eyes locked on his. "Oh my God! Is that the only reason I'm finding out about your day job *now*?"

"No. I knew I had to tell you."

"Get your own lawyer, you ghoul. I'm not the only one in town."

"You're the only one who's her daughter. You could do this for her. Then it would be for both of you."

"You made me dinner to seduce me into producing some paperwork? You must be some kind of an idiot. *I* must be some kind of an idiot. Fucking hell! I'm not going to help her, or you, prolong this. And I'm *not* bringing it into my office. There's nothing down there, and you've got no business mixing in the affairs of my family!"

"This is my family, too."

She levered herself up from the floor and drew her chair away from the wall, replacing it at the table. "And what if I was a doctor? Would I have ever heard about these assignations with my mother in a hotel room? Am I just lucky that I went to law school?"

"If you'd been a doctor, Bridget, I would've had to come right out and *ask you* to support your mother. But I thought maybe it'd be easier for you if you thought you could offer some kind of a service. Then you could show some compassion behind your own back."

She pulled her face away and blinked rapidly as if someone had waved smelling salts under her nose. "Wow," she said. "I'm marrying you."

"You still have a choice with me. But you're stuck with your mother."

"I know that. My mad mother. And my mad sister. And my dead father. I know all that. But how am I supposed to apply all this great information you're giving me?"

"You could use it to conclude that changing the way your father is remembered—even a little—is worth whatever loss of face it causes you."

"I'm not losing face." She stared at him, her eyes reddening. "Is the lake going to spit him out, John? Will he come back from the dead with fucking garlands on him? *Think*." She made pyramids out of her fingertips and pointed them beseechingly at her own mouth. "If my mother finds out my father was persecuted for no reason, she'll go berserk. She'll jump in the lake herself. Maybe she's not even aware of it, but the possibility that he was wrong and that he knew he was wrong is the only sliver of light there is for her in any of this!"

Bailey was pacing near the door to the apartment, as if aware from the tone of their voices that calling out her own need might earn her a slap. The suggestion that leaving David in error was the safest thing had never occurred to John. He was untutored enough in family dynamics that he still believed the truth was good for everyone. He got up and took the leash down from the coatrack and the dog stood on her hind legs. "I know everything I've done here is out of order," he said. "But this is a second chance for everyone. Do you think between the two of us we have the sense to know what to do with that?"

"How much of this is about us?"

"I don't know," he said.

He went down the stairs with the dog. When he got to the front door, he heard her call his name, but he went out into the street to leave her alone with her thoughts.

4.

THE NEXT DAY WAS A SUNDAY, AND JOHN WENT TO Howland Street. He had his shoulder bag with him, but there was nothing in it for Howard's use; John's library hours had lately been taken up with his other research. He let himself in and heard Elvis Costello on the stereo. *I can't change what's written on your face tonight.* He'd nursed the hope that Howard might be out running errands and that he could turn from his purpose, but his employer appeared at the top of the stairs. For the first time in many months, he was properly dressed.

"Oh," Howard said. "Do we have something? Did I forget?"

"You didn't forget anything."

"So this is a surprise visit?" His hands flopped to his sides. "Oh . . . You're quitting."

"No," said John. "Not exactly. Not that."

"Well, don't stand down there like a Jehovah's Witness, come in."

He climbed the stairs and followed Howard partway down the hall. "You're in civilian clothes," he said, and he looked at his watch. "It's not even noon yet."

"I'm working," said Howard, vanishing into the bedroom. Things smelled better. "I'm getting up now, I'm showering, dressing, and then I'm sitting down at my desk."

"You're actually writing?" said John. "That's incredible."

"Incredible means *not believable*."

"Well, it is incredible." John went into the kitchen and plugged the kettle in, listening to Howard move around in the front room.

"One scene a day. That makes it manageable."

John brought a tray into the front room, set it down on a clean surface and marvelled at what a little motivation had done. "It really looks good in here, Howard. Did you hire someone to clean?"

"No." Howard poured for both of them and John leaned down to take his cup. "So, you need money?"

"You owe me money, yes," said John. "But that isn't why I'm here. I wanted to ask you—"

"How much do I owe you?"

"Three months, plus receipts."

"Okay." He wrote a figure down on a scrap of paper that John knew would disappear before long. "So what is it then?"

John reached into the shoulder bag and took out a sheaf of paper secured with an elastic band. He unsnapped the elastic and about a hundred hand-written pages unfurled in his hand. "I want you to look at this."

Howard took the pile and hefted it in his hand. "More improvements to my play?" He laughed and John laughed, and then the both of them were laughing uncomfortably and staring at the mass of paper.

"It's something I'm writing," said John.

"*You're* writing."

"Yes."

His employer lifted some of the pages up at a corner, raised his eyebrows. His hairline shifted back half an inch. "Wow. What is this? Is it a novel?"

"No. I mean, even if it is, I'm not writing it to publish it."

"Then what?"

"It's a gift. I think." Howard was nodding, not understanding. "It's something I want to say."

"To . . . ? Who?"

"Can you read it? Tell me what you think?"

"What takes a hundred pages to say?" Howard sat down on the couch and laid the manuscript on his lap. He covered it with both hands and waited for John to sit across from him. "You really wrote all this? When, for God's sake?"

"Over the last month or so. At night, when Bridget was sleeping. Sometimes in the library."

Howard reached for his tea and brought the cup to his mouth, but abruptly put it back down on the side table. "I struggle for seven years to write a two-act play and you bang off a novel in a month in your spare time?"

"It isn't a novel."

"Right, it's a *message*."

"I need you to do this for me. I need your advice."

"Get an agent."

"*Damn it*, Howard." He'd stood, and suddenly found himself trembling. "I'm friendless now, except for you. Do you understand? You are my friend, Howard. Say you'll do this, or say you won't, but spare me your angst."

Howard remained on the couch, his hands up, warding off the surprise of John's anger. "Okay, yes. I'll read it. I'll read it tonight."

John Lewis headed back downtown, a line of deeds trailing behind him. He hoped to find Marianne still in her room. He was worried he'd have to walk the perimeter of the site calling her name as though searching for a lost cat.

The lobby was full of the same marooned-looking people, standing around with their bulky luggage or sitting in some tourist finery and eating dry snacks out of communal bowls. Hotels were purgatory—who would choose to be in one? He thought that if Marianne hadn't already been crazy when she took her room two weeks ago, she might be dancing at the brink now.

To imagine there was a time before this, when he wasn't strapped to so many outcomes. What a world that was. He could have refused, in that world, to accompany David Hollis to the docks. But David had not asked him for a favour, he'd asked him for company. And in giving his company, his attention, it felt to John that he was now permanently employed and endlessly failing to hold up his end of something. Was it to bear the truth? To bear a lie? He was a toy of the gods. Without his act at the docks he could imagine Marianne's stay here aborted, because he would never have felt the obligation to be here with her. But maybe that, also, was not true. Possibly only a failure to be born would have saved him from being wrapped up in these lives, his nonexistence the only guarantee that there would be a rapprochement between mother and daughter, that these dazed, grief-stricken weeks would, without him, turn into something to laugh about. That to-be-wished-for harmless conclusion to what might forever after have been referred to as *that adventure.* Remember when? *Oh, Mother.* Now he dreaded the clashes that were coming Marianne's—and therefore his—way: the inevitable appearance of Bridget, sniffing betrayal everywhere; encounters with officials and semi-officials; perhaps a phone call to a lower-mid-level paper-jockey with a sliver of power somewhere at Queen's Park. He felt it couldn't lead any-where but to a loss, a collapse. But it was set in motion now: the bait was in the water and Marianne would close her jaws around it until something was wrenched into the light—the truth, no matter its punishing frankness, a hook in her eye.

He'd gone to the lobby café to collect a toasted club sandwich for Marianne and an appetizer order of cala-mari for himself, and when he got to the room, she was in a hotel robe—she'd finally sent her own to be laun-dered—and clearly she hadn't slept. He hadn't regis-tered that there were curtains in room 3347 (of course there would have to be) but if he'd ever seen them, they'd faded off his mental scrim long ago. Now they were drawn, and Marianne was watching television, sitting on the corner of her bed.

He put the food containers down on the desk. A single line of late-afternoon light bisected the room where it pushed through a crack in the two west-facing curtains; it lay across Marianne's lap like a flower stem. "I brought us a late lunch," he said. "In case you hadn't eaten."

He held out the sandwich container to her and watched with some amazement as she took it without comment and began eating one of the toothpicked wedges with complete indifference. *The Young and the Restless* was on. He took the calamari to the same corner of the other bed and sat mirroring her there as he nibbled on the cooling pieces.

"I used to watch this when I came home at midday to meet the girls for lunch," she said, her voice trailing in from somewhere. "They went to school just around the corner on Robert Street, and I'd walk back from the university and put this on while I waited for them. I worked in the same building as your father—"

"Sorry?"

"In the spring," said Marianne and she turned her wan features to him. "David and I would have a picnic with the girls and then walk them back to school. And the thing is, the plot hasn't changed much at all. I'd be willing to bet this is the same story line."

He looked from her to the television, imagining distantly that wherever her mind was, its confusion was coded there on the screen. Two men were scowling handsomely at each other. "When's the last time you looked outside?" he asked her.

"Every ten minutes or so. Nothing is going on."

"Why did you close the curtains?"

"I needed some time to myself." There was a little smile on her face. "You can open them if you want."

He did, and the orange afternoon light flooded in and soaked up some of the gloom. It was almost four o'clock, daylight fading. "I think you should turn that off. Something might be happening."

She felt for the converter. "Really. Like what?"

"I've been doing some research."

"What's your hourly again?" He wondered for a moment if she could be drunk. She seemed dangerously becalmed, as if in proud possession of some terrible, confirming news.

"Are you okay?"

"I'm fine. I've been sitting alone here with the television and room service for"—she looked at her watch—"twenty-nine hours."

"You're *mad* at me?"

She got up and put her food down on the desk, wiped her hands on the robe. He saw now by the light of the desk that she'd been crying. Of all the many emotions he was not schooled in, women's tears were the most difficult. They meant something he was rarely right about. She was standing in front of him now, red gooseflesh under her eyes. "Are you with me, John?"

"Am I with you?"

"Yes. Are you with me, or are you off making plans of your own? Where were you for the rest of yesterday? Where were you this morning?"

"I didn't know I was on call."

"You're on call. You didn't get when the getting was good: you're on call." She waited a moment, then dropped her hands. "I need a shower now." She got up and went around him into the bathroom.

He followed and spoke to her through the door. "I went to the library and looked into the heritage laws. And I found a couple of things. For one, we'd need a minister. I mean, like a minister of culture." He listened to the interrupted sounds of the water coming down. "Marianne?"

"That took a day?"

"I'll wait until you're done."

The bathroom door floated open, curls of steam tufting its edge. "We'll talk now," she said. He pushed the door a little. There was pale steam on the mirror, and through it he noted that the shower curtain was an opaque yellow. He went in and looked around the tiny room, wondering where to put himself, and decided to sit on the toilet with his back to the shower. Her bathrobe was a shapeless pool of terry cloth at his feet. "Close the door. Go back to the minister."

"There may be someone else to talk to first. I called city hall and found out who—there's a man in charge of planning for the city."

"You're not talking about Jack Thomas, are you?"

"You know him?"

"I hope you have a suitcase of unmarked twenties to give him."

"I think we should go talk to him. Maybe he'll feel like being a hero. You know, good PR."

Marianne laughed. "Sure. That's the kind of fellow he is." She turned the shower off. "Before you run for your life, pass me one of the towels above the toilet." He brought one down and put it into Marianne's extended hand. "So this is my decision? To play the grieving widow?"

"Well . . ."

She pulled the curtain open. She was wrapped in the white towel, but before he could look away he saw, to his regret, that she had Bridget's small, rounded shoulders. "What else is there, John?"

"If this doesn't work, then we talk to the minister. To get what's called a 'transfer order.' It means that, for a specified period of time, the province can lay a claim on private property in order to investigate something that might fall under its protection."

"Like the *Commodore Walker*."

"Like that. But you need someone to make an official submission. A lawyer, someone like that."

"A lawyer."

"Someone in a position to—"

"I have to consult a lawyer."

"The submission has to come—"

"I'm sure you handled that brilliantly."

He lowered his head and she stepped out of the tub and leaned down in front of him to retrieve her bathrobe.

"I feel human again," she said. "How do you feel?" He lifted his leg to free the half of the robe that was tangled behind it. The towel hit the tub and the air in the room shifted as Marianne pulled the bathrobe on. He felt as if he were drowning in vague transgressions. She went out and then reappeared with an armful of clothes and stood staring at him until he understood that he had to leave.

He crossed to the north window, leaning on his elbows and feeling light-headed from the bathroom steam. Once he'd confessed a wish in himself to *give comfort* and thought it something anyone who was capable of loving could do. Never had he thought himself incapable of love—not even now—but what if only the wish to console consoled? What if there was nothing else to be done?

He looked at the site for the first time in a day. No more of the wooden object had been exposed and there was no one around it. It was as if a giant inhalation had occurred down there two nights earlier and nothing since. Nearby, the excavation was continuing and the depth of the hole was beginning to vary in places. He imagined that certain structures would go into some of the deeper holes—support beams buried under the complex, or boiler rooms. It was clear, whatever their intent down below, that they were aware that the long brownish slat they'd exposed three nights ago was something unusual. Whether out of interest or fear, they had respected it. John wondered what was being said, who was being consulted.

Marianne, in fresh clothes, was standing behind him. "So I'm guessing here that Bridget probably didn't love the idea that she was of more use as a lawyer than as my daughter."

John stood up straight behind the window. "I hadn't thought it through."

"There's something for your gravestone." The light had changed angles now and it was quieter in the room, an intimate atmosphere, disturbing. "I wish I understood how people of your generation love each other."

"Probably the same way everyone else does. With some difficulty."

"And you love Bridget."

"I don't think I can explain how I feel to you."

"I'm gathering you're not explaining yourself at home either, since you've spent the better part of two weeks lying to my daughter concerning your whereabouts. . . . Is all of this for her own good, John?"

"It was supposed to be. In part."

"How."

He ran his palm over his cheek; his hand was wet. He'd eaten only a few of the calamari and now he regretted it. His stomach roiled with grease. "Do you have any idea how angry she is?"

"At?"

"Everyone. Especially you."

"She takes one stab, over the phone, at talking to me and then she gives up. What right has she got to be mad at me?"

"That's ridiculous," he said. "Do you really think she has to be in the same room with you to have a right to be pissed off?"

"Fine. Then what is it?"

"She's not angry because you're living in a hotel. It's because you don't trust her. You won't tell her anything until it's too late. You paralyze her."

"She paralyzes herself."

"You could have told her what you were planning to do down here. Maybe she would have wanted to be a part of it. Maybe she would have wanted to understand what you were going through."

"She doesn't understand?"

"I don't think so."

"And is this an official message?" She pulled out the desk chair and spun it toward him, but she thought better of sitting, and instead rested her hand on its back. John's eyes shifted from the chair to her hand, and he understood that she didn't want him standing over her. But the gesture meant something, a kind of attention forming. He hopped up on the ledge, a space that belonged to her.

"The two of you have been alone, more or less, in the same city trying to get over the same thing. How many times have you even seen each other since the funeral?"

"People cope differently."

"This isn't coping. It doesn't strike you as strange that half of your remaining family is five kilometres away and you're alone in a hotel room?"

"*You* strike me as strange."

He leaned against the window and crossed his arms over his chest. He had the immediate feeling that he now owned the room, that he could say anything. "You try to nail me to the wall ten times a day, Marianne. But I just hear you changing the subject."

"I don't have to stay on topic with you, I'm sorry. You're not the reason I'm here."

"I don't think you know why you're here."

"And you do."

"I do," he said. "You want to prove 'them' wrong. *Those fuckers*, I think you call them."

"I am going to prove them wrong."

"I thought you were here to prove David right." Her hand moved along the back of the chair, slowly across the whole length of it as if removing a layer of dust. "If Bridget thought you were here solely out of love," he went on, "you probably wouldn't be doing this alone."

Her fingers opened and closed on the wood. "Alone would be very pleasant compared to being lectured by you."

"It's not worth the risk to anyone else."

"I think you should watch your mouth."

"Why don't you tell me what to say then, and I'll say it."

She pushed the chair in, and there was nothing between them. "I'll tell you. For one thing, you don't call *me* 'ridiculous.' And for another, you don't presume to understand the suffering of a person twice your age when you've barely lived yourself. You don't talk to me like this."

"There *is* no way to talk to you. You don't hear any-thing. Why do you think David confided in me?"

The rest of the colour drained from her face. "Get out." He remained on the ledge, watching her as she reached for the chair again, and then her body jerked and he moved his feet in time to avoid being struck. The chair ricocheted off the wall and crashed to the floor beside her bed. She stood there, breathing heavily. "I'm not defending myself to you! Get out of this room!"

"I'll go," he said. "But I'm coming back in the morning."

"Fuck you. I won't be here." She stood now with her head lowered, transforming before his eyes into her bull self. He could see the round, glowing edge of her eyes behind her brow.

"Yes you will," he said.

He didn't see her arm move, but he felt the blow to his mouth as if a third person had materialized between them and he lurched backwards, stunned. There was the smell of iron in the middle of his head. He found his balance, came forward, and put his hands up to block another blow, but there was an empty column of air in front of him. There was blood in his palm: he was cupping it out of his own mouth.

He could hear Marianne sobbing in the bathroom.

He backed up and righted the chair, sat in it, the whole expanse of the room empty in front of him. His head was clanging.

She came out into the hallway in front of the bathroom, mopping her eyes with a clump of tissue. "You hurt me," she said. "Is that something you think David wanted you to do? To do harm to me?"

"I'm bleeding, Marianne."

She went back into the bathroom and ran water. He slid his tongue over his bottom lip. It tasted like meat. It felt like everything that had brought him to this moment had been abruptly erased. She brought him a cold, wet facecloth and he sat down on the bed and pressed it against the swelling. "I'm sorry if I hurt you," he said, feeling idiotic.

"I loved my husband, John."

He spoke with the cloth against his mouth. "You loved him, but you didn't accept him."

"I was married to him. I carried two children for him. I shared a bed with him for almost forty years." She took the cloth out of his hands and looked at the deep red blot. She rinsed it and brought it back to him. "I don't know what else I should have done."

"You could have taken him at his word. You could have believed in what he believed in. Because you loved him."

"Fine. I could have. I didn't." She swallowed. "I did everything else, but I didn't do that." She sat down beside him on the bed. He felt her shoulder against his. "Okay, John? I didn't do that."

## 5.

JOHN LEWIS FELT THE SIDEWALKS OF ANOTHER CITY spreading under his feet. Leaving the hotel and wandering north into what he knew was the burial place of ancient waters made him feel insubstantial. Howard had once told him that the ancient Jews thought of all human souls as being the shattered portions of a divinity that had been destroyed by sin. The Jewish messiah, conjured by saintly action, would come and collect these fragments and remake the One-Soul. This was at least how he'd understood the sources he was reading, sources John had collected for him for some theatrical subtext Howard had long since abandoned.

Still, this oneness that had been strewn into the bodies of human beings was an idea that, at this moment, made sense to John. Except the source wasn't divinity and its many parts were not souls; to John it felt more as if he were a player in a story made up entirely of extras, each of whom had a line to speak. All the great books and legends were nothing held against this ongoing tale with no main character and no ending. He recognized now that its only action was its telling.

For once, it felt as if there was nothing he could do and no point in trying. Everything that had been set in motion was going to continue to its end now. Inevitability had an invigorating quality to it, the way touching bottom often did. It was refreshing, but painful, like a sudden hail.

The street lights came on like the whole city having an idea, and John continued north along Yonge Street. His stomach was sour. He bought a bottle of water to wash out his gut and wandered without purpose. Above Carlton, he stopped into one of the used bookshops with the dirty magazines in the back and browsed the mystery section, thinking he might find something to take to the all-night Fran's nearby. Normal-looking men drifted in and out of the restricted section, thumbing idly through the wares. No one seemed to care, so he went back as well. The silence among the men there was unique. Not even men standing at urinals were so much in their own worlds as perusers of pornography. It was a pious silence, completely at odds with the raunch on the covers—a strange form of communion.

He cycled back into the front of the shop and bought a Patricia Highsmith mystery called *The Tremor of Forgery*. *No relation to my current day job*, he thought. The back cover promised detailed descriptions of a male writer struggling in a long-distance relationship while stuck in the middle of Tunisia with an unfinished novel. It sounded sufficiently distracting.

At Fran's he ordered the mac and cheese. Comfort food. He sat in silence and read the book. He drank four cups of coffee, despite his stomach, with plenty of cream and a teaspoon of sugar in each. He had a drifting memory, his Aunt Cecilia telling him he'd get pinworms if he ate too many sweets.

The book—especially a scene about the writer finding a body outside of his hut one morning—disturbed him more than he was counting on. He went home in the full dark and slept on the couch again. He dreamt he bought an impossible camera with nothing but a slip of acetate behind a metal frame, a camera that recorded the face of anyone who held it. If you picked it up, your face would appear, salted among the many already on the acetate, and you'd see, in the picture, the other men and women who'd once held this machine, their faces now reacting to yours. As if you meant ill by joining their company.

~

When he arrived at room 3347, the door was already open. Marianne was hunched over the *Toronto Star*. She looked up when he walked in. "Hey."

"Hey."

"How's your mouth."

"It's still working, I guess." He tipped his face down to her and she touched the pad of her thumb lightly to his lower lip.

"I got you good," she said.

"It hurts."

"I guess you can't tell people you were slugged by your future mother-in-law."

*Future*, he thought. He wasn't ready to find any of it funny yet, and he turned his attention to the paper. He saw the scene from the window reflected in her lap. "What's that?"

She turned the paper toward him. A headline in the middle of the first section read HISTORY A SLAM DUNK AT UNION SITE. She twisted the paper back toward herself and read, "'Worker Inger Wolfe was the first to see what appeared to be the rib of an old boat. "It was a big surprise," said Wolfe. "Why would anyone bury a boat?" A spokesperson for Union Arena said that the item had been carefully photographed for the city before being removed.'" She held out the paper, but John was already at the window. Nothing had changed below; he could still see the cresting shape of the wooden rib exactly where it had been the night they uncovered it.

"It's still there."

"Of course it's still there."

"Why would they have told the *Star* it was already gone?"

"Why do you think?" said Marianne. "If there's nothing left to look at, then no one's going to be nosing around it, right?"

"It's not that smart to fib to the paper of record, is it?"

"It is if you can get away with it. They'll wait to see if anyone asks any questions. Then it'll be full steam ahead."

She shrugged, and he had the sense that she was ready to give up, that it had all become just a little too much, with the newspapers getting involved and minor city officials being prodded. He took the paper from her and folded it, put it on the ledge. "We have an appointment," he said. "We might as well keep it."

The cab left them at the bottom of Nathan Phillips Square on Queen Street, after a five-minute drive in which Marianne said not a word to him. They walked up through the cold white plaza toward new city hall, where Jack Thomas had his office. Two hundred metres to the east was the red-brick old city hall, downgraded now to a traffic court. It had been deemed unsuitable for the city of the sixties, which had built itself something that looked like a broken ice-cream cone with a tumour in the middle. The plaza was made up of wide, square concrete panes floating over an unseeable depth. The inch-wide cracks between the panes suggested that they were movable, that if you stood on the wrong one, you'd be sucked down into a tar pit that flowed under city hall. On one of these squares, they passed a sparrow lying on its back— it looked dead, but John thought he saw its beak yaw open. He stared at the bird, unsure if he'd seen correctly, and then startled when the hollow chest suddenly expanded in panic.

He shuddered as he entered through the heavy wooden door to the refrigerated interior. No one signed them in, and they took the sleek silver elevator to the second floor. Thomas's secretary checked them off on her schedule and then admitted them to the councillor's office to wait.

There were two chairs facing the desk, but neither John nor Marianne sat. John stood in front of the pictures on the wall—the standard ceremonial shots of oneself with higher-ups. To be pictured with a person of better standing allowed you to borrow significance, to suck power, to be Someone. It seemed to John, based on the offices he'd been in belonging to various lawyers and deans and medical specialists, that Pierre Trudeau (not to mention Bruno Gerussi and Karen Kain and Terry Fox) had been photographed, at one point or another, with half the population of Canada. Anyone without a memento of a dimly lustred Canadian celebrity truly lived off the beaten track.

"God, that's Robertson Davies," said Marianne, pointing at one of the pictures.

"Is that good or bad?" Thomas was about thirty in the picture; his famed high forehead had not yet been glossily revealed and was more or less covered in the thin furze that passed for his hair.

"It just means he paid for something," said Marianne.

"Well, I did buy the book," said Thomas from the doorway behind them. "I actually read it, too."

"Sorry." Marianne offered him her hand. "I'm Marianne Hollis."

He smiled, shaking her hand, and repeated her name.

Thomas sat them in front of the impressive wooden desk, and laid his thin arms on top of his blotter. He gestured to Marianne to speak and after glancing at John, she laid out, as calmly as she could, the bare details. The history of the area, the potential value of the find, the minimal work stoppage that would be required. John had never seen her as supplicant to anything, and the quiet performance moved him and made him sad for her. He was not sure it was having any effect on Thomas, however, who listened stonily, occasionally jotting something down. Then he stood up and raised his hands palms out, indicating to Marianne that she'd said enough. "We know all this," he said. "But here's the problem." He snapped open his briefcase and slapped the *Toronto Star* down on his desk. "The problem is the cat is out of the bag."

"It's not a secret. Probably two dozen people on that site saw it."

"It's the kind of thing the mayor would prefer not to be lectured to about." He opened the paper smartly and read from the story. "'Calls from the mayor's office were not returned. Gerald Lanze, Dean of Urban Studies at the University of Toronto, when asked to comment, said "the mayor has a sorry record when it comes to city heritage."'" Thomas closed the paper. "Unfortunately, now it has to be dealt with smartly, by which I mean *intelligently* as well as *quickly*, or they'll make hay. They'll talk about how this mayor doesn't care about the city's history."

"He doesn't."

"He does, Mrs. Hollis. But he doesn't want the pink pages to tell him what his business is. So it's too late. Union Arena won't hear from his office, and whatever that thing is, it'll be wood chips by the time the *Star* sends someone to do a follow-up. If they do a follow-up. Page A-15 doesn't speak to this being a priority for the paper."

"There are two other papers in town."

"Not for this kind of thing." He stood and held out his hand to her. They'd been in the man's office for all of seven minutes. "I'm sorry, Mrs. Hollis. I wish I had better news."

Marianne shifted in her seat. He seemed to be waiting for her, though, so she said, "It wouldn't take long to see for sure if it was something of interest. If the mayor wanted—"

Jack Thomas came around the front of the desk. Under the main light in the room, his high fontanel glowed. "Look. This city is only a hundred and fifty years old—"

"It's two hundred, actually. Two hundred and four, to be exact."

"You're right. I'm trying to make a point, though—two hundred is nothing. In just about every American city, not to mention every city and town in Europe, you know what they do when they find something two hundred years old? They toss it out. It's not that special."

"Maybe not to a place that's been there for hundreds of years. But we're talking about something that goes back to the beginning here, in *this* place, and I find it strange you aren't interested in it."

He made an understanding face. It was hard to manage the needs of a big place like a city, said the face. The face probably meant it. Thomas said, "I *am* interested in it. I am. I didn't become a city politician because it was my dream job; I did it because I feel involved in what this place is, as well as what it can be. But that means the time and energy we have as a municipal government has to be balanced and based in reality. Things have to be weighed against each other, and that site—" he stared over their heads in the general direction of the arena, as if he could see the money boiling up out of it through the walls "— that site is going to be a completed arena in *seven months*, by the middle of June, in time for the NBA draft, or the league is going to levy a twelve-million-dollar fine. And as financial guarantor, the city will have to pay at least half of that. Taxpayers' money. I know it sounds crass, but that trumps the *possibility* that there is a ship buried in that dirt."

Marianne shook her head. "You're letting a corporation tell you what to do with your own history."

"Mrs. Hollis, the city is a corporation as well. The citizens are our shareholders. And the vast majority of people in Toronto would not want to risk their investment in Union Arena for something like this. And I want to tell you: if all the little local lobby groups and environmental subcommittees hadn't delayed the groundbreaking for as long as they did, then something unexpected like this wouldn't be quite so difficult to accommodate. But as it is, three or four days of work stoppage down there could result in a hefty bill for us. I'm sorry."

Marianne rose slowly from her chair and pushed it in against the desk. "Thank you for seeing us, then," she said, without offering her hand. Thomas nodded. He disappointed people daily and he was used to it.

"What about the province?" said John.

"What about it?"

"Can't the minister of culture do something?"

"Yeah," said Thomas, already moving papers around his desk. This boy was not his problem, the widow was his problem and she was leaving. "The minister of culture can cut ribbons. He's got nothing to do with this development."

"I thought heritage issues were a provincial thing."

Thomas helicoptered a sheaf of papers into a recycling bin. "I didn't catch your name."

"John Lewis."

"John Lewis, whoever told you the minister of culture for Ontario had anything to do with a hole in the ground owned by a consortium of private businessmen told you incorrectly. Their permits are municipal, their licences are municipal, all variances are processed through city hall, and all guarantees come straight from the mayor's office. The only thing the minister of culture has to do with Union Arena is showing up on opening day, if he's lucky enough to get a ticket."

"I thought there was such a thing as a transfer order," he said. Marianne was waiting in the verge of the door with her coat over her arm.

"Come on, John," she said. Thomas waited behind his desk with a fixed smile on his face.

"Isn't there a transfer order?" John repeated.

"Like I told you," said Jack Thomas. "The provincial minister of culture has nothing whatever to do with city business."

They rode back down to the lobby in near-silence. It was midday now, and outside the wind was biting, speeding

315

up without impediment through the square. "I'm going to go and pack my things," said Marianne. "I don't want to be there when they pour the foundation."

"I'm sorry," said John.

"Don't be."

"I am, though. For everything." He made a hopeless gesture with his shoulders and she mirrored it, questioning. "For upsetting you."

"Do you know that I once would have denied you could have any effect on me. But I won't say that now."

"Then I hope you'll accept my apology."

"I will," she said, and she left it at that.

John offered to come back and help her in whatever way she wanted, but she refused his aid. She went to the cabstand and held her hand up for a ride.

The sudden emptiness of the afternoon was jarring; it felt, as John walked back through the nearly empty plaza, that his mind was bled. Where to go? He was hungry, he was thirsty, but his body felt full of something and he knew he'd change his mind the moment he chose to do anything.

He walked idly toward Bay Street and thought he would go down to Queen. His eye, however, registered movement and he realized he was seeing the form of the dying sparrow again, lying in the middle of one of the concrete panes. He went over to it and leaned down, hoping it was over now, that its earlier spasms were the last firings of a system shutting down. But then he saw its eye roving round and it spread its clawed feet and gaped silently. How could something be this nearly dead

for—what was it?—half an hour, and in all that time it
hadn't worked out this simple thing, this dying. "What is
wrong with you?" he said aloud, and the bird's skyward
eye stammered. He straightened and backed off, standing powerlessly before it. The square was as empty as it
had been before, as if no proper citizen would have truck
with the business done there. Behind him was a garbage
can; he retreated to it and fished out a sheet of newsprint,
went back to the struggling form and covered it. He took
a deep breath and stepped as heavily as he could bear to
on the faint rise, the sound of a heart in a shirt, and he
crushed it and hunched over, his eyes stinging, and vom-
ited onto the clean surface of the white plaza.

~

He walked west along Queen Street, away from the centre of town. On the northwest corner of University and
Queen sat a little building called Campbell House. It
occupied a postage stamp of grass and looked out on
nothing that had been there when its lawns had first
been laid. At some point in its past, some cherishing
landowner, now dead, had fought off the parcelling of
his little estate to an interest of some kind. Maybe a tiny
hermit's cabin on his grounds had been put forth as hal-
lowed, a place the loss of which would spell the end of
something important. That battle was lost, of course, as
so many battles to save buildings had been lost in this
city, and it was worse in all directions from that place
where a little blot of history in the form of a house still

remained. Buildings raised in the fifties thundered up in places where there were once familiar landmarks: toll booths, favourite old shops, cooperages with big working grounds under which lay the bodies of horses loved and worked to death. Brands and logos, private meeting places, corners everyone knew by nicknames, flakes of colour falling from the brickwork of a painted letter in a name on an advertisement for a cure. Voices heard from the street. A century ago, there was no past to abandon. Maybe that was better. Those citizens had only wanted to live, among their people, in places they had built for themselves.

He worried that his true way of being in the world was embodied in this disconnectedness he felt now. Other human beings had a gravitational pull, but he was not magnetized to it. It was a force that could be negated by heartsickness, and he felt that perhaps he would scatter into the higher air now, like a smoke ring. And then he had a lifting-up thought, the kind of thought that could presage despair, and in a flash he saw everyone he knew busy in the act of making, himself included. Heads down, brows knit, eyes turned away from the great dark. Making a life, making hope, creating forms to live in: houses or books or stories for telling, for passing down. To make something was good: it was an acceptable form of paying incomplete attention. A perfectly human thing. He felt what must have been real love, thinking of Marianne surrounded by her talismanic ephemera. To have been permitted into her kind of making—that was something, wasn't it? And Bridget struggling along with the everyday despite what must have seemed to her like cruelty on his part—that also was a gracious thing to show him. All this willingness to live *despite* and *without* was a thing he had never actually chosen, and he'd been watching these women struggle in it with something—it now seemed quite clear to him—that was close to grace.

He felt himself finally grieving for David. Like all the dead, he had towed behind him into that other world all his instincts, all his beliefs and plans. The pictures, or whatever was down there, were husks of something that emanated from David Hollis. John had nothing like that, no last things.

He could, if he chose to, go despite and without and find what these absences held. He could go somewhere and be on his own—think the rest of this through. David had told him the prints of the original photographic panorama were in the Foreign and Commonwealth Office in England. Those pictures, at least, existed. They were the fuse that had lit David's thinking, his dangerous thinking. It had continued to burn down in John's mind.

He'd gone another two blocks when his cellphone rang.

"Something's happening," Marianne said. "They've started again."

He imagined that Thomas had picked up the phone the moment his door closed behind them. "Are you all right?"

"It's not the same people." Her voice was different again, and he recognized that she had turned to him.

"What are they doing?"

"Digging. With little shovels. Handheld shovels."

He broke into a trot and hailed a cab and kept her on the phone as he was driven south. People were pacing things off. By the time he got to the doors of the hotel, a roll of yellow tape had been produced. "I'm in the lobby," John said, running to the elevators. A moment later he was standing in the window with Marianne Hollis, staring down at the scene she'd been describing. Two of the people down there—young women, it appeared—had begun to hammer thin wooden stakes into the ground at regular intervals around the wooden rib. They watched the women trace the outline of a rectangle around the exposed shape. One of them brought a line of jute from one stake and tied it off against the one directly opposite: the beginning of an archaeological grid.

Marianne put her hand on his shoulder, and leaned against him a little. His stomach flipped. "My God, John. Did Thomas change his mind?"

"No," he said. "He lied to us about the minister of culture. He didn't realize we'd done our research."

They stood in the window, watching. By the late afternoon, the whole area had been measured off and squared with jute, sixteen lengths of it slicing the air above the boat into one hundred squares. By five, the first two squares had been cut down, the dirt moving along a conveyor belt into a hopper, with three people on each side of it, sifting. A wonder.

Neither of them moved from their spot. At six o'clock, Bridget showed up, still in her office clothes. She took in the sight of the room calmly, shaking her head only a little, and set down on the desk the transfer order with the minister's signature on it. Then she moved to the window, and as John slipped his hand into hers, she took in her first view of the world below.

*Six*

~

# HALLAM OF TORONTO

~

*Summer 1856–Winter 1857*

## I.

THE TOP OF ENNIS'S HEAD WAS GONE.

"That's unfortunate," he said. "A poor collodion layer that time." Hallam stared at the picture, a stillborn thing unable to say its flaw or purpose. Ennis's eyes were clear in the picture and Hallam could even make out the evening's stubble on his chin. But above his eyes, his brows flared up like black smoke and vanished into featurelessness where his forehead and hair ought to have been.

"I poured it over the entire plate."

"Yes," said Ennis, "but it flowed back. It's not a science at this stage. It's an art and you need to develop a feel for it."

"I don't see how a person could make a living at this."

"It isn't gilding, Jem. As you know, the materials are relatively inexpensive."

He looked down ruefully on the malformed results of his many attempts at creating a likeness of his patron in photography. In them, Mr. Ennis appeared variously like a troll emerging from beneath a bridge, or a ghost evaporating at sunrise. Hallam's ministrations had helped Ennis somewhat (he had added a decoction of sarsaparilla to Ennis's diet of pills and gargles, and although not held in much esteem by his contemporaries in England, the decoction fairly jolted Ennis upright), but these pictures suggested the man was in final decline. Once or twice the exposure was right, but the image would not register beyond faint pinpricks, and another time the collodion was properly set but the silver was streaked and Ennis appeared in a fragmented blur, as if he were rushing past a window. Hallam found himself with nothing but second thoughts.

"They are not true likenesses," Hallam said.

Ennis coughed hard and reached for a chair. "It is hard to make a picture of me I'd send home to Mother."

"Your mother has passed on."

"One of the signal difficulties. We have a generous hour of June light left, Mr. Hallam. Shall we try again?"

Hallam prepared another plate behind the curtain. The strong smell of ether made him want to sit down. Mr. Ennis hobbled into his other room and returned with two cups of refreshment, and Hallam tried to decline but took a small draft on strong advice. Ennis had considerably watered Hallam's down with cider, which delayed its brutalizing effects. They toasted the late senior Mrs. Ennis, and then Hallam silvered his plate, put it into its holder, and slipped it into the camera. Mr. Ennis took his place below the skylight and, through the glass, Hallam made to centre him.

"Think out loud, Mr. Hallam. About the variables to consider."

He stood straight and answered in a clear voice. "The light. It's bright and direct on the subject from two sources. No extra illumination needed."

"All right. Exposure time?"

"Maybe half a minute. Focal length of ten feet. I'll set it up."

"There's one more thing."

He couldn't think of it.

"What's your frame? What are you going to put in it?"

"You. What else?"

"But what's the point of treating the camera as if it's nailed to that spot on the floor? It's not a window, Jem. Move it around." Hallam put his hands on it, as tenderly as possible, and turned it a little. "Good lord," cried Ennis.

"I don't know what you want me to do."

Ennis took his teacup out from under the chair and took a long swallow. His condition strictly proscribed drink of any kind, but this was not the right moment to broach the subject.

"The camera is *not* an eye. It's a dumb machine. The human eye is a mechanism for seeing, with the operator built right in. With the camera, the operator must be attached. The camera has no interest in anything. Your choosing what to make it see is the only human thing about it."

Hallam lifted the tripod off the ground. The whole apparatus was heavy, much more solid than an instrument of light had any business being. There was good wood in it. He held it in his hands and moved to his right, then stood it back up. In the viewfinder, the illusion of Mr. Ennis's set burst apart, and he rotated into profile as the rear of his studio room came into view, along with the jumble of newspapers in a pile by the wall, a broken cartwheel, a mirror, and the muslin curtain that led to his bedroom. "I guess this is more interesting," said Hallam.

"You guess."

"It's more like the way you'd stumble on something . . . a scene of some sort."

"Take it then."

The light was both dimmer now and more aslant than it had been when he'd made his last abomination of Mr. Ennis. But there was light reflecting off the muslin, however soiled it was, and he intuited that he would have to be careful not to expose the curtain too much lest the light burn the plate. A fair impression of Sam Ennis would take . . . twenty-five seconds? Thirty. He moved the table into position and placed the camera on top of it.

"You'll have to refocus," Ennis said. Hallam had been on the verge of ruining another plate. He got the viewing glass and focused with it, pulling the lens out and pulling it in until he supposed he had it, and then replaced the plateholder. "Are you sure?"

"I must admit—"

"You're not seeing clearly yourself." Hallam nodded. Ennis stood to demonstrate something but immediately took his seat again. "As the test is one of relative comparisons, just ensure that I am as blurred in the glass as I am when you look at me without it. Then I will be in focus."

An odd science. "All right, completely still now," Hallam said, and his subject took a deep breath and became motionless. He took the cap off the lens. "Thirty seconds is my guess," he said. "My calculation." Hallam imagined the light travelling from Mr. Ennis to the plate, and the plate drinking it in, the silver changing state, the image from the real world lodging itself in a strange permanence. He counted down the seconds, then replaced the cap as quickly as he could.

"Forty-five is what I would have said," said Mr. Ennis getting up from his seat.

"I accounted for the reflection off the curtain."

Ennis turned and took in the scene from the camera's point of view and then regarded the younger man with an equable expression. "See? A dumb machine run by a clever one."

In the exposure room, Hallam uncovered the developing tray with its acrid bath of pyrogallic acid. It was dark, like a moonless night, and the now-familiar smell of the acid rose in their nostrils. "You really need to vent this room, Mr. Ennis."

"You should have been with me five years ago when I was making my pictures on copper. This little room was a chamber of mercury fumes. This is a sea breeze compared." He choked on a laugh and Hallam felt the air crossing his face from Ennis's waving his hands in the vapours. "Anyway, it's the bromines you have to be careful of. *The angel of death*, some of my fellow picture-makers call it. You spill your bromine and you might as well rip up your floors."

"I wouldn't think there's anything in here you'd care to get too close to," said Hallam, although he was certain that Ennis had already been exposed to too much of at least one of his chemicals. On top of his pleurisy, his dropsy, and whatever undiagnosed venereal complaints Ennis already had, he'd noted the classic symptoms of mercury poisoning. When he'd seen Ennis yawn once, he noted small leukoplakias on the inside of his cheeks, red-mottled sickly white sores. And the older man's teeth were loose in his head; they frequently hurt, although knowing a chemist was a great boon to him (caraway seeds added to his pipe tobacco were an anodyne, although he preferred his other additives). His mercury symptoms had been eclipsed by his recent diagnosis, but nothing could disguise the damage his way of life was doing to him.

"There I am again," said Ennis. "Like we've come across me in a bath."

"Unlikely."

"Now, now. Once you figure out how to silver your plates the rest of this will come easily."

"And once I learn how to focus and calculate light and set up the frame and so on."

"And perhaps a few other variables." Two minutes passed slowly. Hallam had placed a wet kerchief against his mouth to filter the fumes, but it was all but useless and he'd discarded it, deciding to take his punishment like an authentic picture-maker. The Irish cider, as he'd come to think of it, was certainly helping. "Into the fixer," Ennis said, dropping the picture into the hypo and washing it with water. Then he struck a match and lit the lamp. And there, at last, he was. As Hallam had seen him in the real world. It was as if he'd spoken his name to the camera, and now here was the picture, saying it back.

"There we are," he said. "In all our glory. A little under-exposed, but we can varnish it and turn it into an ambro."

"It worked," Hallam said, either drunk or awed. "I actually made that."

"You feel the power of minor godhead, don't you?"

Hallam fished the little picture out of the glass tray and held it aslant in the light. "Remarkable," he said examining it. "Is it possible I have a talent?" Ennis laughed, but withheld his answer. Hallam marked a thread hanging out of one of his sleeves in the picture, the distinction between a grey hair and a black one on his chin; the smudge of filth under a fingernail. And his face . . . his face. "How is it that your eyes are closed?"

Ennis tilted his head at the picture. "Maybe you shook the camera."

"I was holding the camera against myself quite steadily, as you yourself showed me, and you had your head firm against the headrest, did you not?" Hallam squinted hard at the picture. His subject's closed eyes were as crisply rendered as any other part of him. "I think I am drunk," he said.

"You needed to be, clearly. You'll have to carry more liquids than the average photographist if you really wish to take this up successfully." He considered his image silently for a few more moments, slanting the plate back and forth in the light.

It had never struck Hallam before what a new world it was when you could hold a miniature version of yourself in your own hands. It was unsettling to think how civilization had crept through almost two thousand years of innovation, and only now people were suddenly able to copy themselves.

"I look like a dead man in a chair," Ennis said at last. "Maybe you will be a phenomenological picture-taker, Mr. Jem Hallam. Your subjects will sit for you in the present, and you will produce pictures of their eternities . . ."

He leaned the picture against the back wall of the exposure room and they both regarded it admiringly. "Although if that is my eternity," said Ennis, "perhaps it won't be so bad."

~

June 15, 1856

My dear Alice, my dear Cecile and Jane,

I imagine that by the time I finish this letter, it will be a lengthy one. I hope you are not daunted by it. I am making it to give you some of myself, as much as I can for now. There have been so many reversals here and it would be unkind to make you contemplate them such as you would if I dwelled too much on the details. In short, good fortune would have made me a more honest man in my reports to you, but I have rooted, it would seem, in a luck-deprived place, and many men like myself, armed commonly with expertise and hope, have not been able to overcome the difficulties to be found here.

In another letter, which I hope will arrive in time with this one, I have written to my father of the specifics, so you will not have to feel you are guarding secrets. In short, I have sold our shop and am now engaged in a photography business. It is not so low a calling as others will have you think. In France, fortunes are being made in it, and men command studios the length and breadth of dance halls with their names in carved wood hanging over the street. It has come lately to America and there is still opportunity to be a first-caser if one is quick about it, and I believe I have been. As my father has often said, the sick are never in short supply, but then there is only so much physick they can take before their health is recovered, and the privations and the growth of this city were both grossly overestimated. It does ill to have hopes for others' misfortunes, but druggists must stand by in solemn citizenhood and hope for the public to be struck low as often as possible. One hopes without lasting damage (for we need them to get sick again!), and with a recovery that makes them happy we exist.

I have never felt too much concerned with that undertaker's "interest" shown in my family's profession—it is a fact of life that people will fall ill. But I have found that short of the streets here flowing ankledeep with tepid filth, and the rain and cold crashing down day and night, and diseased vermin gnawing in all seasons within the walls of this city's houses, there could not be enough sickness here to keep the men who are bound to treat it in any form of fettle.

Photography, however, is not needed at all and appeals only to human curiosity and vanity, and, you may not be greatly surprised to learn, these qualities are in greater supply than the average catarrh! This new craft creates and sustains an interest among those who are exposed to it (and there, dear Jane, is a handsome photographist's pun for you) and a great call goes out to have likenesses made once it is shewn how inexpensive it is. You might pay a portrait-painter six pounds for a finished image of yourself, but it is possible to have a dozen identical images of anything you care for made on paper now, as small as to fit in an enclosure, or large enough to be placed in a frame and put on a mantel. Before now, making daguerreotypes was as expensive a proposition as a painting, but no more. We make pictures on glass and print them off as if they were lithographer's stones.

I can do nothing but beg you to have faith in me. Everything I do, I do in the true wish of making good on my commission here, even though it may not appear on first (or last) flush that I am. I appear, I am sure, to you all as a wastrel. There may even be fear that I have fallen. I assure you my honour is intact. There is an economic weather here that I know you cannot feel over the ocean, but established men have not been able to batten their doors against it. It does no good to be the second man on the block at all—you must be the first. (And, I tell you, I will never forget what it felt like to be tenth.)

Do not feel that I have misled you. I love you so painfully that if I had to stand before you and explain myself, I could not speak it. It is only by the will of God that I am not home, broken in spirit. Although I know my father will offer to send you all here, I must ask you to wait, as we must not be in such a precarious position that we would have to turn around the instant you landed. Please be patient. In the meantime, I have made you a portrait of myself in the form of the city that will be your future home. I know I have made it sound inhospitable, but it is very much like a field of stone under which a rich, fertile soil is waiting to be turned over and seeded. We shall seed it. This is where I live, my darlings, and with the aid of these images I herewith enclose, you can place yourselves in your imagination beside me as we go together to the market to buy our beef and pie for Friday supper. You will go with me from my rooms to where I work, and see the street and the sky. It is summer here now, and although this fickle city almost wrecked your father and beloved, it has its charms, and I will show them to you. The camera makes my mind's eye yours, and in this place we can be together.

I crush you to my heart.

Papa

## PLATE ONE

Come, enough now of words, they make flat aspects of
the fine dailiness of things. Here now, it is the morning
of June 6, and I have awoken in my rooms on Duchess
Street. It is just after seven in the morning, and there is
a cool air over the macadam. I have set up my camera at
the window to show you what I see every morning on
the south side of this little street. The camera is sitting
on a crate on top of my breakfast table and it takes me
but twelve seconds to get the view. So now you see what
I am seeing at my morning window. That is Mr. Baby (I
know, what an unusual name) standing on the sidewalk
in front of his room. I have, just after this image, called
to him and waved. He has done the same. See his hand
from where it is frozen at his side for all time rise up into
the air and halloo you all. Look in the window on the
second floor of the building (made of fine yellow brick,
which is as expensive here as it is at home—Alice, you
would wonder at the streets of yellow brick in some
parts of this new town) and you will see the little dog
belonging to a gentle old couple whose names are
Taylor. The dog is louder than they are. Mr. Taylor has
a plot in the back of their building where he grows peas
and cabbage, and come this September, I expect when
the wind is coming off the lake, we will all in these
buildings smell Mrs. Taylor's stews.

Now I will have my cup of tea and together we will
go down into the street.

PLATE TWO

We are standing in the street! No worry of speeding
traffic behind us—we have a couple of minutes. We're
facing west on this little street toward George Street
and, beyond it, Nelson Street. Just down there, far on
the left, you can see the side of the Mechanics' Institute,
a very handsome building we will pass shortly that faces
onto Church Street, a street of many churches, you may
be surprised to hear. Come to the plankwalk and we'll
go in that direction. See how tightly nailed together the
walk is? Not just a jumble of boards, is it? More like the
oaken floor of a gentlemen's club, as if some folk dancing a tarantella might come cascading down it . . .

## 2.

In Hallam's first exposures, the city had been at the beginning of a mild, welcome summer. Scruff and vetch had pushed through, little meadows filled in between houses, on empty lots. A cold May delayed new growth on the rose canes, but when he photographed Bishop Strachan's estate early in June, the bishop's man had already cropped the lawns. As the month went on and summer began, the blossoms from the chokecherries had already fallen and birds noisily trimmed the tiny fruits. He realized he'd watched the season changing in blinks of time. His image of the wall in Clarence Square, with its purple clematis, appeared at first to be damaged—black spots caused, he thought, by blobs of collodion detaching from the plate. But these turned out on inspection to be bumblebees ducking into the flowers. He found himself photographing water at the end of June, during the summer's first heat wave; captured bathers at the bottom of the Scarborough Bluffs, wading into the cool lake, leaving their blankets abandoned in the grass. A pond under the shade of huge willows hidden above the Davenport portage. He tried to capture a place his wife and daughters could look forward to living in, and yet a part of him felt an ugly certainty that he was creating a little dream for them, one neither they nor he would ever realize. What he did not photograph and what he did not say impeded. Winter was long over, but still the constabulary brought unidentified bodies to Potter's Field, men and women who had perished not from exposure (for the nights were pleasant now) but from any number of privations of the unexpected city: hunger, disease, violence. He walked past a form lying under a white sheet in the park behind St. James' Cathedral: that a person could seek comfort in the shadow of such a place and be refused was a stark truth of the city. He could not communicate this—how it made him feel—he could hardly understand it. But for the first time he thought he could understand the cruelty displayed to him by the Cockburns. Those men had seen the possibility of falling. He felt certain that they had, at one dreadful point, goggled the depths and pulled back. Now he had as well, and he thought he would ruin another man in order not to have another view of it.

He turned away from the unknown dead in the park, crossed King Street to the south side, and from that vantage photographed the beautiful and noble bell tower of St. James'.

By mid-July, when he brought his finished package to the post office on Toronto Street, he had finished a portrait of the place that was going to be his home, and he felt it resisted him just a little less. The summer was in full furnace now: the funk of tar and horse manure floated low over the city, grilling meats too, all of it a stew of scent to assault the nose. Inside the high-ceilinged new post office, a battery of fans was a blur of motion and the stone took the drafting air and cooled it somewhat.

The clerk at the desk weighed Hallam's package. The pages in the man's rate book skirred under the moving air. It was going to cost nearly ten shillings the fast way, the clerk told him, holding the book open.

"It's a gift."

The man shrugged. "In a matter of two or three years, you could telegraph your message under the sea for next to nothing. There's a man in New York going to do it."

Hallam wondered at the image of his wife standing in a telegraph office in London, waiting for his words to form under the hand of the operator, the staccato bursts of his drowned thoughts coming through without emotion. He was glad there was no temptation in that form yet: it felt cowardly enough to send these still images of a world she could not touch or smell. At least, in print, she could hear his voice. Although that voice, and those pictures, were bringing news of a place that was now so much like home to him, and yet not hers, not theirs, and did the pictures say that it would never be? He had to hope she would sense that he all but belonged here now; would somehow know it by his act of uttering it like this. *This is me now*, said the pictures, and what they couldn't say was what he really meant.

The man collected Hallam's money and stamped his package, laid it among other boxes and fragile-looking handwritten envelopes. He told Hallam it would be three weeks, at least—a veritable flash from here to there.

~

Hallam had left off the return address: his first picture had been taken from a window he could no longer look through, as he no longer lived there. At the end of June, he had completed, with Mrs. Rowe and Mr. Ennis, a move back to the shop on King Street. It was to be both home and place of business, no matter the local regulations. He and Ennis had given up their warrens. Now mail coming to Duchess Street would end up in the dead-letter pile at the post office, his name in the *Globe* under the uncollected-letters listings. He went back to the shop, its face much different from when he had photographed it; at night its windows were covered from inside with fabric bought from Crystal Hall. In the front was Hallam and Ennis's room, in the middle the studio, and at the back, accessible by a door leading into a small garden and then the alley, was Claudia's private chamber and the makeshift kitchen. (That King Street was one of the first to benefit from the new gas lines being laid throughout the city meant that the "store" had one of the first gas-burning stoves—a lucky thing, as having to burn coal in the small room where Claudia slept would have meant her waking with soot caked in her nose.) Front and back rooms had the benefit of doors; if they left the studio open on both sides, a breeze sometimes pressed in, but for most of the hot summer the two bedchambers were as still as coffins. There was no way to vent the darkroom—made of a plywood box attached to the side wall in the studio—and they had forbidden Ennis entry into the little space for the sake of his lungs. Claudia, who insisted her health was the best of any of them, did the developing in the dead of night, with the studio doors shut up. She'd warned both of the men not to enter that room after ten in the evening: developing the plates in the middle of the hot summer was something that if done unclothed gave the operator a better chance of survival. That both men had once seen her naked was left out of the discussion. Hallam lay with his back against the rough-hewn wall separating him from the quiet susurrations of her work late at night, his eyes open. Somehow, being together in his room on Duchess Street was a transgression so open that he could measure it; it had a name. Now he was alone with his thoughts. The image of a thin hand of light harassed him: it travelled under both studio doors and picked out her body in gleaming phosphor. He would squeeze his eyes tightly shut only to have them spring open again with sleeplessness.

She was alone in the studio when he came back from the post office, and all four doors were open, the light and air swimming through. It was a violation of the city code to use a place of business as a residence, and during the day the nighttime curtains were thrown wide and their sign put in place. Hallam and Ennis's room was converted to a lobby with evidence of the company's wares on the walls and in scrapbooks on tidy tables. In the morning, both men's mattresses were dragged through the middle room to Claudia's chamber. The bead curtain from Ennis's house hung in her doorway now; the faintest sound of rattling would alert any of them to a customer's curiosity and a quick *employees only, ma'am* would prevent them from being discovered.

They did not have the benefit of Mr. Ennis's skylight to effect the passage of light into the room, but the front, south-facing window was almost as good. A series of three mirrors brought light in off the street and into the middle of the shop. (In mounting the ligatures for these mirrors, Hallam was reminded of his first meeting with Ennis, when the man, still hale, dragged Hallam reluctantly into a new life.) Being indirect, it was a softer light, and exposures were longer and therefore more uncertain. It became the practice of Hallam, Ennis, and Rowe to propose outdoor portraits, and in this offering they were unique among city photographists. On this afternoon, however, Claudia was posing two children in the brightest shaft of light in the middle of the room. A boy and a girl, each holding a white garland, while their mother stood utterly still beside the camera, as if her own movements could smudge their memory. Children told to stand completely still invariably seemed frightened. Hallam strode into the middle of the scene, smiling.

"Who are these adorable children?" he said, and the two of them startled.

"Mrs. Fitch, this is my colleague, Mr. Hallam."

The mother held her hand out daintily. "Mrs. Fitch," said Hallam, "it's against nature to photograph blossoms out of their element."

"But they're from my garden, sir."

"I don't mean the flowers. What are your names," he said to the children. One of them murmured Elizabeth, the other Thomas. "Beautiful names. Do you know I have a garden full of hummingbirds out back? With bright light and two very nice and comfortable chairs?"

"Mrs. Fitch would like a studio portrait," said Claudia.

"We have two studios, though," he said, continuing to smile warmly. It had become his job to sell; Mr. Ennis was too ill to present himself as the true proprietor, even though the equipment and expertise were mostly his. Claudia looked at Hallam mildly; that she was alone meant Ennis was only feet from them in her room, asleep, or awake and suffering on the mattress. Now that he thought of it, he could hear the man's breath coming unevenly through the curtain. "It's up to you, of course, madam, but don't dismiss the possibility of a picture in nature that will be alive for years to come."

The decision being left entirely up to her (would Mr. Fitch have been so open to her wishes?), Mrs. Fitch was not against it. They carried the camera and a tripod onto the sidewalk and went down the narrow alley to the garden behind the gate. Mrs. Fitch admonished the children not to let their clothing touch the walls, and Hallam congratulated himself silently for having had the presence of mind to scrub those walls and repaint them. The two children could have sidled all the way along without threat to their summer linens.

They went into the garden and the children sat on the two white-painted iron chairs; a throw pillow on each seat prevented small legs from burning. Mrs. Fitch approved; the change of location meant that the exposure time would be a mere fifteen seconds compared to forty inside. It meant the children could be themselves, and children appearing to be real children meant eager visits to Hallam,

Ennis, and Rowe from other parents. He posed them and Claudia offered him the camera (she had a natural sense of what the mother would have wished: that Hallam had arrived and taken on the appearance of her employer dictated that he be the "expert" who took the picture), and within two minutes, four exposures were made. On the fourth, he took away the chairs and had the two sit together on the grass at the verge of the flowers. This would be the image that Mrs. Fitch would buy.

She counted out her coins on Hallam's counter inside. Claudia held the children's hands on the sidewalk as they watched the horses trot by on King Street. "Your wife is very good with children," said Mrs. Fitch. He thanked her. That "Rowe" was not another man never crossed the minds of most customers, and among the clientele Mrs. Rowe went mainly by "ma'am." It remained an uncorrected error; it served the business.

"I heard laughter," said Ennis, walking into the studio. In the good light, the whites of Ennis's eyes were the colour of old bone. He watched Hallam put the coins into the locked box they kept in the studio. When Hallam opened the box, he saw the better part of three pounds within. Claudia came in from the street with a paper bag; she'd gone down toward Yonge Street and bought apples. She put one into each hand and they stood in a pleasant silence in the light of the front room, with nothing but the crisp sound of their teeth on the skins.

There were no more appointments for the rest of the morning, and as Hallam no longer went to Jewell and Clow's, he took his paper and coffee into the garden, sitting in one of the chairs out of the direct sunlight. Claudia helped Ennis out into the brightness and sat him in the other chair to shave him. The sun picked up the unkempt stubble on Ennis's face and she shielded her eyes against the light, tucking a torn coffee sack into his collar and then washing his face gently with hot water. He tilted his head back and then side to side, trusting her with the razor he'd stropped, even though she already knew how to prepare a blade and shave a man. He sighed with pleasure, feeling the whiskers come off cleanly, the soap lifting the oils off his flesh and leaving him free to feel the air, the light.

Hallam watched them quietly and felt a prick of shame. Her tenderness with Ennis was a sign of love, a daughterly love. It was as Ennis had avowed: he would never have touched her. Her nakedness in his studio, however strange and inexplicable it had been to Hallam, had been a sign of her trust, and Ennis's position behind his camera was a promise of succour. Although his awareness of the truth as it had always been made him feel he'd disgraced himself, Hallam was also aware that these two people were the entire ship of his life now, and he had accepted this. He felt, for once, that there was a plan for him. If he'd only allowed himself to be bent by another will earlier than this, his suffering might have been less. There were a great many things he was supposed to be, that he ought to have been. But this life had always been waiting for him, it now appeared, waiting to be lived, and not even his fumbling judgments, his benighted actions, could affect its unfolding.

Claudia towelled Ennis off, and he seemed fresher, more alert. He drew Claudia's arm down to him, pressing it against his chest and belly, and kissed her on the shoulder. "I am human again, for the moment."

"You think a shave entitles you to change species, Sam? Maybe later, after Jem has bathed you properly. Right, sir?"

Hallam started from his thoughts. "Beg pardon?"

"When it is dark enough that you won't be visible from anywhere, but still light enough that you can tell the dirt from the hair, I'd like you to put Sam in the tub out here and get him washed up. I want us to take pictures of ourselves, tomorrow."

"I should be remembered as I am," said Ennis.

"Probably so," said Hallam. "Show fidelity to the subject." Claudia stared patiently at the two of them, grown men afraid of a bath.

"Jem, you'll scrub this man until he gleams. He'll feel better." She fingered off a dot of soap under Ennis's ear. "And *you'll* feel like living a while longer."

"'Tis hot," said Ennis to himself. Fifteen minutes in the sun and he was flagging. The sun gave vital nutrient, but a body too ill to make use of it will sap in the light. Claudia went in with the cloth and brought it back out, dripping and cold. She instructed Ennis to go back into the dark and lie down. In an hour, they would wake him up for his medicine. He shuffled back inside without aid, and yawned deeply at the door before vanishing into the inner gloaming.

A haze filled the sky between buildings. Claudia moved the coffee bag off Ennis's chair and sat down, her eyes on the doorway. It looked cool there, though she knew better. For some time, Hallam had been used to a shared silence with Claudia. In the two months they had lived together in his small flat, they'd had no choice but to respect each other's quiet. He went about now reading the columns in the *Globe* unselfconsciously. He glanced up at a windy sound and watched a huge bee stumble onto the lip of a pale purple iris (what some people here called a fleur-de-lys, but which was, in fact, a true iris and not a lily), and it tucked itself under the soft upper lip of the petal. Its black, exposed behind throbbed with seeming delight. He stared at it sleepily, mesmerized by being so close to such a communion.

"Any call for a talented domestic?" called Claudia.

"I don't read those classifieds," Hallam said, and he looked up to see her smiling at him. He turned back to the paper. "But there is a new shipment of French velvet at Gordon & McKay."

"Am I to make you both handsome pink smoking vests?"

He snapped the paper smartly. "There are also new whiskies at Leask's."

He continued reading, but the words just passed beneath his eyes. He could sense her gazing at him. Her look felt like a word spoken through honey. "I called you *Jem*," she said. "Did you notice? Before?"

"Did you?"

"And I call Sam *Sam*. Do you even know my first name?"

"I know your first name, Mrs. Rowe."

"Are you able to form it with your lips?"

"I could if I—"

"Try it. Claaaw . . ."

He turned his face down further, anxious not to be made to laugh. "I know your first name perfectly well."

"For two months you called me Mrs. Rowe, in the privacy of your own rooms—"

"*Room*," he said.

"*And* without there being the slightest chance of anyone hearing you be *familiar*."

"I am just more comfortable—"

"With someone whose life you saved, just about. Why the formality? Aren't we partners? In business?"

He nodded vigorously—yes they were, that was certainly true. But some barriers one did well to observe, although he could not put it to her that way. "Maybe it is right to think of ourselves as just that, though. Equals in a business concern. Perhaps that demands a certain kind of mutual respect."

"And calling me Claudia does not show respect?"

"If I get into the habit of it, and it shows in front of our clientele, then perhaps not. We don't want to appear immodest."

"It's not 1820, Jem Hallam. You can call a woman by her name."

"Well, yes," he said, reddening. "I'll work on it."

"It would be wonderful if you two would settle on nomenclature and let a sick man sleep," came Ennis's voice from inside. Claudia burst out laughing.

"Sorry! Mr. Ennis! Sir!"

She waited a moment, gazing into the room where he lay, then rose from her chair and put the coffee bag down closer to Hallam, where he remained in the shade. She arranged her dress around her legs and sat on the cloth. Insects looped in slow paths around the two of them. "I don't mean to make myself unpleasant," she said, looking up toward him in his chair.

"You are baiting me, Mrs. Rowe, which is unkind."

"You would have to be a hook to be baited, Mr. Hallam. Or a trap."

He flattened his paper on his lap. For a moment, he had the illusion that the two of them were sitting on the deck of a boat moving slowly across the lake, a weekend sojourn to Rochester, perhaps, to pick pears. "How would I be a trap, Mrs. Rowe? Or you to me, or Ennis? My formality is not a form of caution. I'm just more comfortable this way."

"I've been too familiar, then. I apologize." There was remorse in her words, but not in her voice. "Do you want me to go back inside?"

He shook his head. "It's only that it is not becoming for us to—I think you know." He believed she found his squirming discomfort a delight, and he marked her mock-serious face staring up at him. "Mrs. Rowe, it's bad enough . . ."

"I know," she said, and she lowered her voice. "Don't misunderstand me, Mr. Hallam. I know you will go home, in time. I presume it. But in the meantime, we are shipwrecked, and I *must* have a friend! I am being quite plain and you needn't fetch out your slide rule to measure my intent. I'm a social person; I like to laugh, I like to dispute. And I don't want to choke off that part of me because my erstwhile patron is coughing blood in the next room and can't have a drink with me, and the only other person I have to talk to is standing daily on ceremony for fear of falling pell-mell into boiling sin! Be my friend, Jem Hallam. If you had anything to fear from me, I could not talk to you like this anyway. Don't be full of worry."

"I am *not* full of worry."

"You are an old woman full of worry. Tell me something you would tell a friend and let me listen. You can do that. I will lie back here under the bees and dragonflies and you can talk to me." She lay back and waited, but he stared over his crushed paper into the air.

"I can't believe you would say I haven't been a friend to you."

"I take it back. Now tell me a story and make it a good one."

"I don't know what it is you'd like me to say."

"How about I give you a word, then—no, I will give you two words, two nouns, and you will extract by association from your memory a pleasant personal experience that tells an unthreatening morsel of yourself. All right?"

"I think you will find me uniquely uncreative."

"It is not a creative task, Jem, it is one of filing. And since you were born, it seems, with the mind of a clerk, it shouldn't present too great a difficulty." He nodded his silent, exasperated consent and she paused for a moment, then said, "*Key*. And *horse*."

He let the two words into his mind, and saw them both as objects. A series of keys: grey iron ones, little silver ones for jewel boxes and personal diaries, house keys, a heavy rusted gate key that fit into the lock of a swinging metal pasture door. He heard it shut with a bang. Easy to get to the horses then—his grandfather's Shetlands—but also the gleaming black horses he saw daily in the streets in Camden Town—not just the hacks and hansoms, but the big brown drays dragging heavy tanks of water to a fire, or once in a while an escaped palomino darting over the cobbles from someone's sheds, its eyes wild. Metallic *keyness* and large, hard, nostril-clouded *horseness* went clanging and galloping through his mind like a magic lantern show where someone had pulled the slide through too fast. He tried to recall whether he'd ever unlocked a horse, or seen a key shaped like a pony, and then all at once his mind stopped turning over and he was standing as a boy of perhaps ten in front of the house he lived in with his parents until he was sixteen, the house in Clapham. Pale grey stone; vines climbing the walls; it was early summer, and close and hot. He remembered wondering why he'd been brought to this house, fearing that he was to be dropped off there, as he had been at a boys' farm the previous summer, but that was in the countryside, and although he had found the roughness of the other boys a shock, he'd enjoyed himself, and this: this looked like employment of some sort. He asked his father what was happening, and his mother hushed him.

Shortly, being drawn by a broad-chested cabhorse, came a man, who stepped out of his cabin and walked sullenly over to Hallam's father. "I've been to the solicitor's," said the man. "It's in order."

"Tell Mr. Sullivan we hope that with his new capital he will make himself a good start."

The man nodded, and handed Hallam's father a small yellow envelope. Then he began walking back toward his cab. He stopped before the door a moment and turned back. "Mr. Sullivan's capital is being poured out in little rills from one hand to the other, in order of largest debt to smallest. He is broken, Mr. Hallam, but I will pass on your warm thoughts anyway."

"Horrible man," said his mother as young Jem watched his father empty the contents of the envelope out into his hand. It was a single black key. The three of them went to the door. His father told him they had a new home. That summer (Hallam remembered as he told Claudia the story), he had been sent back to the same boys' farm. But was that still part of the story of key-and-horse?

"Go on," she said, and he continued, time sliding away from one spot to another, enjoying the taste of memory moving over his mind's palate. He felt the pull of a trout on the end of a fishing line, the smell of the coniferous forest, and the light slanting down hard between branches. All of this was somehow in him, and as he spoke it, it was as if it were the light itself falling on a plate and seizing that surface—yes, this was what making a picture was like, it was a form of telling.

He looked up and saw Claudia Rowe staring at him, her mouth almost in a smile, and the horses in his mind bolted from the stable and hit the streets in disarray. "It's time for Mr. Ennis's pills," he said.

"I don't get two words of my own?"

"I haven't had the time to think of them yet."

"Then take the time and let me know. I'll go raise him." She pushed herself up and swayed a little, dizzy from lying down in the heat, and then went into the house.

PLATE NINE

We are in King Street now, and the rain has finally
stopped. You must see the Golden Lion, as it is known,
a shop that would be at home on Camden High Street.

(I had intended to give you this picture, thinking of
you standing with me near the end of our little tour, but
in amazement I tell you now that I have had to retreat to
offices across the way, the bulky camera tucked up
under my coat. Just a mere half-mile from where I had
been standing began a rally of calls that a *bear* was in the
street! As if on a Sunday promenade. So think of us
now, caught up in an unplanned adventure, making for
cover. Cecile is in my arms chattering like a monkey,
and the four of us have bounded up the stairs in the
building behind us. By good luck we're in the offices of
the *Leader*, whose clerks have thrown open their doors
and allowed us to crowd in at the windows with them.
And there she is: *Ursus canadensis*, as a learned gentleman says beside me, the common black bear. You may
be displeased to learn: the sight of one of these gargan-
tuan mammals lumbering down our civilized byways is
not entirely unknown. Especially in inclement weather,
the whole city smells of dirt and forest and it all seems
much of a muchness to a bear. This is my third *U.
canadensis* this year. So let us take a picture and we will
try to catch two beasts in one snare: the golden lion, the
black bear. The light is poor under a purpled sky and I
cannot get a fast image, but you see him anyway, there

behind the sign for Paterson's Dry Goods. He is in no hurry. Some brave souls are returned to the street, believing that they are not to the animal's taste— although I fear for the man in the berry-coloured suit standing in front of McNab's. I am afraid the animal is nothing more than a greyling ghost in your picture: as if the camera itself were struck with wonder at the sight of him.)

Now he is gone, let us go back down to the street— come Jane, come Cecile, now we can go down to squint in the windows of the Golden Lion. The sun is co-operating at last. Jane, you will have that dress in red that I have seen there in recent days, thinking of you in it, the fine silvery brocade at the neck and hem. And Cecile will do justice to a pair of white gloves with the small bone buttons, which I know are there lying in the velvet at the bottom of the case. And for your mother—am I to say what your mother will wear? No, let us all go down together, down to the Golden Lion, and we will help her choose a summer frock that will force the rain to stay in England for a change! Come now, the coast is clear.

3.

THE FIRM OF HALLAM, ENNIS, AND ROWE, Photographists, continued to develop its moderate renown, and the three of them were pleased to mark how commonplace it was during the summer months for people to arrive demanding that their portraits be taken out of doors. By now, both Mr. Bryant of St. George's Square and the photographists who worked near the Exchange were advertising out-of-door exposures as well. Hallam had a bitter idea of what sorts of tactics the Cockburns might have used had they been photographists themselves, and tried to think what he could say to Bryant and the Exchange men to scare them off, but nothing short of firing muskets outside their places of business would do, and Hallam knew they could not afford the gunpowder. Three firms offered the purity of "natural light," and there was nothing anyone could do to put a trademark on it. Ennis joked that they should advertise that the sun shone brighter on King Street because of the class of person that walked there.

Instead, they found a leg up on their competition through an insurer who did business just down from the

Golden Lion. There was no better way, said the man, to prevent fraud than to have the original state of things recorded in good copy, with both the owner of the property and the insurer in agreement on what was being insured. Thereby, no unscrupulous homeowner, having set off or suffered a fire, could claim what didn't exist. The poor insurer could bring out a proper illustration of what was lost and what, therefore, a firm such as his would have to be liable for.

This work meant Hallam had to hire a horse and bundle up a massive quantity of equipment to some location to photograph a house, an outbuilding, a new bank, a set of silver cutlery, even, once, a vegetable garden. Or rare tulips, at the behest of a Dutch couple with long memories. He carted people's belongings from one room to another to find light enough to photograph by, sensitizing plates in a little portable darkroom that brought his face too closely into contact with his chemicals. Photographing anywhere outside of the studio was an onerous process, and an expensive one, and it made him a little sick at heart to think of the money being spent by people to establish the verity of their riches. But no one would pay them to photograph the poor or their ramshackle houses. To survive, they would have to invest in the interests of the rich.

In the evenings, Hallam converted their foyer back into his and Ennis's room and drew the curtains on the inside of the window. He lit a lamp and kept it low. The summer ended with their routines established: Hallam administering the various compounds that kept Ennis's illness manageable as Claudia doggedly developed the day's images. Hallam would give Ennis a small, hot brandy-and-water, then go to see the prints Claudia was fixing and hanging on lines strung from wall to wall for drying. He liked to listen to her padding barefoot back and forth between the development box and the line, silently clipping the prints in place. As the fall came on, demand for portraits dropped off as the call for insured property went up. More families came to the city, and their belongings were the last things to tie them to home. You could have them doubly insured—for money as well as for memory. And so while the leaves began to fall on the light-diminished streets, trees of memory budded inside Hallam's old store. He'd help Ennis out of his chair to stare at the images of mantel clocks, standing lamps, gold watches, heavy keystones, and winding staircases. Bits of the lives of people intent on holding dear these dumb objects that spoke of their worlds.

Ennis was visibly weakening. The medication muted his pain and slowed the progress of his death, but it made his mind drift. Beneath these effects, the same man lived, but at a remove. It was as if he were drowning and only with great effort could draw himself to the surface to breathe their air. They didn't show him their concern, but went on feeding him and covering him up at night, reading to him when it seemed he could listen— stories of escaped slaves in the Toronto dailies, bits of news from the world beyond out of *Brother Jonathan*, or even the Bible, which brought his childhood to him in drafts.

When Ennis slept, Hallam stayed with him, closing the studio door to let Claudia have her space to herself. He listened to Ennis's wet, uneven breathing—the morphia, when they had to give it to him, depressed his respiration, but Hallam was experienced enough with it to know how to prevent bringing the man too close to breathlessness. Beyond that room, through two walls, the footfalls and bedtime sounds of a woman whose life Hallam had saved. There it was, bald and true: in all likelihood he was the reason both she and Ennis were still living. He had succeeded in extending his humanness, even though his actions were not unambiguously moral. He knew, without being able to say it, that his humanity extended through others, but how was this to be squared with what he owed those he was connected to most intimately? If, say, he had to choose between saving the lives of two strangers and rushing home to save the life of one of his children, which would be the right choice? Wasn't he *making* this choice right now? Was he a good man or a very bad one? He afflicted himself at night with these questions, even as he listened to Ennis fading in his sleep, this man on whom he spent some of the money that could have gone home to his wife and children. *He will die no matter*, thought Hallam. Ennis's body was a furnace that burned money.

And yet Hallam felt he belonged in this place, with these people. He had not drifted here; a measured pace of choices had delivered him, and directly. Something that galvanized him had emerged from the wreck of his plans. That there was another life! How unique to be spat out of a storm onto dry land and lashed to purpose. It was not to be wished for, one did not expect such a thorough rusticating by the gods only to be handed the machinery for another try. The Lord had seen fit not to let him serve in his chosen manner. He would have to accept the new life.

Claudia opened the studio's back door, and Hallam lay in his bed and listened as she lit the lamp. There was no hour at which she would not work if they needed her to. She was indefatigable. She flowed through the single-chambered heart of the studio in the dark behind him, and it did hurt to think of her. Many times since the move to the store, he'd allowed himself to imagine rising in his bedclothes and going in. He imagined entering the little plywood development box and taking her hand without a word. She'd bring it to her mouth and kiss his fingers, lay his hand on the tabletop to return to the print she was washing, and he'd follow her to the hanging lines. Then go with her through the door to her room, watch her draw her nightclothes over her head and lay them unhurriedly over the back of a chair. Maybe there would be a thread of cool coming through the door that opened onto the garden. They would feel it on their feet.

"Mr. Hallam," she called through the closed door between the rooms. He lay utterly still, as if she'd witnessed his imagining them abed, and seen the phantom of herself covering him with its shifting body. Then he regained his senses and answered her. "I hear Sam labouring," she said. "Is everything all right?"

He got out of his bed and lit Ennis's light. His face
was damp, and Hallam got him up to sitting. "Maybe a
cold cloth," he called. She came with it and Hallam
wiped the man's sallow face; Ennis did not wake, but
sighed with discomfort to feel the cold.

"Why is he worse at night?"

"His body's busy with other things. Digestion, blood
wash, cells to be swept out. In daytime he can beat the
sickness back, but at night there's not the energy."

"Most people die at night," she said quietly.

"They do. Their eyes are already closed."

She stood and looked at Ennis, whose breathing had
normalized, then took up his candle. "I want to show
you something."

In the studio, she moved the candle over images drying on the lines, and they bloomed in its small light. She
had been developing the pictures of an entire street of
buildings—Front Street from Yonge to Church, the
north side—on behalf of the Board of Trade, which was
considering purchasing all of that land from the current
owners, including the popular American Hotel, which
stood on the northeast corner at Yonge Street. As she
passed the light in front of the drying photos, curled as
sleeping bats, he pulled them open and a building, a
doorway, a store window unfurled in front of him.

"These took you less than three hours to make, correct?"

"About that," he said.

"I'm having an idea." She moved the candle away from
the photos and held it between them. Her face looked as if
it were floating, the way he now realized it sometimes

came to him in a dream. "We could make ourselves indispensable. Between the two of us, we photograph every street in this city, every building and corner and street lamp. The parks and the rivers. Print a set but keep the glass for ourselves. Make the city a gift of the photos. There will be archives here someday, and libraries, and back in England they might want something exhaustive to catalogue their holdings. We could be the only ones with a complete set, and we'd add to it as new things appeared in town. Like a directory that comes out each year."

"It's a lot of glass," he said.

"The first set of prints would be a gift, the second would cover all our costs. After that . . ." She wore an expression of childlike pleasure on her face. "We could do it in two weeks, between our regular appointments. I've already calculated the outlay."

He took the candle from her hands and led her back into the front room where Ennis remained unmoving. He drew a box out from beneath his bed, lit his standing lamp, and took out the glass he'd used back in June for the pictures he took for Alice and the girls. For what reason he'd kept them rather than scrubbing them and returning the valuable glass to inventory, he wasn't sure. Maybe the glass was a lock of some kind that would only be opened when reunited with its mirror image. But now his selfishness could serve them all a purpose. She drew a chair over to his bed and unwrapped the muslin that protected each pane. She folded the onion paper over their backs and held them up in the air with one hand while bringing the lamp in at the right angle.

"I've already started," he said. "Not as thorough as you're suggesting, but there's some of it done."

"For your wife," she said quietly.

"My girls as well."

"I was wondering where all that glass had gone." She took them up one by one and read their negative images silently, translating for her eyes the bright spaces as dark, the black windowpanes of buildings as clear, light-crossing windows. Pink nodding heads of roses rendered funereal, the greys keeping to themselves. "They're beautiful," she said, her voice almost a murmur. "They must have loved them very much."

"They're a lie."

She looked over the edge of one of the plates at him.

"If we do what you suggest," he said, "I want to photograph the city as it is. Not as an advertisement for emigration."

She laid the plate she was holding carefully in the box. "How would that be a gift?"

"A true mirror is a gift for someone who wishes to see." He covered the box again and carried it, straining with its weight, into the studio. "We could use some of these," he said. "To be exhaustive, we'll have to take many more. But I think it an excellent idea, Mrs. Rowe." He placed the glass cache behind the developing box, in plain view.

"Your family, Jem. Have you not told them everything?"

"They know about my new work," he said. "But not all of it. No doubt their letters to me are in the dead-letter drawer at the post office."

"You should collect them." He didn't reply. "Are you ashamed?"

"I am not ashamed to be alive."

"Tell them everything. You've done nothing wrong. In fact, they'll think you a hero, making something of nothing, and being a good guardian to people who were strangers to you."

She recoiled a little to see his face. The dimness and the shadows could have made him appear a way he did not intend. Had he spoken, she would have known for certain if he was upset, but instead he pulled the lamp farther away and said good night to her, retreating to his room. As he pulled the door to, he said, "We should begin right away," and she managed only a quiet *yes* before she was alone again in the studio with only her candle.

In the days that followed, leading into the first crispness of September, they brought their outfits into the streets of the city, trying to capture the last of the good seasonal light to make a portrait of a place neither had ever dreamed would be home. In the store, when he was well enough, Ennis was put to work cataloguing the images as they were developed, marking in the pages of a city mapbook purchased from the Consumers' Gas Company all of the streets and structures they recorded. A little scientific method was applied: Claudia broadly photographed streets and made a record of every road, avenue, lane and byway, riverwalk and horse path, pier and rail. Once her omnibus images were committed to paper, the three of them decided together which details needed more specific documenting, and then Hallam would set out a day later to complete the study.

Out of her sweeping vistas emerged his cornices and doorways, the sturdy face of a bank building, a racquet club with high dormer windows, the columns in front of the post office (which he did not enter), church scaffolding, iron fences, close-ups of tin signs and wooden hoardings, scalloped keystones and gold-plated store names. Then he turned his camera to the ground and stared at horrors. Tatterdemalion children worn out from eating hard bread; mad forms against lampposts, stinking of spirits and harbouring rumours. He photographed a pyramid of horse manure melting at its edges into the rainwater, the streets a mixture of mud and ordure. On Caroline Street there were houses like the one Claudia had lived in, their collapsed or ruined parts cut away like the corners of burnt toast. The more he documented, the more it seemed the city was a patchwork of damage enlivened by defiant architecture and freshly painted signs. He could have gone on at ground level, but he pulled himself away and instead detailed the three varieties of gaslamps, the nine sorts of hitching posts (two wooden, five iron, and even two kinds in ceramic). Sometimes he went inside a building and took an image of a hammered ceiling, or a chandelier, if there was enough light and he could cajole it into the right corners; once he even captured the thin uneven stairs that led to an upstairs backroom. When he returned to the store, Ennis went through the heavy mapbook, slowly tracing a red line down the middle of each completed street, then inscribing over the outlines of buildings which aspects had been pictured, which interiors. It took a full share of his energy to do this, but he desired to work, and they would not stop him.

Hallam and Claudia took three weeks all told in September and October and made a tower of prints, more than three hundred images in all—Toronto as a whole and in pieces. Hallam dreamed that they took their images and went throughout the city gluing them over the original subjects so that the whole place was transformed into a vision of itself. When he told Ennis and Claudia about the dream, they nodded sagely, because that was what they had done, in fact, only their city stood in a pile, waiting to be constructed in the mind of a witness.

Now they culled, seeing what had to be pictured in close, what could stand a summary view. That image of a school being built was more important than the block it stood in: any mayor would be pleased to show a visitor to the city such constructive activity. Paper sales signs pasted up on brick and sometimes even over store windows told a better story of the city's business fortunes than did the glittering, but mute, windows with their finery: NOTICE SELLING OUT ALL AT FAIR PRICES said more than a dusty interior where the last of the previous season's wares were lingering.

There were also the people (an absence noted by Ennis, who wondered out loud why his colleagues returned each day with images of a ghost city), and both Hallam and Claudia spent a single bright cold day in the

middle of October taking portraits of the city in motion.
Here they got two men in heavy greatcoats standing on
the sidewalk outside of the market, their hands folded in
front of them and bowing toward each other like
Chinese emperors, lost in conversation. (Hallam
stopped a few feet on and carved his pencil down to
write a bit of overheard talk on the back of a broadsheet:
"You take care around a live goose! She's got a knob of
bone in her wing, sure to break any bone in *your* body.")

In another picture, a man in a coke hat stood in front
of a store with his arms crossed (a man in front of his
store always brought a frisson of grief to Hallam: you
didn't stand in front if there were customers inside).
Outside of the Exchange, they photographed the common sight of a gaggle of top-hatted men standing around
in a tight group, some smoking pipes, all talking, many
with the day's newspaper crumpled in a fist. A boy waiting on them at street level, ready to be called on for
brandy, water, tobacco. Two women pushing prams in
long skirts and heavy shawls—they became a grey blur.
Working men carrying lumber up a flimsy wooden plank
to a church, others carrying tarry buckets of stinking
creosote. It was a wonder they'd ever got clear shots of
anything in town without this welter of humanity always
in the lens.

At the end of the month they were done and they
called on the mayor's deputy, Colonel Thompson, at the
wooden city hall to present him with their gift. He was
a small man (Napoleonic, some called him) who preferred not to meet with the general public, but the

announcement of a gift could rouse him from his cottage and bring him into the municipal offices. Deputy Thompson shook hands firmly with Hallam, glancing over at Claudia, and instructed his secretary, a man named Russell, to prepare two whiskies and for the lady a hot water with lemon. Thompson sat behind his desk and lay his thin arms on the surface as if gauging whether they covered more of the space this morning than they had done previously.

"My man tells me you want to make a presentation." The whiskies came smartly. Hallam hefted a large leathern portfolio up onto the arms of the chair he'd been invited to sit in, and Thompson regarded it eagerly. He had not sat for a portrait, but perhaps these people had it in their minds to make one of him. Hallam untied the covers and lifted one up. Thompson strained forward.

"A picture?" he said.

"Many, sir. A complete record of the city as seen in the fall of 1856."

"Oh." The deputy came around his desk slowly, either bewildered curiosity or distaste spreading across his wide face. Hallam lifted the first image, which was the waterfront taken from a small pushboat about five hundred yards out into the lake. Beneath it was a close-up of the customs house, then Front Street facing east toward the jail, with its good shops lining the north side into the distance. "Is my house in here?" said the deputy mayor.

Hallam and Claudia traded a glance. "It may be," she said. "Which street are you on?"

"College Avenue," he said. "Below the gardens."

She reached over Hallam and lifted up a heavy sheaf of photos, then let a few drift back down onto the pile. "We have two views of College Avenue. The gardens themselves"—she held this one up—"and then the view south from them straight down to the water."

"Let me see that." He took the second picture in his hands and held it up to his face, the light from the window behind his desk illuminating it. He mumbled under his breath, and then exclaimed, "Ah!" and held the picture out to them both. "There! Look! That is my house. Shortened by perspective, but that is it! Right there." He poked the image with a stubby finger. "Isn't that a pip!"

"It is an almost complete photographic catalogue of the city. We felt city hall would want to have it for their archives."

"Can you make another of these?"

"Yes," said Claudia quickly. "They're done with the collodion process, sir. It's repeatable, you see."

"Honestly." Colonel Thompson stared at the considerable collection in front of him. "You say it's complete?"

"I would imagine it is nearly complete, sir. Myself, Mrs. Rowe, and our colleague Samuel Ennis used the gas company's register to keep track of what we were recording. And anything that is not present, or if another view is desired, can easily be accommodated."

"Honestly," the deputy mayor repeated, seeming awed. "Russell, get in here."

His man reported immediately. "Sir?"

"On which street do you have your rooms, Russell?"

"Queen Street, out by the university. Almost at the university."

"It is a long street, boy. Say exactly."

"I am at Shaw, sir—817 Queen Street."

The colonel excitedly waved his fingertips over the portfolio as if to make a rabbit appear. "Come on, come on then, show him his building."

Hallam's stomach sank. Claudia shuffled the images slowly, trying to keep them from sliding out of the case and onto the floor. They had numbered them on the back, and given them legends, but it would be quite a task to reassemble the collection if it should fall while the deputy mayor shuffled through them with dirty hands searching for his favourite pub. "This is the closest view," she said quietly.

Thompson took the photo from her and handed it over to his assistant. "See the detail in that!" he said. "Find your window! I wager your window is there, maybe even with you in it, you lackadaisy. Smoking in your undershirt." He clapped Russell on the back. "Find it?"

"Not yet, sir."

"Well, they can go out of an afternoon and make you a picture in a nonce, they said so." He turned expectantly to Hallam. "Yes?"

"Sir, the reason we're here today is to present, as citizens, a good record of our city *to* the city. And perhaps to suggest there are other agencies that may have use of such a clear historical record as this."

"Who?" Thompson took back the unsatisfactory picture of Queen Street and tossed it back on the pile. "The Lord Mayor of Buffalo?"

"The Home Office," said Claudia, "in London."

"There are libraries," Hallam offered, "here, and in Britain, and there will be archives here as well, one day."

The deputy mayor's face had fallen further with each suggestion. "Of this great frog pond?" he said. "This groundhog meadow? London has art galleries and museums and important institutions. Why would they need two unholy hundred pictures of a swamp with buildings on it? The originals of which, I doubt I need to add, were already *in* England in 1793. The originals, don't you know."

"This is an important city in a new colony, sir. One day, they will want to know from where its greatness sprang."

"Do you believe that precious young Victoria Regina would have dropped such a place from her imperial loins so far out of view if she wished actually to *look* at it? Son, we're lucky we're not an island, or we'd be boarding convicts—not to say that we aren't already. As it is, what few amenities there are here are to assuage the horrors of those stuck in this place, not for the creation of another Bayeux Tapestry. Go out and take some pictures of people's houses and you might be able to tout those for a bob or two, but my archives—madam, excuse me for saying so—are too full with empty whisky bottles."

"Actually, I think I do see it," said Russell, his head tilted at an angle over the portfolio. "For some reason I recognize it better upside down."

"See what I'm saying?" said Thompson. "We are *bouleversé* in this new England. Let me look, boy."

Russell held the picture up and indicated a sliver of pale light against the front of a building seen in the far distance. "I recognize that little black abutment below as my downstair neighbour's flowerpot. That's how I know it."

"You are a details man," said Deputy Mayor Thompson. "You'll do well back in England."

Claudia tied up the portfolio and laid it flat on the man's desk. "I'm sure there will be many in the city's employ who would like to see their various abodes pictured in the most modern portraiture. We will leave it to you to call them in."

Thompson grinned winningly, like a boy being given a live snake. "An excellent idea."

Once back on the street, Claudia muttered "jackanape" under her breath and then linked her arm in Hallam's. He startled to be touched in daylight.

"Mrs. Rowe?"

"If we have to survive by selling civic employees pictures of their own houses, so be it. That idiot might make us a living after all."

4.

BY DAY, ENLIVENED BY THE LIGHT, ENNIS COULD SIT
and sometimes converse. The air was too cool now,
however, to place him in the garden, so Claudia covered
him in a shawl and put him in her room whenever they
had clients. The insurance work kept up, and either she
or Hallam would report to someone's house on Jarvis
Street to trail through and photograph paintings or sil-
verware in well-lit rooms. It was dismal work, but it kept
them alive.

At suppertime, the curtains drawn, they'd convert the
front room into a dining area and Claudia would serve
the simple meal she'd prepared for the three of them—a
stew with meat cooked to disintegrating tenderness or a
mincemeat pie, if she hadn't been out and behind a camera all day. Claudia and Hallam would be silent, not
sharing the thoughts they were having, sitting with the
near-silent Ennis, his eyes glassy from various anodynes:
that they were seeing a common vision of his brief
future. This was supposed to be her calling later, thought
Claudia, this store of tenderness at the end of a life. But

when that time came, she was supposed to be old, too, with much to look back on. As it was, life had offered her an alternative: she was to be young, with a phantasm for a husband, and the man whose life demanded her compassion had been a stranger a year earlier. Still, she applied herself to his suffering.

For Hallam, it was simpler: Ennis was him. His was the honourable death that awaited every worthy man, but it had been transformed into something vulgar. And yet, as for Claudia, it was the only meaningful horror in Hallam's life. Everything else was at a remove, like a story you could remember, but not where you'd heard it. Sitting with this substitute for the life he thought he would one day lead left his marrow cold.

When Ennis chose to speak now, the two of them listened quietly. He was not cogent. He spoke in mad, skirling non sequiturs, working over a practical matter of costs and expenses in the same breath as he speculated on the outcome of a foot race between Galileo and Prince Albert. Or he'd speak a perfectly sensible line, only it would be many months out of date: in this way they learned the complete truth of the life he'd lived alone in the west end. A whispered invitation to a Mrs. Gates contained suggestions they had only imagined. It saddened Hallam, not because it confirmed his suspicions of lewd conduct, but because it underscored the impossibility of Ennis's situation. Drifting farther into the fog, Ennis looked toward shore and saw dreams of himself as a man. It was all coming to an end.

At the beginning of November, he began moaning in his sleep; awake, he asked clearly for drink or black smoke. Hallam felt it could do no harm; it would either hasten death or shield Ennis from pain while cutting him off from the real world.

Claudia knew where to find what he needed. She appeared at the back door of the building with two men, characters Hallam had thought he'd seen the last of when he and Claudia moved Ennis into the store with them. They were named Charter and Lovell, dissolute men with the shambling aspect of the near-dead. They'd known Ennis quite well, were part of his circle when he had his west-end rooms, and, Hallam understood, were also men that Claudia had once known. "Normal" was an agreement struck among people: being in the minority as one who did not indulge made Hallam feel as if he were a naïf, a man without references to anything beyond his own experience. These four had become intimate with something he was merely educated in, and his little forays into opium-eating were tourism compared to smoking the drug. A drop of laudanum was given even to babies.

Charter unfolded a filthy rag, within which lay his kit. He had a long face like a horse's and Hallam imagined that it had melted over time while hanging above a spirit lamp. Charter's kit contained a long pipe with a metal bowl on top that looked like an inverted hornet's nest. There were some scissors, a wooden rod, and a few pieces of yellow rock sugar. Lovell had a pillbox in his pocket that contained the sticky black drug. "Does the doctor want to apply it?" he asked Hallam.

"I'm not a doctor."

Lovell laughed hoarsely. The sound of the man's voice, or perhaps the smell of the small opium cake, roused Ennis and he glanced about sleepily. *Maybe this'll do no good*, thought Hallam. *He is floating already in a tincture of death.*

"Mr. Charter?" Ennis said.

"Here, Sam. With Mr. Lovell."

Lovell leaned in and said something below hearing in Ennis's ear and Ennis said, "*Heavenly.*"

The men prepared the dose; the smell of the flame gave Ennis enough strength to get up on his elbows, but the one called Charter laid his hand along Ennis's flank and gentled him back down on his side. "We drowse when we smoke," he reminded Hallam. He turned nearly completely around and gazed at Claudia. "You remember."

"I do," she said. Her face was pale and she stared fixedly at the pipe.

Lovell spiked a pill of the dark brown substance on the rod and held it in the mouth of the metal bowl over the flame. The paste bubbled after a moment and turned yellow and, as if he were knitting a scarf, Lovell pulled the molten drug away from the bowl, stretching and twisting it, bringing it back down into the main mass and then pulling out more threads. The smoke began to billow out; it had a sickly, creamy smell like apples baking, and Lovell quickly pushed the whole mass back down into the bowl. Ennis had not forgotten what was required of him: he put his mouth against the end of the pipe and sucked deeply. They could hear his lungs rasping, and his eyes flew open in rapture. "Ah," he said loudly, and his ecstasy was embarrassing to Hallam. He exhaled slowly. "My dear life." He looked around him, his eyes yellowed behind the slow-billowing smoke, and he smiled, beatifically, at them. "I am being sunned," he said.

"What is that, Sam?" said Charter.

"Sunned." He raised an arm in benediction. "The light is pouring through me. My impurity turns to gold."

"What is he saying?"

Hallam took hold of Ennis's wrist and lowered it back to the bed. "Silver, Mr. Ennis. Do you not mean silver?"

"No," said Ennis quietly, and he was beginning already to sink into sleep. "Not me, Mr. Hallam. Mine must need be gold to be certain."

His eyes closed and Hallam turned to the men and decided not to explain Ennis's alchemy to them. "Perhaps you can prepare more of that. In case . . ."

"Yes," said Lovell.

Charter looked up at Claudia as he made another, his eyes as jaundiced as a miner's. "Mrs. Rowe? A taste?"

"No," said Hallam. "She's not interested."

"Then she has changed greatly," said Charter.

Claudia crouched beside the two men, watching the shape of Ennis's pupils behind his closed lids: he was dreaming furiously. "Thank you for coming to him."

"It'll wear off within a couple of hours," said Charter. "I'm sure Mr. Lovell would be prepared to sell the remainder of his supply."

Lovell proffered the small pillbox. "These two pipes

we are giving in honour of our friend. But I couldn't give the rest of it."

"I understand," said Hallam with distaste. "I presume it's easy to make, just as you did it?"

"Just don't let it catch fire," said Lovell. "It's nasty burnt, even if you're a habitué."

"I know how to do it," said Claudia quietly. "I'll do it." She held her hand out for the materials and the men wrapped everything up again in the rag and placed the drug in her hands. She gave the kit to Hallam. "Pay them please."

A figure was named and Hallam paid the amount asked without haggling. Charter held his hand out and Hallam shook it, but Charter held it firm and drew Hallam close.

"Is he better off here, sir? Away from his friends and out of his water? We were all fast in the Ward, we were a family. But now he gets to die a dandy, does he?"

"We're his friends as well."

"You're not living off his talents, though, *oh no*," said Charter. "That's a pretty thing. You probably poisoned him."

Claudia put her hand over Charter's arm. Hallam's face was frozen in the fear that the man intended to stay until he did some harm, but with Claudia's touch he withdrew. "William," she said. "You're a good friend, both of you are." Charter was shaking with emotion and glanced back at Lovell. Then he rooted in his pocket and took out the bills Hallam had given him. He peeled off a pound note.

"Buy him some beef and tell him it's from us."

"Mrs. Rowe and I can more than ably—"

"Thank you," said Claudia, closing the bill in her hand. She kissed both men tenderly on their cheeks and without another word (but one look back at Hallam), they left by the door they'd come in.

"A new brand of unchecked depravity," said Hallam, watching them exit the alleyway onto the sidewalk. He drew the curtains against the sight of them.

"They felt a duty and they came," she said. "You can't fault them for that."

"You were tempted," said Hallam.

"It's not easily forgotten."

"I will administer it. When he needs it."

"Whatever you want. But it takes some specific skill. You may want me to show you."

"I'll manage."

She pulled one of her blankets up over Ennis and he shuddered, feeling the air move over him. He opened his eyes halfway. "What is it, Sam?" Ennis's gaze drifted over to Hallam.

Hallam approached the bed. "Is there anything you need?"

His voice was low. "We are lucky men, Mr. Hallam."

"Yes."

"Do you agree?"

"Yes, Sam."

Ennis closed his eyes again.

"What was that?" asked Claudia. Hallam lifted his eyes to her but could think of nothing to say. "What did he tell you?"

He went out of the room as if a gust of wind were behind him and tried to think of something to occupy himself. There were plates to be scrubbed, account books to be written up, but Claudia followed him through the studio into the front room.

"Stop," she said. "Don't walk away from me like that."

"We have things to do." He stood behind the counter stupidly riffling papers.

"Oh, how you have fallen, Jem! From the great heights of your promise to this: procuring dope for a dissipated Irishman and providing for a slattern. Isn't that what you think?"

"I don't think anymore, Mrs. Rowe. It does no good to think."

"The terrible thing for you, *milord*, is that you don't understand how a man of your standing could love people like us. We're not worthy of your care, and yet you give it. What must that mean?"

"It means I am capable of charity. I am a Christian."

"You may be. But I think you are a Torontonian."

"Ah," he said. "And Torontonians are naturally those whose hearts flow with the milk of kindness?"

"You miss my point, Jem. You're home. You've landed in a place you resisted with every fibre of your spirit, and yet this place feels more like you every day. You've given and taken succour because you belong here, among the shipwrecked and the damned. You've lost hope," she said, "and yet you've behaved like a citizen."

"I have a family, Mrs. Rowe. I have people at home."

"I know," she said. "That's why you're so heartless with me. I understand that."

"You don't understand enough."

"You are Hallam of Toronto. Otherwise you would be gone by now. It is more than me and Ennis and your confusion that keeps you here. I've seen it in the pictures you've made. Your camera is not as uncomprehending as you claim to be."

"What it comprehends and what it feels may be two different things, Mrs. Rowe. You won't transform your hopes into mine in desperation."

"But I see you won't leave."

"I may not, but I won't remain without my people either. I belong with my children and my wife. They will come here, eventually."

She stepped toward him and he instinctively moved back, despite there being a wooden counter between them. "Tonight you will *cook opium*. In a pipe. For a dying man. And afterwards, you will sleep unevenly, suffering with your disturbances and aware of me two rooms away. They may come, but they will not find *you* here."

"Leave me!" he said, but she did not budge. "Leave me, Mrs. Rowe. If you are so prescient of my mental state, then you know it's cruel to talk to me like this."

"I'll go," she said, "now that I know you've heard me." She went back through the middle room to Ennis.

He made to close the door to the studio, but heard a voice say, "Hello?" weakly. Then the voice again: "You're closed?" and Claudia returned, to Hallam's surprise, with a man he'd never seen before. He stood beside her in the flickering candlelight she held in front of her.

"We're shut for the evening," Hallam said. Their visitor wore an expensive coat and carried a staff. It had begun to rain and he held his hat tightly over his midsection, trying to keep water from dripping on the floor.

"Is this a private home?"

"I have a permit," said Hallam, grasping for something that might sound unassailable. If the man was a city official, however, they were in considerable trouble.

"Unusual," said the man. He unfastened his top two coat buttons and slid an envelope out. It was a long, thin brown envelope, sealed with wax. "My name is Alexander Burton. Are you Jeremy George Hallam?"

"Jeremy?" said Claudia.

"Yes."

"And that is Mr. Rowe in the next room?"

"Mrs. Rowe," said Claudia. "I'm a partner in the business."

Burton peered over his thin spectacles at her, processing this. It was amusing, what things became quite normal in the new world. "So you are," he said. He broke the seal on the envelope. "Your mule of a deputy mayor tried to sell me a set of photographs he said you took for him. They're your work?"

They both nodded, dumb with anticipation. They were probably going to jail, Hallam thought, that was the logical end to all this.

"He was willing to take two shillings for them." Mr. Burton broke the seal on the envelope and pulled out a parchment. He spun it smartly toward Hallam. There it was, a summons. A blue ribbon at the bottom was attached to the paper by another wax seal.

"What's this about?"

"I'm a colonial undersecretary for Upper Canada, Mr. Hallam. A committee has been struck on Her Majesty's wishes and next year the Province of Canada will be established in place of your eastern and western federations. Your city will be one of five vying to be the seat of government."

"And?"

"A city that thinks to photograph itself—"

"We took those photos under our own direction," said Hallam. "We had no intention of breaching anyone's legal right to anything."

"I beg your pardon?"

"He's underslept," said Claudia, stepping forward with a conciliatory smile. "We have all the plates from the selection you saw at Colonel Thompson's office. We can make ready a huge cross-section of the city for whomever wishes to peer at it. Our survey is exhaustive."

"That dreary anthology? It's no wonder Thompson kicked you out, ma'am. You'd sooner convince the queen to put the capital in James Bay. No, you must find a way to convince the adjudicators in London that this city has what it takes to be a world-class capital. You must be honest without being dismal." He turned his attention to Hallam. "I want a portrait of Toronto. Can you be artful?"

Hallam stared up at Claudia. "*She* can be artful."

Alexander Burton cast an interested look at both of them. "I can visit one of your competitors if you like."

"No," said Claudia quickly. She took the paper and read it. "One hundred pounds?"

"That's the local commission's budget. Whatever you can get them to part with after material costs is yours."

She offered her hand to the man, who stared at it bemused. Then he shook it. "Consider yourselves the parents of this city's future and then make good on that duty. Impress your queen with your intentions, and you'll bring fame to this place. Imagine *that* as your legacy, eh?"

"How many undersecretaries are there?" Claudia asked.

"Forty," said the man, replacing his hat. He leaned in toward them. "But I'm one of the important ones."

5.

IT WAS GOING TO BE THE MOST PRESTIGIOUS HOTEL
in the city, better even than Sword's. Charles and Marcus
Rossin had bought up the southeast corner of York and
King streets in 1855, and by March of 1856 the bricklay-
ers were raising the walls. It would have all the most
modern amenities: water closets on each floor (and some
rooms with their own), gas lighting throughout, proper
heat in the winter. There would be no bad rooms, no bad
views, and the restaurant on the ground floor would
serve the best fare in the whole province.

But it was neither the rooms nor the service that
appealed most to the firm of Hallam, Ennis, and Rowe. It
was that, at five storeys, the Rossin House was going to
be the tallest building in the city, with an excellent aspect
on the lake to the south, the centre of town and its diminishing thoroughfares east and west, and a good clear
view all the way to the hills rising beyond the village of
Yorkville. The city entire could be taken in simply by
standing on the rooftop and rotating in a slow circle. One
could enclose the place in an open-armed sweep.

The Toronto Committee for the Establishment of a Permanent Capital in the Province of Canada accepted Mr. Burton's nomination of the firm for the job of photographing the city. Hallam, on his advice, had visited the committee with a portfolio of fine pictures, and some of the grander images he'd taken for the survey he'd done with Mrs. Rowe. A front-on view of the customs house looming over the street like a great sentinel impressed them terribly. "Why not ten more of these?" asked one of them, and Burton had replied, "Because the queen needs glory, not income."

Income, however, was something the Rossin brothers needed, having fronted the construction costs at twenty thousand pounds, and they required a fee of ten pounds just for access to the roof of the Rossin House. Plates and collodion would come to another ten pounds, and each of the six members of the committee commanded an honorarium of eight pounds. Fifteen fair copies of the report, plus a master set of the photographs, came to nine and three. Then there was passage to England for the presentation (to be undertaken by the uninspiring chair of the committee, an ex–city councilman with an ape's forehead named Hartford Gough) at an additional cost of fourteen pounds, plus a per diem of eight shillings a day, or two and a half more pounds to cover the stay. Total: eighty-five and nine. Leaving fourteen and three for Hallam, Ennis, and Rowe.

It was still a profit.

The Rossins gave them the morning of November 23, 1856, a Sunday. Hallam and Claudia made three trips each with equipment: Ennis's best camera—the Palmer & Longking bellows—a standing tent for all chemical processes, a five-gallon bottle of distilled water, four baths, and bottles of solution any one of which, should it be dropped, would do permanent damage to the new hotel. (They carried up the jar of formic acid wrapped in three layers of muslin, between the two of them.) It was four flights of stairs each way to the rooftop and back, and by the time they came out the door onto the flat roof, nearly an hour had passed and they could barely stand. They paused in an exhausted silence and collected themselves. The roof was covered with fresh pebbling on top of a layer of cold tar. Church was in, and as a result the city appeared abandoned to all its edges. An eerie silence prevailed.

"Will they be impressed with a city no one seems to be living in?"

"Perhaps it will make them sentimental," said Hallam. "As if it were a museum dedicated to their favourite architecture."

The narrowest dimension of Rossin House was its north–south width at just over ninety-one feet. Therefore Hallam made a circle within this limit, calculated its circumference at two hundred and eighty-six feet, and divided it into twenty-two-foot sections. By setting the height of the camera and the focal length of the lens so that each individual view of the city would bisect the circumference of the circle in twenty-two-foot intervals, they would make a panorama of the city in exactly thirteen exposures.

"I'd forgotten calculus mattered in your field," said Claudia when he'd done mapping the circle.

"Apothecary is measurement first, physick second."

"I suppose none of it's any good if you don't know the line between relief and death."

He chose not to respond. Thus far in his life, that line was ceaselessly moving. He put the camera in the centre of the circle under a deadened sky. Natural light would not be enough for crisp exposures; any remaining city life—horses, people, pushcarts, dogs—would slur to grey near-invisibility in the fifteen-second shutter openings. Claudia got behind the camera and pointed it due west. Justice Elmsley's house, with its high white walls, stood near the left edge of the frame, beyond the piano and coach manufactories that abutted King Street. A pile of brick lay in the street in front of the coach factory. The city was forever a work in progress: Hallam could not imagine a future when the streets would not be pock-marked in regular intervals by butts of brick and piles of wood, forged and cast nails being ground underfoot for future generations to chance on, along with the broken ends of tobacco pipes and smashed beer bottles. He checked the focus: the trees in front of Upper Canada College were moving in a slight wind and he wanted to wait to ensure they appeared as a crystalline expanse of bare limbs, but the wind would not die down. He retreated to the preparation tent and made up a plate, put the holder into the camera for her, and Claudia Rowe made the first picture. She passed him the plate and he went immediately back into the tent to pour the acid on it, wash it, and fix it. The first image, in ghostly negative, was done, and already his nostrils were stinging.

Hallam moved the markers to the right and watched his business partner concentrate on her measurements, although little would change between exposures, and he found himself in a reverie of admiration for her stillness, her application. He had watched her change: the Claudia Rowe that must have existed before she came to Toronto was certainly all but gone, and this durable creature had replaced her—a human being known more to him than anyone. He could tell her mood from the back, simply from the curve of her spine. He would not—at least not now—trace that thought past its fulcrum to its other conclusion. She made the photograph and stood up behind the camera, exhaling as if she'd surfaced from a dive. "Next one," she said, and she began to turn the camera again, angling it into a view of the city ajumble with houses and churches, appearing northwest across King Street. She changed the plate, slipping the new one inside its protected sheath into the body of the camera. He stood outside of the frame—in all of these pictures he would be an unseen, barely felt presence beyond the edge, just as she would be the unknown consciousness registering with a living eye the artifact of what was seen. She took off the lens cover and together they counted to twenty and another flat world of roofs and windows, streets and doors burnt into reverse-life on the glass.

They traded places and Claudia moved Hallam's markers along the edge of the circle while he adjusted the sights to get the fourth picture in view. It presented a vision of a temporary city against a more developed one behind, and he snorted with derision as he framed it. "What?" she said from the roof's edge.

"This is an idiotic composition."

She came to look in the viewfinder. Through it, dusty York Street, with its storefronts facing off like combatants in the desert, rose north toward Osgoode Hall at the top of the street, its golden dome as pompous as the Brighton Pavilion's. From the way he'd framed the picture, with York Street almost centred, the hall was a hallucination in the distance, a dying man's dream of Mecca. "It is a little subtle, isn't it? Perhaps a few dead dogs lying in the street would complete it," she said. "Beggars with missing legs."

"I think an empty street creeping with horsehair and grit is comment enough on all that," he said. "And to think it's the last major piece of architecture one might see on one's way to purchase a lady's favours."

Somehow it looked to him as if a dragonfly could shatter it, that illusion of the city's standing in the real world. A feeling he couldn't name began creeping through his guts. He made the picture. The next view showed a mass of houses and tenements ranging off to the northeast, but he paused behind the camera and then stood up. The lake framed his head, the best light of the day reflecting off its surface so she could not make out his expression. Then he picked up the entire apparatus and moved it to the right, off the centre of the circle. "You'll ruin your perspective," she said, holding a new plate out to him.

He set the camera down and pointed it due north. "Look at it now."

In the previous view, the edge of a row of threadbare bungalows—mere logs held together with creosote and crushed stone—would have stood at the bottom left edge of the frame, with the churches and banks of the older part of the city the centre of the picture. But here, he'd made these shacks the entire foreground, with the eastern wing of Osgoode Hall visible in the distance behind them.

"That's rather ugly," she said. "Move it back to where it was."

"Shouldn't the committee see that the city has housing options for persons of all levels of income? It makes us look progressive, I think."

She held her head sideways. "Did you show this Toronto to your wife and daughters? Do they know about it?"

"No. But now, I think, perhaps they should."

"Be honest then, Mr. Hallam." She passed him the masqued frame and spread her hands wide. "By all means, take it." She stepped to the ledge. In one of the doorways of the shacks below stood a large woman in a white housedress. Claudia hallooed her and the woman looked up, frightened to hear a voice from above, and tentatively waved. "You are going to be the subject of an important social document, ma'am," she called down. "Do you think you could smile?" The woman did not, but Claudia heard Hallam slip the lens cover off anyway. She imagined the constabulary collecting in the street below. "Satisfied?" she said to him. "Can we get back to earning our meagre wage?"

He replaced the camera, and went into the tent to prepare three plates. In quick succession he made all three images: north-northeast through the mix of little tanneries and cooperages, better houses and side streets above King Street, then northeast where most of the major churches swam into view. It appeared as if he wasn't paying attention to his own measurements, just turning and counting the quarter-minute, turning and making the image. Perhaps he was getting a chill—the air off the lake was bone cold. "Stop," she called to him. "Slow down, they'll dry out before I can fix them." But he took the view of King Street to the east and began the turn to his right. "Stop it, Jem! That was an important picture, that one especially."

He suddenly pushed back from the camera, standing up stiffly, and it teetered before righting itself. Claudia had sprung forward to catch it, but then found herself with his eyes on her, his mouth contorted into an expression of disgust. "Do you want them to make this a city all the world will admire? So more people will come to the Great Capital and seek their fortunes and then spend their bodies in the lake? This isn't a little thing, Mrs. Rowe, we're going to influence what people do with themselves. And what would you like to do with those frauds who put dreams of cheap land and temperate seasons into your husband's head? That's who we are now."

"A good life is not impossible here."

"A good *death* is not possible. Except for those who arrived here with their pockets full. The ones who followed them, who are made to clear their roads and pay the rents on their lots, they're paying tithes! They can't go back home. Could Sam? To die at home with his people? If he took the money for passage they'd starve for lack of his income by the time he got there."

"You think people are helplessly acted upon, Mr. Hallam. That's only true if you prefer to see it that way."

"I am deserted here!" he shouted, opening his arms. "And with no choice but to make the fat children of Jarvis Street look like suckling pigs in suit jackets and sundresses, and to tart up this beshat fairground of a city so other credulous people like ourselves will come here and strap themselves to its engines!" He wrenched the plateholder out of the camera and pulled the exposed glass out of it. He held it up, burning the silver, and smashed it on the roof.

She stared at it, lying in pieces like a broken eye, cauling over. "Good. Go on and topple it, Mr. Hallam! Lay it waste. Let's make a picture of it at its most wretched, and then they can put the capital in gay Kingston and Toronto can wither back to forest and we'll all be done with it. After all, you'll be in England feeding bonbons to your children, so what could it matter to you?"

"Oh, I am going back to England."

"I know you are."

"I am," he said. He stepped forward and a larger section of the broken plate cracked beneath his boot. Its report came back to them a second later and bore with it a

strange silence in which Claudia Rowe understood at once
what he was saying to her. He saw her mouth form a word
and then go slack. "I'm sorry," he said. "I leave just before
the official close of navigation. In two weeks' time."

She looked as if she'd been struck, then lifted a hand
and let it fall back to her side. "You are truly—what a
hateful . . . Tell me where the money for that is coming
from?"

"The committee."

The bells at St. James' began to toll eleven. As if
echoing them, St. Andrew's and the Apostolic Church
on Bay Street rang out, and then behind them St. George
the Martyr, like a call rolling out across the city. Church
was out and the streets would begin to fill again. He
approached the camera, but she put her palm flat against
the lens and held it, as if silencing a child. "So they're
going to use our profits to send you home?"

"No," he said. "I'm going in place of Mr. Gough.
They thought I might make a better impression."

She laughed sourly. "A traitor in their midst."

"I'm not charged with making the decision, Mrs.
Rowe. Only with showing the evidence."

She was shaking her head at him slowly, in disbelief,
and he began to turn the camera to the right, pushing
against her hand, which she released after a moment. His
face against the camera, he waited for further opposi-
tion, but there came none, and he directed his eye toward
the world below King Street, and saw, off the corner of
the roof, the Royal Lyceum. His hands were shaking.
Yes, the Royal Lyceum, he forced himself to think. A

strange place for an opera house, squatting between two main roads, but he knew it to be successful, with the Americans booking it and even the occasional French or German company. He'd seen *An Invalid of Britain* there, and thought it a little long. And yet, what would it tell the adjudicants in London, to see this giant brick shed set within a rookery of half-built, half-demolished buildings? It would tell them it was a city forever no longer what it had been, but not quite what it was turning into. What kind of place was that to anoint a capital? A place always in the process of being erased?

Claudia hadn't moved and he put her farther to his back after taking the southeast view, forcing the sound of her breathing out of his mind, and pointing the lens over Wellington Street in the back of the hotel. Here were the pretty estates of Boulton and Baldwin—fine estates, four-chimneyed mansions sitting on neat squares of now-dead grass and surrounded by a babble of filthy buildings. Had these houses tumbled from the stars and landed there at random? Their inhabitants looked out toward the lake and the railway, their faces turned away from the squalor. What they must think about, when they saw that lake. Not what he thought. It was just a pretty waterway filled with trout and pickerel and bass to them, and there were nuthatches squeaking and clambering down the trunks of the silver maples at its edge. The people in those houses had no idea, no idea at all, did they? No, they did not see this tabula rasa lake that he saw in the ground-glass viewfinder, the lake flat-on waiting to be named by action: something to be crossed, to be tamed, to be survived. He waited a moment, hearing a train coming from the west, and with the light on his side at last, made a fast exposure of the train crossing in the background, with Tinning's Wharf, mills, and houses directly behind it.

He heard horses on King Street conveying people back from Mass to the hotel or their homes, and the soft sound of the distant hooves on dirt became sharp as they got closer and crossed onto the macadam at Bay Street. Her silence was becoming unbearable now, and although he pressed on and turned the camera to its final view, he could not keep himself from looking at her, and then could not—if he were still human—go back to his work. She stood riven to her spot, staring insensate at him, her face greased with tears. His hands dropped to his sides. "When were you going to tell me?" she said.

"Mrs. Rowe . . ."

"And I'll go to Potter's Field, will I?"

"That is a faithless thing to say."

"Of course you won't know if I do, will you? So you can tell yourself anything over your toast points and newspaper. Which newspaper will you be reading then, I wonder? Not one with the notice of my passing, I'll wager." She began for the door that led back down to the fifth floor of the hotel.

"Mrs. Rowe, you will be taken care of," he said, but she held a hand up, her back to him, and he was silenced. The door closed behind her. He could hear, within, her footfalls diminishing.

All around him, in the streets below the hotel, people were returning to their houses. Bishop Strachan's stable gate was open, his man waiting within to welcome his carriage home. Gradually the streets were filling. It was a day of rest, but people would be visiting each other; cooks in the townhouses below prepared the Sunday hams. When some doors closed, a good English life unfolded behind them. Much of the rest of the city felt the cold. He pulled the cap off the lens, counted to fifteen, and replaced it.

Hallam walked back through the streets toward the store, his overloaded cart in front of him. A fine mist-like snow had started to fall and it seemed to make the equipment and the glass plates heavier than they had been before, less willing to travel over the uneven road. It had taken ninety minutes to get all the equipment down to the street by himself, and his back was drenched with sweat that had begun to freeze. He was still upset with himself for having let slip in a moment of anger that he was going to England. He had not meant to punish her with this information. He'd already made arrangements for her, having paid the outstanding amount on her husband's insurance at the Bank of Toronto out of his savings. Now that the policy was paid up, it would take another year before Claudia could engage the coroner to open an investigation into her husband's disappearance and perhaps six months to reasonably conclude he was dead. After which the policy would be paid in full, a total of six hundred pounds. He found himself admiring Mr. Rowe for having had the sense to buy such a good policy.

Ennis was wrapped in his blankets on his front-room bed when Hallam got back, but Claudia was not home. He checked to see if Ennis was sleeping and saw the pupils behind his thin lids shuddering. The cold had sapped his own strength and he decided he would take a nap. He lit a small fire in the little grate by the door, not caring that the smoke issuing from the front of the store and drifting over the sidewalk could alert people to the fact that there were human beings within: he was too tired and too unhappy to care.

He fell immediately to sleep and he was back on the roof of the Rossin House, his camera pointing south toward the lake. The little train that had passed on the rails in front of the wharves came from the right and passed behind the houses on the left. Immediately as it vanished, it reappeared on the right again. He watched it with quiet interest and noticed that on each passing it had one less car, and before long it was down to nothing but an engine and a single car, and then the engine, and after that he could hear it passing, but it was gone.

It seemed a reasonable idea to walk from the roof down to the ground and visit the lake, and this he did, stepping from the parapet onto the air and then down a foot and then another, following the shape of a stairway through the space between roof and ground. Reaching the bottom he continued south, pausing to let the invisible train pass, and then on to Tinning's Wharf. The lake was as still as glass; he walked out onto it. He moved across it, staring down into the gleaming surface. There was something below, but the sun was too bright on the water and all he could see was himself and the sky above him. He would have to lower himself to his belly to annul the shadows, and once he did he saw that he was in the sky of another city. He was looking down on Toronto. It was Toronto, but it was not the place he was living in, not the place he was dreaming. It was full of marvellous conveyances—train cars that moved on macadam all by themselves and towering buildings clad in glass. And people, a shocking number of people. He drifted down from this sky, and he saw in the windows of the buildings the very pictures he had made of the city, and they were the windows the people of this city looked through! He saw people he knew in the streets, he watched them. Presently, he was among them, and he tried to speak to them. *Do you not remember me?* he tried to say to one woman, but in his head all he could hear was twittering. He went down closer to the ground, past people's legs and feet, and then he hit the ground and shattered it and he was in water; cold, dark water.

He woke without startling, his eyes snapping open, and he saw the shadow of the room beside him against the wall. There was the sound of paper shuffling. He sat up and Claudia was beside him in a chair, wrapped in one of the blankets he'd covered himself with when he lay down. She was reading a letter, one of a number that lay in her lap. His feeling of remorse flooded back. He wondered for a moment if he was still asleep, but just as soon as he thought this, he realized he could smell her, her scent mixed with the warm wool smell of the blanket.

He knew she was aware of him, his wakefulness, but she continued reading silently, and neatly moved a sheet from the front of a small sheaf of paper to the back. After a moment, she lay the paper down in her lap and covered it with her hand. "They don't know where you are," she said. "They don't know what's become of you." She flipped a couple of sheets and he threw his blankets off. "This one is dated September 14. Two months ago and already sick with worry."

He grabbed the letter out of her lap and took the envelopes as well, swinging his feet down hard to the cold floor. He glanced at them quickly, the sight of Alice's handwriting a reproach that made his stomach coil.

"How could you not have written to them?"

He shook the letters at her. "This is none of your business at all!"

"But beautiful Christ, you're alive and they don't even know it! Why let them think you're dead?"

He stood up, his frame looming over her, and he hurled the bundle of letters toward the grate. "Because I am," he said. Blood buzzed behind his eyes and he swayed. "These are not letters to me."

She looked at them, the shadows of the grate's black bars moving over them wavelike, like the shape of sand under water. She wondered if a spark could jump from behind the grille and ignite the paper and then the shop. If Alice Hallam's unconsolable handwriting would be the agent of their deaths. "I agree," she said. "The man they write to is gone. So will you not let them think differently then? When you are there? You will permit them to move on with their lives?"

"I would like to see my children."

The invocation of Cecile and Jane silenced them both. But she could not stop herself from recognizing that he had not mentioned Alice. Something travelled across her scalp. She got up and collected the letters off the floor, squared them neatly and went into the studio to put them somewhere safe, then stood in the darkened room by herself. When she returned he was still staring at the space the letters had lain in, as if they were still there. "You love me," she said. "You can say as much. It doesn't have to change anything, but it would help us both."

"I cannot."

"You have not said what you plan to do once you have said your piece to the London committee. I have been afraid to ask you. But you seem not to know, so I will say to you now: I want you to come back, Jem Hallam. Do what you need to do, see whomever you must see, but then come home. Return to me."

He went and sat on Ennis's bed, pausing a moment to feel the man's hand. It was freezing cold. "You will have the shop," he said to her. "And I've paid your annuity. I don't intend for you to suffer because of my choices."

"No, that would be unlike you." His consistency had stopped surprising her. It was a quality she shared, but it didn't seem to serve her the way it did him. He sat before her, bed-rumpled, his hair sticking up, and at a loss for what to do with his limbs. He took her blanket off the chair and laid it over Ennis. "If you want your letters back, ask me. I've put them beyond reach for now."

"His hand is cold," said Hallam quietly. "But his body is burning up."

"It requires fuel to die," she said.

~

In the night, Ennis worsened, and the two of them hovered over him, applying alcohol to his chest and trying to get him awake long enough to drink water. His eyes were rheumy, swollen red, and his face was thick with edema. They asked him if he had pain, and he nodded or whispered that he did. Hallam mixed morphia into hot water and they put as much into him as they could. Hallam had begun to fear that Ennis would die in the night. Sleep is a leaf on death's tree. He didn't like being in the dark now—the cold without, but waves of heat pouring off Ennis and the candlelight spreading its black-and-yellow tail on the wall. He felt as if he were in a tomb. They sat on either side of him, each holding a hand, trying not to make eye contact over the man's gleaming body. His eyes opened and closed, unseeing, the eyes of an ancient tortoise, and one of the last times he spoke, he said to Hallam, "Take care of my children."

Around three in the morning, Ennis began to thrash, a wet rattling sound coming from his chest. "Do something for him," Claudia importuned, but Hallam, ex-apothecary, didn't know what could be done. His old supplies were gone, the morphia was useless, and the city was sleeping. She rushed back into her room and returned with the last of Charter and Lovell's supply. She told Hallam to sit him up and she prepared a pipe, inhaling the smoke but holding it in her mouth and passing it into Ennis's through his sweat-dank lips. His chest swelled and the smoke came out of his nose. She handed the pipe to Hallam and her eyes were on him and he understood that no one who had loved Ennis could not be a part of this sacrament. A sweet clovey taste in his mouth—it brought back to him the flavour of his laudanum waters—and he opened Ennis's mouth and pushed the smoke into him. They both saw his body subside. Hallam put his hand on the pipe and would not let Claudia take it again. He blew a second dose into the man, and again Ennis's body settled, like something drifting under the surface of water, darkening, and suddenly Hallam could feel the water from his dream, its cold against him, and the weight of his own body being taken down. When he tried to breathe, every pore in his body took in a watery air. He was porous, open. He saw Claudia and his skin leapt: she was smoke, he saw that she was moving through him. He put his hands on his rib cage to feel the air and saw her slip between his fingers. She emerged out of his back as if he were a needle threaded with her. Some distant sense told him that Ennis had died and he saw the man's mouth was blue and slack. He trailed his fingertips down Ennis's forehead and closed his eyes, the skin cold. "I need to lie down," he said, and he backed himself up to find his mattress. He looked at Ennis lying there, eyes pointing upward,

Claudia beside the dead man, her body fitted to his side, her arm over Ennis's chest, and he looked down at himself and saw her thin arm draped over him as well, her fingers trailing against his side. Had she said to him that all her men were ghosts, or had she only thought it and he'd heard it nonetheless? Where was he? Sleep overtook him.

## 6.

Samuel Ennis was buried in the necropolis three days before the end of November, before the ground would seize up for winter. They were surprised to see how many people came: word had gone around. It was a relief to Hallam to know that Ennis would be remembered, at least as long as those who knew him could speak of him. And then, like all people, his memory would drift down time and become smooth before it broke apart. The gravediggers made a clean, deep hole partway down a hill overlooking the Don River. Hallam held Claudia's hand as the men lowered the plain pine box into the grave.

Over the next weeks, he settled his accounts and brought Claudia to a solicitor on Toronto Street. The man prepared a document that would come into force the day after Claudia's husband was declared dead. On that date, the deed in the store would pass to her. Until then, Hallam gave her power of attorney over all aspects of the business. They agreed on a dividend of five percent of net sales in the store to be sent to Ennis's family. The first instalment was three pounds eight, which they sent as a bill of exchange in sterling to the family in Kenmare, Ireland, with a letter explaining their connection to the late Samuel Ennis.

Claudia accompanied Hallam dumbly on his rounds, saying little except to comment on the mildness of the winter or to remind him of something he needed to do. He believed that she had accepted what was about to happen, but he worried also at her quietness, and he braced himself for a collapse. That he thought her brave embarrassed him—he had no right to imagine her as courageous to lessen his own guilt and grief. She was stricken: it only seemed to be bravery.

At the store, he began to pack what few things he had. The original plates for the panorama would come with him—the committee insisted on this, saying the queen's survey had paid for all materials. But the more he thought about it, the more he approved, and he asked Claudia to wrap all the plates associated with their views of Toronto, the detailed registry, his own images, all of it. There were institutions in England that would care to have this catalogue of pictures; they would not be misused in a country where history obtained. She wrapped them all individually in muslin, and when muslin ran out, in newspaper, which in two layers was nearly as cushioning as cloth. His own belongings fit into a sack and a valise. She used his original steamer trunk to pack the glass plates. The trunk would have to go down to the harbour in a hack; it was too heavy for them to lift even together.

December came, and with it the holy season. He took her to Sword's for supper and afterwards he danced with her. He remembered himself walking outside, as he had done almost a year ago, coming back from Ennis's cottage, and seeing the people within behind mullioned windows, talking and raising their glasses. He'd imagined he was within their company and he was struck by an instinct to go outside and find the man who had just arrived, thinking the place closed and foreign, and tell him he would soon be inside as well, full of dinner and with friends.

*There are people around*, he would tell the man, *who will find they need you and they will fold you into their lives. You will become necessary.* But thinking this, he wondered if he had actually made others necessary to himself. He certainly had become indispensable, and yet he knew he had withheld himself. From Ennis because he feared the man's appetites. And from Claudia . . .

He'd finally realized that he did not understand himself enough to fully take in another human being. Having children with Alice was, if not a form of knowing, then one of expression: it joined them well enough, gave them likeness. But being in another place, alone and outside of the dailiness of his whole life, had immersed him in himself in a way he'd never imagined. There was too much of him. There was too much of others. A great simplicity lay under it all, and yet when he had been younger he lived in the presumption of that simplicity, that knowledge of being a living thing among others, never having to see what armoured that beingness. Now he knew the cost of being connected to others, and he grieved knowing it.

He would never be able to explain this—not to Claudia, not to Alice. He only wanted to drowse a little

in his life, as most people did, and carry along as if he'd
gotten lost in a forest for a while, where the sounds of
animals were too distinct for comfort and the scents too
strong, and then the sounds of home came piping in
through the boughs. The wish was for home and the
wish was a weakness.

He was leaving in three days, on a saint's day, the
Immaculate Conception.

On Sundays and Wednesdays, the packet steamers left
for Oswego. Hallam would take a train from there to
Boston, and thence across the Atlantic. Lines of hacks
and people on foot converged on the two docks at the
foot of Yonge Street, where the boats would arrive with
those who had just made the trip, to exchange themselves with those going home. A common sight now,
those emerging from the boats, their legs weak on
the gangplanks but their faces grateful for an end to the
journey, and on the shoreline their new countrymen
and -women watching them. Those faces were familiar
to them and yet also changed in a way the new arrivals
could not name but would come to know, as they saw
their own faces, over the coming months and years,
transform with experience.

On busy shipping days, the sky over the lake grew
dim with greying steam and smoke, a stirring vision of
industry, the world arriving on their shore. Hallam and
Claudia watched the lake approach them (so it seemed)
as their driver brought them down Yonge Street toward
the wharves and it loomed through the front carriage

window under a high bright December sky: one of the last perfect days for sailing before shipping would close for the winter. Already there were slugs of ice in the harbour, a slushy marsh not yet solid.

Hallam was dressed as a gentleman, a gentleman at last: a black greatcoat and a top hat, white gloves in his pockets. Leaving as he'd arrived, with a whiff of formality. He imagined he might be vomiting within hours, the top hat sitting on a deck bench, abandoned as he rushed to the railings. He hadn't known he'd hate the ocean until he first crossed it, and now he dreaded the trip home, the long rolling motion of the boat on the water, the endless sea, the nights a huge dark expanse.

Stevedores pulled the massive trunk off the back of the hackney and took it below. He watched it vanish into the hold. "I think they could drop it once or twice without too much loss," Claudia said. Another man took Hallam's sack and, finding his name on the manifest, promised him it would appear in his room.

They stood together in the crowd that milled about in front of the wharf, too many people for solemnity or even quiet, which comforted him. He did not want to see her upset, and he carried himself with a bright cheerfulness that communicated everything between them had been settled when, of course, it hadn't and never could be.

"Do you think you'll actually be sitting down with the queen?"

"I doubt it," he said. "I imagine she doesn't even know they're looking for a new capital."

"What will you tell them? I imagine you standing on the table and stomping your feet. Will you be disagreeable?"

He smiled faintly. "I'll be polite and let the pictures speak for themselves."

"I'm sure you will," she said. She waited a moment, moving from one side to another to let people pass. All the kinds of goodbyes people made were around them, brief or tender or tearful. "There's no need of a scene, Jem, so you can relax. It would be nice to have a friendly goodbye."

"Yes," he said, relieved. "I'd like that."

"The only thing is, I can't let you go while I still hold a debt. You never gave me my words. Could you not have thought of two words for me?"

"I could. At least."

"Then I'll take them now, while there's time."

He put his valise on the ground at his feet and crouched down to open it. He brought out a gilt-edged copy of *American Notes*, which he'd bought at Churchill's especially for the journey. He took the stub of a pencil out of his pocket and opened the book to the endpaper. "I owe interest by now," he said.

"How much?"

"Let's say a hundred and fifty percent."

She raised her brow. "That's five words. It might be hard to find a story with all those words in it."

He wrote on the endpaper and tore it out, folded it neatly in three, like a letter. "I don't think it will be that hard, Mrs. Rowe. I've been listening to you talk for almost a year now, and five words is nothing for you.

Put this in your pocket." She took it from him and tucked it away. "Leave it there until home."

"So this is what I am to have of you?" She patted the pocket.

"At least that."

"Neither of us imagined this life, Mr. Hallam, but we did well by it. Tell me you agree with that."

"It was different from what I was expecting."

"But it was good just the same, it was worthwhile. Was it not?"

He smiled for her, but it felt as if the wind off the lake was blowing right through him. "It was magnificent."

The crowd moving onto the boat was thinning and he felt that he was gone already. A shadow of his self was standing here on the land, while all of his substance had moved below decks already.

"You're going to shake my hand, aren't you?" she said, bringing him back. He held his hand out, and she stared at it for a moment and then took it in hers. They did not shake as men do, but stood facing each other, clasping hands. "Goodbye, Jem."

"Goodbye, Mrs. Rowe," he said.

From the foredeck, he watched her walk back up toward Front Street, her hands in her pockets, with the others who were staying. From the waterfront, they converged on Yonge Street, the shadows of buildings lying against the cobble in sharp, sunlit relief, the broad form of the crowd funnelling into a thick line, like a liquid being poured somehow up, and she melted into their company.

*Seven*

~

# CONSOLATION

~

*Toronto, November 1997*

## I.

HOWARD HAD NOT WANTED TO MEET AT HIS APART-
ment. There was a café at the top of his street, and
when John came in he was already there, sitting alone
with his coat on. John made a small show of taking his
off and laying it over the back of the chair. The manuscript was sitting in the middle of the table,
giving off rads. Howard regarded him with knitted
brows.

"You okay?" John said.

"Am *I* okay?" said Howard. "What'd you—walk into
a door?"

"Oh this." John touched his lip lightly. It was numb
where it had swelled. "Something like a door." He stared
at the manuscript, the open secret lying dumb in the middle of the table. "Can I sit?"

"Go ahead," said Howard, watching him into the
chair. "So . . . you really wrote this, huh?"

"I don't think it's finished."

"That's a yes, though."

"Yeah."

Howard stuffed his hands into his coat pockets. "What happens next if it's not finished? Does this Hallam come back?"

"I don't know."

"When are you *going* to know?"

"I have some more research to do," John said.

"Am I paying for you to do that research as well?"

*Ah*, thought John. "I did this on my own time, Howard."

"Ennis is me, right?"

"Why would you think that?"

"The grotesque savant who passes his knowledge on to his acolyte? And then dies a noble death?"

"You're not dead, Howard."

"I'm just asking."

The waitress was a waif in combat boots. She signalled she was ready to take their order by silently cocking a hip at them. "I'll have crow," Howard said.

She blinked at him. "We don't have that."

"Coffee, then."

"Me too," said John. The girl went away. "Why are you angry?"

"I'm not angry. I'm . . . gobsmacked. Here I was, paying you to do *my* research, and you squeeze this out of yourself in your spare time? I can't write a play to save my soul . . ."

"I didn't show you this to make you feel bad."

"I know that." His employer looked shrunken in his chair, staring down at the tabletop. When at last he raised his eyes to John's, his pupils were the size of pinholes. "So tell me, please, what the hell are you doing? What in Christ is this for?"

"Howard, can you lower—"

"Where does this come from? All of this was in your father-in-law's diary? Surely there were no bloody drugstores in that thing."

"There was no diary," John said. He waited for Howard to process that.

"No diary."

"No."

"Why the hell would he have lied about that?"

"He was sick. There wasn't time to be honest."

"*Time?*"

"He had enough left to point at something, but not to name it."

"Its name was *Nothing*."

"No. It was more like *Not-what-you-were-thinking*."

"I haven't led a very interesting life," said Howard. John watched the man's eyes search the crumbs and salt flecks on the tabletop, as if they could constellate into something meaningful. "How do you know all this?"

"He told me."

"When."

"The morning he died."

"*I lied about the diary, fare thee well?*"

"Not like that."

"Then like what?"

"I asked him and he told me when I was driving him to the Hanlan Point ferry docks."

Howard leaned away, and his forearms drifted back off the tabletop and fell into his lap. The waitress came with the two coffees.

"That was a joke, right?" she said.

Howard looked up at her as if she'd floated down from the ceiling. "What?"

"Crow. No one serves crow."

"Plenty of people serve crow, miss. You just don't serve it here."

She screwed her lips into a moue and put down the coffees. "Is there anything else?"

"Thank you, no," said John.

Howard leaned back over the table. "You *drove* him to the ferry." John nodded. "You drove him to the ferry and he got out of the car and bought a ticket and got on the ferry and then jumped overboard and died? And you were the one who drove him there, John? You?"

"Yes."

"And does anyone in his family happen to know this?"

"No."

Howard laid his hand on the manuscript again, more lightly now, and pulled it halfway across the table. "And now you want to give them a gussied-up version of what might have happened here in place of all the things you know? My Christ, you're a dark horse, John."

"Should I keep it to myself, Howard? I was writing it for myself. But now I think I should give it to them."

"Well, if you're really asking for my opinion, I think you should get plastic surgery and change your name.

Then run for your life. Aren't you an accessory to a crime or something?"

"I didn't do anything wrong."

"Well, if driving your fiancée's father to his death wasn't wrong, and keeping what you know to yourself wasn't wrong, and shacking up with Bridget's mother—"

"I'm not shacked up with her!"

"Then trying to fix a lie with another lie isn't exactly right. Is it? Because that's the math here, correct? Multiplying negatives?"

"David Hollis was a good man."

"A liar who despaired, a good man? And what are you?"

"He deserves to be remembered differently."

"You think this will turn that particular lock? John: he made it all up, and now you have too. This is just going to add to the overall *badness* of this situation."

"No," said John. "I'm a witness."

Howard looked around wildly. It struck John that he'd suddenly woken the man up. *Do you think you're awake?* David had said, and John had not been sure. But now: this alertness, this pain.

"So . . . what?" said Howard. "You hand them this . . . this *alternate* lie, and they thank you? And everything is fixed? That's terrible."

"I thought, of everyone I know, you'd be the one who'd understand. I thought you had faith in this kind of thing."

"In a lie?"

"In a certain kind of lie."

He watched Howard run his fingertips over his forehead, his eyes downcast. *For one thing*, thought John, *I'm
out of a job*. But that felt fine, it was part of an inevitable
stripping away. He remembered the feeling—he'd had it
before: that willingness to remove oneself from everything
known, everything familiar. Then (so he'd once believed)
what was essential would stand out against the background
of everything lost or left behind. His had never been a talent for acknowledging what was gone; he'd trained himself
to accept absence as a kind of emphasis. Now the nature of
loss, the way it operated on people, seemed to him a much
more muddled thing. It lacked an organizing principle. If
he was going to have clarity again, ever again, he would
have to stand away from grief, just as he'd had Hallam do,
sending him away from love. Even if he were coming back,
first he'd have to leave. To ensure that all this mattered, it
would have to be abandoned.

At last, Howard said, "So what kind of lie is this, John?"

"A comforting one."

Howard blew a slow gust of air through pursed lips.
"Then show it to them. If that's what you need to do,
and you're willing to accept the consequences, show it."

"I'm glad you agree with me."

"I'm not agreeing with you, John."

Howard still had a hand on the thick bundle of papers
and John nudged it a little closer to him. It startled
Howard, and he instinctively took his hand off it.

"There's one more thing I want to ask you," John said.

## 2.

TWO DAYS LATER, HE WAS AWAKE AT SIX A.M. IN A hotel-room bed, with his fiancée and her mother sleeping two feet from him. *What a shit I must have been in a past life*, he thought. A faint light filtered in through the blinds. He called Bridget's name as quietly as he could.

She opened her eyes and focused on him instantly.

"Is she asleep?" he said.

"What time is it?"

"Just after six." He shifted himself up onto one elbow. Any change in position made his lip throb. He saw Marianne's back hunched up under the covers, her face turned away from them. "She's sleeping." He lifted the blankets on his bed and moved over. Bridget looked at the empty space and quietly crept from her mother's bed to his. He lowered the blanket over her and tucked it around her back. She lay facing him, both hands under her chin. "So?" he said.

"Nice lip."

From this close, her face was broken into planes of light. He'd touched every part of that face. "How are you?"

"All right."

"I'm glad you came."

"Good."

He shifted toward her under the covers and pulled her hands away from her face. She resisted a little, but let him push up against her. He kissed her on the forehead, then tucked his face down and found her lips. She kissed him only a little, showing him she was being a reluctant sport, but he put his hand on the small of her back and she let herself return his kiss harder (pain shot into his back teeth) before she retreated from him. "She's four feet away, John."

"She's asleep."

"People wake up."

"God willing," he said.

She backed off further. "What does that mean?"

"Nothing." He wanted to touch her more, feel her hair in his mouth, her chest against his. All the things that had no need of words were wonderful, and sometimes he thought if people would only shut up, these supernally simple things could find their level. She asked him what he was thinking, and he lied and said, "I know she didn't seem that grateful to you last night, but she is. I think in the middle of all this, it's hard to know how to act. For her."

"This is still my mother we're talking expertly about?"

"Sorry."

"I wasn't expecting flowers."

"You deserve them, though."

Marianne had held the transfer order in her hands and read it top to bottom. "They *have* to stop?" she said, and Bridget reassured her that they did. Further work on the site would happen on government time, no doubt a source of joy to the management of Union Arena. Marianne had folded the paper and put it on the desk, then laid her hand on it briefly as if confirming its reality to herself.

"It won't change anything," said Bridget, turning on her back. A puff of warm air travelled the space between them, carrying the scent of the inside of her shirt to him. "If a little underling like me can get an order done, then think of what their lawyers must be cooking up. There are a hundred ways to get it overturned."

"It won't get overturned."

"You don't know anything." She stared upward, and after a moment closed her eyes. "This is an insane situation. I should be packing her up and taking her home."

"Not yet."

Something in his voice had signalled to her that the subject had been changed. She opened her eyes again. "What is it."

"Something else."

"How much worse is this going to make me feel?"

"Some."

She was trying to sit up now, but he put a hand on her hip and gentled her back down under the sheets. She lay facing him, frightened.

"I drove your father to the docks," he said. "That morning. He asked me to and I did."

She blinked a few times, even smiled at him. "What do you mean?"

"I drove him to the ferry, Bridget. I picked him up at your mother's house and took him to the lake. We'd arranged it the week before, and if he didn't call me to say he'd changed his mind, I was to pick him up at seven in the morning and take him down." He saw how hopefully alert she was to the possibility that she'd somehow misunderstood what he was saying. He saw her memory of the day dissolving and this utter, dread shape replacing it. He'd arrived back at the apartment with lattes—so early for him. He couldn't sleep. This is what he had told her, and he'd seemed a little unwell to her. They'd gotten back into bed.

"We made love, John . . ." Tears pooled under her cheek.

"I know."

"How could you?"

His hand lay on her hip, such a quiet intimacy but for the violence he was doing to her. "I was terrified."

"God, John." She pressed her face into the sheets, rolling toward him as if dead.

"I loved you so much that morning."

"Oh my God," she said, and she threw the covers back and ran into the washroom. He lay there, staring at the space where she'd been, the imprint of her body slowly vanishing. He lifted his eyes a degree and saw Marianne watching him from the other bed.

"What did he say to you? On the drive."

"Marianne . . ."

"I'd like to know."

He listened to the water running behind the wall. "He said he'd woken you. But that you fell back to sleep before he left."

"Yes," she said. "I slept through his death."

"I don't know what to say."

"No one knew how it happened," said Marianne. "The police checked with every dispatcher in the city. We knew he must have gone in a private car, but we figured he'd hitchhiked and we'd never know."

"I was with him."

Marianne regarded him silently for a long moment. "Good."

"Good?" Bridget's voice came from the foot of his bed. John kept his focus on her mother.

"We have it all now," said Marianne. "The drive, the woman at the docks who unwrapped a chocolate bar for him, the ferry captain." She looked up to where Bridget was standing. "And now we have John."

"Who agreed to drive your husband and my father to his death."

"He would have gone anyway," said John. "Without me, if he had to. You know that."

Marianne sat up and slid her legs over the side of the bed, facing him where he lay. "Tell me what he said."

He turned on his back. The ceiling had swirls of sharp-looking stucco on it, and it looked to him like the surface of water, moving, shifting. He spoke as quietly as he thought he'd be permitted to. "He only wanted to talk about the morning. The places we were driving through. We didn't talk about—I didn't say anything. I wanted to buy him breakfast, but he wasn't hungry."

"He was never hungry," said Marianne.

"He just wanted to stay in the car."

"Was he frightened?"

"No." His mind drifted back to the morning and he saw the sun on the road, felt the warmth in the car. The last of the morning's coolness leaching away. "We drove down the Bayview Extension and the sun was on the water. He talked the way he would always talk to me— noticing things, being reminded of things. I think I was the only one who was scared. I'm sorry."

There was no sound from the other bed. He was going to go all the way now, this was what Marianne wanted from him.

"Why are you sorry?" said Bridget.

"When we got to Lakeshore, I was suddenly angry at him."

"Why are you sorry?"

"Why were you angry?" said Marianne.

"I just was," he lied. "I felt there was nothing I could do. He wouldn't let me get out of the car. He touched my face and got out." He breathed out heavily. "He told me he loved me."

"Come here," said Marianne, and he raised his head and saw her holding her hand out to her daughter. Bridget took it, soundlessly weeping, and got into bed with her.

He lay back down. "I watched him walk to the booth. I had to back the car up to see. He was walking slowly to the ticket booth. He bought his ticket. He leaned against the iron railing while he waited for his change, and then he went through the turnstile.

"I stayed there, waiting for his ferry to come in to the city. One started over from Hanlan's—it was small against the island, coming out. I wanted it to take forever, but it got there in ten minutes and it docked.

"When it pulled out again, I got out of the car and bought a ticket, and I went through and stood behind the gate that goes to the wharves and watched the ferry going over. It was the size of a toy when it was in the middle of the lake."

He listened to them breathing in the bed. The room felt then like a huge, empty place to him, where any sound he might make would travel outward forever. A cry for help or a prayer drifting from him into heedless space. The silence was broken by the sound of one of the women rising out of the other bed, and he felt a weight on his own and a hand in his. He looked down the length of himself to see Marianne sitting beside him, her eyes looking toward the windows.

By half-past-eight the site was busy with men and women who had nothing to do with the excavation of the arena. The three of them took turns dressing in the bathroom and went down to the street with nothing in their stomachs. Just before they'd left the room, the phone had rung and Bridget answered it, saying, "What?" and "Who is this?" She listened to a voice, and held her hand over the mouthpiece. "Do you want to talk to someone who wants to know what you have against professional sports?"

"No."

Bridget hung up. "We better get the newspaper."

In the lobby, they had time to glance at the *Sun*. The headline, over a crisp picture of an apartment building, read TOT DIES AFTER FALL. Above it: SHE'S NO FAN— LOCAL WOMAN HOLDS UP CONSTRUCTION OF UNION ARENA.

Marianne whistled quietly.

"Should we get you to a safe house?" said Bridget.

"No. Let's get out there," she said.

At the gate to the site, Marianne showed a ministry representative the transfer order, and he let them through on the north side of the enclosure. On the other side, they stood at the periphery of the huge brown moonscape for the first time. The ministry had brought in a long white lab truck, and personnel went back and forth from the truck to the gridded dig carrying papers, instruments, and samples of dirt in small vials. Apart from the ministry crew, there were interested bystanders—members of the public—some with note-books, others with cameras. John presumed that the major papers had sent out a few of their lesser stringers to cover the dig, but he doubted anything else would ever be written about the find. Marianne walked up onto the site and stopped in her tracks when the wooden rib came into view. John and Bridget joined her there, at the edge of the yellow tape that blocked off the work area. A man nudged John and whispered to him, "All this for a lost two-by-four."

The activity within the closed area was organized and thorough. The cutters took the individual squares of dirt down a foot at a time, the sifters went through the dirt and recorded anything of interest. By eleven, thirty squares were down to the two-foot level and the cutters had approached the inside edge of the wooden rib. Near it, they found more rivets and bits of wood. Six of them conferred and after ten minutes moved the markers to remake their rectangle, placing the remains of the boat in the middle. It was slow sport. John went to get sandwiches an hour later and came back to find Marianne standing on her own. Her eyes were fixed on the space in front of her, one hand splayed unconsciously over the middle of her chest. She silently took the sandwich from John and began eating.

"Where's Bridget?"

"She went inside."

"The hotel?"

"What?" She broke off her contemplation of the dirt. "No, the truck there."

He let her return to her staring. "You don't want to—"

"No, John."

Under that ground, so unhallowed that it had been the repository of the previous century's garbage, was the only thing that could hold Marianne's attention now. He had an instinct that she shouldn't be in a public place, but what was in front of her was happening exclusively in public. And the men with the notebooks, the curious few who'd been admitted just for asking, those who nosed around and dismissed it as a pile of dirt, and those who lingered—all these were gone from her view. It was her alone with this emergence, the inch-by-cubic-inch thing that was the post she'd tethered herself to. He put a hand on her shoulder and then left her there.

Across the site, the machinery they'd seen milling around for two weeks was all parked neatly in files, shovels and sledges lowered to the ground like grazing cattle. There were no workers anywhere on the site, despite the fact that the excavation took up less than a twentieth of the area available. He presumed a better case could be made for damages if the work stoppage was total, and no doubt they'd raise insurance issues too. It was very quiet within the barriers, except for the sound of the rubber tread on one of the sifting machines.

He wondered how he would begin to tell someone what had happened to them here. *After the death of my girlfriend's father, I was part of other people's grief.*

Bridget came out of the truck with a man behind her. She introduced John to Dr. Jarvis, the dig chief. "I'll go down and talk with your mother," he said. They watched Jarvis walk down to the dig and start to explain something to Marianne. She listened, nodding.

Standing beside and just slightly behind him, Bridget said, "Do you want to know what he told me in there?"

"Just the conclusions."

"The clay is dropping four inches per foot."

He took his eyes off Marianne, who'd turned to Dr. Jarvis and was listening more intently now. "I have no idea what that means."

"This is all fill," she said. "Clay is underneath. There's organic matter, then sand, and then clay—the lakebed. Dr. Jarvis says that if the grade at the old shoreline turns out to be really steep, then the boat might not be in one piece. It could have been cracked up in the storm, and if it broke apart then the heavier sections could be deeper. The stowage could be under Queen's Quay for all we know." He watched Marianne walking toward them with Jarvis. "Are you seeing someone?" she said. "Besides my mother?"

He whipped around. "What? Come on, Bridget."

Marianne looked exhausted, as though she'd spent the morning waiting for a child to be pulled from a well. "They're going to stop," she said. "Just for the rest of the afternoon. Dr. Jarvis says they have a machine that can look through the dirt. Is that right?"

Jarvis nodded, his eyes moving from John to Bridget. "You clocked him something good, huh?"

"I should've."

"How can it see through dirt?" asked Marianne.

"It knocks on the ground and listens."

"What a clever machine." The representative from the ministry was waving people back from the hole with big circular sweeps of his arms. Marianne let the stream of people gather her up and the others fell in behind, walking toward the Lakeshore gate.

When she was out of earshot, John took Bridget by the wrist and drew her away from the crowd. "You haven't looked me in the eye for five hours."

"How can I look you in the eye, John?"

"Tell me one thing you've done since your father died that was *for* him? That wasn't about saving face or proving someone wrong or backing off from everything?"

She took her wrist back sharply. "You arrogant bastard. I don't have to justify myself to you. You were the one behind the wheel."

"All he wanted was some of your attention."

"I gave him that, and more." The hotel was piled up behind her, its windows reflecting the city in discrete frames. He wondered if Marianne had backtracked to find them, but he couldn't see her.

"You might have taken notice, but not because you wanted to."

"Christ." She stepped toward him. "You've only been around for seven years, John. Do you think I haven't been through all of this already? That we haven't all been through this? I went to digs, I saw him pull old muskets out of the ground like they were rabbits from hats, and turn up lost gravestones and cellars. I got dragged to these things plenty. I was standing three feet from my father when he uncovered Simcoe's first parliament in this city. I can tell you all about that. Would you like that?"

"You can try me."

She crossed her arms; she didn't want to be pushed into giving him anything. "You know who Simcoe was?"

"Remind me."

"He founded the city. Around 1800."

"1793."

"Whatever. He built a parliament somewhere near the lakeshore, at the eastern city limit. No one really knew where it was, but Dad figured it out. He made a couple of maps that showed the old shoreline and the new one and he figured out where the old streets were. He had scrolls of paper with old drawings on them. I remember him laying them down in a parking lot—with rocks in the corners to keep them from blowing away—and showing me and Mum and Alison where we were.

"We'd gone there with some of his students—there were a couple of politicians too, and a reporter, and we were beside a car wash near King Street and Parliament. This was 1981. I think it was 1981. There was a backhoe there, and some white rope tied to stakes, laid out in a square."

"Just like they have here, right?"

"That's right, John. Just like they do here. So don't try to pull emotional rank on me, okay?"

"Okay."

"Are you coming back to the hotel?"

"What happened next?" She'd already turned to follow her mother, but when she saw he'd not budged, she faced him with her hands in her pockets. "I want you to tell me the rest of it."

"I don't remember the rest of it."

"You do though."

She looked down to her right, her jaw set. "He told us he'd settled on that spot because he'd put all the information he had in a pile and looked through it and figured it couldn't be farther south or north, and Parliament Street was where it has been for two hundred years. So that had to be the spot, or it was nowhere. Okay?"

"Were you excited?"

"I was cold. It was December."

"Go on, Bridget."

She brought her face around to him. "He asked the guy, this Iranian guy who owned the car wash, if they could dig, and he said go ahead. He just waved his hands at the ground, like it was the craziest thing he'd ever seen. They started digging, and the backhoe put big chunks of the asphalt in a pile, with dirt and bits of garbage. Dad's students were sifting through it with white gloves. The backhoe kept putting big scoops down on the ground. Dad told us we were looking at dirt that was more than a century and a half old. Then someone shouted, and we all looked. There was a flashbulb and then a student held up this little thing the colour of a waterstain—you know, like in a sink."

"What was it?"

"It was a swine tooth," she said. "A tooth from a pig. We passed it around and looked at it. It had dirt packed so tight in the crown that you couldn't scrape it out. Then the backhoe blew its airhorn and we all looked into the hole and Dad hollered. There was a wood floor under the steel claw. Dad was surprised because he thought it would be farther down.

"We all stood at the edge of the hole. It was five feet deep, with a wood floor at the bottom, and no one was saying anything. Then the owner jumped up and down and shouted for us to keep digging and Dad waved the machine on. I remember the look on his face."

"He was ecstatic."

"Yeah." She pulled a strand of hair out of the corner of her mouth, that beloved gesture. "It took an hour and then there was a whole room there, and the white ribbons surrounding the hole were like walls, except we couldn't see them. We had to imagine them. There was a brick outline around the edges of the floor and a pair of stone steps. We all stood on them, in a dip where people's shoes had worn it away. Dad told us there would have been a hand-painted sign above our heads that said this was the parliament. He said the men and women who walked across that wood floor built the whole city.

"One of the students gave him a clay pipe she'd found in one of the piles. It was very pretty. You could see that someone had made it by hand. It had a little lacy pattern around the bowl. Dad gave it to me."

"He did?"

"He put it into my hand and closed my fingers over it and he said, 'The past really happened.'" She couldn't look at him.

"Can you hear yourself, Bridget? It matters. To you. At the very least, you can say that."

"I've lost it, though. That pipe. How could it have mattered to me if I lost it?"

"You held it in your hand. You know something most people don't."

"Yeah. I know he died for a piece of clay I lost and a chunk of wood nobody in their right mind gives a fuck about!"

He tried to go to her, to draw her to him, but she stepped away, as if she were being pushed by a force field. He stood before her, helplessly, and held his hands out to her. "This whole place erases itself every day, it kills itself, Bridget . . . do you understand? It gets wiped clean like a hotel room. When your mother leaves the Harbour Light, they'll vacuum up every molecule she's left behind, and the next person who comes by won't ever know she was there. They're going to do the same thing behind this wall."

"My father is still gone."

"No, Bridget. He's alive in a thought you're having, and I'm having that thought too. The thing in your hand, that you held. There are some things you can bring back to life."

She backed away even farther. "She won't know where I am . . ."

"Go then," he said.

"You shouldn't have faith in me. I doubt I even brought that pipe home. I probably tossed it back into the dirt. Because that's the kind of person I am. Right?"

"I don't know, Bridget. I never thought so."

"Are you coming with me?"

"Not yet."

She turned away from him and began to walk to the lights. She stopped at the crosswalk and looked back at him, but said nothing. He stood with his hands at his sides and this seemed to tell her something, and she crossed at the light and continued toward the hotel.

## 3.

HE WANTED TO HAVE PICTURES WITH HIM. THE ONE taken with his cousins at a baseball game, a couple from the fridge: Bailey as an apricot blur in the snow, running insanely in a circle; the famous summer picture of Alison and Bridget's bare feet in the sand, toenails painted twenty different colours.

There was a framed photo over the fireplace of Bridget with David, taken in the springtime of his death. When he thought of David, John always imagined him with more flesh on his face, but this picture corrected that memory. The dead are always first recalled as their healthy selves, and after they're gone the photographic evidence of death on their faces shocks. In this picture— which Bridget cherished—David's eyes retreated into his face, and brown blotches marked his cheeks. His skull looked as if it had shifted under his skin. John knew that David had not killed himself out of shame—Marianne had always been wrong about this. But John had never known why he had chosen that day, in particular. Now he realized that any morning in David's last month would have provided its reason through a glimpse in the mirror. They'd always wondered what he was thinking, and now it seemed clear to John that he was thinking, *I'm already gone.*

He pushed out the back of the frame and cradled the glass in his hand, carefully separated it from the picture. He put the empty frame in a drawer and slipped the photo into a book with the others. He filled a single suitcase with his things and brought it down the stairs. The cab came five minutes later and John got in and gave the driver Howard's address.

~

In the hotel, Bridget had chased a single reporter out of the hallway and then locked herself and her mother in the room. They ordered hamburgers from room service and stood in silence at the windows, eating them. An hour later, at three o'clock, a second vehicle entered the site and unloaded what looked like an oversized lawn mower, and a man wearing earphones began moving it over the earth. It had begun to snow and the brown cloddish earth looked like a cake dusted with sugar. The mower operator started near the exposed wood and moved in a long spiral along and out from it. They saw Jarvis and one of his assistants standing in the background with their arms crossed against the wind, while a third man came out of the lab every two or three minutes to shout something to the mower, who would then move a few feet in some direction and lower the head of the machine again.

There was a knock at the door, and on her mother's nod Bridget went to the eyehole. "Is it John?" said Marianne.

"No. I think it's a reporter."

"It is a reporter," came a man's voice from behind the door. "The *Globe*. I know you don't hate sports, Mrs. Hollis. That's not my angle."

"What *is* your 'angle'?" said Bridget through the door.

"Can I come in? I'll leave if you tell me to."

Bridget opened the door and a man passed her a business card. It read RICHARD LOWINGER, CITY DESK. Bridget handed the card to her mother.

"What do you want, Mr. Lowinger?" Marianne said.

"I just want to ask a couple of questions, if that's okay."

"What's your foregone conclusion? I'd like to know that first."

Lowinger raised his eyebrows at her and then started when Bridget shut the door behind him. "I don't have one," he said. "But I'm interested in your husband's work. I covered his Simcoe dig in '82. He wrote me a note to thank me."

"Fine," said Marianne.

Bridget passed him to stand with her mother. "I thought it was 1981."

"Eighty-one, then." He went over to the window and looked out.

"They're using sonar or something like that," said Marianne.

The sounder was focusing on an area closer to the white lab truck. They moved the truck back twenty feet, to the edge of the site. The area they were examining was now about fifteen feet south of the rib and thirty feet east of it. "Jarvis was right about the drop-off, I think."

"Can you explain?" said Lowinger. Bridget told him what she'd told John. "So this thing could still be somewhere out in the lake?"

"They don't know," she said. "The point Mr. Jarvis was making was that if it broke apart on a shallow grade, it would all still be in one place. And if it's not all in one place, pieces of it could be anywhere, under any of the buildings down here."

The reporter turned to Marianne. "Do you really believe there's a boat down there?"

"Are you interested in the boat, or my husband? And his 'struggle,' as you'll probably want to put it."

"Both," Lowinger said. "There isn't one without the other."

"Why don't I dig up my husband for you then? Since they're taking care of the boat."

Lowinger tried to take the comment in stride and failed, coughing into his hand. Marianne went to sit on the edge of the bed. She waited for Lowinger to draw up a chair, and placed herself face to face with the man. He was David's age—her age. Yet another man sitting in front of her with an instinct. When she noticed Lowinger had not leaned away from her, but was patiently waiting, she began. "Three years ago, my husband David had a twitch in his hand that wouldn't go away."

Bridget stood in the window, listening to her mother and watching the progress below. It began to snow. For a while, she sat with them and added her own observations to her mother's, but she returned to the window, impatient for the workers below to finish. An hour after that, she watched the ministry team load the sounder back into its truck and leave the site. Marianne handed Lowinger a photo from her desk, and he tucked it into his notebook. "Is there anything else you want to add?" he asked her, and she said no. He got up from the chair to ask Bridget, but she was already heading to the door.

"We'll have to continue this later," she said. "They're done."

In the lab truck, one of the computer operators showed the results of the sounding. Its readings revolved onto the screen like a radar map, an underground X-ray. They recognized the long, thin rib, which tapered and broke off about eight feet south of where it had surfaced, turning from red to orange in the program's chromatic language of depth. Around it, in sweeping circles, were bits of material: inorganic objects originally in the landfill and displaying in all colours, and some that were identified as part of the boat. These retreated in a pattern from the wooden rib, fading to a greeny yellow.

The sounder had sniffed along in larger circles, and then caught the beginning of a longer shape in dark green, about thirty feet from the protruding wood. The sweeping became ellipsoidal, and the shape extended, deepening as well, dark green to violet: the far boundary of the machine's vision. Marianne muttered an awestruck sound as the lost boat ghosted into view. "What is it?" said Bridget.

"Lake steamer," said Dr. Jarvis. "No later than 1870."

"So it could be from the 1850s?"

"It could be."

A breath-held silence enveloped them all as a ship's deck, shimmering like tropical water, expanded on the screen. Compartments below decks were barely visible, skimming under the solid wood as much darker shapes, their bearing walls appearing as a purple-streaked black. There were six of them in the truck, crowded around the fourteen-inch screen. "You getting this?" Marianne said to Lowinger. The man was writing furiously.

Finally, a heavy rectangular object hove into view, back under the decking. "That's it," Marianne said.

"Screwhouse," said Jarvis. He sounded depressed.

"No, that must be stowage. Christ," she said in quiet wonder. "Is that the front or the back of the boat?"

"We're waiting for someone to bring in a schematic," said the doctor. "They haven't built one of these things in a few years. It must be the screwhouse. These steamers had gearboxes the size of a garage."

"If it's the back of the boat, it could have been stowage," Marianne said. The operator had frozen the screen. "They would have centred it so it didn't skew the boat right or left, and kept it at the back to keep her stern low."

The doctor didn't seem concerned one way or the other. "In any case, it's academic."

Now it was the reporter who spoke up. "The ministry will abandon the dig because what they're hunting for is twenty feet down?"

"Twenty-six," Jarvis said.

"The Union Arena people can get down there in two hours," said Lowinger. "Look at the shit they have over there just waiting to be pressed into service. Get the minister to appropriate one of those big earthmovers and let them dig. There's nothing 'academic' about it."

"You're right," said the doctor, "they could be down there by morning. But that's not why it's academic."

An hour before this, John was stacking his things in Howard's spare room. He locked the door behind him and began walking south toward the hotel. Snow was coming down in drifting clumps, a damp and sticky cold. As he walked, Marianne was sitting on the hotel room bed, talking to Richard Lowinger, and Bridget was at the window, watching the sounder on the site below.

"We met in 1964," Marianne was saying. "I'd moved from Montreal with my parents and I was enrolled in English at the Scarborough Campus of U of T. The school had just opened and it was like having a university in a forest. David was teaching there—geology, although he'd trained as a lawyer—and he held his classes outside poking around the bases of trees. How a man who didn't know a drumlin from a sand dune ended up teaching 'Introduction to Landforms,' I don't know.

"There wasn't as much of a taboo around asking out a student then. I suppose nothing like it could happen these days, and I guess I understand. Except sometimes the person you're going to love comes from somewhere unexpected and you don't really have much say in the matter. We got married the same year we met."

"She was pregnant with me," said Bridget. "She was a bad girl."

The reporter didn't write this down. Marianne continued.

"David was at the university until his death. He brought them a lot of fame, but before he died they turned their backs on him. All because of this."

"Why?"

She was silent a moment, thinking. "He thought modern people were the loneliest people in the history of the world. And the thought that another time was under the one we live in was moving to him. Because it's a kind of company for us, all of us marooned here in the present."

"There are a couple of boarded-up houses on Elm Street, just near Bay," said Bridget. She came over and sat on the bed beside her mother. Marianne covered her daughter's hand with her own. "He got permission from the city to go into one of them. The windows were covered in wood, but he had a flashlight. There was still carpet inside, and wallpaper on the walls—this embossed wallpaper with flowers. Dark squares where people had hung pictures. We went up the stairs—there was nothing wrong with the house, but Dad said one of the hospitals owned the land, and the houses had been designated historic, so it was a stalemate. He knew the names of all the people who had lived in the houses since they were built, in 1873. We walked through the house and he was talking to me as if the last people to live there were still around, just out for a few hours. He told me the man who owns this house probably works not too far from here, in the business district. Perhaps a banker. At night they hear the horses on the cobblestones outside. It's a normal, everyday sound. There are no parking garages on the other side of the street; there are gardens there and a gate with a key that everyone on the street has a copy of. I had a thought: he and I were as real as those people had been, who lived there once. And our being alive and their not being alive somehow wasn't that much of a difference between us."

Less than five kilometres away, John crossed onto Bay Street. He passed the houses that Bridget was, at that moment, speaking of and continued down toward Queen Street.

Marianne said, "He got commissions and the university always took a cut of the fee and a lot of the spotlight. His classes were always full. He had a sweet tooth. What else do you want to know?"

"Why did he kill himself?"

Bridget turned instinctively to the reporter, but Marianne squeezed her daughter's hand. "I imagine he was unhappy, Mr. Lowinger. He was sick. And he was probably frightened. He didn't tell me, so I don't know." She stood up. "Do you want a picture of him?"

"Sure."

Marianne searched on the desk for a photo and Bridget marvelled at what she'd just witnessed: her mother had charmed someone. John had rubbed off, whether Marianne knew it or not.

"I don't know why heritage is such a hard sell here," said Lowinger. "It just is."

"You know what David said?" The reporter waited. "No one wants to hear the story of a whore's childhood."

Lowinger opened his notebook again. He finished writing and looked up into the quiet room. "Is there anything else you want to add?"

"We'll have to continue this later," Bridget said. "They're done."

A moment later they emerged into the snow on Queen's Quay, and John Lewis crossed Richmond Street heading south.

## 4.

THERE HAD NOT BEEN GRASS UNDERFOOT AT
Richmond and Bay streets in more than two hundred
years, but as John crossed through the intersection he
felt grass beneath him, and it was June in another time
and place. He was almost used now to this feeling of
slippage—his waking life had begun to obey the laws
of dreams and anything could draw his thoughts
away—the sight of cobblestone revealed through
cracked asphalt in the side streets near Bathurst, or the
smell of bread baking on McCaul. His mind was a net
of awareness.

Now he was in a nearly empty park; the air was
warm and the scent of chocolate hung in it. He could
hear the sounds of excited children running in and out
of the wading pool farther down the hill behind him.
He took his sandals off and drowsed a little in the
greeny light.

A woman entered the park off Roxton Road with her
dog. She leaned down and unsnapped its leash, and the
little apricot-coloured animal bolted into the park, head

low, its ears flapping. The woman wore an orange one-piece dress with ribbons of light blue swimming through it. Her sunglasses pushed back in her summerlight hair. She called to the dog, but it wasn't listening. John watched the little animal hit an open patch of grass, drop down into fourth gear, and start running in mad circles, *hurf*ing at the woman whenever it got within range of her. It was a tremendous display.

The woman clapped her hands with joy. "Oh yeah, you're ferocious! Who's a ferocious girl?"

Two more rotations and the dog broke off again and made a beeline for John. He was still the only other person in that part of the park, sitting on a green bench in front of the abandoned bocce pits, a box of wooden balls at his feet. The dog came right up to him, her tongue pulsing in her mouth.

"She's coming," said the dog.

"Bailey! Bailey—*get over here!*" The woman was running now, whether worried for him or the dog, he couldn't tell. "Sorry," she said. "She doesn't go to anyone! I'm amazed she just ran right over here."

"It's okay," John Lewis said. A few strands of hair had slipped out from behind her ear and she tucked them back. He would beg her not to cut her hair in the years to come, but it was a nuisance to her. "You don't cut the roses because they grow too tall," he'd say to her one day, and she'd reply, "Actually, green thumb, you do."

"She's famously timid," said the woman. "You must smell like fresh hamburger or something."

"My cologne," he said, and she laughed quietly, the first time he ever heard that laugh, a snap of surprise and delight.

He was something of a sight, sitting alone on a bench with a box of wooden balls at his feet. It made her curious. "Are you from the neighbourhood?"

He pointed west. He lived on a street called Shannon, just off Ossington. "I got an apartment there just before Christmas. This is my first summer down here."

"Do they play bocce in your old neighbourhood?"

"I just bought them," he said, and he hefted the big box into his lap. "A nice old man on the street was selling them in his lawn sale. Ten bucks."

"Ten bucks! They cost like a hundred and fifty new. Why would he sell them for ten bucks?"

"He said the guys he played with were all dead."

She screwed her mouth into a sly grin. "Is that true?"

"Probably."

"So you're just sitting here with them? Commemoratively?"

"The old Italian men play here. I see them all the time, and I don't know how to play so I figured—"

Now she laughed out loud at him, bending over at the waist and catching her sunglasses as they tumbled from her hair. "You're not!"

"They can always use some fresh blood."

"What's your name?" she asked once she'd collected herself. He told her, and she said Bridget and they shook hands. "Well, John, it's Sunday and they're all in church, so you might have to take lessons from someone younger and not as Italian."

She tied up the dog, and now he was crossing King Street where the late-November snow was falling a little harder, bursting bright in the streetlights. Soon they'd turn the kliegs on in the site and in his future, Bridget showed him how to toss the target ball. The game was a little like curling, she said, except the "house" was the little white ball. He didn't know curling. "What kind of Canadian are you?" she said, grinning at him, and she explained it a little more and it would take only one more meeting for him to fall in love with her. How was it that this sleek beautiful creature was allowed to appear in *his* world? It was the beginning of happiness, and he did not think, as no one does, that folded into that sweetness, like a seed, was its end.

He let her beat him nine to three. "Good move," said the dog, who wanted to sleep against him and curl up at their naked feet after they made love. John walked them home. She lived just a couple of streets away and there wasn't much time to leave the right impression.

"Me and my roommate are having some friends over next weekend. Just for some beers," she said. "You'll like my friends. They're all *very* sporty."

"Lawyers like you?"

"Hey, I'm not a lawyer yet."

"So there's still hope," he said, and she whacked him.

"You're cute, eh? But you need a haircut." She studied him a moment longer. "Although you shouldn't cut your curls off," she said. "You have nice black curls. Are you Jewish?"

"No, but I work for a Jewish guy."

"It rubs off?" They turned onto her street and Bailey strained against the leash. "She's thirsty."

He brushed a clump of snow off the dog's face and then turned to stand in front of Bridget. He pulled her against him and their summers and winters spun before him against the backdrop of the street.

He stood there on Crawford, holding her to him in desolate love. "Puppy!" Bridget called over his back. "Don't run off." He released her, and she looked at him with excited eyes. "Will you come next week?"

"Yes," he said. He saw the kliegs burst under the lowering sky and he pushed his hands down in his pockets and continued south.

~

It was academic—the fate of the indigo and violet boat on the screen—because the lawyers for the owners of Union Arena had already shut down the dig. Paper covers rock. Out on Lakeshore Boulevard in the near-dark of five p.m., a line of eight cement mixers was waiting to enter the site, and a crew had assembled at the back of the excavation where the machines had sat silently for two days. Bridget looked on unsurprised and took her mother's hand. "Let's go back to the room."

"I want them to do it in front of me."

"They will."

"There could be cameras here," said Richard Lowinger, "in five minutes."

Jarvis came out of the truck, squinting across the expanse at the pale headlights flickering on. "They won't let any reporters in here now," he said.

"They don't have to be inside the site in order to see," said Lowinger, looking up at the buildings that ringed the hole in the ground. "Cameras are quite portable."

Marianne separated from her daughter and went back up the steps, holding her hand out to the student who'd interpreted the sounder results for them. "I want you to show me exactly where the strongbox is. Out here."

"*Gear*box, Mrs. Hollis," Jarvis said.

"I want to see where that shape is, whatever you want to call it."

"Go ahead," said the doctor. "Show her."

The young woman led Marianne thirty paces from the door and stopped. "How far down?"

"At least twenty-five feet, ma'am. The farther down, the less accurate the reading."

"But you're sure it's right under here."

"Near here, yes."

Marianne stood on the spot and faced the lake, smelled the blade of frigid air that sheared off it. The construction wall blocked the view, but Marianne could still see it: the street and the buildings, traffic lights, the cold-contracted streetcar lines, the thin ribbon of grass and then concrete along the water's edge, the water and the islands a kilometre out—islands where, David once said, Indians had hunted wild pheasant. There had been fox out there as well and black bears when the islands still connected to the mainland. In the shallower

water, lake trout in schools. She closed her eyes and saw
the reel of time go backwards: the roads and condominiums scattered to dust and dirt, and the brick and stone
the city planners had used to make the lake smaller
drifted back to its undisturbed sources and the water
came up to her feet. She saw the afternoon storm that
made the captain of the *Commodore Walker* consider
turning back toward Kingston, and except for the unpre-
dictability of winds that might have blown him clear to
Rochester, he would have. David's diarist was aboard—
she had to believe this—returning from England where
he must have dissuaded the queen's committee from
choosing Toronto as the new capital of the Province of
Canada. He was standing on the deck with the rest of the
passengers, his photographic cargo below, returning to
source, all of them watching the city approach. The
irony of being at sea for two weeks in all manner of con-
ditions, and only now—perhaps half an hour out of
port—a monstrous lake tempest. They came into the lee
of the island and the lake grew rougher. Usually the harbour guarded the city and any traffic against the wind,
but it was a northeasterly system and they began to ship
water, the hull creaking and the boat shaking violently.
They made for Brown's Wharf, tacking against the wind
to keep it in line, to keep the boat from launching over
the breakwater and landing in a vat at Gooderham &
Worts. Here it comes now—Marianne saw it fighting
the wind. She felt Bridget's arm on hers. "Come on,
Mum—"

   "They're almost in," she said—

—trying to come around, but the wind is pushing them past the wharf, the bosun calls everyone to deck, it's safer to stand out in the cascading rain than to remain below and they can see the city rushing up now, the rockfall lining the bottom of the esplanade that keeps the macadam from silting away, and everyone is moved to the stern as the captain tries to slow her down.

She hears the crack and her name called, a hand on her arm, the prow of the boat grinding into the rocks and the soft bodies at the back of the ship thrown to decks; she hears *Mrs. Hollis* and she can see the man coming forward from the stern, rain sluicing off his hat, the boat is cracking and dipping quickly. No one can see for the rain, he cannot go below and also live, everyone is rushed front and there is no way to shore but through the freezing water. In they go, clambering to land and then standing drenched on the other side of danger, the place they call home—*this is home!*—and Marianne sees the city pushing forward, the roads unfurl in front of her, the condominiums break through the man-made earth, and soil covers it all in strata of piled dirt and garbage, the lost scene of the broken ship and the voices in the towering rain. She is standing over it, witness.

"Mrs. Hollis, I know I can't make this any easier for you." She took in a man in a yellow hard hat. "If it counts for anything, I did want you to find what you were all looking for."

"Go pour concrete on him then. Go on—"

"I'm sorry," the man said, and she thumped him on the chest. Bridget sprang forward in time to keep her from leaping at him. The man lifted an arm to signal someone in the distance behind them, and Bridget drew her mother away.

*"Awake long?"* November 1996, *more than two years ago now. Christmas music in all the commercials.*

*"A while. I drank my pills."*

*"What are you reading?"*

*"Some reminiscences of a pioneer."*

*"Which one?"*

*"Seton Thompson. I think the British came over to drain bogs and rivers. It feels as if that's all they really wanted to do here. Drain stuff."*

*"Maybe they'd drained all the good ones at home."*

*He put the book down in his lap—this book that she can still find in the house, shelved with the rest of his touch-stones—his gaze fixed on the wall across from them.* "History is just a long story about a fight with water, you know? You have too little and you can't eat so you bend a river, or you have too much so you bury one to build houses, and then there's too many people and too much competition, so you cross some water to get more resources or find more places to put people and when you get there you don't like where the ponds and ravines are, and so on and blah blah blah."

*"And that's your man's story? He came over and drained rivers?"*

*"They'd done most of that by the 1850s, or they were in the middle of it. No, he came over to make money and send it home to his people, or bring some of them over. He had a family. A couple of young children."*

*"It doesn't end well, does it?"*
*"He doesn't say how it ends, Marianne."*
*"No, he wouldn't have, would he?"*
*"That's always in someone else's diary."*
*Frost on the inside of the windows.*

## 5.

WHEN JOHN LEWIS ENTERED THE HOTEL LOBBY, A knot of people stood on the marble floor in front of the bar, their necks craned. He heard, "That's just outside of here," and he pushed in and got near the front. The bar's television was tuned to an aerial view of the Union Arena site, a view he knew well, although it was from a different angle. After a moment, he figured out that the shot was being taken from another building, one adjacent to the hotel. The report carried the live proceedings of what seemed to be Marianne conducting a seance. She stood apart from the rest of the group (he easily made out Dr. Jarvis and Bridget, and as he was looking at Bridget, she stepped toward her mother) and beyond them, in a phalanx, stood the diggers and plowers and stampers-of-dirt, all at the ready. Marianne stared out at the south wall of the site. There were cement trucks standing on Lakeshore; you couldn't hear the slow rumble of their barrels turning, but he understood their presence to be sinister just the same.

He went up in the elevator and used the key card Marianne had given him to enter the room. He snapped on the television and could see from the window that it was all happening in real time. He had the strange sensation of being in three places at once: the actual place, where he stood and witnessed; the electronic place that confirmed his witness; and the place in memory where he knew how that earth smelled, what the people he loved were saying to each other. He was woven into all the layers of the story and could not be unravelled from it.

For some reason, the television's reality was the most immediate—he retreated into the room to look at the screen. In watching it, he was tied to hundreds if not thousands across the city who had tuned in to this odd dumb show. It may not have mattered to them when they'd read the one or two little squibs that had appeared in the newspapers, but this was the news on *TV*—this was happening to everyone, at the same time. A woman alone on a patch of ground for some reason, surrounded by people who seemed frightened to go near her. Something about this mattered, that is what the image said. Here is *our* present passing at this very moment.

Now a man in a yellow helmet approached Marianne and they spoke. John was only a little surprised to see her shove him.

He heard the sound of machines changing gears, chunks and rumbles. The first cement trucks were entering the site. The ministry group had pulled back and the construction workers moved themselves into place. Men with spades and rakes stood nearby. A moment later, Marianne and the others disappeared from view, hidden behind the wall, but he was certain they were still there; some form of decency demanded they be allowed to watch the unhappy proceedings. The trucks went directly to the southwest corner of the site, and he knew now for certain that the ground was not ready, that this was not the foundation being poured: it was an assertion of who belonged here, who owned this dirt, even if it meant breaking the concrete up in a week to lay it properly. Three of the trucks lined up in a fan pattern above the exposed rib of wood, and at once they tipped up their tanks and the white mixtures began to flow out. The three streams met and became a pool, spreading. The men with the spades shoved the slow-coursing mixture forward, and the men with the rakes levelled it. From above, on the television and through the window, the ground looked as if someone had knocked over a huge bottle of whiteout onto it. An unfolding, soothing nothingness. A surface becalmed.

As with people so things also had an inclination to vanish; they were by nature truant. The world below this one was accomplice to its own passing. It kept no names for its legion things; it had no sentiment for them. Boats and dead pets and lost shoes became layers of earth; wooden carts, yellow brick and stamped tin ceiling tiles, cherished knick-knacks and empty liniment bottles and gutta percha photograph cases and ceramic dolls with their painted eyes rubbed almost clean—all things co-operated with extinction; only people held them tight. He imagined with sudden clarity David Hollis aboard the spectral *Commodore Walker*, holding on through the wrack and smash of the storm, the water pouring down in sheets through gaps in the deck, and John felt his terror, his anticipation of release, the sound of ruin so near.

John collected a couple of books from the room and for the last time, descended the thirty-three floors to the ground. When he left, the first shift of cement mixers was backing up onto Lakeshore Boulevard to make room for the next.

Lowinger had left before they began to pour. When he saw the cement trucks begin their stately march onto the grounds, he quickly shook Bridget's hand and held his arm out to Marianne, but she refused it. Lowinger, in an awkward gesture of fellowship, tried to lean forward to squeeze her upper arm, but Marianne caught him in an embrace and he teetered against her, his ear against her mouth. Bridget did not hear what she said to the reporter, but when she released him he was nodding absently at her, enchanted or frightened or both.

The line of white trucks moved like metal elephants onto the site, and Bridget took her mother's hand and pulled her finally away. In the hotel, Marianne paid the bill. The clerk behind the desk said, "I hope we'll see you again."

They went up silently to the thirty-third floor. Marianne's face was grey and her eyes dull, and Bridget wanted to get her back to the house and make her something to eat. The business of letting go would begin in earnest now, and at last she felt ready to be child to this broken heart.

At the door, Bridget took the key card out of her mother's hand and slipped it into its slot. The mechanism drew back smoothly and they went into the stale-smelling room. Under the scent of dried clementine skins there was now a persistent funk of unwashed laundry and sleeping bodies. The lights were already on.

Bridget saw Howard Rosen before her mother did. She'd only met him once before, but his long grey hair was too distinctive to forget. He'd risen with the sound of the door and was waiting patiently to be noticed, his arms at his sides. His presence here closed a circuit that had opened for Bridget when John told her he was not coming back to the hotel. Howard's presence would provide both the question she could not formulate at that moment as well as its answer.

"Excuse me?" said Marianne, and Rosen stepped forward, holding out a key card of his own.

"John gave me this——"

"John?"

"I'm sorry," he said.

Bridget stepped forward. "This is Howard Rosen, Mum. John works for him."

"I know who Howard Rosen is," she said. "Why is he here? Why are you here? Where is John?"

Rosen lowered his still-outstretched arm to his side. The gesture told Bridget that there was an order to things that would have to be followed now and that

Rosen would be deciding that order. "Could we all sit down for a moment?"

He retreated to Marianne's bed and sat on the end of it, and Bridget pulled out the desk chair for her mother, who sat and looked about the room as if it were unfamiliar. "Are you going to answer my mother's questions?" said Bridget. "Why isn't John here?"

"He's reduced me to errand boy," said Rosen. He spread his hands to take in the room. "This is my errand."

"And what is 'this'?" said Marianne. She continued to scan the space for clues, taking inventory. She noticed an empty space on the desk. "Where's my monograph?"

"He's borrowed a couple of items. He'll return them—"

"*Borrowed?*" She wagged a hand toward the phone. "Call him, Bridget."

Rosen leaned forward on the bed, a hand out. "Marianne? Mrs. Hollis? Listen to me, please. You know what I do, yes?"

"You are a supposed writer."

"Okay, that's fair. I've been writing a play about an imaginary family for about seven years. I have no real model for such a thing. Actually, I have no idea why I ever chose it as my subject matter."

"What do your failings have to do with anything, Mr. Rosen?"

"John never had a model either." He reached down to the floor beside the bed and brought up what Bridget recognized as John's shoulder bag. It frightened her to see it. He drew a thick manila envelope from it and handed it to Marianne. She stared at it in her palm.

"Where's John?" she said toward the packet. She looked back up at their visitor. "I'd like to speak to John, Mr. Rosen. Many things have happened here today, and I don't understand why he's not here. When will he be here?"

"This is the end of something, Mrs. Hollis," Rosen said. "You need to understand that."

For a long moment no one moved, and then Marianne leaned down and put the manila envelope on the floor.

"Start with telling us where John is," said Bridget.

"He's left for the airport."

"Goddamn it!" She went around her mother and strode to the window, hiding her face.

"He flies tonight for England."

"What the hell for?" said Marianne.

"Research," said Rosen. "That's what he told me."

Bridget spun toward him. "You've sent him to England? You don't even have enough money to pay him what you owe him."

"It's not for me, Bridget. It's for *that*." He touched the tip of his shoe to the package.

"Which is?"

"It'll be better if you just read it."

"Why," said Marianne.

Rosen stood and suddenly his face was bright scarlet. "Because I can't fucking explain it to you, that's why! It's for you, he says. He asks me to deliver it, and now I have. I've done my duty. Now yours is to read it and get on with your lives." He scooped his jacket off the bed, but Bridget rushed to block his way to the door.

"Hold on—you're not going anywhere yet." She stood in front of him with her arms crossed. "I thought John worked for *you*."

"I thought that too."

"When is he coming back?"

"I'm sorry for your loss," Rosen said over his shoulder, and he backed up to go around Bridget the other way.

"Let him go," said Marianne. Bridget looked over to see that a sheaf of paper lay on her lap. She was barely aware of the sound of the door closing behind her. Marianne was riffling the paper: pages and pages of John's handwriting. She handed Bridget a small white envelope. "This was in the envelope too. It's addressed to you." Bridget took it and tore it open, slipped out the thin white card inside and read it. She muttered *Jesus*, and dropped it onto the bedspread as if it were burning.

"What?" said Marianne.

"The bastard."

"Bridget?" Marianne laid the pile of paper on the desk and rose to hold her, and Bridget stood stiffly in her arms.

"What the fuck is going on?"

"It's just us now," said Marianne.

Bridget drew away. "So I get a greeting card and you get . . . what? A full accounting?"

Marianne turned half the pile of paper over and they both stared at it. The line at the top of the page said, *As if beckoned by a strange gesture of hope, the spring came in*

*earnest the week after Mrs. Rowe moved into Hallam's rooms.*
Bridget looked up at her mother. "Who's Hallam?"

"Maybe this is the man who wrote your father's diary."

"This is not a diary."

"Well, maybe that's good," Marianne said. "You don't get to find out the ending in a diary."

"We know how this ends," said Bridget. "Everyone vanishes in a puff of smoke and no one ever remembers what they said or did. And the last ones get a few extra minutes to see if they can make any sense of it all. Do you like that ending?"

"I prefer it to nothing." Marianne pulled the sheaf of paper off the desk and slid it into its envelope.

"This is John's talent, isn't it? Sowing chaos."

"I don't know what his talents are anymore," said Marianne. "At least he didn't leave without saying goodbye."

"The result is the same."

"No, it isn't, love." She put her hand against her daughter's cheek, and Bridget did not pull away as Marianne thought she would. If anything, she felt her daughter turn her face minutely into the heat of her palm. "Take me home now. Please."

Bridget stirred herself and went to begin collecting her mother's clothes from the drawers and stack the few remaining books. A couple of large paper bags with handles accommodated everything. They'd send a cab for the lamps.

They brought everything out to the elevators and waited, watched the numbers rising and falling in the wall, not speaking. When one of the doors opened Marianne said, "Hold on," and apologized to the people within who stood with their belongings looking embarrassed. "Let this one go," she said to Bridget, and she went back down the hall alone. In the room, she found John's note, on the bed where Bridget had dropped it. There were five words on it: *I hold you to me*, and Marianne put it into her pocket, in case her daughter wanted it at some more forgiving time, in the future.

*The birds returned and it was time to lay in the spring bulbs again. Almost a year since she'd last done this planting— but with David of course, sitting nearby, still alive, yet alive, a mug of tea in his hand. Then the summer came on afterwards with its unseemly optimism. But this did not distract her from the fact of his life ending. It would not be put aside, not even for a second. It was like having a distant memory in her mind that would not leave her, although this was a memory that had not yet formed. It was waiting to take its final shape. The sensation that accompanied it was filled with an emotion, but not an emotion she would have called sadness. She suspected it was something that animals felt, something completely removed from life's orders, a primal thing, unspeakable.*

*She had been anxious about summer's coming again, the first summer without him. Last year, he'd wanted to be with her wherever she was, to sit in the garden, at the table, to lie in bed. A quiet, staring creature who sometimes stopped in her world to report something. If it occurred to him, he might say that bees and birds were responsible for everything beautiful. Or that shit was the key ingredient in the food chain, and then laugh and wipe his mouth. Laughter was the ultimate* thereness: *if he could do it and she could hear it then* he was alive in the ceaseless present and she might be crouching down by the tomatoes and saying to herself, The moment is still here, *and she would think she was not storing a memory, she was actually living.*

*He was still walking on his own, although she worried how he'd cope anywhere without her. Since the spring, when he'd absconded with John for that roadside drink (it was almost funny now—almost), she'd kept a closer eye on him, and he'd seemed more willing to be watched over. An afternoon conference at U of T—where he'd finally present the work he'd spent the entire year pulling together—made her nervous, but they'd deal with the physical challenges then. Now, he was already losing motor function and he'd stop in his tracks sometimes and need help to get restarted. If she put herself in front of him and let him lean his chest against her palm, he could begin moving again with her mediating gravity for him. She'd feel his heart fisting madly behind his rib cage, and he seemed so fragile sometimes that she thought her palm would pass right through his bones and she'd be standing there, holding his heart in her hand. At night she'd sleep with her fingers wrapped around his wrist, ready to wrestle him away from whatever thought it had a claim on him.*

*She realized that the feeling she lived with then was the same as the one that came suddenly these days when she was nearly asleep and heard a sound in the house: all her senses immediately present, a pointed awareness that subsided when the rational mind arrived on the scene and told everyone to disperse. Except for that entire spring and summer it would not. A low-level hum of danger ran under everything; it would spike for the most banal of reasons. Seeing a cupboard full of plates, or hearing the sudden sound of a tin can landing in the garbage. As if these moments full of their meaningless orderings somehow held the code for reality and she had never noticed it until then. Once, she'd nearly fainted with horror clicking shut the soap compartment in the dishwasher.*

*She'd thought of killing him. She remembered this more freely now. She told Bridget this after everything at the Union Arena site was finished, and Bridget said she understood. She told her daughter that on more than one night she'd sat awake in a chair on his side of the bed, watching him breathe in his sleep, his face a little sunken, like a death mask, and seen how simple it would be. Doubling, or even tripling, his loraʒepam before bedtime would depress his breathing and she could do the rest. Or just lower the head of the bed and let the various creeping fluids drown him.* This is love, *she'd thought, and she imagined she was mad. But rationally mad. Who wouldn't think of this?*

*Long after the end of that autumn, when she was back in her own house, she wondered how much of what she'd thought in that bedside chair had crept through the ether above his head. Between them, they'd married his sickness and allowed its offspring into the world. Something in both David's life and his death inhabited them all now, long after simple grief had faded from their lives. It had changed them, and if this was what David had wanted from his death then she had it now, even though it was small solace, or no solace at all. But if it was the last thing he had to give her, heart of her heart, then now—moving on in her life—she could not refuse it.*

For Anne, Benjamin, and Maxime

For William Dendy and Jane Jacobs

*Raconter, c'est témoigner . . .*

THANK YOU

To Steven Heighton and Claudia Dey, to Michael Helm especially, and to Anne Simard profoundly.

To Rebecca Silver Slayter and the rest of the *Brick* sprites and editors.

To Maya Mavjee, Pat Strachan, Ravi Mirchandani, Scott Richardson, Martha Leonard, and Ellen Levine.

This is a work of fiction based on fact; for its sources, background, some commentary, and acknowledgements, please visit redhillconsolation.blogspot.com.

THIS BOOK WAS WRITTEN BETWEEN 1999 AND 2006
IN THE CITY OF TORONTO

A NOTE ABOUT THE TYPES

Pierre Simon Fournier *le jeune*, who designed the type used for the principal text of this book, was both an originator and a collector of types. His services to the art of print communication were his design of individual characters, his creation of ornaments and initials and his standardization of type sizes. Fournier types are old style in character and sharply cut. In 1764 and 1766 he published his *Manuel typographique*, a treatise on the history of French types and printing, the intricacies of typefounding, and on what many consider his most important contribution to the printed word—the measurement of type by the point system.

The display heads in *Consolation* are set in a digitized version of Didot. The original fonts were designed by Firmin Didot in Paris in 1783. Didot's types defined the characteristics of the so-called modern roman style with their pronounced "thicks-and-thins": substantial stems flowing into extremely thin hairlines. This contemporary version of Didot retains the features that make such types superior for book work and its delicate lines are enhanced in display uses.

BOOK DESIGN BY CS RICHARDSON